TENNIS SHOES
ADVENTURE SERIES
TOWER OF
THUNDER

TENNIS SHOES
ADVENTURE SERIES
TOWER OF THUNDER

a novel

CHRIS HEIMERDINGER

Covenant Communications, Inc.

Cover illustration by Joe Flores

Cover design copyrighted 2003 by Covenant Communications, Inc.

Published by Covenant Communications, Inc.
American Fork, Utah

Printed in Canada
First Printing: February 2003

10 09 08 07 06 05 04 03   10 9 8 7 6 5 4 3 2 1

ISBN 1-59156-177-9

For my Web site guests.
The greatest fans an author could ever have!

NOTE FROM THE AUTHOR

This novel, like other "Tennis Shoes" novels, makes many speculations about the ancient people, cultures, and circumstances surrounding scriptural events. Much effort has been made to provide chapter notes and other details in the text of the story to teach and educate readers on what is written in ancient texts and what has been taught by modern prophets and scholars. Nevertheless, my purpose (and the purpose, really, of *all* historical fiction) is to take such information and use it as a stimulus to my own imagination, and to fill in the blanks where specific information is not available. In this light, the reader is advised to keep this story in its proper perspective. It is a work of fiction. By presenting it to my readers, my hope is that, if nothing else, the ideas presented herein will open up our minds, clear the slate, and remind us how much we *don't* know, so that when the Lord finally fulfills His promise to "reveal all things" (D&C 101:32), we will find ourselves to be teachable, humble, and eager students.

PROLOGUE

Jim

I've always considered myself ravenous for knowledge. Ever since I was a young adolescent and embarked upon my first adventure with Garth Plimpton, I've tried to soak up everything there possibly was to know. Of course, I could never lap it all up the way Garth could. He always used to say to me, *"Jim, don't you see . . . ? Don't you realize . . . ?"* I never did unless he explained it. It's always been a great comfort to have people like Garth in my life.

Yet even he has his limits. It overwhelms me to realize how little I will *ever* know while I remain behind eternity's veil. I wonder if our state of incurable ignorance can sometimes be equally frustrating to God. Well, maybe "frustrating" is the wrong word. But think about it. Undoubtedly there have been thousands of human beings who've approached the heavens in prayer, hungry to know the deep mysteries of the universe. Yet if my impressions on the subject are correct, our very nature may limit our capacity to receive such information. I wonder if there's only so much that the Lord could ever reveal and still have it comprehended. It would be rather like me trying to describe the nature of life on land to a sea creature that has only known the darkness of the deepest oceans. Even if this sea creature were highly intelligent, how well would it really be able to get its mind around my description?

"What is wind?" the sea creature might ask.

"Well, wind is like . . . sort of like an ocean current," I might reply. "It makes the air move around."

"Air?"

"Yes, that's the environment that creatures on land live in. When it blows it makes wind."

"Blows?"

"Moves around, I mean. It makes the leaves rustle on plants and causes the clouds to move across the sky."

"Clouds? Sky?"

"Yes, clouds are . . . well, they're water vapor that's lighter than air and therefore floats in the sky—"

"Water can float?"

"Yes, when it's a super-heated vapor, but—"

"Super-heated *what*?"

"Vapor. Vapor is . . . well, it's in the air. It floats in the . . ."

About that time the blank look on the sea creature's face (assuming it *has* a face) causes me to sigh in futility. My pupil just doesn't have the equipment or the experience to understand.

If this is how difficult it is to explain life on land to a sea creature, imagine how difficult it must be to explain the realities of eternity to a mortal human being. Our Heavenly Father has started to explain it on several occasions, but He usually qualifies it with something to the effect of, "If I say too much, the knowledge will be fatal." Okay, He doesn't say it quite like that. Rather, it's ". . . *no man can behold all my works, except he behold all my glory; and no man can behold all my glory, and afterwards remain in the flesh on the earth*" (Moses 1:5).

I think Joseph Smith summed it up best when he said, *"But great and marvelous are the works of the Lord, and the mysteries of his kingdom . . . which surpass all understanding in glory, and in might, and in dominion; Which he commanded us we should not write while we were yet in the Spirit, and are not lawful for man to utter; Neither is man capable to make them known . . ."* (D&C 76:114–116).

So I guess I shouldn't feel so bad when I read in the scriptures things like "one eternal round," or multiple "heavens," or "there is no space in which there is no kingdom" or "past, present, and future are continually before the Lord." Even if such things were explained to me, I undoubtedly wouldn't comprehend. My little brain might even short-circuit. And perhaps it's not *necessary* to understand such things while still in mortality.

But what I find most disconcerting is how little I know about my own planet—its history, its beginnings, the role of dinosaurs, ice ages, Neanderthals, and other events and circumstances that may have occurred before the days of Adam and Eve. And what about the history of the world *since* Adam and Eve? As I think about it, I know such a minimal amount of information that it's almost embarrassing. This is especially true about life in the days just before and after the Great Flood. The scriptures hardly provide any information at all. We have some names, a few events, but that's about it. For instance, what was life on earth like before the days of Noah? What was the earth's population before the rains fell for forty days and nights? Was it anywhere near the population of today?

Think about how little we know about some of the early prophets. The scriptures suggest that many were some of the most important men ever to walk the earth. Prophets like Melchizedek, Enoch, Seth, and Methuselah. For some of these men, all that we know amounts to a couple of paragraphs. For others, it's even less. And yet we acknowledge that these men were some of the most important people in the history of the world.

In some cases we're specifically told that more information will be forthcoming, but sometimes my impatience causes me to feel I might self-combust. I'm sure the real key is to study and be obedient to the revelations we already have. But *oh!* How I look forward to the day when I, or the Church as a whole, may be judged worthy to receive more!

Which brings me to the beginning of this story. Or rather, it brings me to the day that I bade farewell—again—to my son, Harry.

On that day my longing for knowledge of the mysteries of God was greater than ever. Harry was home from his mission to Greece less than seventy-two hours and suddenly he was off again—off on another impossible exploit. I also said good-bye to my old friend, Garth Plimpton, and my son-in-law, Marcos. I left the three of them alone in the depths of Frost Cave. When I returned home I discovered that my youngest daughter, Steffanie, was also missing. She'd gone after them. I'd have thought that I would have seen her in the cave—passed her on the way down. My suspicion is that she may have hidden when she saw me, knowing that I'd have done everything in my power to stop her.

The next few weeks were almost unbearable. I couldn't even imagine what my loved ones would face or where they were going. They'd gone in search of my stepdaughter, Meagan, along with a most remarkable addition to our family—a young Jewish maiden from the first century A.D. named Mary. Also in their company were my young niece and nephew, Joshua and Rebecca Plimpton, and a Roman soldier named Apollus Brutus Severillus. I felt entirely powerless to offer assistance. A transformation in the Rainbow Room had created an amazing conduit, a gateway to the corridors of history. And the only key to controlling this conduit appeared to be a small, whitish stone in the hands of my son. Or at least it was in his hands when I last saw him. But by the last week of September, I'd still heard nothing. Neither had Melody, or my wife, Sabrina, or Garth's wife (and my sister), Jenny.

After the kidnapping of Joshua and Rebecca at Lagoon, it was Jenny who received most of the focus of the media and police. I almost regretted having called the authorities. There was nothing they could do. There was nothing *anyone* could do—at least not anyone in this century. But we endured the interviews, interrogations, and even a few accusations. That's a whole story unto itself—discuss all the ways and means that we dealt with the attention—but suffice it to say that we passed all scrutiny and lie detector tests. (After all, they never asked us, "Do you think Joshua and Rebecca may have been taken to a different century?")

Also, Garth's disappearance a week after the abduction didn't help matters for Jenny, despite her assurance to the police that he was searching for his son and daughter. When they asked where, she could only tell them that it was "outside the country."

We'd also received phone calls from the parents of Ryan Champion in Arizona. Their son was supposed to have started school at BYU a few weeks before. They were sick with worry, and felt sure that Ryan's disappearance was related to the disappearance of Meagan and the others. I realized that soon we'd have to tell them everything we knew. That included Frost Cave, the Rainbow Room—and the whole works. But I decided to wait just one more week to see if we learned any new information.

However, unbeknownst to any of us, my family was about to learn more about the mysteries of time and space than we'd bargained for. Events more mind-boggling than anything we'd previously experienced were about to unfold. Such events would reveal more about the history of the earth than I'd ever imagined—more than anyone in the modern world had ever known.

It began on an unusually cold Sunday evening toward the end of September. It was the season's first snow. I couldn't remember the last time we'd had snow so early in the fall. That is, if you could call it "snow." Actually, what the sky had poured down upon the residents of Provo, Utah, was more of a thick, heavy sleet, but it was enough to coat the lawn and streets with an inch of icy slush.

The four of us were gathered together that Sunday night at my home, just as we'd gathered together every Sunday for the past few weeks. Although some of the media and police attention was finally dying down, our private lives were still being regularly invaded, and we cherished these times to get together and offer one another comfort and support.

Actually, there were the *six* of us gathered together. Besides Melody, Sabrina, Jenny, and myself, there was also my infant son, Gid, and Melody's adopted son, Carter. Melody had also brought along her little hairless dog, Pill, who seemed to go everywhere with her these days, partly to serve as a comforting companion, and partly because he was getting quite old and she didn't like leaving him alone.

Sabrina and Jenny had gone all out to prepare a wonderful meal consisting of pork roast, mashed potatoes, JELL-O salad, cheesy cauliflower, and homemade rolls. But as usual the occasion was pervaded by a grim undertone of tension. As dinner got underway we tried to speak of pleasant things, things that pointed toward the future and happier times. One of the subjects was the adoption of a second child for Melody and Marcos.

"We're going to file the papers as soon as Marcos returns," said Melody. "This time they promised us it would be a girl."

"Isn't that what they promised the *first* time?" asked Jenny.

"Yes," said Melody. "But then the opportunity to bring home little Carter came up, and I just couldn't resist those big brown eyes."

Those big brown eyes were nearly covered in mashed potatoes at the moment as Carter practiced using his spoon.

"That'll be wonderful," said Sabrina, her tone subdued.

A moment of silence prevailed, and it was clear we were all thinking of our loved ones.

"Well," said Jenny as she started to lift a few dishes from the table, "I'll get started on these. I think I'd like to get home a little early this evening."

"Jenny," said Sabrina, "why don't you stay here tonight?"

"Thank you, Sabrina," she said, "but I'd like to get ready for tomorrow. My family could arrive home any day, you know, and I'd like to have things finished."

Jenny had undertaken a renovation of her living room and several bedrooms, just to pass the time. Just to keep from losing her mind.

"You'll have plenty of time to get things ready," said Sabrina. "I can't bear to think of you going home to that empty house on . . . well . . . on a Sunday night."

Jenny paused, but her eyes were downcast. "You forget, I'm an old veteran at this." She carried the dishes to the sink.

Indeed, she'd come home to many empty houses in her life, waiting and wondering about the well-being of her husband. Garth had been away from her for nearly a year during part of the time that they'd lived among the Nephites. He'd gone off to serve as a missionary. Only later did she learn that he'd been imprisoned at Jacobugath. They'd also been separated while Garth was searching for Meagan and Harry in Judea in 70 A.D. But on both of those occasions her domicile hadn't been entirely empty. She'd at least had her children with her. I suspected that my wife would prevail in convincing her to stay, but she would probably have to ask several more times.

Having finished my supper, I got up and wandered into the front room where I could look out the big bay window at the front yard and street. It was a place where I often stood, anticipating the moment when Harry, Meagan, and the rest would come strolling up that front sidewalk. The temperature had dropped a few degrees. The sleet was finally starting to look more like snow. After a long, green summer, the world was finally white again with the advent of winter—not an especially cheerful thought for someone awaiting the return of many of the people most dear to him.

Then I realized my lawn was not *entirely* white. I stepped up to the window for a closer look. There were footprints in the lawn's slushy surface that revealed the still-green grass underneath. The foot-prints came from the street, crossed the yard, and seemed to go around back. *How strange*, I thought. Someone had trespassed on our property, most likely within the last few minutes. I was afraid it was reporters, but of late most of them had been pretty responsible. The paparazzi-type journalists had mostly moved on to the next big story.

I also knew that kids sometimes used our property and the adja-cent property beyond my back fence as a shortcut to school. As a result, they'd broken a few slats on the back fence. I'd managed to catch several of them in the act and kindly asked them to find another pathway. But even if the culprits were kids, it was still most unusual. Today was not a school day.

I wandered back into the kitchen where Jenny was starting to load the dishwasher. She saw me coming, and interpreted my approach as meaning that I wanted to give her a supportive hug. She looked like she needed one, so I did. But during the hug I peered over her shoulder into our backyard. The back porch light wasn't on. I preferred it that way. A light would have further obscured the dark background, creating harsher shadows. As it was, there were many places where a trespasser might hide. The former owners of our house had taken the liberty of planting many trees and hedges. That was one of the reasons we'd bought it; my wife wanted to exercise her green thumb. But at the moment, I realized it left me at a disadvantage.

"Did anybody see someone cross the lawn and climb the fence?" I asked casually.

Melody was finishing up feeding her son. She sat just inside the sliding glass doors and was in the best position to see such things. She shrugged and shook her head. "*I* haven't seen anyone."

"Do we have another trespasser?" asked Sabrina.

"Maybe," I said, still studying the yard.

"I *told* you that you should get a Doberman," said Melody play-fully.

I smiled, rolling my eyes, and wandered back into the living room. It occurred to me to grab up my coat and follow the tracks to see where they went. But first I wanted to study them again through the front window.

What I saw raised the first real flags of alert. Several *additional* sets of tracks had appeared. I couldn't quite tell how many they represented. Maybe three or four people. They'd crossed in just the brief time that it had taken me to walk to the kitchen!

My first instinct, as I suppose would have been *anyone's* first instinct, was to throw open the front door, run around to the side of the house, and shout a few choice, but stern words. I even went so far as to grab the front doorknob. But then I stopped myself.

My track record at following the promptings of the Holy Ghost was not particularly impressive. I'd ignored many such promptings over the course of my life in favor of impetuousness, or what I felt to be superior intelligence. Once or twice I'd even ignored such promptings out of sheer laziness. Perhaps it was a sign of my spiritual maturity, or perhaps it was because this particular prompting was stronger than usual, that I decided to listen and obey.

I returned to the kitchen. Jenny was the first to notice the pallor in my complexion. "What's wrong?"

"I think we should get out of the house," I said awkwardly.

That got everyone's attention. They looked at me with concern.

"What's going on?" asked my wife.

"I don't know," I replied evenly. "But we should leave here— *now.*"

It's surely an amazing thing—and a phenomenon that may only exist in an LDS household—that with just those few mood-altering words from the priesthood holder of the house, my family was instantly on their feet. No further questions or clarifications were asked or demanded—at least not yet. They all started scrambling to gather up coats and car keys.

"Where should we go?" asked Melody, lifting Carter into her arms. The toddler started complaining loudly at losing the opportunity to finish his JELL-O.

"I—I'm not sure," I said, a little flustered. Then with confidence, I said to my daughter, "*Your* house." I said to everyone, "We'll all meet at Melody's house in Salt Lake."

Melody nodded and turned to Jenny. "We'll take my car."

Jenny agreed, throwing her apron on the counter. I'd already found her coat on the hook beside the front door and was waiting to wrap it around her shoulders. She gave me a last look of alarm, then she gathered up Melody's dog while Melody put a coat on little Carter.

"We'll take the Camry and meet you there," I told Jenny and Melody. "Don't stop for anything and don't go anywhere else."

My daughter nodded uneasily, trying to steal another glance out the front window before she and Jenny made a dash for the vehicle parked in the street in front of our property.

"Go, go," I said.

I couldn't resist watching to make sure that they made it okay. My nerves were on edge as Melody took the time to strap Carter into the car seat in back. I wished that I'd advised her to just get out of here—strap the kid in a few blocks away. But she managed to do it in lightning speed. Jenny had climbed behind the wheel to make the escape even hastier.

Sabrina entered the living room as they pulled away. Little Gid was now strapped into a baby seat with a blanket thrown over the top. They were both ready to go. I took my wife's hand and pulled her toward the door leading into the garage.

"Did you actually see someone?" she asked. Questions were acceptable now—they did nothing to slow us down.

"No," I said, pulling open the door. "I'll explain on the way."

But I never got a chance.

My wife gasped. A man was standing behind the door. He was adorned in ancient leather and metal—a gold-colored helmet on his head, a shining metal sword in his hands, and a bloodthirsty scowl on his face. Three other men were in the garage behind him, similarly dressed in leather and jadestone bands, but their helmets were copper colored. Other elements of their uniforms also appeared less ornamented. The intruders had entered the garage through the side door at the back. I'd always tried to keep that side door locked, but my efforts were inconsistent, and now I was paying the price.

The warriors entered, forcing us to back away, our minds swimming in apprehension. I had no idea who these people were. I certainly recognized that their garments were ancient, but they were of a make and style that I'd never seen. The silver breastplate on the first man was enormous. At the base of it was a kind of cummerbund of black fur, lined with jade. I half-wondered if such a breastplate might stop a modern bullet.

The first man's face was the most curious of all. It was ashen-white, beardless, and pocked with scars. He was in his early fifties, perhaps. No hair at all was visible beneath that helmet. A small nose was squished against his face, and puffy lips surrounded a pair of protruding front teeth, as sharp as a canine's. His tiny eyes were crystalline blue, burning with a cold fire. An odd thing occurred to me. It struck me that if you gave this guy a black robe or cape, he'd have passed as a typical Bavarian-style vampire.

He backed us all the way into the living room, his men pressing in behind him. We said nothing, our hearts beating wildly. It was the blue-eyed vampire who spoke the first words, which he directed to one of his men after he noted the wide view through the bay window.

"Pull that drapery!" he commanded.

The soldier did so clumsily, as if he'd never worked curtain strings before. The vampire's eyes scanned the living room. I realized he was looking at the portraits on the wall. Portraits of my family—of Renae, Harry, Steffanie, and Melody. There were others with Sabrina and Megan. When he came to a portrait of my niece and nephew, Rebecca and Joshua, his eyes stopped cold.

"Is it here?" he asked me, his eyes still fixed on the portrait. His voice was hoarse, as if the question drained him of energy. As if he'd already asked it a million times without receiving the answer he sought.

Having no idea what he was talking about, I inquired, "Who are you?"

The vampire yanked an eleven-by-fourteen picture off the wall that featured all the children of both Garth and myself—including Mary. We'd taken it just before Harry went into the MTC. He turned and indicated specific individuals in the portrait. "The girl, Mary, and the girl, Rebecca, and the boy, Joshua—are they here?"

My mouth fell open. The words took the breath out of my lungs. In the distance I became aware of the drone of fire sirens. The soldier's inefficiency at closing the curtain had left a three-inch slit that allowed me to gaze across the rooftops to the south. An unusual glow lit up the sky in that direction. Was it just a coincidence that the home of Garth Plimpton was over in that neighborhood?

"How do you know Mary, Becky, and Joshua?" I demanded. "Who *are* you?"

With the portrait still in his hands, his eyes started crawling over every inch of the room, as if he secretly hoped that the thing he was searching for might be sitting out in the open, as plainly visible as any other piece of furniture.

"I am the king of Morōn," he stated, making the last "o" long, much like the name of a land that I remembered from the book of Ether. "And I seek that which they stole from me long ago. Something that I created with my own hands." At that instant he smashed the portrait against the corner of the wall, shattering the glass. My wife shrieked. The king pulled the photograph out of the frame and held it up to my face, using his other hand to draw his sword and move the blade toward my stomach. "*Where are they?*"

Little Gid started to cry beneath the blanket.

I was stymied. I struggled to find the words to reply. "I—I don't know what you're talking about. Mary, Becky, and Joshua aren't here. I believe . . ." I considered my next words carefully. I felt certain, considering their obvious origin, that they would understand. "I believe they're still in the ancient world."

For a moment, time seemed to stand still for the king and his men. I wasn't sure at first if my words had made sense. Then, slowly, I realized they'd made more sense than I could have expected. And because the statement was so surprising, so unconventional, it appeared that it was also *believed.*

Anger was percolating and building inside the king. He turned his wrathful gaze onto one of his men.

"What does this mean?" he asked, his tone poisonous and threatening.

The soldier was a young man of twenty or so. He looked like a relative—perhaps the king's son. As he answered he was trembling. "He—he lied to us. The prophet lied to us *again.*"

The king's fury continued to mount, like pressure behind a volcano. At last it exploded. With an earthshaking roar he raised his sword high overhead and brought it down again. It landed on our piano bench, splitting it in half. I shielded my wife and crying baby from flying slivers of wood.

"*Twenty years!*" raged the king. "Three prophets! And they've all lied time and time again!"

Another soldier spoke, this one much more self-assured than the first. He also showed a family resemblance. "The seerstone is useless," he spat. "None of our shamans have divined a single revelation from it."

"*No!*" the king insisted. "It has *great* power! I've witnessed it with my own eyes! I've seen it in operation in the young girl's hands. It's the *prophets* who have betrayed us!"

My infant son was screaming loudly now. Sabrina took him out of the baby seat and hugged him close to try and calm him down.

"But Father," said the last soldier, leading me to conclude that all *three* of these men were the king's offspring, "we are closer than we've ever been before. We've found the place of the young girl's origin." He indicated the half-crumpled portrait in his father's hands. "We've found her home."

The king stuffed the portrait inside his cloak and boomed, "But we haven't found the *sword!*" His anger was so virulent that I thought he might kill one of his own sons. But the rage was directed elsewhere, and the new object of his wrath froze my blood.

He looked at my wife with the screaming infant and commanded arbitrarily, mercilessly, "Kill that whining pup before I lose my mind!"

My wife drew back in desperation. "*No!*"

"*Do it now!*" he shouted.

The command was directed at the first son—the one whose intestinal fortitude seemed to be lacking. The man's hand reached for the dagger on his belt. At that point my mind lost all capacity for rational thought. A savage, parental instinct took over. I flew at the man before the dagger had been removed from his belt. We crashed together against an oak pillar near the window. The flower vase that it had supported fell onto his head. I heard him grunt in pain, but almost as quickly, I felt other hands grabbing my shoulders.

But it was the actions of my wife that surprised and impressed me the most. In the confusion, she bolted toward the door with Gid still in her arms. The remaining son tried to cut her off. I glimpsed her grabbing a small bronze statue from the shelf beside the front door. It was the statue of a cavalry scout that I'd received on my mission.

Many years ago I'd done with it exactly as my wife was about to do. She swung it at her attacker. It impacted his head with great force—the force of a mother defending her young. The man staggered and fell, and my wife escaped into the snowstorm. The next image I saw was the broken half of the piano bench as it was swung down on my face.

I blacked out after that, mostly anyway. My head was throbbing and my thoughts were distorted and confused. I remember the smell of smoke filling my lungs, the roar of flames in my ears, and the echoing voices of . . . Melody and Jenny?

"Come on!" they yelled. "Jim, you have to help us! Try! Just try!"

They were dragging me. I helped as best I could, pushing with my heels, but the delirium was overpowering. The next thing I remember was the cold shock of icy slush against my body as I was laid onto my front lawn. I could hear more police and fire sirens, very close. In fact, they were pulling up in front of my house. Melody's face fell into focus—and Jenny's too! They'd come back! But the greatest relief of all was seeing the face of Sabrina. Little Gid was still clutched in her arms, and tears were streaming down her face.

"Jim!" she pleaded. "Can you see me? Can you understand me?"

Conspicuously absent were the faces of the vampire-king and his sons. I could only speculate that they'd fled into the night at the sound of the approaching sirens. Their existence now seemed more like a dream. But then I looked at my home. Fire had engulfed the front room. Flames were shooting out of the broken bay window and the windows of several bedrooms. The place had been set aflame. Because he couldn't find the thing that he sought, the king had determined to slay me, kill my family, and destroy everything I owned. If my wife hadn't escaped, and if my sister and daughter hadn't returned to rescue me, he likely would have succeeded. Apparently he and his sons were also determined to destroy everything owned by Garth Plimpton, because his home was also burning. I knew of only one object that could inspire such insanity. But it was an object that I thought I'd destroyed more than a quarter century before.

Who were these ancient strangers? The vampire-king claimed to have created the thing he sought—created it with his own hands. Akish? *No. It couldn't* be. Yet he'd mentioned the Jaredite land of

Morōn. This was Akish's home turf. But how? Why? There were far more questions than answers. And most alarming of all, why was he seeking Mary, Joshua, and Rebecca? What could they have done to incite the wrath of one of the wickedest men who had ever lived?

Undoubtedly this king would continue his search for them, conceivably to his dying breath. Where *were* they? How could I warn them? How could I save them? And yet if the three of them really possessed the object I feared, would there still be anyone left to save?

This wasn't *possible!* I'd destroyed it once! How could it have returned? Such thoughts threw my mind back into a delirium of pain—a pain that went far deeper than the concussion in my skull. Even deeper than my fear of Akish and his sons. I had to face the facts. The devastating possibility.

The sword of Coriantumr was back in our lives.

PART I

CHILD
OF THE
COVENANT

CHAPTER ONE

Mary

I will write in the manner of the people of the latter days, though I am a woman of the meridian of time. In my day there was not so much emphasis upon the description of simple, subjective things, such as the coolness of an evening breeze upon soft skin, or the meaning of the subtlest expressions of the human face. In my experience, the people of my era, the Jews and Greeks of the Decapolis in particular, wished only to read the facts—the "truth" and the quicker that one event might lead to the next, the better. But I have grown to love the artful, seemingly superfluous detail of the storytellers of the modern age. And particularly the style of the writers of English—the only language that I have so far learned to read. So I will try my best to communicate in these colors, hoping that I may be granted the power to speak as much to the spirit as to the mind, and that not a letter or even the stroke of a letter may be misunderstood.

My name is Mary Symeon. I was named for my grandmother, Mary, and for my great aunt, Mary, the mortal mother of my Savior, Yeshuua. Or as His name has come to be pronounced in the latter days, Jesus.

I was born in Jerusalem in 54 A.D., the daughter of Symeon Cleophas, bishop of the Jerusalem Church. He was a man of modest means who raised me plainly to be the simple wife of a nice Jewish boy. But all of that seems blurry now. If someone asked me today where I would call home, I might be hard pressed to answer, for I have "dropped in" on more centuries than any plainly raised Jewish girl ever should. And at the time of this story, I was as far from my roots in the first century A.D. as I ever had been.

Let me start at the beginning.

No, no. Let me not start at the beginning, for that might raise more confusion than my mind can bear. Let me start in the middle. Or better yet, let me start toward the tail end of Rebecca Plimpton's account. Everyone has read that account, I presume. Please tell me that you have, because I'm much too exhausted to give a stitch by stitch summary of such happenings. Instead I'll try to say it all in a single breath. Are you ready?

I'd just escaped the jaws of death by jumping off a cliff inside a cave tomb in the nineteenth-century ruins of Petra in the Sinai Desert and fallen through a hole in time along with ten-year-old Rebecca Plimpton and twelve-year-old Joshua Plimpton, where we were immediately swept up by a tornado and hurled through history until we finally landed with a thud in the middle of a flat, desolate landscape while little blue streaks of lightning flashed around, and looming in the distance was a tower that looked like the Tower of Babel.

All right. (Let me pause to take air.) Was that plain enough? Surely not. But the reader can't be any more confused than myself or the two children.

In truth, what lay before me was amongst the strangest sights I had ever beheld. And I should point out that the notion of it being the "Tower of Babel" was only speculation. Its multiple tiers reminded me vaguely of the ziggurats of Babylon. I mentioned this to Joshua, and he, in turn, "ran with it" (as they say in the modern vernacular). Thus, we drew our conclusions regarding Babel.

It was the construction's sheer height and breadth that astounded us most, straining our imaginations. Its summit arose into heaven, but its base was so far distant as to be obscured by the curvature of the earth (a concept I had learned by reading of the voyages of Christopher Columbus). I was convinced that I had never seen anything so high as this framed by the hands of men. No, not in any century, future or past. And who was to say how far away it rested? Miles, leagues, kilometers, acres (I was still having a time of it keeping straight all the various means of measuring distance)—it was impossible to tell how many of these distances stretched between ourselves and the structure's base.

Joshua, Rebecca, and I stood together upon the parched desert floor, frightened and amazed, our hearts furiously pumping, our minds swirling with awe. It was sunset, the start of a new day. (I never could get used to the illogical modern notion that a new day started at sunrise.) The sky in the west was the color of purple aster, soft and illusory, while the sky to the north was sullenly gray, blending almost seamlessly with the stark, gray land. Now and then a many-fingered flash of lightning—normal "white" lightning this time—appeared in that direction. I could tell that a storm was moving steadily toward us.

The vertigo of our amusement-park-style ride inside the tornado hadn't entirely left my senses. Joshua noticed that I was unsteady on my feet and thoughtfully came over to support me.

"Mary, are you all right?" he asked.

But my unsteadiness was not entirely from vertigo. My emotions were overwhelmed, to say the least. It was equally so for Becky and Josh. Only moments ago we had faced a vicious killer who had sought to murder us with his sword. We'd felt certain that by leaping into the void we would be sent home to the twenty-first century. But we had waited too long. Becky had warned us that the time "window" to the modern era was very narrow. Her inspiration was that we should leap precisely at the setting of the Judean sun on that October day of 1842, but our struggle with Akish the sorcerer had delayed us. The consequence of that delay was now apparent as far as the eye could see. A minute later it was Becky who became the most distraught of all.

"The stone!" she cried. "It's gone! I lost it!"

If the weight of dread already on our shoulders was not enough, these chilling words were the final grains that brought us to our knees in desolation.

"What happened to it?" Joshua demanded of her. "How could you lose it?"

"Akish ripped it off my neck," said Becky. "He was trying to keep me from falling over the cliff. That's when I bumped the sword and made it fall with us."

I again glanced at Akish's sword lying against the cracked earth, its silver surface winking in the purple light of the lowering sun. The sight of it filled me with revulsion. Only a minute ago that weapon had nearly been the instrument of our deaths. But my revulsion went deeper than this. We'd all stood there watching, our feet seemingly glued to the earth, as that sword had cut down that villain, Todd Finlay. We'd watched in horror as Akish set its tip against Mr. Finlay's small silver statue, the metal becoming suddenly molten hot and climbing the bronze-colored blade. It was doubtless the power of demons—a power that Akish had certainly utilized during every phase of the sword's creation.

At the moment the weapon looked harmless enough. Still, in my mind it might as well have been crawling with maggots and festering with disease. Every instinct of my flesh told me that it was a thing of corruption and that the lightest touch of my finger would bring this corruption into my soul.

"What are we supposed to do now?" Joshua fretted. "Without the stone, how are we supposed to find another doorway to get us home?"

I glanced skyward. Clearly we could not use the "doorway" that had brought us here. Unless of course we could catapult ourselves back into the heavens.

Tears came to Rebecca's eyes. She began rocking back and forth, on the verge of hysteria. "I don't know! I don't know!"

I went to her and held her tightly. "It's all right. It will be all right. God knows we're here. That's what's important. Don't panic. Nobody panic."

I was speaking these words to myself as much as to the children. We were as helpless as ants under a magnifying stone in this terrible place. Or at least that was how it would be when the sun came up in the morning.

Joshua began untying the camel-hide belt at his waist. We were each arrayed in Bedouin mantles, burnooses, and the typical sacks and bundles of desert travelers. The contents of those bundles, however, weren't typical at all. From his own bundles Joshua brought out American money and a Roman coin, his school ID card, my driver's license, a small tube of Vaseline Lip Therapy petroleum jelly, a solar-powered calculator, a blue ink pen, tweezers, and a little battery-powered penlight. Oh, yes, and there was also some red lipstick, black eyeliner, rouge powder, a little mirror, and an extra pair of pantyhose. No doubt I was at the height of my powers of inspiration when I brought along pantyhose.

In Becky's bundles there was also some hand cream, a sewing kit, and a nail file. I'd tried to throw most of these items away long ago, but Joshua was still convinced that they might be valuable for trading. To credit him properly, we had managed to barter a fingernail clipper, a hairbrush, and some chewing gum for a ride to Jerusalem during the first half of our adventure. Presently, however, there were no traders in sight, and we'd have certainly preferred it if our pockets and bundles had been filled with date cakes and other food.

Joshua and I were both wearing a water pouch, though Joshua's was nearly empty. We had enough for two days at most. The coming rains might leave puddles to aid us further, but by the look of the chapped and fissured ground, Mother Earth was thirstier than ourselves and wouldn't leave a lot to spare.

Having finished checking our inventory, Joshua arose and asked, "Which direction should we walk?"

The children looked to me. And why not? I was the adult, after all. I might have assumed such a leadership role earlier if not for Becky's stone. Not surprisingly, I missed the stone more than ever.

I looked up toward the distant tower. And then I pointed in the exact opposite direction. "That way."

Joshua started to object. "That way? *But we don't even know if there's a city that way. Or water, or* anything.*"*

"Joshua," I explained, "if that really is the Tower of Babel, it's not a place that we would wish to be. The people of Babel were wicked. Hideously wicked.*"*

Josh stewed about this, then sighed in resignation.

Rebecca remained on her knees. "I'm so tired," she said drearily. "It's almost dark. Shouldn't we wait until morning before we leave?"

"Not unless we wish to become like a hen's eggs in a frying pan," I replied. "We need to find shelter—and quickly."

Joshua arose and went over to the sword in the dust. "What about this thing?"

Becky stood and we joined Joshua around the silver blade like a circle of curious children around a venomous serpent, keeping well out of range of its strike.

"I'm not sure we should leave it," said Joshua.

"We have *to leave it," said Becky. "That sword is cursed. I can feel it just by looking at it. It's just the opposite of a seerstone or a Liahona."*

"Akish will be looking for it," said Joshua. "A guy like that wouldn't work so hard to create such a thing and then forget about it. I wouldn't be surprised if he falls out of the sky any second.

We glanced upward, flinching, like three Chicken Littles, fearing the collapse of heaven.

Josh added, "Or if not Akish, some other wicked soul will come along and find it."

"I say we bury it," said Becky. "Make sure no one finds it."

I pondered this, then shook my head. "I don't think we could bury it deep enough here to prevent the winds from uncovering it in time. Besides . . ." I studied the sword more intensely. ". . . I have a feeling that it has a way of 'calling' people. Almost like . . ."

"A radio?" said Josh.

"Precisely," I replied. "Like it can send out a beacon for the wicked of the earth to come and find it."

"We need to drop it in the ocean," said Josh. "That's the only way to be sure that we can get rid of it. Or else drop it down a crevasse or something where nobody would be able to get at it for thousands of years."

"Or launch it into space," said Becky. "Or melt it down and destroy it."

"Meagan told us that your Uncle Jim already destroyed it once," I said. "It was always Mr. Finlay's objective to go back in time and find it."

"How did Uncle Jim destroy it?" asked Josh.

I sighed wearily and shook my head. "Meagan never told us."

Josh straightened up, looking brave. "Well, if Uncle Jim can do it, I'm sure I can do it. I'll be the one who carries it."

"You can't!" cried Becky. "None of us should touch it!"

"Did Uncle Jim touch it?" asked Josh.

Becky and I thought about this. Obviously Jim had carried it with him for quite some time.

"Here's what I think," Josh continued. "If we leave it here, it's gonna find us again. It's like that horror movie where the guy cuts off this dude's hand, and then the hand keeps crawling after the guy who cut it off, seeking its revenge."

I rolled my eyes. "I fear you're being overdramatic."

Josh became animated. "Think about it! If that sword really is evil, then it hates our guts. We're the ones who separated it from its master. As soon as it finds a new owner, I'll betcha anything it will inspire that owner to come after us. The sword will hunt us down like dogs."

Becky shook her head emphatically. "We can't take it! I think Mary is right. It's sending out a signal. Instead of drawing wicked people to itself, it will draw wicked people to us!"

Josh scratched the red hair on his head. "Hmm. Good point." He shrugged. "Then I guess we're toast either way. So I say we carry it and take our chances."

Again the children looked to me. I mulled over the arguments. My leanings were toward leaving it to its fate, but I wasn't completely comfortable with that. And yet, was it right to let it fall into the hands of an unsuspecting passerby? Was it really limited to attracting the wicked? Perhaps it was capable of corrupting anyone. *Or was I being as overly dramatic as Joshua? I think I would have settled upon the notion of leaving it right where it was, but Joshua saw my moment of hesitation and took advantage.*

"Let me make this easy on everyone." He reached out toward the sword. "Josh, don't   " peeped Becky.

But Josh ignored her and snatched it up in his hands. He stood erect and felt the weight of it. He ran his finger along the flat side of the blade, his eyes fixed on the shining metal surface. Becky and I watched, unmoving. I observed Joshua's face, almost expecting his countenance to change, perhaps darken, a demonic glint appearing in his eyes. There was nothing like that. There was no change at all. Josh looked at us and smiled crookedly, almost sheepishly.

"You shouldn't have done that," said Becky.

He huffed. "Someone had *to do it."*

"What do you feel?" I inquired.

He considered the question, then shook his head. "Nothin'. I don't feel anything. I think we're all overreacting about this." He held it toward us. "Here. You guys try it."

"No!" Becky and I snapped in unison.

"Ah, shucks," said Josh, playing it up. "This is ridiculous. It's just a stupid sword. A piece of metal can't be evil all by itself. It needs to have somebody evil controlling it. I'm sure for us it's no different than Mary's penlight or my Roman coin. Just some copper, a little gold and silver, and a couple jewels—that's all it is. Might even come in handy if we need to chop down a tree or something."

"Well, I don't want anything to do with it," said Becky.

I breathed a heavy, acquiescent sigh. "All right, Joshua. But I would feel much better if you wrapped it in one of your bundles. An uneasiness comes over me every time I gaze upon it."

"I'm not sure I have enough material," said Josh, but he set to work and asked if we might be willing to carry some of his other things.

Becky and I divided up the various articles from his pockets. Josh tore off one of the baggy pockets of his cloak, and used half of the burnoose on his head. When he was finished, he'd managed to cover all but the jeweled knob on the gold-plated hilt. He even devised a kind of strap that allowed him to carry it behind his shoulder.

"It's lighter than I thought it would be," said Josh. "I don't even think it will slow me down."

But even if Joshua's burden felt light, my own definitely did not. It was now my responsibility to find a way out of this morass. Even if we managed to find a settlement in the direction that we were headed, what did we expect to do after we arrived?

Food and shelter. That's all I cared about right now. Only after we obtained the necessities of life would I allow myself to hope for anything more.

We started on our westward journey. The thunder continued to rumble in the north, but it no longer looked to be moving toward us, almost as if the clouds had stopped. I took this as a sign of God's support. If we had to walk all night, at least we wouldn't be walking in the rain.

Rebecca stayed close to me, but she wore a very glum expression. "This is all my fault," she said. "If only I hadn't lost the stone."

"I doubt very much that you could have prevented it," I replied.

"But I always knew what to do when I had the stone. I could always follow its guidance."

"Well, we always have prayer," I replied. "I don't recall that it has ever let us down before." I gave her a wink.

This made her smile a little. It also made me feel much better.

We continued plodding forward. The night fell over us like a funeral shroud. My mind turned again to Harry. To say "again" may be misleading since he was never entirely absent from my thoughts. Had I remained in Salt Lake, had none of this occurred, and had our lives gone on without interruption, Harry would have been home from his mission to Greece by now. We would have been in each other's arms, making our future plans together. But this was not to be, and, instead, I felt consumed by my own private grief.

But should I call it grief? In reality, it was my thoughts of him that gave me strength. It gave me the energy to go on. I felt an unusual connection to Harry's soul. I'm sure it sounds foolish, but I'm going to say it anyway. Over the last two years I felt as if I knew when Harry was happy or sad, succeeding or frustrated, weary or invigorated. I wondered if he sensed the same connection, though it may have been exclusively the gift of a woman.

But tonight I felt something different. I felt he was near. Does that sound silly? I felt as if he was as close to me as the breath of night or the smell of rain. But of course I dismissed such feelings, knowing that no person could have been farther away.

It was still dark when Becky announced that she could go no farther. We cuddled together tightly under the desert stars and awaited the rising sun. It would not be a welcome arrival, for I knew that in a place like this its rays could be lethal. Nevertheless, I would accept it with hope, like the coming of any other dawn, for it would be our first day in a century so near the dawn of time.

NOTES TO CHAPTER 1:

There are few subjects more intriguing, more captivating, and more likely to contain errant speculations than the subject of the early history of the earth. It has been called a favorite topic for high priest group meetings (according to the unfortunate stereotype), as well as a favorite playground for theological intellectuals. Sometimes it becomes a primer for fringe groups who claim special or exclusive understanding. Those who delve into the subject exhaustively are often categorized as "far out" or "on the edge," while those who don't study it at all may be defying the Lord's directive to "search the scriptures" (John 5:39). Yet who can deny that the subject ignites our curiosity, stretches our imagination, and sometimes boggles the mind?

In this novel many speculations are made about life in the early history of man's sojourn on earth. The author has attempted to be thorough in his research, utilizing the scriptures as well as statements from General Authorities, scientists, philosophers, and details from ancient apocryphal texts. Nevertheless, it must be recognized that very few actual details on these subjects have been revealed. Primarily the information comes in broad sweeps and must be taken on faith until more information comes forth through the light of revelation. This makes a novel of this type a fertile field for a healthy imagination, but it also means that it should not be considered a serious resource for a definitive understanding of the subject of early biblical history. However, it is hoped that it may be a resource that stimulates further investigation, and celebrates faith. Without a doubt, it is a reflection of the common hope for so many Latter-day Saints that one day the Lord may find us ready and willing to receive additional revelation through the mouth of His prophets.

CHAPTER TWO

Harry

For Steffanie and me our peaceful, reflective, almost *relaxing* journey in the midst of liquid light became a violent thrust, like a boot kick to the lungs, or the blast of a firehose—or better yet—like an explosion from the spout of a great blue whale. That analogy seems most accurate, because as soon as my eyes became cognizant of my surroundings, I was twenty feet airborne, my legs kicking furiously above my head, as if trying to dig their heels into solid sky. But the only thing worse than the sensation of flying is the unmistakable sensation of coming down. And in fact, I twisted my body around just in time to see a slab of red stone flying upward toward my face.

By a miracle I managed to land on my shoulder and backpack—not that I didn't expect a hefty bruise. Most curious of all, I became aware that the fine spray of water on my face and hands felt, quite suddenly, steaming hot!

To avoid a scalding I threw myself to the right and rolled end over end three times before I felt I was far enough from the splashing heat. Out of the corner of my eye I also saw my sister Steffanie—or rather, I heard her scream. Like myself she was also in midair. But *unlike* myself, she was fortunate enough to land in soft dirt.

I looked back toward the source of steam and sucked in my breath in consternation. I was only a few yards from the blowhole of a geyser.

A geyser! That pillar of silver light had transported my sister and me through a network of energy and out of the exit spout of a geyser!

Yet I didn't feel soaked. Nor did I feel as if I'd just emerged from a boiling, geothermal cavern. If I had, my flesh would have been hanging off my bones! Somehow that cushion of energy had protected me until the very moment I was ejected.

The geyser looked similar to Old Faithful in Yellowstone National Park, which I'd visited once when I was twelve. Its roar filled my ears, and the foaming water splashed all around the slab of red stone that encircled it. After another five seconds, the fountain began to weaken as the geyser was drawn back into the earth.

I started crawling toward Steffanie, who was trying to sit up, still dazed and disoriented.

"Steff! Are you all right?"

She gave me a cloudy look, as if the sight of me didn't quite register. She joggled her head and tried again.

"Harry," she said groggily. Suddenly her eyes lit up. The reality of where we were and how we'd gotten here settled in. She laughed, overcome with relief and wonder.

"Holy moly!" she exclaimed. "Now that was a *trip!"*

I can't say that I was as enchanted about this situation as my sister, but I was grateful to have survived with nothing more than a bruised shoulder blade.

She grabbed my shoulders. "We just got ejected out of a geyser! Do you realize how totally cool that is?"

I winced as she touched my bruise. "Right. Totally cool. So nothing is broken on you? You can stand up?"

"I think so." She brought her shoulders forward to adjust the weight of her backpack, then pushed herself to her feet. I did the same, though not with as much vigor. She saw me favoring my arm again.

"What's the matter?" she asked.

"That's the arm I landed on."

"Hmm. Next time you really ought to come down on dirt rather than stone. Much softer."

I gave her a strange look. She grinned and she put an arm around my good shoulder. "Buck up, little brother. We made it! It's just like old times. Oh, I've missed you, Harry. I thought your mission would *never* end. I think you and I were *meant* for adventure. Don't you?"

"Sure, Sis," I replied, still working the muscle of my upper arm.

"Well, I'm excited. It's good to be here."

"Good to be *where?*" I replied, surveying the landscape.

There appeared to be several geysers and hot springs all around us. To our right bubbled a mudpot the color of Hershey's chocolate milk. Above us trickled a tiny stream whose edges were striped with blue and green algae. The foul egg smell of percolating sulfur filled my nostrils. It looked like any tourist site in Yellowstone, except for the absence of trees or wooden walkways. At the edge of this little geothermal valley stretched a line of rolling hills, verdant with prairie grass and speckled with wildflowers. A few trees poked up as well, but they were scrubby, desert-looking things, much like the foliage around Judea and Galilee.

"I thought you said this was where we'd find Meagan and Mary," said Steffanie.

"Not exactly," I replied. "I mean, maybe. Yes, we'll find *somebody* here. I'm just not sure who."

My sister looked perplexed. "I don't follow."

I pulled the white stone from my pocket—the same cloudy white stone that I'd found at the base of the pillar in Frost Cave. I stared into it and heaved a sigh. "Neither do I. At least, not entirely. All I know is that when I look into this, I see things. That is to say, I *know* things. One of the things I knew was exactly when to jump into that pillar."

"So where did it take us?"

"I—uh—don't know that either."

"So what you're saying is . . . this stone told you to come here and find *somebody?*"

I nodded sheepishly.

She rolled her eyes and began pacing. "And you're sure this isn't all in your imagination?"

"Trust me, Sis. I'm not sure how, but there's a power that I can access through this stone. A *good* power."

"I trust you," she assured. "If a newly returned missionary isn't sensitive to such things, I'm not sure who is. But a *stone?*"

"Dad and Uncle Garth think it's a seerstone."

"Like a Urim and Thummim?"

"Something like that."

"Let me see it."

I gave it to her. She rolled it around in her fingers, squinting to study its milky, pearl-colored surface. She closed her eyes and cupped the stone tightly, as if willing it to tell her something.

When her eyes opened again, she looked disappointed. "I don't get it."

I reached out and she handed it back. "Uncle Garth suggested that my ability to discern things with it is a gift."

"A what?"

"You know. Like the gift of tongues or prophecy or whatever."

"And you have the gift of being able to perceive information from this stone?"

I shrugged. "Apparently so. And one of the things I feel strongly is that Meagan, Mary, Apollus, Becky, Josh, and Meagan's boyfriend, Ryan, have divided into two groups. Marcos and Uncle Garth went in search of one group while you and I went in search of the other."

"But we don't know who's in which group?"

"Not exactly."

"Wow. This is crazy! So one group could have five while the other has one? Or four and two?"

"No," I said. "It's three and three. I'm confident of that much."

"Why won't the stone tell you who's where?"

"It's not the stone that tells me *anything*. It's just a conduit. And I'm not sure why I don't know who's where. I might still be able to learn. That is, I might learn how to concentrate better to see things more clearly. I've only had it a couple of hours."

Steff still looked impatient. "How are we supposed to search when we don't know who we're looking for? What do we ask people? 'Hey, have you seen a Roman warrior and two children? Or maybe a Jewish maiden with one girl and a blonde-haired man about eighteen years old?'"

"I'm hoping the stone will help me know where to search," I said.

"So where are we? We could be anywhere from Nephi to Cumorah, right?"

"Actually, the range is a little wider."

"Like from Panama to Alaska?"

"Wider," I said.

"Anywhere in the *world?*"

"And unfortunately, any century."

She looked exhausted already and we hadn't even taken one step. "Okay. Fine. I can handle this. So I guess the first order of business is to figure out where we are." She faced a gap in the hills that looked like a natural trail. The water from the spring flowed in that direction. "Shall we get started?"

She straightened her backpack and started walking.

"Wait," I said.

She turned back.

I continued to clutch the stone. Hesitantly, I pointed toward the right. "I think we should go this way."

Steff walked back toward me, her blue eyes sparkling. "Cool. The stone told you that? This is almost like having our own Liahona."

"Actually," I said dryly, "I just thought we might have a better view from higher ground."

She slapped my arm playfully.

It *was* good to be with her again. I'd been so consumed by missionary labors for the last two years that I'd almost forgotten what it was like to be lost in a new, unexplored world. Not that Greece didn't feel like a new world much of the time, or that a missionary doesn't frequently feel lost. But just being with Steffanie stirred so many old memories—memories of Zarahemla and Bountiful, Ephesus and the restless Mediterranean Sea. And the best thing about it, I didn't have to learn a language. I assumed the gift of tongues was still standard issue for a time traveler. Learning Greek had been no cakewalk, and I wasn't eager to repeat the experience. During my first frustrating weeks in the MTC, I remembered thinking, "Why couldn't the world just get together and adopt one language and make it easier on everybody?" Such was my naïveté. The challenge was getting everybody to agree on which one.

We began to climb the ridge to the right. The way was rocky, but it wasn't really that steep. Just a steadily ascending trail. The morning sunlight glistened through my sister's blonde hair and a steady breeze tossed it about. The clouds were high and billowing, quickly changing shapes as they rolled toward the southeast. It really was a gorgeous day, whatever day it was.

I asked Steffanie, "So what does your fiancé, Michael, think about this?"

"About what?"

"About you coming here and leaving him behind."

"Oh," she said obliquely. "I'm not sure."

I raised my eyebrows.

She added, "I just left a message on his answering machine. I told him I'd be gone for a while. Among other things."

"Other things?"

"Yeah."

She paused for a long time. So long that I was left with only one conclusion.

"Are things okay between you two?"

"Sure, I guess so. Okay as they *ever* are."

"Are you sure . . . you *want* to get married?"

"Of *course* I want to get married. What makes you say that?"

"Well, gee, Sis. You're certainly dropping enough hints that you might not be too excited about it."

She sighed. "I want to get married. I'm just not sure I want to get married to *him?*"

"Really? You don't love him?"

"Oh, Harry, don't ask me that. I *do* love him. Or at least . . . I *thought* I did. I don't know."

"If you don't know for sure, then it's a pretty safe bet to say that you don't."

"Thank you, my all-wise and knowing brother. But I don't think that's true. Everybody has doubts. Doubts are healthy. We're *supposed* to have doubts. It forces us to think things through as thoroughly as possible. Haven't you ever had any doubts about Mary?"

"No," I said.

She gave me a crusty look.

"Okay, yes," I confessed. "Sometimes. But they don't last very long."

"But you *do* have doubts, right? So there! What do you have doubts about?"

"Hey, we were talking about *you*. Not *me*. What doubts do you have about Michael?"

She looked at the ground. "I wish I knew. I think when I started dating Michael, I was looking for someone who might bring me down to earth. You know what I mean? I do have a wild streak, in case you haven't noticed. And I love a good fight. Maybe I thought Michael could sort of . . . you know . . . tame me."

I pulled a face. It was an odd speech. *Wild streak?* I wasn't quite sure what she meant by that. I knew that Steffanie was known to concoct a few strange perspectives. She got a big kick sometimes out of philosophizing things to death. But in no way would I have classified her as having a wild streak—at least not in any way that people usually defined that term. My sister had one of the strongest testimonies I'd ever heard. Then again, she *did* have a point about never backing down from a fight. Steffanie had a competitive drive that wouldn't quit. And considering her height and stamina (she was almost five-foot-eleven) she rarely lost. But it wasn't just sports. She hated to lose *any* contest, whether it was basketball, Monopoly, or Tiddly Winks. She'd fight to the death if she thought she had to. Because of this, everything I'd heard about her fiancé made me think he was the perfect choice. Michael Collins didn't seem to have a competitive bone in his body. In one of Steffanie's letters she'd called him the most "easygoing, levelheaded person she'd ever met." It was a perfect example, in my mind, of how opposites attract. Apparently I was wrong. It was no easy task to hold my sister's attention, and for poor Michael it was probably just a matter of time.

"So Michael's not much of a lion tamer, eh?" I said.

"No," said Steff sadly. "Not much. Oh, Harrison, he's a good man. Really he is. I just don't think I'm cut out to marry an accountant."

"So on the answering machine you told him the marriage was off?"

"Not in those words, but . . . I think that was the gist of it." Tears started to form in Steffanie's eyes.

I put my arm around her. "Hey, it's okay. Life goes on."

She became intense again. "I don't know what I want out of my life, Harry! Am I hopeless? Am I really hopeless? I *am*, aren't I?"

"I'm afraid so," I deadpanned. "Completely hopeless. But you gotta go with your heart, Steff. And if you're having serious doubts about marrying this guy, maybe you should listen."

"So what kind of doubts are you having about Mary?"

"I told you. None."

"That's not what you said. You said 'sometimes, but they don't last long.'"

"I was just trying to sympathize."

"Oh, give me a break. What are your doubts, Harry?"

"Nothing serious. I just . . ."

"Yeees?"

"How come you wanna know this? Don't you hear enough gossip in life?"

"I told you something personal. Now I want you to tell me."

"It's nothing. I just . . . wonder sometimes if we have enough in common. That's all."

"Don't be ridiculous," scoffed Steff. "You think Melody and Marcos had anything in common? Look at *them*."

"Okay, maybe it's more than that. I think . . . *man*, this is hard."

"You're doing fine.

"I think . . . it's all been . . . too *easy*."

"What do you mean?"

"I don't know. Sometimes she just seems so . . ."

"What? Come on. Out with it."

"Predictable!" I blurted. "There. I said it."

"Do you feel better?"

"No. In fact, forget I said it. I *love* Mary. I always have. And I know that she loves me. Sometimes, in fact . . . I think she loves me too much."

"*Too much?* Are you serious?"

"A little." I closed my eyes tightly. "Aaagh! Listen to me. I sound like a jerk."

"No. Keep explaining."

I drew a breath and let it all out. "It's like I just feel too *sure* of everything. Almost from the day we met, I knew that Mary was in love with me. She came with me back to the modern world. She lived at my house. She does everything I ask. She was faithful to me during my entire mission. I don't even think she ever dated anyone else. Did she?"

Steffanie shook her head. "Absolutely not."

"There. You see? I've felt my obligation from day one. She expects me to marry her, and that's it. End of story. If I don't, I'll be a total heel. A complete loser."

"You don't *want* to marry her?"

"That's not what I said! You're not listening. I just wish . . . I had to *work* at it somehow. Does that make sense?"

"Perfectly," said Steff, her expression a little darker. "I know the drill. And frankly, Harry, I'm a bit disappointed. I thought you had a little more spine than the average male—"

"Oh, here we go. Gee, I'm sure glad I told you all this—"

"What is it about guys?" Steffanie kept ranting. "Unless they think they're 'winning' your love, they lose interest. Then half the time, even after they've won, they lose interest anyway."

"Don't give me this. Girls are the same way—"

"It's all about conquest, isn't it? Oh, it's infuriating! So *what* if Mary knows exactly what she wants? Is that such a bad thing?"

"I didn't say it was a bad thing. I just said . . . Has it ever occurred to you that Mary might have the same doubts? I mean, does she really love *me?* Or have I just been in the right place at the right time?"

"Give me a break, Harry."

"All right, forget it. Forget I said anything. I *love* Mary. I'm going to marry her. Case closed."

"You sure make it sound romantic."

"Conversation closed, too. Let's just find them."

We continued climbing toward the summit of the hill, hoping that we might see something on the other side that would give us a better idea of where we were.

"How long do you think it will take to hone in on their location?" asked Steff.

"I don't have the foggiest idea," I replied, my mood still a little testy.

"So we could be here for weeks?"

"I don't know. But if we don't keep moving, we might . . ."

My voice trailed off like an echo hitting a soundproof wall. The sight on the grassy plain below us left me breathless, almost gasping. We continued to edge forward in silence, eyes wide, until the full vista was spread before us like a vision from Dante's *Inferno*.

On the verdant plain about two miles distant a battle was about to commence. At least that's how I interpreted it. There were two distinct bodies of men facing one another on opposite sides of a lazy river. There were *thousands* of them. Maybe *ten* thousand living, breathing soldiers. The river was about twenty feet wide, but from the looks of it, not much more than ankle deep. But the *character* of the armies was what struck me. This is what gripped my chest like a taut band between heart and lungs. It was like nothing I'd ever seen. Well, let me be more specific. The character of the army on the *east* side of the river was like nothing I'd ever seen. The army on the west appeared to be fairly ill-equipped— no cavalry, no catapults or any other kind of artillery. They were arrayed in rags and dull earth tones. The army on the east, however, had horses and catapults and even *elephants!* Soldiers and animals, artillery and wagons were arrayed in the most brilliant colors—shimmering purple, sky blue, blood red, and emerald green. I might have mistaken it for a traveling carnival if not for the dazzling reflection of golden war shields, silver and bronze swords, and multispiked javelins.

As Steff and I finally halted, our eyes still wide, I tried to determine the nature of the scene before us. At present there was a kind of pregnant anticipation. Cavalry and archers on the east side of the river were still joining in formation, lining up in two tidy rows, as if making ready for the assault. I thought I could hear chants and jibes on the wind, insults being hurled from one side of the river to the other. The army on the west looked cocky enough, but not nearly as disciplined. I judged that they were a fairly tough rabble, but with uneven rows and sometimes unequal knots of infantry. They seemed to be *daring* the horses and elephants to make their charge. The actual number of soldiers on both sides looked fairly equal, and yet to casual observers (as Steff and I obviously were), it looked anything *but* equal. The army on the west appeared as if they were about to find themselves in the middle of a genuine bloodbath.

Okay, I've described the scene in the foreground (if two miles away can be considered a foreground). Now let me talk about the *background*, because this was no less awe-inspiring.

Rising in the northeast, just right of the horizon line, was a tower. I'm gonna capitalize that. There was a TOWER. This thing was *huge!* I couldn't have wagered a guess as to how high. Or how far away. The hills in the foreground blocked the base of it. There was also a dark gray cloud obscuring the summit. The top of this monstrosity appeared to have its own *climate!* The structure was a kind of block-shaped pyramid with different levels, but it was too far away to describe specific details, except for its color—black. This thing was as black as coal. Well, that may not have been accurate. It was too distant to perceive if there were other colors. But when I started to imagine *people* at the top of that colossus, I felt a wave of vertigo. The sight was so breathtaking—and *freaky.*

"Harry," said Steffanie, a tremor of fear in her voice, "what *is* that? Where are we? What's going on?"

I shook my head. What made her think *I* knew the answers? Yet the sight of that tower did evoke one idea. How could it *not?* It was the most obvious presumption of anyone familiar with Western civilization or the book of Genesis. But the concept was dizzying. Was it possible? Were we actually staring at the *Tower of Babel?*

"Are you thinking what I'm thinking about that tower?" said Steffanie, as if she'd honed into my thoughts.

"I am," I replied, "if you're thinking 'Tower of Babel.'"

She became excited. "Then it *did* occur to you!"

"Of *course* it occurred to me. How could it *not* occur to me? But how can we be sure?"

"If it *is* the Tower of Babel, what century would that make it?"

"Don't ask me. Two thousand B.C. Three thousand B.C. I don't think archeologists are sure either. To most of them the Tower of Babel is a myth."

"Three thousand B.C.? You mean that pillar in Frost Cave may have thrown us back *five thousand years?*"

I nodded uneasily. "If my impressions are correct, that pillar of energy is capable of sending us anywhere in history. As well as to any location on the globe."

We heard the sound of a trumpet—very loud. The blast reverberated in our ears and made us instinctively crouch down behind some brush. It wasn't exactly a covering, but it would at least hide us partially from spying eyes.

Following the trumpet blare, each army became deathly still. The ranks of infantry and horsemen stopped forming. There were no more cries or jibes, just the haunting moan of the wind. But after a moment, a voice rang out. A *loud* voice, as if it were amplified by a bullhorn. Steffanie and I could hear it well enough, though at times we had to strain our ears.

"Sons of Japheth!" the voice bellowed. "Your rebellion is at an end! Your kinsmen have abandoned you! Beyond you is the wilderness of Joktan. You cannot survive in Joktan. Mardon, Prince of Shinar, has cut off your escape. Will you now submit to the will of your king, or will you be destroyed?"

There was an eruption of angry voices. The men dressed in gray and brown rags on the west side of the river started stirring like a hornet's nest, obviously in defiance of the voice.

"There's going to be a battle," I said.

"Gee, Harry, do you think so?" asked Steff, sounding more alarmed than sarcastic.

My mind was furiously drawing conclusions. *Sons of Japheth.* I'd heard that name before. Japheth was one of the sons of Noah, right? Shem, Ham, Japheth. I'd also heard the name Shinar. During the last couple months I'd reread Genesis during personal scripture study. I felt sure that this was where I'd seen it. To verify the hunch, I slipped the backpack off my shoulder.

"What are you doing?" asked Steff.

Without answering her right away, I unzipped the pocket at the very back and pulled out my missionary Four-in-One. The volume was considerably dog-eared after two years of frequent use. I'd marked it up just the way I liked. As neatly as you please, I turned to Genesis, chapter eleven.

"Here," I announced, and started reading at verse two: "*And it came to pass, as they journeyed from the east, that they found a plain in the land of Shinar; and they dwelt there. And they said one to another, Go to, let us make brick, and burn them thoroughly. And they had brick for stone, and slime had they for morter. And they said, Go to, let us build us a city and a tower, whose top may reach unto heaven . . .*"

I looked up again at Steffanie, whose face appeared thoroughly enchanted. We turned simultaneously to gaze at the tower again.

"Wow, Harry," she said. "You found that fast. I'm impressed."

"Two years on a mission will do that to you."

"What about the name of Japheth or Mardon? Who were they?"

"Japheth was the oldest son of Noah. But I've never heard of Mardon."

"'*Sons of Japheth*,'" Steffanie repeated thoughtfully. "Does that mean the guys on the west are his descendants?"

"That's what I'd guess."

"So who are the guys on the east? The ones with the elephants?"

"Don't know. Descendants of Shem or Ham, I suppose. But we'd have to—"

Another flurry of trumpet blasts erupted from the eastern ranks. The critical moment had arrived. The archers on the front lines of the eastern army fired a volley of arrows into the midst of the sons of Japheth. It looked like a thousand silver needles. Flames were put to several catapults and the springs were released. As the ordnance flew through the air it looked like little more than a smoking flicker, but when it exploded among the ranks on the ground it was like an explosion of napalm, igniting ten or twenty soldiers at once. Arrows were also expelled from the ranks of Japheth. We heard a blood-chilling roar as the infantry on both sides of the river collided like two ocean waves. Horsemen on the east galloped swiftly through the rows of archers. The river boiled as men crossed frantically to and fro. The clashing of weapons reminded me of the sound of water sizzling in a pan of hot grease. A cloud of pale dust and black smoke was stirred up, obscuring our view of the northernmost part of the action, but the battle in the south—closest to our position— remained plainly visible. I heard the shriek of horses and the screams of men. Living things were falling everywhere, either from being struck by arrows, firebombs, or swords. I saw a horse collapse along the edge of the river. Like the hyenas of Jericho, a cluster of Japheth's warriors lunged in on all sides of the fallen man, no doubt chopping him to bits.

Steffanie's eyes were riveted. She looked almost catatonic with shock and revulsion, but then she turned to me and said in a subdued, ominous tone, "Maybe we should get out of here, Harry."

"And go where?" I asked.

"I don't know. But if that battle starts moving south, I don't want to be here."

"I doubt anyone would retreat toward us," I said. "They'd go southwest, along the river. Or north."

"They might think it's safer in these hills."

I shook my head. "They'd head toward those hills in the north, where there's more brush and trees. The safest place for us is probably exactly where we are. And yet . . ."

"What?" asked Steff.

"Sooner or later we have to talk to *somebody*. If a few soldiers wander this way, it might be the best thing that could happen. How *else* are we going to find the others unless we start asking questions?"

"That brings us back to our original problem," said Steff. "What questions would we ask?"

We watched the theater of death and destruction for over an hour. My prediction for the battle's outcome was proving accurate. The sons of Japheth were being systematically eliminated, stomped out like cornered bugs. Eventually the army on the east charged in with their elephants. The beasts were arrayed in brightly colored armor from tusk to tail, an unstoppable line of battle tanks. This appeared to be the final blow to Japheth's morale. Pockets of warriors started fleeing north, just as I'd anticipated. But a larger number were actually fleeing west—exactly in the direction of this so-called wilderness of Joktan. From here the region looked like a vast wasteland, flat and featureless. Obviously there would be very little water or resources for anyone who tried to escape in that direction.

About this time I began to notice something quite interesting. It was a bird. That might not seem interesting at first, but the way the bird was acting definitely evoked curiosity. As far as I could tell, it kept diving in and out of the action like a Japanese Zero. Then it would fly back to a knot of horsemen at the rear of the eastern army. The bird would land among the horsemen, then fly off again to some new area of the conflict, as if giving reports of the battle's progress. But this was ridiculous. What kind of strategy report could be offered by a bird?

After watching this for a while, I began to notice a pattern. The bird would fly over specific groups of warriors who were retreating from the battle area, then let out a piercing squawk. I soon realized that I wasn't the *only* person watching that bird. Some of the commanders within the ranks of the eastern army were apparently using it to direct troop maneuvers. I could have sworn that once—when the raptor squawked at a group of ten or so soldiers trying to flee into the trees—a group of cavalrymen immediately turned their horses and took up pursuit. Amazing as it seems, I started to believe that this bird was helping orchestrate command decisions on the ground. Its job seemed to be locating stragglers. Apparently the eastern army was determined to let no one escape.

The battle started winding down. I noticed some of the warriors of Japheth throwing down their weapons and surrendering with raised hands. These men were being frogmarched toward a gathering place on the plateau, just right of the knot of horsemen who controlled the bird. Other sons of Japheth were executed on the spot. I assumed these were some of the rowdier enemy warriors whose "rehabilitation" was deemed unlikely. Several of the elephants must have been trained to trample men underfoot, because right before our eyes one burly pachyderm was unleashed on a squadron of captured men in the southwest corner of the battle zone. Steffanie's stomach gave in. She turned away, shuddering.

"Let's get out of here, Harry," she insisted. "These people can't help us. They're worse than jackals. They'd sooner kill us."

I was starting to agree. Yet I hesitated another moment, scanning the desert toward the west. A small group of Japhethite soldiers were escaping behind a sandy ridge. Their position would have been invisible to the eastern army's commanders, but it was perfectly visible to us. It occurred to me that a small group of stragglers like this, battle weary and alone, might be good prospects to become our allies.

But then I saw the bird. It swooped down over them and let out an obnoxious squawk. Several more times it descended upon them. One of the warriors fired an arrow at it, missing horribly. Sure enough, from the grassy plain, several horsemen armed with silver-tipped javelins began riding in the direction of the ridge.

I watched the bird start flying back toward its master on the plateau. Then it did something alarming. After a sharp correction in flight, it began flapping toward *us!*

"Uh-oh," I said. I grabbed Steffanie's arm. "Duck down!"

We flattened down against the dirt behind the brush. But what was the point? There was no hope of hiding from an airborne spy. I glanced up just as I heard and felt the whoosh of its wings a few feet over our heads. I also had my first full glimpse of its appearance. It was a large bird with dark brown wings and a white, spotted belly and throat. I felt sure it was a falcon. A red string or strip of leather was tied to its right leg. It belted out an ear-splitting squawk, like the screech of tires on an old furniture truck, then flapped higher into the air. I swore there was laughter in that squawk. It found it hilarious that we were trying to hide. The raptor swooped down several more times, screeching like a mother hen. Steff threw a rock at it.

"Shut up!" she cried.

But it was no use. I looked over the top of the brush. A dozen cavalrymen were already galloping our way. Only after it was sure that our presence had been noticed did the falcon finally retreat.

"What can we do?" asked Steffanie.

"We can *run!*" I exclaimed.

I seized my pack by the strap and began careening down the hill. Steffanie's legs were carrying her just as swiftly. We charged back toward the geysers. Where else could we run? At least near the springs there were rocks and crags where we might hide. At this point I might have been just as pleased to dive back into the geyser—even if that steaming water was in full eruption!

But there wasn't enough time. It was a ten-minute dash to reach the geysers. After only four minutes, I turned back to see the horsemen coming over the top of the rise. Steffanie saw it too.

"Stop!" she shouted to me, panting heavily. "There's no point in running. We have to come up with a plan—and fast!"

"A plan for *what?*" I asked.

"For what to *say* to them. What are we going to say?"

I fought to catch my breath. "I have a feeling they're gonna want to do all the talking."

"Come *on! Think* of something!"

The horsemen would be on top of us in less than a minute.

"Take out your CD player," said Steff.

"My what?"

"CD player! It makes noise without the earphones, right?"

I was catching on. The only thing that might save our lives now was an immediate blast of modern technology. I reached into a side pocket of my backpack and dragged it out. At the moment a Brad Wilcox talk was inside of it. This wasn't quite the effect I was looking for. I grabbed my CD case.

"Hurry!" raged Steffanie.

The cavalrymen were only a few gallops off. My selection of CDs was rather limited. On my mission we'd been restricted to hymns and the Mormon Tabernacle Choir. I grabbed a CD at random and fumbled desperately to fit it into the player. I yanked out the earphones. Two of the horsemen raised up their ten-foot javelins; one end was tucked tightly under one arm while the fearsome bronze tip was pointed at our chests. They were going to *skewer* us! I shut the CD player, hit Play, and held it high.

My choice of CDs couldn't have been more inspired. From the speakers boomed the first chords of the *Hallelujah Chorus* by Handel. As I opened one eye, several horsemen pulled to a halt. Other horses became frightened, reared up, and spun their riders in the saddle. The soldiers with javelins had also stopped, their faces aghast.

Thank you Mo-Tab, I thought in my heart. *Thank you, George Frederic Handel.* The combination of the two appeared to have saved our lives.

NOTES TO CHAPTER 2:

The Tower of Babel is one of the least understood subjects in the earth's history. All that we know officially of the edifice and the events surrounding it are recorded in the first nine verses of chapter 11 in the book of Genesis. Somewhat more can be learned from various tracts of apocryphal literature, including the book of Jasher, the works of Josephus, the book of Jubilees, and others. But the information is often conflicting and does little to fully illuminate the circumstances and history. Modern prophets have also been reported to have made statements, some of which boggle the mind and create as many questions as they answer. Some of these will be discussed as they become relevant in the story.

But even from the scant information that we have, it's apparent that the occurrences associated with the Tower of Babel were some of the most significant events to occur on our planet. We are told that as a result of its construction the languages of the world were confounded. No longer was the pure, undefiled language spoken since the days of Adam to be the universal means of communication. It is the first major event recorded after the Great Flood, though it is unclear exactly how long the interval between both occurrences may have been. Possibly it was three to five hundred years. Of course, in the minds of many scholars, both the Great Flood and the Tower of Babel are myths and are not considered legitimate historical events, despite the fact that many cultures of the world include episodes very similar in their own histories.

There are reportedly some six hundred "flood" traditions among peoples as seemingly disparate as the Navajo and the Chinese. For instance, records from Ninevah that date back to 1700 to 2000 B.C. tell the *Epic of Gilgamesh,* wherein a man named Utnapishtim received divine warnings of a flood, built a huge ark, preserved human and animal life, sent out birds, and offered sacrifices. For many historians this is actually the oldest flood account on record (Jean Bottero, *Everyday Life in Ancient Mesopotamia*, 214–15 [Johns Hopkins University Press, 2001], 214–15). Like most such traditions, this epic mixes in the people's local deities and flavor, but the essence of the story—a universal flood wherein a small number of humans and animals were saved in a floating vessel—generally remains the same.

Often the legend of a tower to heaven and the confusion of tongues is included right alongside it. Long before the arrival of Europeans on the Island of Hao, part of the Puamotu (or Tuamotu) Islands in Polynesia, the people told tales of a great flood wherein the principal Noah character was named Rata.

After the flood, the sons of Rata who survived attempted to erect a building by which they could reach the sky and see the creator god Vatea (or Atea). "But the god in anger chased the builders away, broke down the building, and changed their language, so that they spoke divers tongues" (R. W. Williamson, *Religious and Cosmic Beliefs of Central Polynesia* [Cambridge, 1933], vol. 1, 94).

The *Popal Vuh*, the sacred book of the Quiche Mayas, tells of a great flood prepared by "Heart of Sky" to punish the disobedient because "*they did not remember their Framer or their Shaper. They walked however they pleased.*" Later it narrates that the language of all the families gathered at Tulan was confused and that none could understand each other's speech (Allen J. Christensen *Popal Vuh*, F.A.R.M.S., 2000); (Brasseur de Bourbourg, *Histoire des nations civilises du Mexique* (1857–59), vol. 1, 72). A similar Andean tradition was recorded by Sarmiento de Gamboa. Like other accounts, it places the confusion of languages after the Deluge (Gamboa, *Historia de los Incas*, 7).

From Fernando de Alva Ixtlilxochitl, a Mexican nobleman who wrote the history of his ancestors in Spanish, we have the following account:

> *And it is recorded in the Tulteca history that this period or first world, as they called it, lasted for 1,716 years, after which time great lightning and storms from the heavens destroyed mankind, and everything in the earth was covered by water, including the highest mountain called Caxtolmolictli, which is 15 cubits high.*
>
> *To this they recorded other events, such as how after the flood, a few people who had escaped the destruction inside a Toptlipetlacalli, which interpreted means an enclosed ark, began again to multiply upon the earth.*
>
> *After the earth began again to be populated, they built Zacualli very high and strong, which means the very high tower, to protect themselves against a second destruction of the world.*
>
> *As time elapsed, their language became confounded, such that they did not understand one another; and they were scattered to all parts of the world* (Ixtlilxochitl, *Obras Historicas*, ed., Alfredo Chavero, vol. 1, ch. 1, 1892).

Many other traditions could be cited, but this is sufficient to illustrate that such accounts all seem to point back to very ancient and real events. If indeed these events really occurred, then we would *expect* the essence of the story to have been preserved in many parts of the world. The persistence of the name of "Noah" is particularly remarkable, especially when you consider the ultimate language differences between peoples, and the extreme local distortions that developed in flood legends. Yet the name survived virtually unchanged in such isolated places as Hawaii (where he was called Nu-u), the Sudan (Nuh), China (Nu-Wah), the Amazon region (Noa), Phrygia (Noe) and among the Hottentots (Noh and Hiagnoh).

A farther compilation of flood traditions is provided on the Internet at: http://www.cheimerdinger.com/towerofthunder/notes

CHAPTER THREE

Joshua

Mary's gonna give me a turn to tell the story, which I think is way cool of her, 'cause honestly, I, Joshua Plimpton, am the coolest! *There's no twelve-year-old quite as cool as me. And I'll prove it by how exciting I tell things.*

That first night that we spent out on the desert after we dropped out of the sky felt very long and very weird. Okay, maybe the "weird" part only applies to me. That probably sounds funny. Let me explain. You see, it was because of the sword. I slept with the sword of Akish cuddled right up beside me. Of course, Becky and Mary were squished up around me too, as we tried to stay warm, but the golden hilt of Akish's creation was kept close to my chest.

At first Mary made me set it away from us a short distance, but it was just so cold and, I dunno . . . It was as if I could sense the sword's heat. I could feel it even though it was just a few feet away. For reasons I can't explain, I knew somehow that just by holding it, I'd be kept warm all night long. Not only did I know that, *but I also knew that it would keep* the *others warm too. They'd be warm just because they were touching* me.

Now let me make one thing clear. I had no illusions about the sword. I knew evil hands had forged it. I knew that it had killed Todd Finlay and that it had almost killed us. I also knew that it might have evil powers inside it, but I really wasn't sure what to make of that. The way I looked at it, a sword was a sword was a sword. It was sort of like that one bumper sticker that reads, "Guns don't kill people; people kill people." I kind of saw the sword the same way. Sure, in the hands of somebody evil, it could do a lot of evil things. But I wasn't evil. I was one of the good guys.

I realized Mary and Becky didn't want to have anything to do with it. And that was okay. I respected that. And honestly, I took their squeamishness very seriously. I was determined to keep on my toes. If I felt like the sword was tempting me to do anything wrong in any way, shape, or form, I'd nip it in the bud before it could do any damage. It was still very much in my mind to destroy it the first chance we got.

But the reality was, the night was cold and that sword was warm. Becky and Mary were already asleep when I reached over and pulled it closer. It felt so good! The warmth went from my hands all the way down to my toes, and I could tell it made Becky and Mary warmer too, because everybody stopped shivering.

After I finally fell asleep, I had a very weird dream. I dreamed about the Nephites and the Lamanites. In fact, I dreamed I was standing on the Hill Cumorah with the sword in my hands. I was defending the Nephites from utter destruction. And I was doing an awfully good job of it, too. I managed to cut down every Lamanite warrior who even came near. Pretty soon they just ran away in terror. I saved the whole Nephite nation single-handedly! It was the neatest dream ever! I'd been thinking for some time now how noble it would be to change history and keep the Nephites from being wiped out. In my opinion I was a Nephite. Sure, I knew my parents were American and all. I was proud to be American too. But I was born in Zarahemla, and a part of me definitely felt obligated to defend and protect my people.

Then came the weird part of my dream. After we won the battle, all the Nephites around me cheered and stabbed their swords triumphantly into the earth. I was caught up in the cheering too, and I rammed my own sword into the ground. But the very instant I let go of that golden hilt, the Lamanite armies turned back from their retreat. They began attacking again! My fellow Nephites all around us started getting slaughtered. And even more bizarre, the Lamanite army seemed larger and more ferocious than before. But the minute I grabbed up that sword—the instant I put my hand back on its golden hilt, the Lamanites halted their attack and retreated. In my dream I tried this several more times, and the result was always the same: Hang onto the sword, and victory was mine. Let it go, and I would get slaughtered.

Yeah, I know what everybody is thinking. You're thinking—Oh no! Poor Joshua is gonna think he needs the sword to save the Nephites and he'll get corrupted!

Oh, contraire! *You really think I was that stupid? I wasn't fooled.*

In fact, I remember waking up right after the dream ended and looking down at the sword. Its surface glistened in the starlight, almost like it was smiling at me. I made a little snort and said sarcastically in my mind, almost as if I was talking directly to the sword, "Yeah, right! It's the bottom of the ocean for you, pal. And don't you forget it!"

No response entered my thoughts. The sword was silent. When I fell back asleep, my dreams were perfectly normal, which is to say, I don't remember them. But I do *remember that when the three of us started to awaken at first light, I felt totally refreshed, like I'd slept for a week. Nobody else was complaining either.*

"We should try and walk as far as we can before the sun gets too high," *said Mary.* "We'll just have to hope that by this afternoon we've found some kind of shelter to wait out the heat of the day."

We all took one drink of water. That was all. Mary was determined to make it last as long as possible. After that, the drudgery of walking across a flat, empty desert started all over again.

After a couple hours some plants began to appear here and there. Also, we began to see the outline of some hills. As I turned back, that tower hardly looked any smaller than when we'd started, but I guessed it had shrunk a little.

By noon we still hadn't found any shelter, but the landscape around us was changing. It was rolling a lot more, and there were more and more plants and grasses, and even a few scrubby bushes. Then around midafternoon, we found something new. It looked like wagon tracks. They came from the east in a line that went directly back toward the tower. We'd actually been walking more to the southeast, which may have been why we didn't cross it earlier. If this was supposed to be an official road, it must not have been used very much. By the looks of it, there were only wheel ruts for two separate wagons. The reason we knew it was headed west was because there were also dozens of horse prints.

"I don't see any camel tracks," *I commented.* "Horses need a lot more water, right? I wonder if that means we're a lot closer to a village or a water well than we think."

"Either that," said Mary, *"or the wagons were carrying a great deal of water with them."*

Either way, it reminded me of how dry my mouth felt. If we were gonna survive, we needed to find water—and soon.

About an hour later something appeared ahead of us. It was difficult to tell at first what it was. Just a dark lump on the horizon. The shimmering heat waves weren't helping either, and they kept its true shape a mystery until we were almost on top of it.

Finally, Becky made a guess. "Wagons!"

She was right. By all appearances it was the exact same two wagons that had made the tracks. They were hidden slightly behind rises in the unlevel ground. They also seemed to be sitting slightly askew, like they'd decided to stop and make camp. I even smelled the smoke and saw a little dark puff rising into the air. But as we drew nearer I began to sense other shapes. None of them were moving. The other shapes were mainly of two kinds—big dark ones and smaller white ones. Mary was the first to identify the bigger ones.

"Horses," she said gravely.

She meant dead horses. I swallowed as the identity of the smaller shapes entered my mind. I turned out to be right. The smaller white shapes were human bodies. All of them dead.

The closer we got, the more sickened we all began to feel. Upon arriving, we felt downright horrified. The horses, the people—they were all dead. The bodies of both men and beasts were pincushioned with arrows. Someone had attacked them—and recently. Vultures weren't even circling yet. Blood on the ground still looked moist. One of the wagons had been burned, though part of it was still intact. The candy-striped canopy was still smoldering. So the source of smoke wasn't a campfire at all. The other wagon sat crookedly in the sand, its front axle split and one of its wheels lying flat. The two draw horses were still harnessed there, lying dead with their eyes open, a few flies buzzing around them. The sight was so awful I can hardly describe it.

"Don't look at the faces," said Mary. "Just keep walking."

I tried to take her advice, but I couldn't help myself. Just seeing a dead person's face for a single instant burned it permanently into my memory. They were such awful, heart-wrenching images! As we walked through the scattered remains, each face frozen in death looked more *grotesque than the last. The white and billowy cloaks of the bodies were blowing in the wind. Many of the people were still clutching weapons. As of yet the smell wasn't that bad, but in the heat of day it would soon become unbearable.*

Tears began to stream down Becky's face. Mary put her arm around Becky's shoulder, trying to strengthen and comfort her.

"Who would do such a thing?" Becky wept. "Why?"

I'd been asking myself the same questions. If the attackers had been bandits or robbers, why would they have killed the horses? Wouldn't live horses have been valuable prizes? Maybe the bandits had been looking for something very specific. The contents of the wagons had been thrown all over the place. Sacks had been torn open and the grain was blowing about like lawn seed. Expensive-looking garments and clothes were strewn everywhere, some of them dangling from thorny scrubs. Colorful ceramic plates and bronze goblets littered the area. I would have thought that some of this stuff was pretty expensive. Maybe the robbers had already ridden off with as much as they could carry. Or maybe they'd found the thing that they were looking for and galloped away satisfied.

But somehow I didn't think this was true. Maybe it was the way that the baggage had been hoisted out of the wagons and tossed aside. Somebody had searched this caravan as thoroughly as possible, and by the looks of how they'd left it, they'd been quite angry not to find the object of their search.

I also had another thought. I couldn't have said for sure, but my gut feeling was that the people who were driving this caravan had been running away. I don't know what made me think that. Maybe it was how out of place the stuff in the wagons looked out here in the desert. Also, the people had been well armed with cool-looking carved bows and shiny metal knives. The weapons were still lying in the dirt beside their hands. I suspected that some of the attackers were also among the dead. Most of the people were wearing white, rough-looking cloaks. But two of them wore bright purple, gold, and black cloaks that looked rather pricey. It was a uniform. I felt sure the attackers were soldiers or the private bodyguard of a rich merchant or king. I might have thought they were bodyguards for the caravan, like samurai warriors, but one of them had an arrow through his neck that matched the arrows in the quiver of one of the dead caravan guys.

The appearance of the attackers was different too, especially the way they did their hair. The caravan people had plain, straight hairstyles, but the bad guys (I only guessed that they were the bad guys) wore complicated braids. Even their beards were braided, and sometimes laced with glass and metal beads and other things. But just like everybody else, the bodies of the attackers had been left in the desert to rot. Whoever had slaughtered this caravan, they'd been in an awful big rush to leave.

My eyes started scanning the countryside. Mary and Becky were doing the same. We were all thinking the same thing—that the attackers might still be close. There didn't seem to be anyone else nearby, but in the west we could now see a lot of hills and many places where bandits could hide.

Becky looked back at the devastation one more time. "What should we do?" she asked, sounding helpless. "We can't just leave these people like this."

It was sort of a funny thing how folks from our civilization couldn't stand to leave dead bodies unburied. It just didn't seem right. But what else could we do? If we stopped now, we might as well have buried ourselves right beside them. Such a job would undoubtedly force us to drink up all our remaining water. It didn't look like we'd find much extra water among the wagons. Two big water barrels were lying on the ground, each one broken open, the contents allowed to seep into the earth. It seemed really weird that they'd sabotage the water, almost as if the attackers had wanted to make sure, in case anyone survived, that they'd never make it back to civilization.

"We have to keep moving," said Mary stiffly. "We have to forget about this."

"How can we forget?" asked Becky, her voice trembling.

"We just have to." Mary was trying to sound brave, but I could tell she wasn't any less disturbed than Becky or me. I knew that she'd seen some awful things back in Judea during the war with Rome, but I still could hear the slight quiver in her voice.

"What about food?" I asked. "Should we at least look to see if—"

"This is a grave site," said Mary. "It wouldn't be right for us to act like vultures and jackals."

"But if there's food," I said. "If there's anything that might help us . . . Mary it only makes sense. How do you know that God didn't lead us here for just this reason? You have to let us at least look."

Mary sighed. I could also see her shudder, but she realized I was right. "Fine," she said finally. "But only food or water. We are not grave robbers and scavengers. Take only what we might need to survive."

Mary stepped away a short distance and left the searching to Becky and me. She'd been taught some very strict guidelines about how a person behaved around corpses and dead bodies, and couldn't quite shake her uneasiness about it.

Becky and I focused most of our energies on the partially burned wagon. The contents of the other wagon—the one with the broken axle—had been completely strewn about. But some of the stuff in the burned wagon had been left. The attackers must have thought that the fire would completely consume it, but they were wrong. After we removed the top layer of burned cloth and debris, we found other stuff underneath.

"Josh, look at this!" said Becky.

Holy Toledo! She'd found three sheepskin canteens! Well, maybe they weren't sheepskin, but they were some kind of skin. Most importantly, they were bloated with liquid.

I went to rummaging in the same corner and pulled out a burlap-type sack stuffed with something that looked like biscuits. A few spilled out. There was a hole in the sack. Somebody's blade had stabbed into it, as if making sure something else wasn't hidden inside. The biscuits were dark brown, like pumpernickel.

Becky snatched one up and bit into it. After she'd chewed for several seconds, she announced through a mouthful of crumbs, "It's delicious!"

I bit into one of my own. My eyes widened excitedly. "They're cookies!"

That wasn't totally accurate. It's not like they were as sweet as Oreos or Vienna Cremes. But they definitely had a sweet, molasses kind of flavor, almost like gingersnaps. Only after I'd snarfed down a couple more did I begin to notice that they were baked into animal shapes—just like our modern-day animal crackers! There were lions and horses and elephants, and even one that looked like a rabbit, and another that looked like a coiled-up snake.

"I could eat this whole sack!" Becky declared.

"Don't eat too much," I said. "This could last us for days."

Suddenly I started to imagine that I was in one of those commercials where the guy gets stuck in a scientific chamber with tons of cereal and an empty fridge—Got milk?

Water would have to suffice. I grabbed up one of Becky's sheepskin canteens, untied the top, and started to guzzle. Then my eyes widened all over again. I held the canteen out in front of my face. Becky saw the white dribble on my chin.

"What is it?" she asked.

"It's milk!" I exclaimed.

Becky grabbed it away to taste it herself.

As I licked my lips, I rethought the matter. "Actually, I think it's cream. It's kind of thick."

After Becky had swallowed and wiped her mouth, she said, "There's something sweet in it. Wait'll I show Mary!"

She took the canteens and climbed out of the wagon. I took another quick look around, but except for another sack containing some kind of grain, there didn't appear to be anything else edible.

I tied the two sacks together with some rope (careful to tie it below the place where the sack of cookies had been stabbed) and slung them over my shoulder. Then I rejoined Mary and Becky. Mary had just finished taking her first small drink from one of the sheepskins.

She smacked her tongue a few times thoughtfully, then said, "Goat's milk." Still, she didn't look entirely certain and added, "It's very different."

Mary passed on eating any of the cookies for now. I think she wanted us to get farther away from the corpses. We started walking westward. Despite our discoveries, our moods were still heavy and depressed. We were also nervous, but as we passed the last body of a dead horse and the last strip of headcloth caught on a thistle, I think we began to feel a little sense of relief. The grimness of death was behind us.

Or so we thought.

Suddenly I noticed a place on the ground that looked very much like a bloodstain. Becky and Mary both reacted as I pulled to a stop. Soon their eyes were drawn to the same bloody spot. I leaned down and touched it with my fingers.

"Joshua, what are you doing?" asked Becky.

"Look," I said. "There's another spot over here."

In fact, I found several more spots, just like a trail. It seemed to lead to the southeast, over a small hill and around the edge of a little ridge.

"I've seen enough blood," said Becky. "I think we should get far away from here."

"Wait a moment," said Mary. "It may be the blood of a person—someone who's injured or dying. I think we should follow it."

"What if it's the blood of a horse?" I asked.

"If it's a horse, that may be even better," said Mary. "The first thing a wounded horse will look for is water. The trail might lead to a river or spring."

Good enough argument for me. The trail of blood was fairly well marked for the next hundred yards. It went over a hill and into the flat area beyond it, but as we approached another little ridge, the drops disappeared. We searched around for a minute or so, then Mary said, "Well, whatever it was, its wound must have coagulated. Let's not waste any more time. Let's move back to—"

That's when we heard it. The sound was as clear as a windchime, but the wind made it difficult to pinpoint where it had come from. There was no mistaking what had caused it. I'd heard this sound more than I cared to say over the last few months with the newest arrival of Uncle Jim's family. It was the cry of a baby.

We held our breaths, waiting intensely for the sound to repeat. It had been so short. Just a peep, really. But it couldn't have been too far away.

"This way," said Mary, making a guess.

We walked toward the next short ridge. At last we heard it again, this time louder. It was more like a wail now—the kind of high-pitched wail that vibrates in the brain and makes a mother sit up in bed and rush to see what's the matter. We ran around the ridge. Three seconds later, I came to a halt. Mary and Rebecca gasped.

Lying against the stones was a woman in a white cloak. The material was coarse and heavy, but it was still fancier than anything worn by the people in the caravan. I might have thought she was with the attackers. But why would an attacker have been a woman? More than that, why would an attacker have a baby?

The woman's face didn't look like it had any signs of life. The baby wasn't quite visible. It was hidden under the puffy folds of material on the arms of her white dress. We knew the baby was in there though, because we could still hear it crying. Mary leaned down to touch the woman's shoulder. The lady looked a little older than most mothers—forty or so. I could see the evidence of her wound. She'd torn off the hem of her cloak and tried to use it to tie off a gash in her stomach. Obviously it hadn't helped much, because she only made it a few yards farther.

Mary reached down and pulled away the puffy folds of material to reveal the little one. As she exposed it, it only cried all the more—so much so that it almost couldn't breathe, its face turning the color of hot lava.

The woman stirred. She was still alive! But she was far too weak to stop Mary from taking the baby away. Mary tried to calm it down. Becky sat behind the woman's head. She nudged closer and laid the woman's head in her lap. My first impulse was to take the canteen off my belt. It still had a little water left, and I knew she must've been awfully thirsty.

At first she looked terrified of us, but I soon realized that she wasn't terrified for herself. She was frightened for the baby. She tried to reach out and take it back, but Mary wouldn't let her. Mary put her other hand on the woman's shoulder to try and offer comfort.

"It's all right," said Mary. "Your baby is all right. He looks perfectly fine."

She'd called the baby a "he." Leave it to a girl to determine a baby's sex at a glance. To me it could've been either one. The woman tried to say something, but her throat was too dry. I put my canteen up to her lips and poured a little water between them. She closed her eyes and her tongue worked it around.

"Give her more," said Becky.

I leaned in to do so, but the woman shook her head. Then she looked at Mary and said in a weak and strained voice, "Not . . . my . . . baby."

Mary looked confused. "Not yours? Whose baby is it? Are you part of the caravan that was attacked?"

She nodded at that, closing her eyes. "Nimrod's . . . guards," she said weakly.

"Nimrod?" asked Becky.

"Don't . . . let . . . find him," she said.

"The baby?" asked Mary. "Don't let Nimrod's guards find the baby?"

"They will . . . kill him."

My eyes bulged. Was she serious?

Her eyes opened again, but only to a narrow slit. She spoke something else, but the words weren't clear. The crying baby also made it difficult to hear.

Mary tried to lean closer. "What? Say it again. Please."

"Don't die," said Becky tearfully. "We'll take care of you. We'll get help. Just don't die."

But the woman could only say two final words. They were hardly a whisper. "Great . . . Shem."

Mary was gripping the woman's hand and at the same time trying to bounce and soothe the baby. She wasn't able to hear as well as Becky or I.

She asked us, "What did she say?"

Becky and I didn't dare reply, afraid if she said more we'd miss it. But after another moment, we realized that no sound at all was coming out of her mouth. We leaned back and looked at her face. Her eyes were still open a little. I waved my hand over them to see if there was any reaction. There was none.

"Becky," said Mary urgently. "Take the baby."

Becky was overcome with emotion. She took the baby from Mary, but she couldn't remove her eyes from the woman's face. Mary laid her ear against the woman's heart, listening for a beat.

"Is she . . . dead?" I asked.

After a moment, Mary raised her head and nodded solemnly.

Becky started to sob, clutching the baby—who was now crying much louder—tightly to her body.

"What did she say?" Mary asked again. "What were her last words?"

Mary's question echoed three times in my brain before I understood it. It felt like my senses were in a blender—everything was moving too fast.

Finally, I shook my head. "Nothing. Her last words weren't anything. She just said 'great.'"

"'Great?'"

"Yeah. Then she said 'Shem.' It's a name, I think."

"It's the baby's name," said Becky. "She was telling us his name." Becky wiped her tears against the baby's swaddling cloth.

I wasn't so sure my sister was right, but it sounded reasonable enough. We had to call the baby something.

"What did she mean by 'Great?'" asked Mary.

"I don't know." I shrugged. "She might have been trying to say more, but that's all she had the strength to get out."

"There were no other sounds? Maybe something that you didn't quite understand?"

"No," Becky confirmed. "Josh is right. That's all she said."

Mary stewed over this.

"Who do you think she is?" I asked.

"*There may be no way for us to know,*" *said Mary, gazing into the dead woman's face. "But if you ask me, the word 'great' refers to herself. She obviously gave her life for this child.*"

I asked, "You think she really was protecting this baby from the guards of somebody named Nimrod?"

"*Who is Nimrod?*" *Becky asked again.*

"*Nimrod is a king,*" *said Mary.*

"*How do you know?*" *I asked.*

Mary looked back toward the tower, its top now almost completely hidden by clouds. "He's the king of Shinar."

"*Shinar?*" *repeated Becky.*

Mary turned back to us. "Yes. Have neither of you studied the Torah?"

I pulled a face. "The what?"

"*The five books of Moses.*"

"*You mean the Old Testament?*" *I asked.*

"*Yes,*" *said Mary. "The first part anyway. In the days of the Great Tower, the king of all the land was named Nimrod." Again she looked at the tower intently. "He was the 'mighty hunter.'*"

I raised an eyebrow. "Mighty hunter of what?"

"*At the moment he's apparently hunting this infant," said Mary. "This woman clearly knew that she was dying. A woman on the verge of death will choose her words very carefully. I think she desperately wanted us to do the same thing* she *was doing. She wanted us to protect this baby.*"

"*But why would the king's guards attack some wagons and kill everybody just to find a baby?*" *I wondered.*

"*I guess it would depend on who the baby is," said Becky, giving a last sniffle and looking into its face.*

By some miracle the baby had stopped crying. It continued to moan a little, but its eyes were closed. It was falling asleep. We all studied the baby's face. It was a cute little face. Several reddish marks—stork bites I think they're called—still showed on the baby's eyebrow and chin. If I remembered right, this usually meant that the baby was only three or four months old. Actually, Shem looked almost exactly the same age as my little cousin, Gid Teancum.

Mary reached toward Rebecca. "Would you like me to take him?"

"No," said Becky sharply. Then she looked at Mary pleadingly. "I mean . . . not for a little while. Is it okay?"

Mary nodded with understanding.

"I think it stopped crying because it's too weak to cry anymore," I said.

Becky looked stricken. "What are we gonna do?"

Mary thought a moment, then grabbed one of the canteens of goat milk.

"Will it drink that?" I asked.

"I don't know," said Mary. "But I'm going to try. This woman was most likely the baby's nursemaid, but they might have kept that milk on the wagon for just this purpose."

Mary positioned the baby and the canteen just right. She managed to pinch off the top so that it would cause the baby to suck, acting more like a rubber nipple. She tried for several minutes, encouraging the baby with soothing words, getting milk all over its face. My heart knotted up in my chest. Was it just too weak?

But then I heard the first sucking sound. Mary's face lit up.

"He's drinking!" she announced.

Massive relief came over Becky and me. I was convinced that everything would be all right.

As Mary continued feeding and talking sweetly to the infant, Becky and I sat back against the ridge.

"Who do you think little Shem might be?" Becky asked me. "Do you think he's a prince? The son of a powerful enemy to King Nimrod?"

"I don't have the vaguest idea," I said. "I'm not even sure its name is Shem."

"But the woman called him Shem."

"It seemed to me the way the woman said it was . . . I don't know . . . almost as if Shem might be the person she wanted us to take it to."

"Don't call the baby an 'it.' It's a him."

"Sorry. Him. I wonder if Shem is the baby's father."

"Well, we may never know now," said Rebecca sadly. "Besides, I like the name. It suits him."

"Better than calling him, 'the baby,' I guess."

She rolled her eyes at me. The baby finally finished drinking and Mary tied the top of the canteen.

"We need to save all of this milk for the baby," she said. "Or at least for as long as we can before it spoils."

"I'm surprised in this heat that it isn't spoiled already," I said.

"I'm a little surprised too," said Mary. "But one should never question a miracle."

"Then you do think that God might have led us here," I said, ribbing her a little.

"I think," she admitted, smiling, "that it's a distinct possibility." But then, true to her character, she got instantly serious again. "We shouldn't linger here. Let's keep walking."

* * *

Mary rigged up a kind of papoose carrier for the baby, then she gave Becky the honor of being the first to use it. After he'd gotten his fill of the goat milk, the baby fell back to sleep. He seemed accustomed to sleeping on the move and hardly stirred for the rest of the day. We continued our journey in the miserable heat. Thank goodness for the burnooses we'd gotten back in Judea, or my poor head and face would have been fried to a crisp.

Our water was almost gone. Unless we found more H_2O before tomorrow, we'd have no choice but to start drinking some of the baby's milk. As I was walking, I said a few prayers that we might soon find a stream or a lake. Just before nightfall, it appeared that the Lord had heard my prayers.

When we first saw the pond it was about a mile away. The surface was a glistening orange color in the light of the setting sun. I guessed it was about three hundred feet across. Actually, it looked more like a mud hole. But despite how it looked, we weren't the only creatures it had attracted. The pond appeared to be a gathering place for hundreds of animals! I counted at least two dozen different kinds—species that I would've never expected to see together in one place! There were elephants, water buffalo, gazelles, giraffes, deer, zebras, wild camels, and rams. I saw ostriches and all different kinds of antelopes with twisting horns. There was even something that looked like a moose. A short distance from the waterhole I noticed several large rhinoceroses lounging about, and other hairy creatures that looked like gorillas and baboons. Smaller animals scurried near the water's edge, though they were still too far away to recognize. I could also see all different types of colorful birds. I'd watched shows on the Discovery channel featuring parts of Africa with many different kinds of animals gathered at waterholes, but I'd never seen anything quite like this. It was as if some types of animals that would one day feel skittish toward one another were still the best of buds.

Rebecca said it best when she blurted out, "It's like an animal convention! *It's better than the zoo!*"

Shem woke up and let out a few concerned chirps, trying to figure out who we were and where he was. But he didn't become hysterical, as I might have expected—just looked around at each of us with a mildly frightened expression. Afterward, his fear seemed to go away, and he looked more curious than anything else. I almost wondered if Shem had gotten used to seeing new faces every time he awakened.

The baby's noises caused something to stir in the tall grasses to the right. Mary stopped abruptly. We stopped with her and listened. I was sure I could also hear rustling to the left. But on the right I could see some of the grasses bending, as if a creature was moving through them. It reminded me of that scene with the velociraptors in Jurassic Park II. Something was out there, and it was obviously stalking closer to us. My heart started pounding. The grasses went still and silent.

"Let's walk quickly," said Mary, "toward the waterhole."

My sister looked again toward the animal herds. "Do you think it's safe?"

I had the same question. Were elephants and rhinoceroses really any less dangerous than whatever was in the grass?

"Just follow me," said Mary sharply. "Move faster!"

Hastily, we started forward, leaving the tall grasses behind. Whatever was watching us from the grass for some reason had chosen not to attack—at least not yet.

We continued toward the water. But my nerves were still on edge. To our right about fifty yards was a herd of four or five rhinoceroses. I'd always heard that rhinos were one of the most dangerous animals in Africa. But shockingly, these armor-plated rascals hardly seemed to notice us. They just minded their own business, munching grasses. There were two ostriches just ahead of us as well, busily poking among some scrubs. As we got closer, they wouldn't even move out of our way! Just lifted their *heads once, then ignored us. It was amazing! They weren't afraid of us—weren't even upset by our presence. The animals seemed to consider the waterhole public property, and no single species felt it deserved to be here more than any other.*

As we neared the water's edge, I saw a kind of animal that I'd never seen before. It looked like a small horse, but it had the head of a camel and a long, stiff mane. These animals, unlike the others, at least showed us the courtesy of moving out of our way, but they weren't in any particular hurry. If I hadn't been so thirsty, I might have even tried to go up and pet one of them. I think I could've petted the elephants too. It was like these creatures had lived around human beings all of their lives, yet I couldn't imagine how that could be true way out here in the wilderness.

After we reached the lake, I volunteered to be the one to wade out into the water and fill our canteens. Mary and Rebecca set out to make a sort of campsite for us on a little ridge overlooking the water. There was a single tree on the ridge and some sticks lying about.

I took off my shoes and waded out for about ten feet, just until I felt it was deep enough that my toes didn't kick up a cloud of mud. The water didn't look particularly appetizing, but the animals were all drinking it, so I supposed it wasn't poisonous. Actually, the water was surprisingly cool. I wondered if it was fed by a spring that came up out of the ground.

I dipped in all of our waterskins, filling them completely. Afterwards, I took a sip. After smacking it around and squishing it against the roof of my mouth, I swallowed.

"Not half bad," I mumbled.

I took a really long drink, then went back to Becky and Mary, who quickly satisfied their own thirsts. Mary suggested that I might put the goat's milk in the water to help keep it from spoiling. Honestly, I was starting to think there was something already in the milk to help with that. It should have spoiled long before now. But after doing what I was asked, I returned to find Mary and Becky gathering sticks.

"Mary says there might be enough wood here to build a small fire," said Becky.

"Why do we need a fire?" I asked. "Are we gonna cook something?"

"It's for after dark," said Mary. "It will help keep the baby warm."

I shrugged. "I thought we were all pretty warm last night."

"You gotta be kidding," said Becky. "It was freezing.*"*

I realized she was probably fast asleep by the time I grabbed onto the sword. She had no idea why she'd slept so soundly.

"It's not just for warmth," said Mary. She looked intently back toward the grassy hills.

"But we don't have any matches," I said.

Mary made a sly smile. "Oh, you children of the twenty-first century! Do you doubt that I can conjure fire?"

I smiled. Mary was likely making fires before I was even born.

"Josh can make a fire too," said Becky. "Right?"

"Yeah," I said uncertainly. "But I'm a little out of practice."

I was embarrassed to say that without my Nephite flint (a little memento that Dad had brought back from Bountiful, and which was right now in my dresser drawer back home), I wasn't quite sure how to go about it. This was a real matter of pride for me. I liked to think of myself as the ultimate outdoorsman, often fantasizing that a helicopter might drop me in some remote part of the world where I could prove my survival skills. (Come to think of it, wasn't that pretty much what had happened to us?)

I helped them finish gathering sticks as well as some loose bark from the tree. The evening air was filled with the grunts, snorts, clicks, and yaps from the herds of various animals as they played in the dimming light. Shem was very alert and even cooing. Becky talked to him, telling him all about her little cousin, Gid Teancum. Mary paused in her fire preparations and leaned over to kiss the baby's cheek. Afterward, Shem touched her face. Mary made a funny gasp that caused the baby to laugh. It was incredible how calm and contented the infant seemed after everything that had happened.

"He's so precious!" Becky exclaimed. "What are we gonna do with him?"

"I'm not sure yet," said Mary thoughtfully. "I have a strong feeling that the Lord will direct us on that." She gazed into Shem's face. The baby gave her a big smile. Mary continued, "I feel . . . that when the nursemaid said the word 'great,' she was most likely referring to the child."

"I don't get it," I said. "Who do you think he is?"

She sighed longingly and shook her head. "I don't know, but . . . I'm starting to believe that this child is the main reason we're here. I believe it's our solemn responsibility to protect and care for him until . . ."

"Until what?" asked Becky.

"Until he's safe," said Mary uneasily. "When that time comes, we'll know it."

Using one of our shoelaces, Mary fashioned a kind of bow that would create friction with two sticks. She made a pile of small twigs and bark strips.

"How long will it take you to make a fire?" asked Becky.

"An hour, perhaps," said Mary.

That seemed awfully long. If I'd had my flint, I felt sure I could've started it in just a few minutes. The sun was setting quickly now. I noticed that the elephants that'd been soaking in the mud on the other side of the lake were moving away from the water. This seemed like a cue to many of the other animals to also begin moving off toward the hills. The grasslands became quieter than before, and I felt an odd sense of tension in the air. I was becoming anxious to get a fire going.

A strange idea popped into my head. I looked down at the sword of Akish and began to wonder . . .

All at once I started making my own little pile of kindling.

Becky saw what I was doing and declared, "Ah! A contest! We'll see which of you guys can start a fire first."

Mary made a determined face at me. She was just being funny. I don't think she took the competition seriously. But for some reason I took it very seriously. I found a stone the size of my palm and polished off the dirt. Then, almost instinctively, I set the blade of the sword against my pile of kindling and struck it with the rock.

I couldn't believe it! An enormous white spark jumped right off the sword blade and landed in the middle of the kindling. Within seconds the spark became a red and blue flame, like a pilot light, crackling and snapping. With their eyes wide, Mary and Rebecca watched as I put on larger sticks and twigs.

"Hey, hey!" I whooped. "Nothin' to it!"

Mary walked over to me, still gaping at my fire.

"How did you do that?" she asked, sounding almost like she was accusing me of something.

"I just used the sword like my Nephite flint," I explained. "Here, I'll show you again—"

"No," said Mary curtly. "Joshua, I don't want you to use that sword for anything. Do you understand me?"

I frowned. "Don't you think you're overreact—"

"Nothing!" she repeated. "I realize we have no choice but to bring it with us, but we will not make it a tool. Is that clear?"

I rolled my eyes. "All right. Fine." My tone was too defensive. I mellowed out and said, "You're right. I'm sorry. I won't use it again. Not even to crack a walnut. Okay?"

"Promise me, Joshua," said Mary earnestly.

"I promise."

It all seemed kind of silly. Then again, I didn't see any reason to rock the boat. Mary obviously felt very strongly about this, and I decided maybe it was wise to trust her. No big deal. I decided that tonight I would set the sword at least ten feet away while I slept, just like Mary had asked me the first night. Besides, there was no need for it. The skies were clear, and we had ourselves a nice crackling fire to keep us warm. In a way, I also felt a strange desire to prove to myself that I could do it —that it had no power over me.

That probably sounds bizarre. Scratch what I said. I was just being obedient to Mary.

As I set the sword aside, I also went down to the water to get one of the canteens of milk. The evening was calm. Not a living thing was stirring out in the twilight. I even stood there for a second, listening and counting the sounds. It was weird. Except for my legs sloshing in the water, and the sounds of Mary and Becky back in camp, I could hear absolutely nothing. No wind, no crickets. It was like I was in a sound vacuum or a big, empty football stadium.

I returned to camp. We said our prayers and got ready for bed. Mary got Shem to drink a little more milk. Afterwards, she sang him a pretty song, and kind of sad, about a mother watching her babies grow up, and the pain in her heart as she watched them marry into other families or go off to war. Mary really did have a beautiful singing voice, and I thought sure the baby would fall right to sleep. But just as I was laying out the sack of grain so that I might use it as a pillow, Shem started to cry.

"What's wrong with him?" asked Becky.

"I don't think it's any mystery," said Mary. She unwrapped part of his bundle. Sure enough, he'd left a nice, runny gift on the cloth.

"Yuck!" I declared.

"Oh, grow up," scolded Becky. "He is a baby, after all. What did you expect?"

"Now what are we gonna wrap him in?" I asked.

"For tonight I'll wrap him in my head shawl," said Mary. "Josh, I'd like you to rinse out his swaddling blanket and set it near the fire to dry."

"Me?" I asked, mildly horrified.

"We have a baby to care for," said Mary. "We all have to do our part."

Becky turned to Mary. "Maybe he'd rather sleep with Shem beside him so that he can get pooped on in the middle of the night."

"No, it's all right," I said quickly. "I'll rinse out the blanket."

I took the cloth from Mary's hand with two fingers. Grumbling under my breath, I made my way again down to the shore. The water may have only been ten yards away, but climbing down the backside of the knoll in the dark was kind of a challenge. The campfire was above me, so it didn't reflect on the ground. Still, I got there just fine and leaned down, supporting my weight with one palm so that I wouldn't get my knees muddy.

I'd gotten the cloth wet and was just starting to swish it around when I saw something move in the darkness. The movement was just on the other side of a swampy arm of the lake that curled around part of the knoll. Despite a thick line of reeds, I could see the outline of several creeping shadows. The hair on the back of my neck stood up. The shadows appeared to be circling around so they could make their way back toward Mary, Becky, and the baby. The way they moved was familiar. It didn't take a safari guide to tell me that these were some very big cats. I thought I could also make out manes. Lions. There were four of them. Maybe five. My heart took off like a buzz saw.

Quickly, I snatched the blanket out of the water and turned. Then I froze like a deer in headlights. In fact, headlights are a good description of what I saw twenty feet to the south of where I stood. The eyes were the color of yellow fire. The creature stiffened the instant I turned. In fact, if I hadn't turned, I was sure it would have already leaped on my back. But what kind of animal was it? The light of the campfire barely skimmed over its back. I could see stripes. Holy moly! It was a tiger!

One of the girls at the top of the knoll let out a scream. The fiery eyes in front of me became distracted, turning toward the sound. I bolted toward the top of the knoll, running wildly toward the campfire. I saw Becky and Mary. They were huddled close together and holding Shem. Something large was standing on its hind legs just on the other side of the fire. A bear! It was massive! A grizzly!

This couldn't be real. I was dreaming. Lions and tigers and bears. It was like a nightmare out of Wizard of Oz. But it was too incredible! All of these species attacking at once? Animals didn't behave like this!

I tripped! My body sprawled forward and tumbled onto the ground. I was a dead man! A tiger was about to pounce! But as I skidded on the dirt—it was the weirdest thing—my hand came to rest on the hilt of Akish's sword. I'd fallen exactly on the spot where I'd laid it. My fingers closed around the hilt.

Instantly, my heart ignited, just like throwing a match on a pan of gasoline. My veins surged with courage and anger. It felt as if my muscles had the strength of ten men. I rolled onto my back. And just in time! The tiger was diving at my face!

I cried out and swung the sword. The firelight flashed on the blade, causing me to blink. It was a strange sensation to feel the sword cut into the tiger's flesh. So clean! Like a Jedi's light saber! As I leaped to my feet, the tiger was on its back, jerking with convulsions. Unbelievable! I'd slain a tiger! A real tiger!

Becky screamed again. I sprang into action. It was like I was a machine! I knew exactly how to move, how to fight. The grizzly was just about to charge through the campfire to kill Becky and Mary. Instead, I rushed between them. I hardly remember what happened. It's like a blur. But I recall hoisting the sword back behind my head with both hands. Then I stabbed down, almost like planting a flag on a mountaintop. I drove the blade into the bear's chest. It shrieked in agony, then collapsed at my feet. The blade slid out of its ribs as easily as Arthur slid the sword from the stone. I turned again just as a hurricane of shadows flew toward me out of the darkness. It was the lions from the reeds! I could also see the stripes of several more tigers. This was beyond everything I'd ever heard or read—beyond anything I'd ever imagined. The predators were working together! They were all rushing at once!

"Stand behind me!" I yelled to the girls, but neither one moved. Curiously, they were gawking at me!—as if I was the thing to fear—not the charging animals.

I lunged forward and met one of the attacking lions as it was in mid-leap, my blade perfectly timed to swipe its neck. I reacted to a sound behind my ear and again swung wildly, stabbing another tiger in the chest. I swung and swung and swung, until three more animals fell, all of them gasping and convulsing on the ground. I was Tarzan! I was Sinbad! I was Aragorn and Conan and Gidgiddonihah rolled into one! There was no stopping me. No living thing had a chance. I was invincible!

Almost as suddenly as the attack had begun, the shadows started retreating. The animals were fleeing back into the darkness. Becky and Mary were kneeling on the ground now, still holding each other. Shem was crying hysterically. The girls' eyes were wide and frozen, as if they were going into shock.

The knoll was littered with six carcasses—some of the most ferocious predators on earth. The sword in my right hand dripped with blood. In fact my whole arm *was drenched in it. Judging by the way that Mary and Becky were gaping at me, I guessed that my face was splotched with it as well. Yet I'd never felt so invigorated. I wanted* more. *I wanted the lions to attack* again.

"Cowards!" I shouted into the night. "Come back and fight! Do you hear me? Come back and fight!"

"Joshua!" Mary snapped, her voice like a clap of thunder.

I felt a rush of temper. How dare *she yell at me! Maybe she needed a lesson too. Maybe they* all *needed a reminder of who was in charge.*

Then I met her eyes. I'd never seen anyone's face so stern. Her complexion was glowing in the firelight. Her teeth and her fists were clenched. I could almost hear her thoughts, like the echo of a war-general's voice: Stand down, soldier! Stand down!

But there was something else in those eyes—something I didn't expect. It was like . . . How can I describe it? Love? Pleading? Compassion? Whatever it was, it hit me deeper and more powerfully than her sternness. It shook me. It was like it woke me up.

I looked at the sword again and its reflection of blood. This time it hit me very differently. I glanced around at the bodies of all the dead animals, some still twitching, some oozing blood from their wounds. Nausea twisted in my stomach like a creeping tarantula. As Mary came to me and wrapped her arms around my head, I started shaking.

The sword of Akish dropped from my hand.

NOTES TO CHAPTER 3:

The animal with a mane like a horse and the head of a camel is actually recorded on the old clay tablets of ancient Mesopotamia. It apparently describes a beast that has long been extinct (Carol Moss, *Science in Ancient Mesopotamia*, 44).

Many of the animals mentioned in this chapter are generally not thought to have ever coexisted in the same region of the world. We usually don't think of lions and tigers hunting the same territory, even though there is ample evidence that this has occurred. (Actually, even today the tiger and the endangered Asiatic lion dwell in the same habitat in India.)

But did a grizzly bear ever coexist with tigers? Or did a moose ever graze the same grasses as a zebra? Or even beyond the story text of this book, did a kangaroo ever occupy the same territory as a hippopotamus? Or did a koala bear ever munch the same foliage as a panda?

If we are to take the story of Noah's ark literally, then the answer is a *qualified* yes. Qualified because the exact number of species that may have existed prior to the Deluge has not been revealed to us in any book of scripture. Nor do we know precisely how the various species would have been categorized or distinguished. Nor do we know how Noah's animals may have fanned out across the earth after they were set free—to say nothing of knowing the full logistics for how Noah would have gathered, housed, fed, or bred these animals before, during, and after the ark came to rest on Mount Ararat.

In fact, for many Latter-day Saints (and probably for most Christians in general) there is often a palpable resistance to such questions, fearing that the answers may fly in the face of modern science. We prefer to accept such things on faith, and plug our ears to the host of biological evolutionists, geneticists, zoologists, and geologists who seem determined to refute the possibility that a person such as Noah may have existed, or that a universal flood may have occurred, or that life on earth could have ever been preserved by something like an ark filled with thousands of animal species that remained afloat for a full year.

However, it should be noted that several accredited scientists, LDS and non-LDS, have gone to great lengths to prove that such an event as the Great Flood and Noah's ark were not only feasible, but scientifically probable. A battery of various issues have been addressed. Some of these include the strata of the earth's crust, genetic diversity, and mircoevolution. (Microevolution is the belief that yes, living things do evolve, but not in the manner Darwin suggested, and certainly not with the conclusion that simple organisms evolve into more complex organisms, such as an amoeba one day becoming an elephant.) Such studies attempt to show that no category of science effectively refutes the plausibility of these events, and, in many cases, strongly supports them.

Detailed analyses have been offered on how Noah might have carried out the complex problems of animal husbandry for so many different species. Using known biological equivalents, these studies show how the dietary requirements of carnivores may have changed in the years after the flood and how the diet of certain herbivores may have become more specialized (as in the case of a koala that eats only eucalyptus leaves). They also reveal how each of these species may have migrated and eventually settled in their present environments. These studies are only speculation; nevertheless, it's quite remarkable how faithful to the scientific method they have been, presenting the argument that we need not doubt a single detail of the Genesis account (John Woodmorappe Ph.D., *Noah's Ark: A Feasibility Study* [Inst. for Creation Research, 1996]; John C. Whitcomb & Henry Madison Morris, *Genesis Flood;* Eric N. Skousen Ph.D., *Earth: In the Beginning* [Verity Publishing: Orem, UT]).

The author of this novel has made conjectures about the sociality or tameness of some of these non-predators in the centuries immediately following the flood, suggesting that their "skittishness" toward each other and their fear of men may have settled in over the convening centuries. In Genesis 9:2, the Lord declares that all beasts will fear mankind, but as with other conditions or "curses" implemented by the Lord, such things may have taken effect over time, through natural processes. Although the idea of the inordinate tameness of animals is only conjecture, it would be well to remind ourselves that after the Savior's coming, "*The wolf also shall dwell with the lamb, and the leopard shall lie down with the kid, . . . and the cow and the bear shall feed; their young ones shall lie down together: and the lion shall eat straw like the ox. And the sucking child shall play on the hole of the asp, and the weaned child shall put his hand on the cockatrice' den*" (Isa. 11:6–8).

CHAPTER FOUR

Steffanie

Steffanie Hawkins takes the microphone!

How many of these adventures have I been in? And how many times have I had a chance to say my piece? Like maybe NEVER!

Well, all that changes here and now. I may be the "middle child" in my family, but I'm by no means the quietest. I only wish the circumstances had been a little more festive.

After Harrison had blown away the soldiers with the first few notes of Handel's *Messiah* on his CD player, they all looked at us and each other with intense curiosity and surprise. After which they promptly confiscated the electronics and bound our hands in front of our bodies.

"What is your clan?" demanded the man who was the apparent leader of the seven riders. Like the others, his hair was tied behind his head in a long, wrapped braid that almost made it look like he was wearing an elaborately decorated coonskin cap.

"Clan?" asked Harry.

"Are you of Shem?" he asked. "Are you of Japheth?"

Harry was at a loss. He replied, "I think . . . Shem."

"As I suspected," said the leader contemptuously. He spat on the ground to emphasize his opinion. He held up Harry's CD player. "Do they fashion these devices in Salem?"

Again stammering, Harry replied, "Uh, yeah. Sure. Salem."

Another of the riders spoke gruffly, "It's as King Nimrod has always said. The people of Salem have great secrets which they hide from the civilized world."

"Well," said the leader, "they won't hide them for much longer."

The meaning of that exchange escaped us, but I wasn't sure if Harry's choice to align ourselves with Shemites or Salemites was very smart. Harry looked at me to see if I felt inspired to make any comment. To be honest, I was feeling a little breathless. And I confess, it had nothing to do with the fact that we'd just run for almost half a mile. Nor was it particularly related to the fear and tension of the moment. I was just . . . simply . . . and totally . . . in *awe* of these *men!*

That must sound so lame. Here we were, facing the very real possibility of death, and my eyes were practically bugging out of my head. I had never in all of my life seen such stunning, gorgeous, majestic, and delicious-looking males. Every last one of them was as beautiful as Fabio and as buff as a young Arnold Schwarzenegger. *Every single one!* You know who they reminded me of? Those paintings of the Book of Mormon. Arnold Friberg had it right! This was it. This was the mold. This was as good as it got. What year was it? 3000 B.C.? Obviously it was long before the likes of Woody Allen and Pauly Shore had polluted the male gene pool. Try as these horsemen might to cover their features under their fine purple and gold riding cloaks, there was no doubt in my mind that they were popped from the mold that God had fashioned when He created the species. These guys were *perfectomundo!*—their jawlines, their chests, their leg muscles, their silky, black hair, their crystal-blue eyes. So much eye candy at once was making me slightly delirious.

The brusque voice of the leader broke me from my trance. "Let's ride! We'll take them directly to Mardon. I'm sure he'll want to know more about *this*." He slipped the CD player inside a travel bag on his horse.

Both Harry and I were hoisted onto the back of a pair of crimson-colored stallions. Seated behind me was one of these living Adonises. I'm ashamed to admit that I found myself gawking more than once at the marble-carved biceps that hedged me in on either side as he grabbed up the reins and spurred the horse to a gallop. But maybe I can be forgiven for my infatuation. I'd devoted most of my life to physical conditioning. I'd earned a black belt in Muso-Ki Karate from Shihan Arakaki in Murray, Utah, shortly before we'd moved to Provo. I'd received a full-ride scholarship in basketball to BYU-Idaho. I was an all-state softball pitcher and had excelled in gymnastics in junior high. I could also hold my own in tennis, soccer, and volleyball. In my junior year of high school I'd also had a stint with female bodybuilding, so I had a somewhat "above normal" appreciation for a well-toned physique. It's not that I was necessarily *attracted* to that kind of male. I just felt a natural admiration for anyone who was committed enough and self-disciplined enough to take care of their bodies.

Who am I kidding? Okay! So I was a pushover for a beautiful man! What can I say? But in the end it was the total package that reeled me in: intelligence, personality, looks, and spirituality. Oh, and *charm*. Yes, I did love a charming male. Which was why, despite my brief crush on Apollus while we were in Judea, I was more than happy to turn him over to Meagan. Charm was definitely not his strong suit. My fiancé, Mike, had plenty of charm, but well . . . I guess it must have been in some of the other categories that I found him lacking.

So why am I saying all this? I don't know! I guess I just wanted to offer a little background on my frame of mind as the soldiers of Shinar rode toward the encampment of Prince Mardon, son of Nimrod.

Honestly, we hadn't ridden very far into the river valley before my infatuation with the horsemen fizzled away. Death and destruction has a way of doing that. Though we were kept mostly to the upper shelf on the east side of the river, I saw plenty of slain bodies, both men and horses, and even one elephant. The whole thing turned my stomach. I looked down and closed my eyes, unable to tolerate the sight. The man who sat with me in the saddle chuckled obscenely at my reaction.

"This one's a touch squeamish," he announced to the others. Funny how utterly unattractive males can make themselves in the twinkle of an eye.

I looked over at Harry on the other horse. He had a look of quiet confidence. This comforted me somewhat. Harry really didn't look as out-of-place among these warriors as I might have expected. He may not have had the tree-trunk neck of a Mr. Universe, but he definitely held his own in physical dimensions. My little brother had filled out considerably over the last few years. It had started during his three-year sojourn in first-century A.D., and accelerated from there. Greek living—both ancient and modern—seemed to suit him.

As we continued along the outskirts of the battlefield, the leader of our squadron of riders asked a foot soldier, "Where is the prince?"

The infantryman pointed north into a haze of smoke that wafted up from the western shore of the river. The equipment and provisions of the men of Japheth were all being gathered into a pile over there and put to the torch. Through the haze I could clearly see a post the height of a flagpole. At the top was a gold-plated sculpture of sorts that was obviously some kind of standard.

Our leader saw it and nodded. Our horses approached with a determined gait. Before we reached the prince's encampment we came upon a large knot of prisoners. They were situated just below a bluff leading up to the area of the flagpole. I heard an awful scream that sent shards of ice up my spine. I realized the men of Shinar were torturing the soldiers of Japheth for information. They were using a brand of some sort heated in the coals of a fire. I heard some of the questions they were asking—questions about the location of another division of Japheth's army. Apparently the voice on the bullhorn hadn't been entirely forthcoming when it insinuated that all of the sons of Japheth had abandoned their kinsmen to defeat.

I looked at Harry, who was also appalled and disgusted. Why, I wondered, did we have to ride past such a scene? Couldn't we have gone around it? As I heard more screams, I shuddered and tried to focus toward the top of the bluff. That's when I finally saw him—the most beautiful figure of a man that I'd ever seen in my life.

He was mounted on the back of a stunning black horse, overlooking the scene of torture and branding with great interest. The hair on his head was pulled back. It was so heavily laden with braids and decorations that it laid behind his shoulders almost like an oriental fan. Even the hair on his crown was tightly curled and frizzy, sort of like an Afro, but he had the same piercing blue eyes as the rest of his comrades. In fact, they were *bluer*. Even thirty yards away and through the smoke I felt I could discern the color.

At first I had no idea of the man's identity. He wore the same purple, gold, and black cloak as the others, but his chest was laid bare. On his ears hung earrings of bright sapphire stones. He wasn't at all what I might have expected from the man who had orchestrated such a bloodbath. He looked very young. Only a year or two older than I—if even that. Yet I still would have never guessed that he was the Prince of Shinar. After all, he was alone—no bodyguards or escorts. I wasn't sure of his identity until the leader of our cavalrymen shouted up to him, "Noble Prince Mardon! Greetings from Arvad, officer of the cavalry! We have prisoners that you may wish to question."

"Who are they?" he called down impatiently from the bluff.

"They are Shemites from Salem, noble prince."

"Shemites?" he said with some surprise. Still, he seemed annoyed that his attention was being diverted from the scene of torture. "Have Lasha or one of my staff interrogate them."

"These you may wish to interrogate personally," said Arvad, and he reached into his saddlebag and pulled out the CD player.

He hit the button just as he'd seen Harry do and immediately the Hallelujah Chorus picked up right where it had left off. The soldiers involved in the branding and interrogation turned toward us with alarm. Even the prisoners looked startled. After Arvad felt that he had made his point, he shut the music off.

Mardon stared at us for a few seconds, his blue eyes glistening. His stare evoked strange emotions inside me. There was no denying his awesome, hypnotizing beauty, but at the same time there was something eerily repulsive about him. Maybe it was the pleasure he seemed to draw as he watched that brand sizzle on human flesh and listened to the screams. The attraction and repulsion was an acute contradiction that I had to untangle in my mind.

He motioned for Arvad to follow him, then turned his horse and rode down the other side of the bluff, deeper into the smoke. We remained in the rear as he led us back toward his tent. After we'd nearly reached the encampment, I happened to look up into the sky and noticed the falcon that had betrayed our position. It came to a landing on the arm of a man on horseback. This man nodded to Mardon who rode on by without giving any reaction. Then the falcon-man looked at us. Like everyone else, he was also a candidate for the next *Scorpion King* movie. But unlike the others, his face had been marred. He wore a diamond-shaped patch over his left eye, almost as if the falcon perched on his arm had clawed it out on some former occasion. The leather patch didn't quite cover the damage. A rather nasty scar curved out from underneath it and ran down his cheek. He watched us malevolently as we rode by. After we'd passed, I heard him mutter something to the bird. He sent it flying off on another spy expedition.

The tent of the prince was not particularly lavish looking. I supposed that the material looked slightly better than the other tents around it, but not exactly the accommodations that I might have expected for the son of a king. Apparently in these circumstances he preferred swiftness and mobility over luxury—or so it appeared.

On closer investigation I realized that being a prince was not without its perks. Among the many officers and staff members who approached him as he neared the doorway of his tent were several women whose attire was anything but modest. For all practical purposes their outfits had more jewelry and trinkets than actual cloth. I realized they were probably consorts or concubines—not only of Mardon, but of all the officers. The women of this country were not a whit less beautiful than the males. In fact, that's an understatement. I'm going to abandon humility temporarily to offer a comparison. I know perfectly well that I am considered by most to be a reasonably attractive girl. My best feature, I think, is the shape of my eyes, curled slightly at the outside corners, which in one of the captions in my high school yearbook were dubbed "exotic." Though at five-foot-eleven I am taller than most girls, I am still quite cognizant of the power that I have over most men. In truth, I rather enjoy it, though I think I am conscientious enough not to use that power to hurt anybody. But these girls were in a totally different league. I mean, these were *super-models*. In fact, they were the most *gorgeous* supermodels I'd ever seen. It redefined in my imagination how beautiful human beings could possibly be. Perfect bodies, perfect faces, blondes, brunettes, and redheads, almond and doe-shaped eyes, tall, sleek, feminine. It was *unbelievable!* And more than slightly intimidating.

Nevertheless, Mardon treated them in the same brusque, impatient way that he treated his officers. "Go away! All of you! Except for you, Mash."

He was referring to one of his officers. Funny name for a person. The man was older, but he had hulking muscles and an odd-looking beard that looked more like a woven carpet. It hung down from his chin about eight inches. The weaves and braids were quite intricate, and it was perfectly squared at the bottom. I noted that many of the other officers had similar beards.

Mardon indicated us, and said to the man named Mash, "These are your kinsmen. They say they are from Salem."

Mash looked over at us narrowly as we were pulled down from the horses. "Salem, eh?" he said with perceivable contempt.

I glanced over at Harry. I hoped again that he hadn't made a stupid mistake when he allowed them to believe that we were Shemites from this mysterious city named Salem. The old warrior, Mash, almost looked dubious of that conclusion anyway.

We were pushed toward the door of the tent.

Arvad said to the prince, "We will wait until you are finished, in case you need me and my men to take them down to the fires. I'm sure we can compel them to reveal more than they were willing to say."

Mardon made a twisted, little smile, as if imagining the scene and relishing it. "Good idea."

Again I looked at Harry. What was going on? What did they expect us to tell them? I couldn't see how this interrogation would possibly turn out in our favor. My brother's expression had altered slightly. Not so confident anymore. I sensed that he, too, was starting to wonder if he had made some sort of mistake.

The interior of the tent was much more lavish than the exterior. The floor was covered with dozens of rugs and furs. There was no furniture to speak of, but there were a lot of colorful pillows with tassels on the corners. They sort of reminded me of the kind of pillows I'd see on the bed of a French king.

Harry and I were forced to sit in the center of the floor. I paid one of the soldiers a lethal glance as he pushed me down. I'd have happily and willingly sat down on my own. But, typical of most goons, he enjoyed treating us roughly.

Mardon was watching me intently, his eyes twitching from time to time, as if things were stirring in his imagination that I had no desire to know about. This caused me to squirm with discomfort. I wasn't sure why he seemed so fascinated with me. Considering the kind of female visual stimulation that hung around here every day, what was the point of leering at me?

One of his staff members handed him the CD player. This seemed to shake him back to reality. The prince sat on a pillow at the back of the tent and rolled the player over in his hands. He even bit it with his teeth, as if checking its genuineness, like a wooden coin. Then, at last, he pressed the Play button.

For the third time today, the sounds of the Mormon Tabernacle Choir shook the air. I noticed that numerous faces were pressing around the entrance to the tent, whispering and speculating about who we were and wondering about the things we had brought. Another pair of soldiers laid our backpacks at Mardon's side. As far as I could tell, the packs had not yet been opened. This privilege, I concluded, was being reserved for the prince.

The player was turned off. I heard more excited muttering at the doorway. Mardon drew a deep breath through his nose, as if he wanted to smell us before he addressed us, then he asked, "What are your names?"

"I'm Harry," my brother answered. "This is my sister, Steffanie."

The news that I was Harry's sister seemed to please Mardon. "You're sure she is not your wife?"

"No," said Harry. "Sister."

"And you are from Salem?"

"Actually," said Harry, "That's not entirely accurate. We're really from a city called Provo. It's waaay far away. Across the oceans. You don't even want to know."

"Don't I?" asked Mardon. "Why did you tell my cavalrymen that you were Shemites from Salem?"

"He, uh, sort of put those words into my mouth," said Harry.

"Typical," spat another man who wore a cream-colored robe. He appeared to be some kind of chancellor or personal secretary. "First they will confess—when they don't feel threatened. And then they will lie."

Did he really think we felt any less threatened then than now? Obviously this guy had never had a spear thrust in his face.

The secretary continued, pointing at the CD player, "This device could only have been built at Salem."

Mardon turned to his Shemite general, Mash. "So? Are they your kinsmen?"

Mash shrugged. "I have not walked the streets of Salem for over a hundred years, noble prince. Not since before you were born. They *could* be my kinsmen." He turned back to us. "What is your father's name? What is your grandfather's name?"

"Well, uh . . ." I could tell Harry was praying hard. This was not the time to say the wrong thing.

I was still digesting Mash's statement about not having visited Salem for over a hundred years. Was this a casual exaggeration? Like saying something is a million miles away? Also, his statement hinted that Mardon was much older than I'd suspected. It had to be some kind of private joke. No way was Mash over a hundred years old.

"My father's name is Jim," said Harry, "and my grandfather is Ronald."

Mash cocked an eyebrow. "These are Shemite names? How old is your grandfather?"

"He is continuing to lie," the secretary proclaimed. "See if he will deny that his music box is a product of the secret knowledge from before the Flood? We have always known that King Shem hoarded this knowledge and kept it from his brothers and their descendants."

This was wild. Secret technologies from before the Flood? How cool! It was even more intriguing to think that one of Noah's sons might have kept these technologies alive in a city called Salem. But Harry wasn't interested in that subject right now.

"I'm gonna be straight with you," he told the prince. "'Cause I really don't want to be tortured later today, if that's okay with you. We're not really Shemites. Actually, we *might* be Shemites, but it's . . . well, pretty likely that *lots* of people where I come from have a little bit of Shem in them. Ham and Japheth, too. My sister and I come from a different sort of land. We really only came here to find my friends and relatives. Their names are Mary and Megan, Apollus, Ryan, Rebecca, and Joshua. Have any of you seen them?"

Nothing like getting to the crux of things right from the beginning. Everyone in the room was looking at Harry as if he was babbling like an idiot.

The secretary's impatience was mounting. "The prince will not tolerate being taunted! He demands that—!"

Mardon raised his hand to silence the secretary. "Shut up, Lasha. I find these words to be quite . . . intriguing. Tell me—Harry—where is this land that you are from?"

"You really wouldn't understand if I explained it," said Harry. "And it isn't relative to the subject—"

"I will judge that," said the prince curtly.

Harry shut his eyes. He blew the air out of his lungs. What was my brother doing? Was he trying to be clever? I realized he'd decided just to blurt it out. Why not? Every other time we'd visited a different century we'd always hemmed and hawed and twisted the facts to keep from short-circuiting anyone's primitive brain. Harry appeared to have decided that telling the truth, for once, was worth a shot.

"Okay," Harry began. "The fact is, we come from the kind of place that you couldn't possibly imagine. I'm just guessing here, but I'd bet that the technology where I live is probably a little more advanced than this place called Salem. I can assure you, no one here has ever visited it, and it would be pretty much impossible for you to get there even if you tried. Suffice it to say, the only reason we're here is because of a miracle. You might even say we fell out of the sky—"

Harry's last statement drew such a gasp of shock and surprise from the listeners both inside and outside the tent that he paused to reassess his approach.

"Maybe that's not the best way to describe it," he said feebly.

"Do you mean to tell us that you are from the clouds?" demanded Lasha.

"Actually, spit out of a geyser might be more . . . uh . . . " He looked at me, hoping I might bail him out.

"We're from a city," I said. "Just like most of you, I'm sure, but—"

"The City in the Clouds!" exclaimed someone at the door of the tent.

I gaped at him, then back at the prince. Now I was totally lost. I had no idea what they were talking about.

"You claim to be from the heaven of the Great God?" asked Mash, nonplussed.

Harry was backpedaling furiously. His "truth" approach had been a serious blunder. "That's not what I said at all. What I mean is—"

Prince Mardon rose to his feet. "I want my tent cleared of all but myself and the two prisoners! And I will have no listeners at my tent walls! Heed my command! Now go!"

Yowza! We seemed to have stepped into it deep. I still wasn't following any part of this. City in the Clouds? Heaven of the Great God? What were they talking about? It was *crazy!* Did they actually suspect that we might be visitors from heaven?

Within thirty seconds the tent was completely empty. It was just me and Harry, our hands still tied in front, and Mardon, Prince of Shinar. Those bright blue eyes— shimmering with cold calculation— continued to watch us as he walked around behind our backs.

"I think there's been a misunderstanding," said Harry in earnest. "I don't think we're the people that you think we are."

"And who do you think that I think that you are?" asked Mardon, his tone as slippery as an oyster.

"Well, it sounded like . . . I—I just don't want you to think we're some kind of . . . well . . . angels."

Mardon raised his eyebrows. "Why would you use that word?"

"Angels? Isn't that a word you're familiar with?"

"Of course I'm familiar with it."

"Well, that's not what we are. We're not heavenly messengers. We're not supernatural in any way. We're just regular people, and we're looking for my cousins, just like I said."

"Then where did you get this?" he asked, still holding the CD player. He walked over to our backpacks. Something in one of the pockets caught his eye. The compartment was partially unzipped. He reached in and pulled out Harrys small Sports brand flashlight. Ah, yes, a flashlight—that good ol' standby for dazzling the ancient mind.

"And this?" asked Mardon. "What is it?"

"It's . . . sort of a . . ."

"It makes light," I interjected. "But it's nothing miraculous. It uses batteries. If you untie my hands I'll show you."

Mardon stepped closer to me, his tongue moving around strangely inside his mouth. Finally he asked, "Do you think yourself more capable of operating such things than myself?"

"No," I said cheekily. "But it just might make it a little easier for you to understand if I explained a few things."

"I thank you," said Mardon in mock politeness, turning away. "But I think not. I've lived for sixty-two years. I certainly have the intelligence to figure it out on my own."

He couldn't be serious. If this guy was a day over twenty-five I'd have eaten my gym shorts. Yet I couldn't let this addle me. I had to reply with cool composure.

"What's the matter?" I asked, cocking an eyebrow. "Are you afraid of me?"

Mardon turned back. He leaned in even closer, his nose an inch from my own. "Should I be?"

"Well, I don't know," I said unflinchingly. "Obviously you must feel threatened by the idea that somebody might know more than you."

His eyes flicked, and then he said with a grin, "On the contrary, I like it when someone feels they know more than I do. It gives me the opportunity to squeeze them of every drop of information they think they possess."

"Unfortunately, in this case that won't be necessary," I replied smoothly. "Why don't you untie me so I can give you a demonstration."

He hesitated another moment, then his smile grew even wider. He reached for his sheath and drew out a bronze knife. He moved the point of it slowly, teasingly toward my chin, still testing to see if I could be intimidated. I didn't budge a centimeter. In one swift motion he directed the blade downward and pulled it back toward him, cutting through the ropes on my wrists. I was free.

I stood up and rubbed my rope burns. Then I held out my hand for the flashlight. The tongue started working the inside of his mouth again as he placed it in my palm.

I untwisted the end. "The batteries go in here." I turned it to show him. "See?"

He glanced inside, then locked his eyes with mine again, and nodded. "I see."

I pointed at the bulb. "This is what causes it to make light. All you do is press here."

I turned it on. The tent was dim enough that the light was fairly bright. Mardon looked fascinated, but not nearly as fascinated as I might have expected from somebody living in 3000 B.C.

"How interesting," he said. "And after showing me this, you still claim that you are not from the sky?"

"If we were really angels," I said tiredly, "why would I be wasting my time standing here talking to you? Why wouldn't I have freed myself and my brother a long time ago and floated away? Or maybe I should just call down fire from above and roast your entire army to a crisp."

He made a peculiar, hissing laugh and shook his head. "You would like me to believe you have such powers, wouldn't you?"

I cocked my eyebrow. Was this guy really this dense? "I don't think you're getting the point—"

He interrupted and said in a sleazy tone, "In spite of your denials, you are, Steffanie, precisely how I always imagined that an angel would look."

Little shivers launched up my back, like worms in my veins. Was that his idea of a come-on? Somehow I managed to keep a straight face. I still couldn't comprehend what he saw in me. I'd seen his other girlfriends. Also, I was fully cognizant of my own imperfections. My nose swooped into sort of a funny little bump on the very end. A pimple was trying to form on my right cheek. Frankly, at the moment I might have wished I was covered with hairy warts. This exemplar of male beauty and masculinity truly made my flesh crawl. Then he said something that led me to believe his statement was not necessarily meant as a compliment. He was totally serious.

"My father always said to me that angels were not the invulnerable beings that the Shemites and other weaklings of the earth have portrayed them to be. He believes they have faults and vulnerabilities like any other creature created by the Great God." He stepped over to Harry. "I wonder—do you bleed like men?"

"We're not *angels*," said Harry. "We're people—and yes, we *do bleed*."

"You're eels!" Mardon hissed. I guessed this was the same as if he'd called us wimps. "My father was right. All my life I have doubted him. But after seeing the likes of you—" he stood over Harry "—I'm beginning to see how his dream of defeating the City in the Clouds is not as foolish as I first supposed."

"What city are you *talking* about?" asked Harry, bristling with frustration.

"*Your* city!" he repeated. "The heaven which floats above the earth! The Tower of Babel is nearly high enough now. When it comes around again, my father's archers and infantry will be ready. I will lead the attack. Then all the secrets of heaven will be ours. Yes, I think my father will be very interested in meeting the two of you."

Harry looked almost cross-eyed with confusion. I was rather overwhelmed myself. It was almost as if Mardon was speaking an entirely different language. Well, actually, he *was*. It was as if our gift of tongues wasn't translating correctly in our minds. Was the prince speaking in metaphors? Was this City in the Clouds a metropolis on top of a mountain? Were these secrets of heaven a collection of technologies that might have existed prior to the Flood? If Mardon was speaking literally, then it was plain that someone had siphoned off a few of his brain cells. If he really was sixty-two, maybe he was already starting to get senile. Could any human being seriously be planning an attack against *God?* Did Nimrod's son honestly think he was going to lead an invasion against the forces of *heaven?* Should I have been looking around for Candid Camera?

I sifted through everything that I knew about the Tower of Babel. I'd always been taught that this tower was built to reach heaven, but I guess I'd never considered exactly what that meant. I mean, if you think about it, how could any dufus believe he could really reach heaven by building a tower? What would he have been trying to reach? The sun up in the sky? Clouds up in the stratosphere? A low-hanging star? Perhaps I was taking for granted the banquet of information available to everyone in the twenty-first century—the relationships of the earth to the sun, moon, and stars. In my day this stuff was common knowledge. But how revolutionary would it have seemed to a resident of 3000 B.C.? Maybe to a totally ignorant, earthbound soul it really *was* conceivable that a high tower might reach heaven. Still, the whole idea seemed illogical.

It was also explained to me that part of the motive for building the tower was to save mankind in case the Lord sent another flood.

Of course, anyone familiar with the prophets would have known the Lord's promise never to destroy the earth again in that manner. But apostates and their descendants might not have accepted such a promise. Still, there was something illogical about that concept too. Yes, the tower in the distance did look massive. But how many people would the builders have realistically felt that they could save? Even if there was a five-star hotel and restaurant at the top, could they have really expected to save more than a few hundred? Even if you could fit several thousand people on top, it seemed to me that it would have made far more sense, and been considerably less expensive, just to build a fleet of arks. These arks could be put into commission the moment it looked like the rain wasn't gonna let up. I felt sure that there was more to this tower story than I'd ever been told—motivations and plot twists that hadn't yet been revealed. At least I preferred to believe *this* rather than believing that Mardon and his people were morons.

"I'm going to try and explain this one more time," said Harry determinedly. "Steffanie and I are not from heaven. The things we carry are not magical tools made by angels or Salem-ites. We come from an entirely separate period in the history of the world. A totally different century!"

"I'm aware of that," said Mardon. "You are from the days of Enoch, are you not?"

Harry drew his eyebrows together, then he shook his head vigorously. "No, no, no. Rewind. Start over. We're from the *future*. Do you get it now? We're from the last days of the earth. From a time when electronics and science and technology like what made that music box and flashlight are as commonplace as swords and wagons are to the people that live today."

Mardon became impatient. "What is this nonsense? How dare you think I would be gullible enough to accept such lies! You are captured spies from the City in the Clouds. I do not wish to hear any more of this pig-swill." He turned back to me. "I'm afraid I will have to bind your hands again, angel girl. It's unfortunate that I must proceed with my torture and branding of the two of you. But I must ensure that when you meet my father you will reveal all that you know about the defenses of the gods."

Instinctively, I positioned myself in a defensive stance, then shook my head. "I don't think so. There's nothing you could learn from us that we wouldn't tell you willingly. I promise you."

"I'm pleased to hear it," said Mardon. "Nevertheless, it would be good for the morale of my men if they could see that denizens of the heavenly realm are treated the same as common prisoners."

My eyes narrowed. I raised up my hands and clenched them in the manner that I'd been taught. "You go ahead and try," I said coolly.

Mardon smirked, then huffed in amusement. "Arvad!" he called out.

Arvad and two of his other cavalrymen appeared at the door of the tent.

"What's the matter?" I said to Mardon. "Can't handle me by yourself? Am I too much 'angel' for you? I guess I should have expected as much from an *eel* like you."

Mardon's expression changed. But it wasn't anger. He looked stimulated by the challenge. He turned to Arvad. "Give me a length of cord."

Arvad handed the prince some rope, about four feet long, to replace the cord that had been cut.

He said to Arvad, "You may go."

Arvad hesitated.

"It's all right," Mardon assured. "I'll bring them both out momentarily, their hearts properly prepared to face the creative procedures of your men."

"But in case you fail to tie that rope back around my wrists," I said hastily, "I want you to promise that you will not torture or brand us, but you will take me at my word that we will reveal anything that you want us to reveal to your father, the king."

I was glad that I had made the challenge in front of witnesses. Indeed, Arvad and the others looked highly entertained.

Harry started to object, "Steffanie, I don't think this is a good idea . . ."

"No, I like it," said Mardon. "I'll even improve upon it. If you can prevent me from subduing you, I will allow you to ride away at sunset with my finest mule under your legs. Is that generous enough?"

"How about half of your kingdom," I said flatly, my eyes focused like a laser on the movements of the prince.

The hint of a frown crossed Mardon's features. The smiles also fled the faces of Arvad and his men. This was no longer a joke. I'd managed to offend them deeply. Chock that up as par for the course whenever I'd had the pleasure of competing against men. But then Mardon's grin returned, now with a renewed edge of malice. He moved to the tent door. Arvad and the others got out of his way, stepping back into the daylight.

"Don't go far," Mardon said to them. "I'll toss her out shortly, trussed up like a festival hog."

Arvad yanked the tent flap shut. Mardon turned back to me, those blue eyes blazing. He raised up the four-foot cord with both hands and snapped it in front of his face. "I fear I've been too lenient with you," he growled. "A single brand across your back hardly seems sufficient. As you've insulted me in front of my officers, I'll now have to deal with you more harshly."

"Prince Mardon!" said Harry urgently. "Why don't you fight a real man? Fight me!"

Mardon kept his eyes riveted on mine, moving steadily forward. "Not interested," he said to Harry. "The contest with your angelic sister is far more . . . interesting."

I clenched my teeth and locked the knuckles and thumb of both my hands in a typical Okinawan style. I took a few steps sideways to keep from being cornered. Mardon cut the distance between us to only about five feet. Then he went as still as a panther. I did the same. Suddenly he made two quick movements, flapping his arms. But it was only a feint, trying to get me to blink. I maintained my posture.

At last Mardon lunged for my wrist. *He caught it!* I couldn't believe it! Was I really so slow? He yanked me forward and grabbed for my other arm. He began twisting the first arm behind my back. *Aaugh!* How infuriating! I thought I was better than this!

But then he made a mistake. After he missed my other arm, he decided to settle for pinning me around the chest. Using my center knuckle, I stabbed him right in the Adam's apple. Instantly, I was released. His hands flew to his throat, as he gasped once for breath. This was no time to sit back on my laurels. I roundhoused the sucker right in the side of the head. Not settling with that, I brought up my other leg and did a front kick, striking his face with the ball of my foot. Mardon, the Prince of Shinar, went down.

He shook himself, stunned and surprised. I returned to my stance and waited.

All at once, Mardon started laughing. "Very good!" he said, still flat on his back. "I'm impressed!"

I stole a glance at Harry, who was grinning at me with pride. The prince started to get up, his feet a little unsteady.

"I've known a lot of strong women," he said. "But none quite as strong as you, fair Steffanie. None quite as lithe as—"

The unsteadiness was an act! Mardon lunged again. I was so *stupid!* I totally fell for it! His shoulder barreled into my stomach. I was crushed to the tent floor, the full weight of the muscle-bound prince right on top of me. I couldn't breathe! Now it was *my* turn to be disoriented. By the time I realized what was happening, Mardon had already cinched the first loop around my left wrist. What was worse, his knee was pinning my other arm. *I couldn't move!*

That's when my brother struck. Harry was my wild card. He threw his bound wrists over Mardon's head and yanked back on his throat. Once Harry had pulled Mardon off my chest, he tried to put him into a stranglehold. But Mardon's anger was fully aroused now. He threw his elbow backwards and hit Harry in the mouth. The prince reached his powerful arms over behind his head and seized the back of Harry's shirt. I heard the shirt ripping as Harry was hoisted into the air and flipped right over the top of Mardon's shoulders. He slammed my brother down on the ground. Then he planted the bronze toe of his boot directly into Harry's stomach. Harry curled into a ball, groaning in agony. There was no doubt in my mind that he was completely out of commission. I only hoped there wasn't internal damage.

This was too much for me to bear. Screeching like a she-devil, I drove my clenched knuckles once, twice, three times right into Mardon's face. I was all over that guy like honey on Pooh. He took a swing at me, but I had my wits about me now and jerked out of the way. While Mardon was off balance, I landed another roundhouse against his ear. I got a little overanxious at that instant, and before I'd finished positioning my weight for maximum power, I tried another roundhouse. Mardon caught my leg. As my kick sent him tumbling to the floor, he pulled me to the floor with him. Somehow he managed to twist me onto my stomach, seizing my other leg. I was now lying on top of him, but my head was toward his feet. That's when the bolt of inspiration hit me. A man can do some foolish things. Did Mardon think himself any less vulnerable than my brother? I raised up my elbow and brought it down just as hard as I could—a repeat performance of what he'd done to Harry, only slightly lower. How sweet it was to hear him make the same wrenched cry as Harry.

I kicked my legs and escaped from the prince quite easily after that. As I came to my feet, guards and soldiers were standing at the tent door, no longer able to resist the temptation to see what was happening. I continued to stand over the prince, my fists still cocked and ready in case Mardon wanted more. But Mardon and Harry were still both recovering on the tent floor. Arvad and his men started toward me, this time with their weapons drawn.

In the midst of all this Mardon started laughing again. There were tears in his eyes, but he was still laughing. He said in a humorously strained voice, "How I do admire a fighting angel!" If this was a feeble effort to convince his men that he hadn't been squarely defeated, it was incredibly lame.

Arvad and the other soldiers paused.

"What are you waiting for!" the prince yelled hoarsely. "Bind her arms like her brother!"

Spearpoints and swords were directed at me from all sides as another cord of rope was wrapped around my wrists.

"I should have known," I seethed, "that an eel can't be trusted to keep his word."

"On the contrary," said the prince, "I intend to keep my word in every possible particular. I will spare you and your brother the requisite torture and branding."

"What about the mule?" I asked. "What about letting us ride away into the sunset?"

"I said every *possible* particular," he clarified. Mardon managed to get up on one knee, his face still straining with pain as he declared, "I am the Prince of Shinar! Do you really think that I'd own a mule?" He faced his secretary, Lasha. "Have the armies break camp! We will start our march for the tower tonight!"

NOTES TO CHAPTER 4:

All discussions of race—from those that stem from prejudice to those that attempt to categorize people based on lineage—eventually take us back to the three principal parents of the human family: Japheth, Shem, and Ham. We know relatively little about these three individuals (though we may know considerably more about Shem, as will be discussed later). It is recorded that they all took wives with them into the ark, and that they all had multiple sons (daughters are not named, though we obviously assume they existed).

The Bible proclaims Shem as the eldest of the three (Gen. 5:32); however, modern revelation proclaims that Japheth was the eldest (Moses 8:12). In either case, Shem is named as the progenitor of the children of Israel and the person through which the authority of the holy priesthood was passed on to Abraham and his descendants. Why Japheth was not given this privilege is not recorded, although we are clearly told in the scriptures—as well as in numerous apocryphal sources—that Ham's descendants were cursed as pertaining to the priesthood. This was because of a specific incident when Ham tried to steal Noah's garment before his appointed time. It is said that this garment was the same garment given to Adam by the Lord in the Garden of Eden, and was the consummate symbol of priesthood authority. Specifically, the curse was applied to Ham's son, Canaan, rather than Ham himself. The scriptures tell us, "Cursed be Canaan; a servant of servants shall he be unto his brethren . . . Blessed be the Lord God of Shem; and Canaan shall be his servant" (Gen. 9:25–26). The JST adds: "and a veil of darkness shall cover him, that he shall be known among all men."

It is well-known that many Semitic (Shemite) nations as well as Indo-European nations arrogantly used these verses for centuries to justify the enslavement of Ham's descendants, whom they interpreted as the African race. Those who promoted this interpretation apparently forgot the caveat mentioned in Matthew 18:7: "For it must needs be that offences come; but woe to that man by whom the offence cometh!" In other words, though the Lord might allow certain conditions to exist, it does not excuse the cruelty of those who put human beings under the yoke of slavery.

It's interesting to note that according to one ancient document this curse upon Ham was to be lifted in the last days. In the *Pirqe de Rabbi Eliezer* it reads, "Because you grabbed it ahead of time, Ham, you cannot have the Priesthood until the end of time. Meanwhile, I will give the garment to Shem, and part of it to Japheth, but you cannot have it" (Hugh Nibley, *Temple and*

Cosmos, [Deseret Book Company, 1992], 128). It has been suggested that this "end of time" might correspond to the revelation received by President Kimball in 1978 which gave the priesthood to all worthy males.

By tradition, the descendants of Shem eventually became the Jews, the Arabs, and (as we learn through modern scripture) the native peoples of North and South America. The descendants of Japheth became the Europeans and the peoples of India, while the descendants of Ham became the Negroid and Mongoloid races of Africa and Asia. This is, of course, a vast oversimplification, but it spells out the basic consensus.

We should be warned that there is no shortage of uninspired pundits and pseudo-scholars who have tried to use such distinctions to characterize segments of the human population with certain gifts, endowments, tendencies, and flaws—usually with the motive of painting themselves as somehow superior. Even those who try to be "fair and objective" about it usually come off as having some social or political motive, if nothing more than to appear inordinately witty or educated. Such studies are typically shortsighted, and even destructive, since people will use them to stamp stereotypes rather than judge individual character.

Yet it does seem apparent that after the history of the world is revealed we will learn that certain peoples were, in fact, cursed or blessed, based on the actions of a specific progenitor. We may also learn that the failure or success of whole nations is the result of one person's righteousness or evil. Although we are ultimately judged by our own choices, the scriptures indicate that personal actions can, in fact, endow generations unborn with specific blessings (Gen. 24:14–19; D&C 124:90; D&C 104: 22, 25, 33, 37, 40, 42). On the other hand, one person's sins can curse generations unborn with specific consequences (Alma 3:15). Fortunately, the scriptures also indicate that "trans-generational" curses can be overcome by an individual's faith and repentance (Alma 23:18; D&C 124:50).

Nimrod, the son of Cush, the grandson of Ham, and the great-grandson of Noah, has always been a shadowy figure in biblical history. Theologians have often been torn between classifying him as some kind of mythical hero, since the Bible calls him a "mighty hunter before the Lord" (Gen. 10:9), or classifying him as a figure of great evil. He was undoubtedly a very important and influential figure, and did much to shape the early history of the earth. He is credited as the founder of both Babylon and Ninevah, both of which grew into great empires that would later conquer the divided kingdom of Israel.

It is a credit to the Joseph Smith Translation that the classification of "mighty hunter before the Lord" is rephrased as "a mighty hunter in the land" (JST, Gen. 10:5). This is more in agreement with all of the apocryphal literature on the subject, which unanimously defines him as a figure of great evil. The name actually denotes "one who rebels" or "come, let us rebel."

The Jerusalem Targum reads, "He was mighty in hunting (or in prey) and in sin before God, for he was a hunter of the children of men in their languages, and he said unto them, *Depart from the religion of Shem, and cleave to the institutes of Nimrod.*" The Targum of Jonathan by Uzziel says, "From the foundations of the world none was ever found like Nimrod, powerful in hunting, and in rebellions against the Lord." The *Syriac* calls him a "warlike giant." The word *tsayid*, which we render *hunter*, signifies *prey*; and it is applied in the scriptures to the *hunting of men* by persecution, oppression, and tyranny. Hence it is likely that Nimrod, having acquired power, used it in tyranny and oppression; and by rapine and violence, he founded the first kingdom since the days before the flood (Clarke, *Bible Commentary* [World Bible Publishing Co., 1986], 1:86).

Hugh Nibley points out that in an age when Melchizedek established a Zion after the pattern of Enoch, the prototype of the true city of God, Nimrod established Babylon—a name that would, throughout history, be used to symbolize the prototype of the kingdom of Satan, the antithesis of Zion (Nibley, *Lehi in the Desert* [Deseret Book, 1988], 154–64).

Prince Mardon, son of Nimrod, is mentioned only in apocryphal works. In the *Book of Jasher* it tells us that he was more wicked than his father (Jasher 7:47).

CHAPTER FIVE

Mary

After the terrifying attack of the beasts in the night, Josh continued to tremble, his soul wracked and his mind torn with confusion. I continued to hold him, and at the same time held baby Shem, whose crying was finally starting to abate. The remains of the bear, several tigers, and at least two lions lay in heaps about us. Joshua remained unconvinced that he had done anything egregious.

"Maybe I did get carried away," he said. "But I saved our lives! I killed those animals before they could kill us! What did I do wrong?"

"It wasn't wrong to protect us," I told him. "What worried me was your reaction—the way that you did it."

"If only you could have seen the look on your face," added Becky. "In your eyes."

"I'm sorry," said Josh, looking at the sword that lay on the ground at his feet, obviously still fighting within himself. "But I felt so . . . so powerful! And if I hadn't done what I did, we'd all be dead!"

"Has it occurred to you," I asked Joshua carefully, "to wonder why these animals attacked us in the first place?"

"Huh?" asked Josh.

"Did it seem normal to you that animals—even lions and tigers— would behave in such a way?"

"How do I know how lions and tigers behave in this century?" said Josh defensively. "No, it wasn't normal. I admit it. Tigers and bears and lions wouldn't normally attack at the same time. At least not on any nature show I've ever seen. Male lions don't usually hunt at all. But none of these animals around here are acting 'normal'—"

"*Have you considered,*" I continued in the same careful tone, "*that the sword may have* brought on *this attack?*"

Clearly it had not occurred to him, because he fell deep into thought. But then he asked, "*Why would the sword do that? It lured these animals to us just so I could* kill them? *What would be the point of that?*"

"*Perhaps to intensify your attachment to it,*" I suggested. "*To increase the dependence that* all *of us might feel toward it.*"

"*I'm not attached to it,*" Josh insisted. "*I could care less about it. But neither of you girls wanted to carry it.*"

I felt an acute pang of guilt. I should have never left it in his custody. I should have taken it upon myself. Or else I should have taken Becky's initial advice to leave it behind.

But no, I didn't feel right about that either. I'd come to appreciate the viewpoint that if we allowed this sword to fall into the wrong hands, it would become an instrument of great evil to its owner, and to anyone else in the owner's sphere of influence. I was persuaded that the best course of action was to destroy it. But to have left it in the hands of a twelve-year-old boy . . . This, on my part, was inexcusable.

"*Will you now allow me to carry it?*" I asked Joshua.

Josh seemed surprised. He hesitated to answer.

"*You?*" said Becky with alarm.

"*Yes,*" I said succinctly. "*I should have taken this responsibility from the very beginning. I will trade with Joshua for some of my other bundles.*"

"*Fine,*" said Josh, sounding irritated. "*It's all yours. It was chafing my shoulder anyway. Good riddance.*"

"*But you* can't *carry it!*" Becky said to me. "*If the sword were to corrupt* you, *where would that leave us?*"

"*Give me a break!*" said Josh. "*I'm not corrupted.* Sheesh!"

"*We should throw it in the lake,*" Becky continued. "*We should just be done with it.*"

My mind was torn. "*Oh, Becky. I'm sure that would seem right. But that would only allow it to hurt someone else. Would it be right to leave a deadly serpent to roam freely in a child's room? Or in your own century, to leave a loaded pistol on a playground? I'm afraid we cannot abandon it. We must find a place to deposit it where it poses no threat to others, or we must destroy it.*"

"But what if it keeps attracting dangerous things to us?" asked Josh. "What if it brings evil people? You said it was our job to protect little Shem. Isn't it possible that it will keep luring to us the very people we're trying to hide him from?"

It was an awful quandary, one for which I did not have a perfect answer. Or perhaps I did.

"We will have to hope," I replied, "that our faith is infinitely more powerful than the evil in that sword."

They pondered this. For Becky the thought brought great comfort. Josh continued to resist the notion that the sword had enticed him to do anything wrong. As for me, I felt overwhelmed with an incumbency to protect all three of these children from harm. In pursuit of this I felt strongly that remaining here was not an option. Besides, I would never tolerate sleeping in the vicinity of all these carcasses.

"Come," I said to the children. "We will continue walking in the coolness of the night air. It will be considerably more bearable than the heat of the afternoon."

"But what about more tigers and lions?" asked Rebecca.

I reflected on this, then said, "If indeed that sword enticed the animals to attack us, then the sword will know that it must try another tactic. I feel strongly that we will have no more trouble in that regard tonight."

They looked at me with apprehension and doubt, but I didn't hear any additional objections. The way our hearts were pounding, I doubted if we would have obtained much sleep that night anyway. My only insistence was that Joshua return to the water to fetch our goat milk, and to cleanse his face and arms of blood.

"What about the blood on the sword?" asked Joshua.

I turned to gaze upon it. Like Joshua's face and arms, it too had a bright sheen of red. "Don't concern yourself," I said. "I will rinse the sword."

Josh nodded uncertainly. He looked toward the water with apprehension. "Are you coming down there with me?"

I was actually relieved to see that a normal, healthy fear of the darkness had been restored in Joshua's mind. I gave the baby to Becky. Shem was very alert, watching us closely, his expression filled with curiosity.

I stepped over to the sword and paused. It seemed so unassuming lying there. So impotent. But I wasn't deceived. Had I really told myself that I *would never touch it? So much for noble intentions. I reached down and grasped the hilt.*

I felt a slight shock, like the shock that one might feel when lifting a woolen fleece. It was painless, but served to remind me that I was hefting no ordinary thing. I paid it no mind, and followed Joshua down to the water.

All at once my mind filled with laughter. Not the sound *of laughter. More the echo of it. The* memory *of it. I stopped in my tracks, allowing for the echo to die away.*

From behind me, Becky inquired, "Are you all right?"

"Yes," I replied, and started toward the shore again.

As I finished rinsing off the silver blade, I thought I might have heard the laughter again. It was familiar to me somehow. Not an evil, melodramatic laugh, but . . . like the laughter of someone that I knew. Someone from long ago. It evoked very strange feelings inside me.

I dismissed it. I was sure it was the product of the sword. But unlike Joshua, I did not say within my heart that I would resist it. In fact, I felt sure that this is what it would have preferred. It wanted its bearers to believe they could grapple with it on their own, relying on their own inner will and strength. But I knew that I was too weak a vessel for that. I needed help. And much of it. Instead, I tried to fill my heart with the voice of the Spirit. I immediately prayed for strength. And gratefully I found it—just enough that I was able to direct my thoughts again to our present situation.

I borrowed Joshua's strap for carrying the sword and the four of us continued our journey under the light of the stars. Becky took responsibility for Shem. The baby forced us to stop again after only half an hour to suck more of the goat milk. For more than half of the night we continued walking, until we gave up out of pure fatigue. I'd begun to notice for some time by the light of the moon that trees were beginning to spring up around us. By the time we collapsed and gave in to sleep, we were within the confines of a rather densely wooded vale, reminding me of nights I'd spent with my sisters in the Forest of Jarden in the Decapolis. North of us I could see the ghostly shapes of cliffs and hills.

I set the sword away from me and shut my eyes. The children and the baby were all fast asleep long before I was. Into my mind came a strange whisper, like something that the wind had carried from the woods, but the source was several places at once.

I am still here, Mary.

My eyes popped open. I looked at the sword, dimly flickering in the starlight.

Should I warn you of the danger? Perhaps I shouldn't. You seem to hate me. Yet I want to help you. Trust in me, Mary. Trust me . . .

The whisper was very strange. It felt almost as if I had invented it in my own mind and dramatized it. But this wasn't possible. The tone of it was completely beyond my personality. I did not respond. I was determined that I would never *respond. Immediately, I began to pray. The whisper fell silent, and I drifted off to sleep.*

* * *

"Mary!" came the urgent whisper. But this was not the sword. It was Rebecca. "Mary, look!"

I gathered my wits. The sun was quite bright. We had obviously slept until late in the morning. Rebecca was pointing fearfully into the woods. Joshua was also awake. Shem was still bundled up in my head shawl and tucked comfortably in a little nest of leaves. He remained fast asleep. I rolled onto my stomach and focused my eyes on the place she indicated.

Horses. The children were watching the approach of several horses through the thickness of the woods. All we saw were snatches, really. And the occasional glimpse of purple and gold riding cloaks. Their approach was very slow and methodical, as if the riders were studying the ground for signs.

"Nimrod's warriors," whispered Joshua. "They're headed this way. They're tracking *us!"*

I feared Joshua's assessment was correct. They may well have been following footprints. Our footprints. At their present rate they would discover us in only a few minutes.

I gestured to the children—I didn't dare even to whisper anymore. Becky gathered up little Shem. The baby yawned—a rather loud *yawn. Becky threw the corner of the shawl over his face and followed as I began to lead them toward the north.*

I paused suddenly. The sword! *I'd almost forgotten it. Quickly I stepped back and grabbed it. We slipped into a ravine and made our way toward the cliffs and hills.*

After a few minutes, Joshua dared to speak. "Do you think I'm right? Do you think they might be tracking us?"

I failed to answer for a minute; then a thought occurred to me and I asked Joshua, "Did you remember to bring the baby's swaddling blanket—the one that you went down to the water's edge to rinse?"

Josh paled slightly. "I-I don't remember. I don't think so. So much happened. I think I forgot it."

Had it really been that simple for them? The more I thought about it, the more alarming it became. Might the soldiers of King Nimrod—the very same men who had attacked that caravan—have approached the waterhole early this morning? Might they have found the baby's blanket while investigating the curious assortment of slain animals? Might they have recognized it? A fresh surge of anxiety sped through my veins. So foolish of us! I should have remembered that cloth! But on the other hand, we may have been very fortunate to have fled from the waterhole when we did. If we'd remained until morning, we'd have been discovered hours ago.

Josh cursed himself. "Stupid! So stupid!"

"It's all right," *I said.* "Hopefully our new direction will throw them off."

"Unless," *said Josh,* "they're better trackers than we think. They might find where we slept and realize we're close. They'll start traveling faster."

I detested pessimism. Especially when it made a strong point.

We arrived at the escarpment of rock formations and followed swiftly along its boundary until we discovered a place where we might climb. The trail was between two boulders. This would shield us from the eyes of anyone below. It might also gain a vantage point from which to overlook the valley.

After climbing for ten minutes or so, the baby began to fuss.

"He doesn't like all the jerking," *said Becky just as she slipped on a stone to emphasize her point.*

"Or he's just hungry again," *said Joshua.*

"We better feed him," *I said.* "If he starts to wail, it will carry quite a distance."

We tucked ourselves into a windbreak against the cliff a short distance from the top. Joshua broke out the canteen of milk and untied the neck. I contemplated taking the baby from Becky to ensure that it was done properly, but she seemed to do it just fine. The baby sucked the tip of the sheepskin contentedly.

"I'm gonna finish climbing to the top and see if they're following us," said Josh.

"I'll join you," I said.

Becky wasn't thrilled to be left alone, but she made no complaint. Josh and I finished climbing to a high point and crawled to the edge of an overlook that revealed the woods below.

My worst fears were verified. The riders from the desert—the murderers in their purple, black, and golden cloaks—were still following our trail. We could still see glimpses of them and their horses in the thickness of the foliage. They were a short distance beyond the place where we had slept. As Joshua had surmised, they were traveling much more swiftly.

"How many do you see?" Josh inquired.

I tried to count the shapes among the tree trunks and brush. I suspected there were almost twenty. Several horsemen entered a small clearing and made themselves quite visible. They were surprisingly large men with an arsenal of dangerous-looking weapons. One of the men favored an odd-looking spear with an assortment of razors on the tip, like a scythe with teeth. He rode a horse with a coat so black that, in the brightness of the morning sun, it looked almost blue. They all wore ferocious and determined scowls. Their eyes searched the boulders and cliffs. Josh and I ducked down to avoid detection.

"Let's return to Becky," I said. "We must continue on."

"If the baby cries now," said Joshua, "they'll hear us for sure."

"Pray that he doesn't."

Oh, but he will.

Just as last night, these words rang in my thoughts from no apparent source.

Joshua saw the strange look on my face. "What's wrong?"

I refused to glance at the sword. "Nothing," I replied. "Pray, like I told you."

We made our way back down to Becky and found her still feeding the baby.

"We must proceed over this hill," I told her. "Come!"

"But Shem isn't finished."

I looked down between the boulders toward the base of the slope. "They'll be riding past this point in a matter of minutes. They'll see us clearly."

"At least let me try to burp him," said Becky. "It's not a bottle, and he drinks it too fast."

Josh pleaded with his sister. "Don't you understand? They'll see us any moment! We'll be killed!"

"Do you want the baby to scream?" asked Becky.

She took the flask from the infant's mouth. Thankfully, he didn't seem to mind. Becky laid him against her shoulder.

"Burp him while we climb!" I whispered urgently.

Becky followed us awkwardly. The jarring movements helped burp the infant more effectively than pats to his back. Air popped from his stomach. He spit up goat's milk onto Becky's burnoose. One burp was so loud that I was afraid it would be as audible as any cry. But as of yet, no riders had appeared below us. If they had tracked us this far, it seemed certain that they would discover the place where we had climbed. Our modern shoes were digging deep grooves into the dirt and gravel. Our trail in several places was visible to the eye! I took some comfort knowing that if they followed us, they would be forced to abandon their horses. This would mean we would travel at the same speed—or even faster since they would have to pause to check for sign on the trail.

Had I taken leave of my senses? *I was with two children and a baby! We could* never *outrun them for any great distance. Our best hope was to hide. Somehow we had to divert them off our path.*

After another minute we reached the hump of the rise. The ridge was like the spine on an animal's back. It descended into another forested valley. I could hear the sound of a river. Along the opposite slope protruded a far greater variety of rock formations. The ground looked harder—less likely to leave footprints. All of this gave me an idea. I needed only to find the right place where I could . . . There! I saw just what we needed. Along the trail that descended to the valley floor was a shadowed hole in the face of the hill. Not a cave exactly. More of an overhang between two large blocks of stone. I adjusted our direction to move toward it.

"Where are you going?" asked Joshua.

"Stay behind me," I said.

We traveled along a diagonal corridor. Our course wasn't directly toward the overhang, but it would pass close by. As we reached a place where the ground beneath us was solid stone, I brought our party to a halt.

I said to the children, "I want you and Becky to slip inside that hole."

"Which hole?" asked Josh. There were actually many gaps and crevasses in the area.

"That one," I said, pointing. "The one with the overhang. Go in as deep as you can so that you are completely hidden in the shadow."

"What about that one over there?" asked Josh.

"Please!" I pleaded. "Do as I advise!"

"What are you going to do?" asked Becky.

"I'll rejoin you in a few minutes. I also want you to do something else."

"What?" they asked in unison.

"Remove your shoes. Remove them here and now. Carry them in your hands. If you do leave a track, I don't want it to look anything like the tracks we've left before this point."

"That's gotta be a hundred yards," said Becky. "It'll cut up our feet."

"I'll carry Shem if you'd like," said Josh.

She handed him over. The children obeyed without further questions. Thank grace for that! Children of the modern century never did anything without a gaggle of questions.

As for me, I retained my twenty-first century Puma sports sneakers and continued to the bottom of the ridge, deliberately kicking up as much debris as possible. I glanced up at the children once before I entered the woods. They were nearly to the overhang, wincing from time to time as their bare feet encountered sharp obstacles.

I slipped into the forest and made my way toward the sound of the running water.

I like your idea, Mary. But you must hurry. Any moment the riders will top the ridge.

I didn't need the sword to tell me to hurry. I was doing plenty well on my own. At last I found the babbling brook. It was a smaller river, only about ten paces across. I deliberately left a careful trail right up to the water's edge—then I hastily removed my shoes.

Quickly, I retraced my steps back through the forest to the rocky slope. I winced several times myself as I stubbed my toe. It surprised me how painful it was. My feet had grown soft over the last two years while living with the luxury of modern footwear. I regretted losing the callouses that I had so diligently developed over the first nineteen years of my life.

As I began to climb, I heard the echo of voices near the summit. They were following our trail as surely as a fox follows a rabbit to its burrow. I took a slightly varied trail as I climbed the ridge, keenly aware that if even one of the twenty trackers caught sight of me, my plan would be foiled.

The final leg of the climb was the steepest, ending at a sort of unlevel platform exactly in front of the overhang. As I'd hoped, the starkness of the sunlight made it so that there was not the slimmest evidence or outline of any shape inside that hole. Shem made a cooing sound as I entered, seemingly relieved to see that I was all right. Becky and Joshua had crouched inside as far as they could, their shoes now back on their feet.

"It's not going to work," remarked the ever-positive Joshua.

"What's not going to work?" I asked, replacing my sneakers.

"Didn't you ever watch Dad's copy of Butch Cassidy and the Sundance Kid? *They tried to do the same thing—outwit the trackers by changing their trail. The trackers figured it out and kept coming."*

"That was a movie," Becky replied. "This is real life."

"I don't know," he said doubtfully. "So far these guys have been pretty dang good at what they do."

The boy is right. It was a clever idea, Mary. But I'm afraid for you.

"Shh!" I spat.

Josh gave me a queer look, as if I'd meant the shush for him. What was I saying? I did intend it for him. I would not and could not respond to the sword. Besides, the first tracker in his purple cloak had just appeared at the top of the ridge. Everyone went stiffly quiet.

The man remained there for a long while, surveying the forest below, as well as studying the ground for sign. Another tracker appeared behind him. It was the person with the scythe shaped javelin. They spoke with one another, but we couldn't hear their words. Several other purple-cloaked men appeared at various places along the ridge. One of the men—a square-jawed figure who reminded me vaguely of the Roman general Titus—gave orders to various soldiers to search this way or that way. But the first two individuals who had appeared remained honed in on the precise trail that we had taken when coming down the hillside.

Shem made another cooing sound. The infant was certainly in high spirits, despite the stomach-twisting tension that gripped the rest of us. He even let out a babyish laugh. I realized such sounds were almost as dangerous as wails to the high heavens. I took the baby from Becky and bounced him gently, whispering shushing sounds and singing softly in his ear.

A moment later all we could see were the two original trackers, the others having fanned out across the slope. The two men paused at the place where Becky and Joshua had removed their shoes, causing my heart stop within my chest.

"It's not gonna work," Josh repeated in a soft whisper. "It's not gonna work."

My muscles remained taut. Then one of the men discovered a shoeprint that I'd left a little farther down the slope. They studied it, then continued climbing down. Becky heaved a great sigh of relief. This caused Shem to make another giggle. I turned quickly toward the baby. How do you tell an infant not to be happy? Just lull him to sleep, *I prayed. The trackers did not hear him and continued to the bottom of the slope. Soon they vanished into the trees.*

"I guess I was wrong," said Joshua, shrugging. "It happens occasionally. Once every decade or so."

"Quiet!" whispered Becky, still nervous about the proximity of the other soldiers. For all we knew, one might have been standing on the boulder right above us.

Now we waited. There was little else to do. I feared we might be forced to wait here until dark. Even then, I'd have been very apprehensive about emerging. In a matter of hours, after they figured out that they'd lost the trail, they would undoubtedly backtrack and likely pass by here again. Again I found myself staring at the baby. What was so important about him? What would incite the King of Shinar to seek him with such diligence? Did they seek to destroy him? It seemed almost reminiscent of the Messiah when King Herod had ordered the death of Bethlehem's infant children.

This thought had barely skimmed over my thoughts when I heard Joshua gasp. We stiffened in apprehension. One of the trackers had returned. He was standing at the edge of the forest, looking puzzled, his eyes following back up the ridge. Had I truly thought it might be hours before his return? It was less than three minutes! And by his expression, he'd plainly concluded that something was amiss. His accompanying tracker was not with him. Perhaps the other man had decided to further investigate the area where my trail had ended. But this individual—this man with the scythe-tipped javelin—had decided that the mistake might have been made earlier on.

The children hardly dared to breathe. The sound of blood pumped in my ears. I glimpsed the face of little Shem. His expression had changed. I couldn't have said why he hadn't felt our tension before, but suddenly he looked quite concerned. Even frightened. He made a worried noise, as if asking us to explain why everyone looked so distraught.

"Becky," I whispered, handing the baby to her. "Try to feed him. Comfort him. Anything!"

The stress in my own voice didn't help at all. Shem made another concerned little moan. Becky brought up the flask of milk, but the baby showed no interest. The tracker had begun to climb the ridge again, double-checking all of the signs.

"What are we going to do?" asked Josh, his voice barely a peep.

Even that noise was too much. "Shh," I said.

The tracker reached the place where Becky and Joshua had taken off their shoes. He stopped and touched the hillside with his fingers. Then he raised his gaze and looked toward us.

Fortunately, it wasn't directly toward us. I'd chosen this overhang because it did not look like much of a hiding place. There were other caves and crags along the ridge beyond us that would have appeared more logical as a place of resort or concealment. It was toward these other crags that he directed his gaze. Our last and only hope was that he would climb past us, focus on these more obvious hiding spots, and never return. He began to move toward our position. Or rather, he began to scoot along the ledge toward the more distant ridgeline.

The boy. Be wary of the boy.

Just as the sword issued this peculiar warning, Joshua whispered,
"The sword."

*I looked at Josh in alarm. He had a desperate look in his eyes. He was
asking me to use it. To defend us with it!*

I shook my head. "No."

You're right, Mary. It shouldn't be the boy who defends us. It
should be *you*. I will strengthen you. You have my promise.

*I wished the sword would shut up! I wasn't going to acknowledge it.
Heavenly Father was the source of all my strength.*

*Shem made a sound as though he would start to cry. Becky began
kissing him and hugging him, trying breathlessly to keep him from crying
out. I'd heard of desperate women among the Jews who, while hiding
from the Romans, had suffocated their own children while trying to
prevent them from screaming. But how could I even consider cutting off
an infant's air supply? Such actions would only cause Shem to scream all
the more as soon as he breathed. Yet I now understood the panic of such
women. If Shem cried out, he was going to die anyway. We would all die!*

*The soldier kept his course, his eyes fixed beyond us, just as I had
hoped. At exactly that instant I saw Shem scrunch up his face and draw a
deep breath. He was about to let out a wail!*

*Quickly, I reached toward Becky's lap and grabbed the baby's face,
pressing my palm against his mouth. I successfully squelched the sound,
but I was hurting him! My instinct to never harm a child overpowered
all else. I released the baby's mouth. The tracker was only a stone's throw
away now. Joshua panicked and grabbed for the sword on my shoulder. As
I tried to stop him, Shem let out a screeching wail.*

*The soldier stopped abruptly, his eyes shooting flames toward our
hiding place. The baby started to draw in a breath so deep that the resul-
tant cry would surely shake the earth to its foundations.*

The man with the scythe-tipped javelin started toward us.

"Please, Mary," Joshua pleaded. "The sword can save us! I know it!"

He's right. I can.

"No!" I said more firmly, my teeth clenched.

The soldier was only a few paces away, lips grinning. The baby screamed. The soldier stopped just short of the entrance. He drew back his javelin. He was going to stab that terrible scythe into the shadow! —as if blindly plunging a trident into the sea to draw out a fish.

Use me now!

I acted, but not with the sword. I shrieked no less loudly than Shem and launched myself at the man's chest. There was surprise in his eyes as I vaulted out of the blackness.

"Mary!" Joshua shouted.

My crossed arms drove into the man's chest. He fell backward, over the side of the ledge, but I was falling with him! Joshua's arms locked around my waist. He pulled me back as the soldier dropped away. The man was airborne for a full three meters before he landed against his crown on the slope below. The way his head bent on impact, the neck had surely snapped.

I stared over the ledge, feeling sickened. The man wasn't moving. Becky emerged from the hole, the baby in her arms. Shem was now screaming and wailing like a Roman bloodhound. We had to run, but which direction? My first impulse was to climb back over the ridge. But that was foolish. Several men had certainly been left to watch the horses. Next, I looked west along the same route that the soldier would have gone if the baby hadn't cried out. But I saw two trackers in purple cloaks in that direction, pointing and scurrying rapidly toward us.

I took the baby from Rebecca. "This way!"

We charged headlong down the slope, approaching the forest's edge. I knew at least one other soldier was nearby, but this was our only possible escape! Despite the screaming infant, I reached the base without tripping. We entered the forest. Joshua made no further attempts to grab the sword. He seemed satisfied now simply to run. He held his sister's hand to make sure she kept up.

"Over here!" I directed, determined that we would not follow the same path to the stream that I had taken before.

Instead, we ran eastward, through what appeared to be a thicker part of the woods. I could hear the river babbling somewhere up ahead, but I *couldn't yet see it. Shem had recovered somewhat from his trauma. He no longer wailed quite so loudly. He was merely content to let out a howl every few seconds.*

Joshua raced on ahead and was the first to reach the river's edge. He looked back. "Should we cross?"

Certainly one would not have drowned crossing here, but it still appeared terribly inconvenient. The baby would get wet and likely start screaming again.

Look to your right.

So far I'd resisted following any advice from the sword. But this time I turned my head and looked. A short distance downstream there appeared to be a logjam. Whether or not the idea had come from the sword, it did appear to be the most expedient way to cross. I led the way through the brush until we found ourselves at one end of the logjam.

A fallen tree had created the small dam. A score of additional branches and leaves had collected around it. Most of the water seeped underneath, pouring over a waterfall about twice the height of a man, and gathering into a pool below. For the most part the top layer was dry and exposed, though it looked terribly fragile. Crossing it might cause a section to give way. Two seconds later we received fresh incentive. Footsteps were crashing through the brush behind us.

"Go!" I commanded Joshua.

He began the balancing act, with Becky close behind. I climbed onto the dam last to keep them moving. Shem glanced downward at the pool below. He showed no fear. Just fascination.

At the halfway point in the logjam was an island of sorts where debris had built up particularly high. Just as we reached this island, we pulled to a halt. A purple cloak emerged from the trees on the north bank. My heart withered. It was the original tracker who'd been with the soldier who carried the scythe-tipped javelin. In his hands was a short bronze sword. On his face was a twisted smile.

We turned to go back, but just then the other soldier coalesced from the brush. Clenched in his fist was a loaded bow, the arrow pointed at the infant in my arms. He stalked closer until one foot was positioned on the south end of the logjam.

What? *I thought to myself.* No snide remark from the sword? *I couldn't help but wonder if it had* deliberately *enticed us into this trap.*

The tracker on the north end—the one with the sword—spoke to us. *"My, my. A woman and two children. I might have expected a more challenging adversary to take up the cause of Terah's son."*

For the briefest of instants, I forgot our certain prospect of death and focused only on the name he'd just pronounced.

"Who?" I asked.

The soldier laughed. *"It's as we suspected. You merely found the child in the desert and became its protectors, am I right? What became of the baby's nursemaid, Amthelo?"*

I replied, almost obliviously, "Dead."

"Serves her right," pronounced the soldier. *"She betrayed King Nimrod, as did Chancellor Terah when he tried to spare his newborn's life against the will of the king."* He changed the subject abruptly. *"How does a tiny woman like you come by such an attractive weapon?"*

He was referring, of course, to the sword.

The soldier on the south, with the loaded bow, spoke to his companion. *"I can kill them all here and now. The first arrow would pierce both the infant and the woman. We can divide the reward."* He pulled back the string.

"Wait!" called the first soldier. *"What if she falls into the pool? I want that sword."*

Reluctantly, the archer lowered his bow.

The man on the north said to me, *"I might change my mind if you toss your weapon over this way."*

I shook my head. If I was to die, I would do them no favors.

The archer sternly objected, *"Why should you have the sword?"*

The first soldier huffed in irritation. *"Very well. We'll gamble for it tonight. Eh?"*

The archer nodded. He slung the bow behind his shoulder and took another step toward us across the logjam. The first soldier also stepped toward us, switching the bronze sword to his other arm so that he might use his most agile hand to grab us.

Becky, Josh, and I pressed closer together, our hearts quaking with fear. We should jump! *I told myself. But would this make any difference? The pool below us was reasonably calm; there was no current to whisk us away. The soldiers would only jump down and wait for us to swim to either bank. We'd be killed just the same.*

"Easy now," said the soldier with the sword, creeping closer.

The archer continued closing in from the other direction. Our choices of action had reached an end!

You're correct. You have no choice. *Use me!* Swipe at the knot of debris in front of you. *Trust me!*

This was the moment. God forgive me. I decided to trust the sword. I handed the baby to Rebecca, reached over my shoulder, and yanked it from the cloth. The soldier in front of us smirked, humored by my show of determination. But he wasn't smiling as I brought the sword over my head and chopped down upon the debris right in front of my feet. The single swipe cut right through a large stick that was supporting a tangled clump of debris.

The result was spectacular! All at once a major portion of the dam was set free. As leaves and sticks spilled over the falls, a wave of the river followed. The soldier with the sword slipped instantly, dropping his sword and knocking his chin on the logjam. He splashed clumsily into the pool below.

My effort proved more effective than I might have wanted. The island of debris under our feet began to move. It was sliding out from under us.

"Fall to the left!" I cried.

Becky jumped, the baby still in her arms. I leaped and did the same, plunging into cold water up to my neck. The same chain reaction took effect under the feet of the archer. The entire top layer of the dam was giving way. The archer attempted to fall in the same direction as Becky and me, but he got his feet caught in a rolling branch and ended up being dragged over the falls. At the last second he grasped part of the original fallen log and hung on, but Joshua reacted quickly. Somehow he'd maintained his balance on the only clump of debris that hadn't washed away. His hand reached into a satchel at his waist. He pulled something out, but I couldn't see what it was. Joshua stepped toward the clinging soldier and stabbed something down on the archer's wrist. I think it was an ink pen. Accordingly, the man dropped. We heard the splash on the other side.

Miraculously, Becky had managed to keep the baby's head above water, but not the rest of Shem's body. She was already pulling herself onto the north bank. I raised the sword out of the river and struggled to reach her, swimming with one arm. Joshua pulled himself along the fallen log and reached dry ground before I did. He helped Becky to hoist me out. In one fluid motion I was able to slip the sword back into the wrapping of cloth on my back. I took the baby from Rebecca. The infant seemed too shocked and traumatized to cry. He just buried his face in my shoulder.

As we began running again through the woods, I clung to that infant like I'd never clung to any child before. I was still beside myself, still marveling and wondering over the revelation of the soldier's words. I was chilled to the bone, I'd just survived two nerve-shattering attempts on my life, but my thoughts were consumed with the reality of what I'd learned about the tiny life in my hands.

Son of Terah. Ward of the nursemaid, Amthelo.

In my arms was the destiny of Israel, the recipient of the great covenant—my own great, great, great (there were too many greats to count!) grandfather!

I was holding the father of the Hebrew nation—Abraham.

NOTES TO CHAPTER 7:

There appears to be little agreement between historians regarding the precise timeframe of the life of the great patriarch, Abraham (or Abram, as he was called before the Lord changed his name). Although by scholarly tradition he is thought to have been born anywhere from 300 to 1000 years after the events surrounding the Tower the Babel, it is clearly established in ancient Jewish, Christian, and Moslem tradition that Terah, Abraham, Nimrod, and the events surrounding the confounding of tongues occurred contemporaneously. This seems to be supported by Genesis chapter 11, which begins the record of Abraham's life immediately after the account of the Tower and the confusion of tongues. Nonbiblical sources include the book of *Jasher, Pseudo-Philo, Legends of the Jews,* and *Chronicles of Jarahmeel,* among many others.

But even when comparing nonbiblical manuscripts, there are conflicting accounts of Abraham's exact role in Nimrod's kingdom. Several portray circumstances that are similar to those the author has presented in this novel (i.e., the life of the infant Abram is sought by King Nimrod, many infants are slain in the effort, and Abram's life is saved by nursemaids, servants, or Abram's mother). Other accounts describe Abram as coming in conflict with Nimrod as an adult. Several documents tell how Abram was cast into a fire by Nimrod and came forth unscathed. It's possible that there is no conflict between such accounts since Nimrod's reign is purported to have lasted for many years—even beyond the destruction of the Tower.

In any case, several themes appear to be common: Terah is a ranking official in Nimrod's court. Terah is an idol worshipper (as supported by Abr. 1:5–6). Abraham's life is sought by Nimrod. And finally, Abraham eventually departs from the realm of Babylon, or Chaldea, and dwells in Haran before the Lord commands him to go to the region of Judea.

Hugh Nibley has suggested that the "Pharaoh" from the book of Abraham and "Nimrod" may be one and the same person (Hugh Nibley, *Abraham in Egypt,* F.A.R.MS., 2000, 226–32).

The name of Amthelo as the nursemaid who initially saved the life of Abram is based on one of the names given as Abram's mother. None of the ancient records seem to agree on this name. While *Legends of the Jews* calls Terah's wife and Abraham's mother Emetelai, *Jubilees* calls her Edna. Eutychius, a first-millennium Christian historian, insists that her name was Yona. The *Book of Jasher* calls her Amthelo. Emtelai, or Emetelai, seems to be the preferred appellation; nevertheless, the author chose to preserve the name of Amthelo in the role herein portrayed.

CHAPTER SIX

Harry

"Here's another fine mess you've gotten us into," my sister said to me as we were placed in the back of an ox-drawn "paddy wagon" (for lack of a better term).

Her joke fell flat. Actually, I don't think Steff meant it to be funny—just ironic. I actually recalled some pretty horrible messes throughout our adventures—volcanic eruptions, forest fires, shipwrecks . . . So far, being a prisoner of Shinar wasn't even in the top ten.

But it *was* one of the more peculiar *messes* that I could recall. The warriors of Shinar literally believed that they'd captured a pair of *angels*. Or if not angels, some other form of heavenly beings. Mardon clearly said that we were being taken to his father, King Nimrod, to be interrogated on the most effective strategies for defeating heaven. As I considered the reality of this, it was all I could do to keep from laughing. And yet it was no laughing matter. Nimrod apparently felt—in all seriousness—that he could wage war against God. The whole thing was unbelievable. Yet here we were, sitting in chains in a portable, straw-lined cage, on our way to the palace of Shinar.

Still, we were better off than the majority of Japhethite prisoners. At least we had transportation. The rest of the defeated rabble were left to walk, despite any battle wounds, and despite any pain caused by the lion-headed brand that was scorched, without exception, into the flesh of each prisoner's back. Any prisoner too injured or exhausted to travel was executed on the spot, his body left as food for the vultures. The captives of Japheth had been marked as Nimrod's slaves for life.

Steffanie and I may have been the *only* captives who had avoided this awful brand. Even the two poor souls thrown into the back of the paddy wagon with us had a blistered and bleeding mark behind their shoulders. They'd also been beaten to unconsciousness. I suspected that they were Japhethite generals, or other ranking officials whose utter humiliation was required by Mardon. Because of our chains, Steffanie and I couldn't get close enough to them to offer assistance.

They'd really overdone the chain thing. The ropes on our hands had been cut, but iron shackles took their place, locked around both of our wrists and both of our ankles. There was also an iron collar around my neck. The two men across the cage also wore wrist and ankle chains, though right now this was the least of their discomforts. One had both eyes swollen shut from the beatings; the other had one leg twisted so badly that I felt sure it was broken at the shin. Apparently this was the fate of anyone who defied the might of King Nimrod and his sadistic son.

"How do you feel?" Steffanie asked me as our wagon started to roll. She was referring to the injury I'd received from Mardon's boot.

"I'll be all right," I replied, though the pain still throbbed.

"What an awful man," spat Steffanie. "A despicable man."

"I'm glad you think so," I said. "Renews my faith in the female race. Nice to know that not all girls are suckers for a pretty face."

"You can be sure of it," said Steff. "I'm only attracted to members of the human race. Not animals. Not total and utter sewer rats."

"Best-looking sewer rat I bet *you* ever saw."

She narrowed her gaze and curled her mouth. "Think so, eh? Well, if this is what good-looking guys are like in this century, I'll happily marry Weird Al Yankovich."

One of the men across the cage stirred. He was an older man with a grizzled white beard. The beard was braided into two points that lay on top of one another, almost as if he had *two* beards. At present it was matted with blood. Even though he was older, by the size of his biceps I'd have guessed he was in better shape than most men in their twenties. We waited to see if he might awaken, but after only a few seconds, he became motionless again.

"Do you think they'll live?" asked Steffanie apprehensively. She knew that I'd seen my fair share of badly beaten and injured men in ancient Jerusalem, as well as back on Lincoln Island in the Mediterranean Sea.

I shook my head sadly. "I don't know. But the younger man on the right is the worst off. That broken leg is swelling pretty badly. He could easily shoot a clot to his lungs. If he starts acting like it's hard for him to breathe, it's probably too late for him."

Steffanie yanked at her chain, following an impulse to go to him, though she knew that she couldn't. "Who do you think they are?"

"Leaders of the army, I'd guess. Could be anyone. The one on the left looks pretty old. Might even be Japheth himself."

"Are you serious?"

I shrugged. "People in this day lived an awfully long time."

"How long do you think it's been since the Flood?"

I shook my head. "Three, maybe four hundred years."

Her eyes widened. "Japheth lived for *four hundred years?*"

"I can't remember. But I know that Noah lived at least three hundred and fifty years after the Flood."

"You mean Noah might still be *alive?*"

"I wouldn't think so. But it's possible."

Steffanie leaned back in wonder. "Now *there'd* be a cool guy to meet. Can you imagine?"

I murmured in agreement. Our mood went somber again. Right now our circumstances were so dismal that it was hard to imagine anything so glorious.

"What's going on, Harry?" Steffanie asked. "Who do these people think we are? Are they really so dense as to believe we're angels?"

"Apparently so," I replied.

"Just what do they think angels *are* in this day and time? It's almost as if they think angels are a whole different *species*—a species as vulnerable and capable of being defeated as any other living thing."

I shrugged. "*Most* religions—even in our day—think that angels are a different species. We're the only religion in the world that teaches that angels are glorified beings who once lived on this earth."

"And what about that business of attacking heaven?" Steff continued. "Mardon was *serious!* Are these people a few fries short of a Happy Meal or what?"

"Either that," I said, "or they're among the most hoodwinked and arrogant human beings in history."

"After meeting Mardon, I could almost believe it."

"I'm not joking," I said. "Think about it. What do we know about the Tower of Babel? They were building it to try and get to heaven, right?"

"That's what I've been taught," said Steff.

"Just how corrupted and twisted does a race of people have to be to think that they can build a tower to reach heaven?"

"Aren't they just trying to save themselves from another flood?"

"Maybe. But I think it's *more* than that. It's as if they're convinced God can be outwitted. As if they think God is just a nuisance to be overcome. Nimrod has undoubtedly deluded everyone into thinking *he's* a god, one more powerful than the God of Heaven."

"That's pretty typical," said Steff. "The pharaohs of Egypt said the same thing. So did the caesars of Rome. And the Aztec chiefs."

"Yeah, but except for someone crazy like Caligula, how many actually believe it about *themselves?* For Nimrod to have undertaken a project like that tower, he'd have to believe he really *is* a god."

"Maybe in an era when men live three or four hundred years," said Steff, "it's easy to become that deluded. In my opinion, *anyone* who stops repenting goes a little bonkers. Satan *makes* them that way. Four hundred years would give the adversary a long time to warp somebody's personality."

We stared through the bars of our cage at the tower in the distance. It really was breathtaking. Yet I still wasn't sure how far away it was. If one of the men across the wagon had been conscious, I might have tried to ask him for answers, but it was still uncertain if they'd ever wake up long enough to tell us anything.

Fifteen riders had been posted around us. I don't think they were so worried about us escaping as they were about keeping others away. Angels were quite the curiosity, and word that Mardon had several in captivity was spreading fast. I heard some of the gossip as various soldiers and officers approached our guards to ask questions. They particularly wanted to hear details of how one of the angels had injured the prince, but our guards remained tight-lipped on that subject.

The night came on swiftly as the army marched until a very late hour. Our wagon had a wooden roof, so I couldn't see who drove the oxen, but it wouldn't have surprised me to hear that he'd fallen asleep at the reins. The soldiers of Shinar couldn't be less tired than the prisoners they'd defeated. Mardon seemed determined to march them until they dropped.

At last, we heard the captains up and down the ranks shout the command to make camp for the night, or for what was left of it. Our wagon pulled to a stop. We watched Mardon's servants throw up the royal tent with the efficiency of circus roustabouts. No fires were kindled, either because the men were commanded not to or because they were too exhausted. Within thirty minutes the army of Shinar fell silent. Soldiers bedded down right where they'd halted—all but the guards posted around our cage.

Steffanie made a pillow from the straw and was soon asleep as well. I sat awake in the darkness, my back propped against the side of the wagon. They'd taken our backpacks and supplies, but there were at least two things that they hadn't confiscated. One was my oil vial, which had become a permanent fixture in my pocket, and the other, in the pocket beside it, was the seerstone that I'd found in Frost Cave. I reached in and pulled it out.

Even in the darkness it emitted a kind of light. I cupped it tightly in my hands and gazed into the delicate glow. I'm not sure what I thought I'd see, or even what I *wanted* to see. My thoughts were so overwhelmed and scrambled that I half hoped the stone would decide for me. That is, I hoped that the Lord would show me whatever He felt was necessary.

It seemed to me that the glow shimmered a little, almost like it was tuning into the desires of my heart. At first I didn't necessarily perceive anything, but then a warm shroud of comfort wrapped around me.

I thought about the loved ones that we were seeking to find. I still wasn't sure who they were. I only knew that we were looking for three people. Marcos and my Uncle Garth were searching for the other three. They'd gone to an entirely different century. I could only imagine what hardships or adventures they might be enduring.

I contemplated asking if I would ever see any of them again, but I think I was too afraid. Better, I decided, to ask if any of them were close by—perhaps awaiting us in Shinar. The glow seemed to go a little darker. My feelings of comfort sank significantly. I shuddered. I realized we were *not* moving closer to them. In fact, I felt we were moving farther *away*.

However, I also sensed that the task they were engaged in was no less important. Then the Lord gave me a small, but wonderful gift. The stone revealed that at least *one* of the people I was seeking was Mary. I clearly saw her sweet face in the surface of the stone—that is to say, I saw it in the surface of my mind. She was *here*, in this century. She looked tired and frazzled, but she was healthy and well. I also sensed that two more of my loved ones were with her, but I wasn't exactly sure who.

There was only one more question to ask the stone, but I was scared to death of the answer. I'd already learned from personal experience that the miracles of God were not always immediate. For three years I'd sojourned on a Greek island in the Aegean Sea. I don't think that I could have borne it again to be away from my family for so long. Nevertheless, I worked up the courage and pronounced the question clearly in my thoughts.

What should I do? How can I save my sister and myself, as well as save Mary and the others? And how can I do it swiftly, before any serious or tragic consequences occur?

Unexpectedly, the seerstone threw me a curve ball. The image that I saw was so completely startling that the air seemed to go cold in my lungs. I saw a face from my past. It was a hideous, repugnant face. The image froze my heart and boiled my blood. It wasn't the first time that I had seen it. It had appeared countless times in my nightmares. Without a doubt it was the most horrifying image of my life, and it had stamped a brand onto my memory that I would have considered far more painful than any brand now festering on the backs of these prisoners.

The face came out of the darkness. It emerged from the shadows at the bottom of a long stairwell. The forehead was angular and a coarse red beard circled the mouth. The man's arms were covered with jet-black tattoos shaped like rams and snakes, leopards and dragons. The tattoos crawled all the way up the man's neck and onto his cheeks. It was those narrow-slit eyes—so wicked and full of hate— that haunted me most. He emerged from the shadows armed with a bow. An arrow was already pulled taut on the string.

And then he let the arrow fly.

I gasped and lowered the stone. My actions were so abrupt that it caused Steffanie to stir.

"Harry? What's wrong?"

"The Scythian," I whispered.

"Who?"

"The Scythian from the stairwell. The man who killed . . ." I could hardly utter it. " . . . who killed Gidgiddonihah. I saw his face in the stone."

"The *seer*stone?"

"I saw it all over again. The critical moment. The instant that the fatal arrow was fired."

"I don't understand," said Steffanie. "Why would you see such a thing? Why would the stone dredge up such a horrible memory from your own mind?"

My heart continued pounding. I tried to calm myself and think. "I . . . I don't know."

"It must mean something," said Steff.

I nodded, though I wasn't entirely certain if it meant anything at all.

"Don't look at it anymore tonight," Steffanie advised. "Try to sleep, Harry. It's been a long and terrible day. Look in it again tomorrow. Will you try to sleep?"

I took a deep breath and nodded again. I wouldn't have wished such an image on anyone—particularly just before they fell asleep. But it wouldn't have been the first night that such a vision had kept me awake. The image had always come before without any help at all. So why would the stone have shown it to me again? And in such vivid detail?

I tried to take Steffanie's advice. I tried to go to sleep. It wasn't only the image of the man in the shadows that staved off slumber. It was the nagging question of why the stone had shown it to me. And Steffanie's words: *It must mean something.*

* * *

"Did you see your city last night?" asked the guard at dawn.

I opened one eye and looked at him. *Finally*, I thought to myself. *A genuinely ugly man.* I'd been starting to think no one in this century looked normal—that is, like someone you might find at a convenience store late at night. Yet despite his oversized jaw and beady eyes, he still had the body of the Incredible Hulk. He handed me a ladle filled with water. I drank it down in earnest, then I said, "What?"

He repeated his question, "Your city. Did you see it? It lit up the whole sky last night."

I must not have been fully awake yet, because I *still* didn't understand. Then it occurred to me. The stars. He was talking about my supposed home—heaven.

"No," I said. "I didn't see my 'city.'"

He refilled the ladle, then used the edge of it to nudge Steffanie, spilling a good portion on her neck. She aroused with a start.

"Better drink this, Highness," he said mockingly. "It'll be the last you get until tonight. And here's your breakfast." He tossed us both a loaf of round bread and a piece of bruised fruit—a pear, I think. He returned to his conversation with me. "You'll see it again tonight, I'll wager. Not that it'll make a difference. I don't expect that you'll be floating back there anytime soon."

"No, I expect not."

"In a few days we'll see it in daytime. It's that season of the year. Nimrod believes the tower is high enough now. Soon he'll be the king of *both* realms."

"Oh, I'm sure he will."

He studied me a moment. "Are you being sarcastic?"

Steffanie replied, "You figured that out all by yourself?"

He glowered at us, then turned to leave.

"Wait," I said apologetically. "What about them?" I pointed to our other two cellmates, still unconscious, though I'd heard one of them stirring earlier.

"What about 'em?" he asked.

"They'll need water."

The guard thought about this, then dipped his ladle twice and splashed it in their faces. He walked away laughing. The two Japhethites awoke, at least partially. The older one used his chains to pull himself back against the side of the wagon. His eyes were still severely swollen. The younger man—the one with the broken leg—opened his eyes and tried to move, but the effort only caused excruciating pain. He went still again, seeming to faint.

Steffanie indicated the departing guard, and asked, "What did he mean—'See it in daytime?'"

"The stars, I think."

"See the stars in *daytime?*"

I shrugged. "I guess so. He asked if I'd seen my 'city' last night. I assumed he meant the stars of heaven."

"That doesn't make sense," said Steffanie.

"I'm just repeating what he said."

She sighed. "This place just gets weirder and weirder."

The Japhethite was looking at me as best he could through his swollen eyes. I tried to think of how to start a conversation. I certainly wasn't going to say "good morning." Asking him how he felt didn't seem particularly fitting either.

I settled with an introduction. "I'm Harry Hawkins. This is Steffanie, my sister."

He raised his arm to rub his eyes. It was a reflex. He winced the instant he touched his bruises and gave up. He made no effort to reply to me.

"Do you understand us?" asked Steffanie, thinking perhaps he was still disoriented.

"Of course I understand you," he replied. His words were a little slurred. He tenderly felt the inside of his mouth, I think because several teeth had been knocked loose. He asked, "Wha' 'r ya?"

"Excuse me?" I said.

He removed his fingers. "What are you?"

"We're . . . not what they think we are," said Steffanie.

The man spit into the straw. The spittle was red. "What do they think you are?"

"Angels," said Steff.

He grunted in amusement, but said nothing more.

"What's your name?" I asked.

"Boath," he said.

I wasn't sure if he'd slurred that last syllable. "Boath?" I repeated.

"Boath, son of Magog."

Magog. I'd heard that name before, but I couldn't quite place it.

"This—" he continued, stretching his eyes to see the other man beside him, "—is my grandson, Partholan." He touched his grandson on the leg, immediately drawing a painful response.

"His leg is broken," I said.

Boath adjusted his head to try and see Partholan's leg more clearly. "Has he said anything?"

"Nothing," I replied. "Nor have they tried to give him food or water."

Boath grunted. "I suppose I should have expected that."

I asked him, "Are you one of the generals of Japheth's army?"

"I am *the* general," he replied, sounding a little irritated that I didn't seem to know this already. But then his chest sank and his tone mellowed. "Which means that the revolt is at an end. My people are defeated."

"What will happen to them?" I asked.

"They will become slaves of the Cushites and the rest of Ham's rabble," he spat. "We will all become the ferrets of King Nimrod." He sighed deflatedly. "Ah, what does it matter? Most of the children of my grandfather, Japheth, *already* grovel at Nimrod's feet, working his slime pits, carrying his bricks. For the better part of five generations they have labored. And that's the monument of their misery." He nodded toward the distant tower, but he barely glanced at it, as if he couldn't stand the sight.

"What about the other division?" asked Steffanie.

One of his swollen eyes opened a little wider. "What?"

"The Japhethite's other division," said Steff. "Isn't there another—?"

"Who told you this?" he growled. Somehow the question had offended him.

"I overhead the soldiers of Shinar interrogating your men as we were—"

"*Shhhh!*" he said, as if this might prevent her from giving away a secret. "How can you know of this?"

"I don't think it's anything they don't already know," said Steffanie. "They were torturing your men to find out where the division was located."

His tone became very suspicious. "Who are you?"

Steff and I looked at one another, unsure how to respond.

"Who is your ancestor?" he persisted. "What are your generations?"

I'd given up on my idea of casually explaining the concepts of time travel. That's precisely what had gotten us into this pickle. I said simply, "We are allies of the people of Salem."

This apparently did the trick, because he leaned back, looking relieved. "So Mardon thinks he knows all about the other division, eh?"

"I guess one of your men gave in," said Steffanie.

"Men cannot tell what they do not know," said Boath. "Even *I* do not know their location. This was my command, so that if I was beaten or tortured, I could not betray them. They will be coming. And they will bring all the young recruits from my homeland, Scythia."

My heart skipped a beat. "Your people are . . . the Scythians?"

He noted my reaction. "Scythia was my mother," he said. "My father named the land for her. What's wrong? Have my kinsmen offended you somehow?"

I shook my head, feeling foolish. The image of the face at the bottom of the stairwell passed freshly through my mind. I certainly couldn't blame this man for the actions of a descendant who wouldn't be born for three thousand years. Still, the name itself was like nails on a chalkboard.

"No," I said. Then I added, "Not yet."

"I wish I could say the same for the men of Salem," he retorted testily. "The people of Salem appear to have forgotten about their brothers in bondage. Are they sending an army to help in our cause?"

"I don't know," I said.

Boath let this simmer, then declared, "The city of Shem has done nothing to crush the tyranny of Nimrod. In fact, many of Shem's seed are his strongest supporters, including his chancellor. Surely you know of Terah, son of Nahor?"

Steffanie shook her head, but I nodded. Again, I was grateful to have reread the book of Genesis in the past few weeks. Terah, son of Nahor, was the father of Abraham.

Boath directed his next question to me. "But have you heard of Terah's treachery against his own house?"

"No, I haven't."

Boath began, "One year ago Nimrod's stargazers saw signs in the heavens. The signs foretold that a son would be born who would rise up to defeat Nimrod and possess all the earth. In the district where the sign was given, the king ordered all pregnant women brought to his palace. He kept these women in captivity until they were delivered. Then he ordered his midwives to slay every male child as it emerged from the womb."

Steffanie's eyes widened in horror. "That can't be true!"

"But Nimrod forgot the district chancellor, Terah. Four moons ago, when Terah's son was born, Nimrod's diviners proclaimed him as the foreordained child. Nimrod commanded Terah to bring his newborn to the palace so that he might slay it with his own hands. For gold and silver Terah did as he was told. He willingly let the king kill his own flesh and blood. This is the depravity of the followers of Nimrod."

Steffanie was still too appalled to respond.

I asked Boath, "What was the child's name?"

Boath shook his head. "I don't know. The name doesn't matter. I only make the point that even innocent babes are beholden to Nimrod's wrath. I promise you that I will *die* before I ever serve him."

"As will I," said Partholan weakly.

He appeared close to fulfilling this promise already. The grandson of Boath rolled onto his stomach, cringing in pain. His grandfather reached out and took his hand. Steffanie and I continued to reel in revulsion at Boath's story. Yet I could have sworn that I'd heard this legend before. My dear friend, Micah, had taught it to me on Lincoln Island. According to his account, Terah did *not* give his son over to death. He fooled the king and his son escaped. Then again, it was just a legend. This story wasn't in the scriptures. No doubt there were hundreds of stories from the first generations of the world that never reached the Bible.

Boath aided his grandson as best he could. He got Partholan's leg in a position to try and set it. It was an excruciating thing to watch. When the actual maneuver took place, my magnificent sister, who wasn't often squeamish about anything, turned her head as if she might throw up. Partholan passed out. Boath managed to strip off a short piece of board from the side of the wagon and ripped up his own shirt to bind it in place. It was a crude cast, but it was the best he could hope for under the circumstances.

Steffanie got up the nerve to ask Boath, "How old are you?"

He replied unconcernedly, as if it were nothing extraordinary, "I have lived two hundred and fifty-seven years."

We gaped at him in astonishment. I might have guessed him to be in his sixties. Maybe seventies. *But two hundred and fifty seven!*

"Are there many men as old as you?" I asked.

"Fewer and fewer," said Boath. "The lives of men have been decreasing for generations. The Shemites say it began in the days of Joktan. I only know that I have outlived all of my sons."

"Why do you think people don't live as long anymore?" asked Steffanie.

"Because the One God has decreed it," said Boath. "My great-grandfather, Noah, was building the ark for one hundred and twenty years. This was the time of probation given to the children of Adam. But since the people would not repent, it now signifies the maximum age of men."

"How far is it to Shinar?" I inquired.

"You're there," said Boath. "This is the land of Shinar. Tomorrow we will arrive at Babel and the base of the tower."

Our eyes again focused on the mighty structure.

"Exactly how high is that thing?" asked Steffanie.

"They say it is more than five thousand cubits," said Boath.

I did some calculations of that in my head. I'd lived among the people of the ancient world for over three years, and I knew that a cubit was basically the length from the elbow to the tip of the fingers—about 20 inches, depending on the arms of the person making the measurement. I remembered from school that a mile was exactly 5280 feet. That meant . . . *Holy cow!* This thing was over a mile and a half high! I'd read somewhere that the Empire State Building was 1500 feet. That meant . . . (My brain was starting to hurt. I really needed a calculator) . . .1500 feet was equal to about 900 cubits. So . . . *Oh, baby!* It was five times as tall as the *Empire State Building!* If it had been standing on the valley floor in Utah County, it would have been as tall or taller than Mount Timpanogos! Had anything remotely comparable ever been constructed in the history of the world? The engineering requirements were mind-blowing! There must have been a million laborers at work during the various stages of its construction.

I studied the structure again, looming larger with each passing hour. By tomorrow I presumed it would block out much of the sky. It was more or less pyramid shaped. Maybe cone-shaped is a better way to describe it—but it wasn't round. Its design was very "cubic," with dozens of tiers and slopes and levels—no doubt accessed by thousands of stairs. The base of it was *humongous*—like a man-made mountain. I'd have guessed that just walking around it took several days. And climbing to the top? I supposed a climber in the best possible shape could have done it in a day or two, but for the *rest* of us . . . I'd climbed Mount Timpanogos when I was thirteen, but it wasn't like I'd climbed it from the valley floor. We'd driven a car a good part of the distance.

Much of the tower was dingy and gray, no doubt from all the bitumen slime that was used as mortar for the bricks. Certain segments appeared to have been whitewashed or "red"-washed, but it couldn't hide its overall filthy exterior. A pall of black smoke hung over the area, adding to its dirty appearance. The logistics of getting materials from the bottom to the top would have been staggering.

At the very summit of the tower was a flat area, maybe the size of several city blocks. In the middle of this flat area was a kind of triangular pinnacle, climbing several hundred feet higher. I was curious where this final pinnacle was supposed to lead. It just went to the top and dropped off the edge. That first step into heaven was, to say the least, a doosey.

We learned more from Boath about the earth's history since the days of Noah, and a few more details of how Nimrod had come to power. Apparently many years ago there had been a spectacular family reunion held in Shinar wherein all the descendants of Shem, Ham, and Japheth journeyed from their inherited lands. Almost two million people had been in attendance. During this festival, Nimrod, who had been designated as the leader of the Hamites, persuaded many influential descendants of Shem and Japheth to join him in building his empire. Immediately after the festival, a war broke out between Ham and Japheth wherein the leader of the Japhethites, Fenoch, was killed. From there Nimrod used his army, now supplanted with mercenaries and confederates, to secure power. He took the children of conquered families and held them as security to force the people to become his slaves. Labor on the tower was begun. Today the entire world belonged to Nimrod, except for a few scattered remnants of Japhethites and the Shemites of Salem.

It occurred to me that this was the only time in history when an obsessed military leader had achieved his dream of taking over the entire world. Alexander the Great had tried, the Romans had tried, and even Napoleon and Hitler had tried, but only Nimrod could claim to have succeeded. He'd vanquished just about everyone there was to vanquish—all but the residents of the mysterious city called Salem.

Boath's energy was finally spent. He fell back to sleep. The muggy heat caused me to nap through much of the day as well. At one point I awakened to see that the scene around the wagon had changed. The army was no longer marching through grassy countryside. Instead, the landscape was covered with farmland and buildings. The arm of a wide, grayish-green river was visible in the east, flowing lazily southward. I assumed this was the mighty Euphrates. The haze of smoke in the air was becoming denser. It seemed to hang particularly thick around the base of the tower. The stench of pollution was increasing—especially the smell of burning tar and oil. The closer we got to the tower, the grimier *everything* seemed to appear. A sooty residue clung to the walls of every clay building. This couldn't have been a very healthy place to live, no matter how genetically perfect your body was. I wondered how it compared to London or Paris at the height of the industrial revolution. Bitumen tar seemed to be the area's most popular fuel, and heavy black smoke rose up from almost every hamlet. We were, after all, in the petroleum capital of the world.

I began to see caravans of wagons and oxen. They appeared to be going to and from the region of the tower, many of them carrying barrels of tar. One of the major deposits of bitumen for the tower's construction must have been in the area, probably down near the river.

Our wagon pulled to a halt late in the afternoon. Mardon had decided to make an early day of it, much to the relief of his army as well as the prisoners of war. Our parched throats were finally provided with much-needed water. They also gave water and some bread to Boath and his grandson. But they refused to give more food to me or Steff.

"You will be joining the prince tonight in his tent," said the guard.

After he departed, Steffanie said to me sarcastically, "Great. The megalomaniac is inviting us to dinner."

"Where are we exactly?" I asked Boath.

"The region of Calneh," said Boath.

Partholan started coughing. It looked like a fever had set in. Again, I felt helpless to do anything for him. Then, all at once, my missionary instincts kicked in. I asked the question that I'd asked a hundred times in Greece, usually to families with sick children.

"Would you like me to give your grandson a priesthood blessing?"

Boath gave me a queer look. "You have the power of the priesthood?"

I nodded. "I have consecrated oil too—in my pocket. If you were to help Partholan to lay his head this way, I might be able to reach—"

Boath interrupted, "You have the priesthood of the Fathers?"

"Yes," I said again, "if by that you mean the priesthood handed down from Adam."

He looked amazed. I wondered if I had overstepped my bounds. I wasn't even certain if Boath was a religious man.

He said finally, "There are none among the sons of Japheth who hold this power anymore. My father squandered it, and I have never had a mind to seek it. Nimrod may claim it, but he does not have the right to it—despite the garment that he flaunts before the people. I am old enough to know the truth. His grandfather, Ham, stole Adam's garment from Father Noah and gave it to his son, Cush, who in turn gave it to Nimrod. I had begun to think that I would never meet another man who held it by legitimate right."

I said again, humbly, "If you wish me to give Partholan a blessing, I'll do it."

Boath hesitated. A range of emotions crossed his face—doubt, guilt, feelings of unworthiness. But at last he nodded and helped to maneuver Partholan's head as close to me as possible.

I took the tiny Hold to the Rod oil vial from my pocket. My chained wrists could barely reach far enough to touch Partholan's head. I pronounced a healing blessing. Afterward, Boath looked at me with a strange reverence, as if I might have awakened in him an awareness of spiritual things that, over the last 257 years, he'd almost forgotten. I think he was about to express gratitude, but the servants of Mardon arrived, along with Mardon's loutish secretary, Lasha.

They unlocked the chains on Steffanic and me, then replaced them with new fetters. A three-foot silver chain was attached to my wrists. We were allowed to wash up a little. That is, they commanded us to wash up, using water from a local fountain. I wouldn't have minded fresh clothes as well, but they seemed to prefer us in our modern shirt and pants, as if it strengthened the argument that we were angels.

Some unusual characters were waiting outside of Mardon's tent. In fact, they looked so out of place amongst the cloaks and armor of Shinarian soldiers that I found myself gawking in astonishment. There were three of them, adorned in leather and bands of blue-green gems. Their features were round and flat—still striking in their own right, but very different from the long, sweeping features on the faces of the men of Nimrod. Perhaps I shouldn't have found it peculiar that they were gaping back at me. Everybody gaped at us. But the expression on these three individuals seemed distinctive from the rest. The army of Shinar still looked upon us with a healthy degree of fear and respect. After all, we were *angels*. But from these men I sensed only a deep and visceral enmity. These guys hated our guts! It was so apparent that I almost wanted to stop and say, "What'd we ever do to you, punk?" I decided to ignore them, and seconds later Steffanie and I were whisked into the tent of the prince.

Mardon sat facing the tent door. All around him were many of his highest-ranking officers. Mash was there, as well as his cavalryman, Arvad. They lounged on pillows and fed on grapes, little round cakes, and other hors d'oeuvres provided by the residents of the community.

In the center of the room, set on a bright purple cloth, was an unusual sculptured mask. It looked like pure gold. If I hadn't known any better, I might have thought that the gemstones in the eyes and teeth were Central American jade. But it was the feathers of its headdress that struck me most dramatically. Was it possible? Could these have been quetzal feathers?

I decided I was mistaken. Surely the feathers had come from a bird native to Mesopotamia. And even if they *did* belong to a quetzal bird, was that so extraordinary? Exactly when did quetzal birds migrate to America? For all I knew, the Jaredites were the ones who had transported the species to the New World.

But then I saw the man seated beside Mardon, and my curiosity intensified again. I thought back to the guard that I'd met this morning—the one who I'd thought was genuinely ugly. I must have entirely forgotten what the word meant. This man was the textbook definition. He was a frightening kind of ugly. His skin was pale and anemic. His checks were covered in pinprick-sized scars. He was as bald as a soccer ball, with protruding ears and small, beady eyes. His two front teeth stuck forward and he had a thin scruff of white facial hair circling his mouth. On the rug beside him was a helmet, plated in gold, which reminded me vaguely of helmets that I had once seen among the Lamanites.

I take that back. It wasn't the Lamanites. Where had I seen them? I couldn't quite put my finger on it. I noticed that Steffanie was also staring at that helmet with familiarity.

"As I promised you!" Mardon announced to the pale man beside him. "Captives of the Heavenly City! Showing them to you seems a very small price for the generous and valuable gift that you have brought to my father."

"On the contrary," said the stranger, "a golden mask is a trifle compared to the privilege of gazing at the countenances of . . . *angels*."

Why was it that his pronunciation of the word told me that he didn't believe any part of it? But if he was mocking the idea, neither Mardon nor the others caught on.

"Join us, Harry and Steffanie," Mardon invited. "I'd like you to meet one of my father's most loyal subjects." He hesitated, already forgetting the name of his guest.

"Shika," said the man, never taking his eyes off mine.

"That's right," said Mardon. "Lord Shika of the land of . . ." Again, the prince had forgotten.

"Syria," said Shika.

"Yes, Syria," Mardon repeated.

Lasha had us sit down on the pillows in front of them. Shika continued to stare at us with burning intensity. "Tell me, Prince," he said, "what price would I have to pay to take ownership of these prisoners?"

"I'm afraid if you had that much money," said Mardon, "my father would have already confiscated it."

After a pregnant pause, he let out a guffaw. Laughter erupted from all of the other officers in the tent. Shika smiled at the joke obligatorily. I could tell he was actually rather perturbed.

"But," said Mardon, "your gold has certainly earned you a place at my feast. And tonight you can ask them any question you wish. Tomorrow, however, you and your men will return to your caravan, and I will take the prisoners to the throne of Nimrod."

"Very good, Prince," said Shika, nodding abjectly. "Perhaps your captives can tell me where it was that they 'fell out of the sky?'"

A visceral uneasiness came over me, as if the Spirit were sending me a warning. Something about this man didn't sit right at all. I didn't have the foggiest idea who he was, but I had the impression that he definitely knew who *we* were.

Steffanie looked at me, indicating plainly that since I'd created the mess about "falling out of the sky," it was my job to clean it up.

"We, uh, landed in the hills near where Mardon defeated the army of the Japhethites," I replied.

"Your garments are intriguing," said Shika. "I think I may have seen apparel like yours before."

"Oh?" said Steffanie. "On whom?"

"Well, I suppose they must have been angels, like you," said Shika. "Perhaps they are acquaintances of yours. I believe their names were—"

I held my breath.

"—Mary, Rebecca, and Joshua."

My heart stopped. I stared wide-eyed into Shika's face. He saw the shock on both of our faces and seemed to relish it.

Shika picked a poppy seed off one of the cakes, put it into his mouth, and asked casually, "Do you know them?"

We didn't answer for several seconds, still gathering our wits. Finally, Steff replied with a shrug, "Maybe."

"Maybe, eh?" he said coolly. "Tell me, by chance have you seen them lately? Perhaps since you fell out of the sky?"

"Have *you* seen them lately?" I asked.

He shook his head. "For me it's been quite some time. That's why, when I heard there were angels in the prince's custody, I decided I had to meet them. To be honest, I was rather hoping that you might turn out to be the very same angels whom I met before. But I suppose that finding their 'acquaintances' would be the next best thing."

"When you saw them last," Steffanie asked, "where was it?"

"In a land very far away," said Shika, sounding nostalgic. "But I was given to believe that they might be in this area. I'd like very much to find them, if you might at all be able to help me."

Mardon interjected, "If there are any more angels to be found in Shinar, they are to be brought to the king."

"Of course," said Shika abjectly. "I would turn them over to the court of Nimrod immediately. But first I'd like to see if they had in their possession an item that they borrowed from me many years ago."

The uneasiness inside me was growing. "What item is that?" I asked.

He shrugged. "A trifle, really. A silver-bladed sword. Not *pure* silver, mind you. Just an ordinary sword. But it is a weapon for which I must confess a certain fondness. If at all possible, I would like to get it back."

I looked deeply into this man's eyes, trying to see into his soul. A silver-bladed sword. I knew all about silver swords. In particular, I knew about the sword of Coriantumr. My father had filled me in on the scant details of Becky and Joshua's kidnapping at Lagoon. He'd mentioned that the perpetrator was named Todd Finlay—a former police officer from Cody, Wyoming, who had caused my father a great deal of trouble over a silver sword. After a quarter century Finlay came back, and his obsession for the sword was as powerful as ever.

Still, this man didn't seem anything like the man my father had described. He'd told me that Finlay was a gawky fellow and that he wore glasses. If Mr. Finlay had looked like someone who'd been dug up from a graveyard, I was sure that Dad would have mentioned it. I decided this was not Todd Finlay. But who was he?

Just before we'd embarked on this journey, Dad, Garth, Marcos, and I had discussed many theories for why Todd Finlay would have taken the children to Frost Cave. The answer that kept coming back was that Finlay had wanted to use them to somehow locate Coriantumr's sword. He would have needed Josh and Becky to show him the route to the Rainbow Room. We decided that Finlay's ambitions would be in vain. The Rainbow and Galaxy Rooms would not have given him what he wanted. It wasn't possible to go back to a time before the sword had been destroyed. We'd felt sure that things just didn't work like that. But that was before we'd discovered the pillar—and the seerstone.

Was it possible that Finlay had triumphed? That he'd succeeded in finding the sword? The thought chilled my blood. But if Finlay had found it, how did *this* man fit into the picture? Who was Shika of Syria?

I looked at Steffanie. Her instincts had also been alerted. I asked Shika carefully, "What makes you think that these 'angels' have taken your sword?"

"Oh, they have it," said Shika. "I'm positive of that. After all, they killed the servant who I gave charge of it. A man named Finlay."

My eyes narrowed. Shika was lying—at least about who had killed whom. But Shika's words at least allowed for one disturbing conclusion. He may have been telling the truth about the sword. Mary, Becky, and Joshua *did* have it. Or if they didn't, they at least knew where it was. It was for this reason that Shika and his goons—the three men outside the tent—were trying to find them. This was why they'd followed our loved ones to this century and time. It was also the reason that Shika had offered gold in return for the opportunity to meet the two angels reportedly traveling with the army of the prince. He'd undoubtedly been hoping that we were Mary, Becky, or Joshua.

Mardon had been following the conversation closely. He remarked, "So my father was right. Angels really are the bloodthirsty murderers that he has always preached."

Steffanie asked Shika, "What made you think that we would know these angels—What were their names again?"

"Mary, Becky, and Joshua," he said patiently, then he shrugged. "It was just a hope." He gave a toothy grin, revealing his deformed front teeth, as if something else occurred to him. "Ah, but maybe it was more than a hope." He began to feel around the pockets of his tunic.

Finally, he pulled out a piece of paper. As his fingers unfolded it, I realized it wasn't paper. It was a photograph. As he displayed it before us, my heart filled with rage.

It was *our* photograph! It was the family portrait from my father's living room—the very picture taken just before I went into the MTC! Steffanie and I were in it, as well as Garth, Jenny, Meagan, and Melody. Also featured were Mary, Rebecca, and Joshua. A cry wrenched out of Steffanie's throat. I lunged for the photograph. Shika snatched it back just as several of Mardon's servants seized my shoulders. Someone else seized Steffanie. One of the servants punched me in the jaw.

"Enough!" shouted Mardon.

Steff managed to break free. She reached over to support me, though the chains on her wrists made it awkward. I glared at the servant who had struck me and tasted a cut on my lip. Then I fixed my gaze back onto Shika. My thoughts were whirling. For Shika to get his hands on that photo, he'd have to have been in my home.

"Let me see it," said Mardon, putting his hand toward Shika.

Shika hesitated, then he smiled and said, "Of course, Your Highness."

"What have you done to my family?" I asked Shika through clenched teeth.

Shika glanced at Mardon and the other officers. He realized that in this company he couldn't answer the question directly, though I think he would have liked to. "Why, nothing. How could I have done anything to them? Your family resides in the Heavenly City, do they not?"

"What *is* this?" asked Mardon, still studying the photograph. "Is it some kind of drawing?"

"It is a frozen reflection," said Shika mysteriously. "Plucked from the surface of a pool. It's a magic that can only be achieved—" He grinned at me. "—by angels."

"If you did anything to them," Steffanie hissed, "we'll hunt you down. We'll hunt you like a rodent."

Shika laughed and said sarcastically, "I'm very worried."

"I hope you are," I confirmed, my gaze as steady as granite. "If you harmed them, I promise you won't find refuge in any corner of time or space. I will find you."

He studied me for a moment. "My, my. You are a vengeful one, aren't you? I like that."

"They're *both* feisty," said Mardon. He eyed my sister. "Deliciously so. This one fights like a tiger. But as you can see, they are not invincible."

"I don't presume," said Shika, "that your father will need them permanently, will he? Perhaps I could purchase them when the king has concluded his interrogation."

"Doubtful," said Mardon. "But if you wish to try, my advice is that you return to your home and bring as much treasure as you possess to my father's palace. He is a bargaining man. Perhaps he will see clear to grant your request."

There was a lethal glare in Shika's eyes. I could tell he liked Mardon as well as a cat likes mud. Still, he retained his composure. "As you wish, noble Prince."

"Now go away," Mardon ordered. "I have given you your interview, and frankly, your appearance disturbs my appetite. Go! Be gone!"

He shooed Shika off like an insect. I could tell Shika was boiling. He was not accustomed to being dismissed. Yet he bowed, paid Steffanie and me one final threatening look, and departed the prince's tent.

"What a strange man," said Mardon to his secretary after he was gone. "Where did he say he was from again?"

"Syria," Lasha answered. "Part of the lands of Aram the Shemite. That is, before your father's annexation."

"I see," said Mardon. "I'll advise my father to send a division of the army immediately. They obviously have wealth that has not been assessed." He picked up the golden mask with the jadestone eyes and popped another grape into his mouth. "Yes, a very strange man."

It finally occurred to me where I had seen a helmet like the one that Shika carried under his arm. It was on the heads of the Pochteca traders who had kidnapped Steffanie, Dad, and me in the land of Zarahemla when I was ten years old. The similarity was not exact, but it was the same idea—a sort of animal face that came over the brow of the head. I knew that the Pochteca were a very ancient organization. I also knew that Kumarcaah, the leader of the Pochteca in 34 A.D., had discovered the secrets of the cave and had used it to transport himself to other centuries and continents. Still, the puzzle didn't quite fit together. Shika was no Pochteca trader. I wasn't ready to draw any firm conclusion about these visitors seeking the silver sword of Coriantumr. Except one. They were definitely not of this time or place.

They were from ancient America.

NOTES TO CHAPTER 6:

The subject of seerstones remains a mystery for many Church members. In this novel they are used primarily as a device for moving the story forward, and are not meant to represent official doctrine on their practical use. (See Notes to Chapter 12 in *Warriors of Cumorah*.)

Regarding the fact that men lived significantly longer prior to the flood, and for some centuries thereafter, the Judeo-Roman historian Josephus wrote the following:

> . . . *Let no one, upon comparing the lives of the ancients with our lives, and with the few years which we now live, think that what we have said of them is false; or make the shortness of our lives at present an argument that neither did they attain to so long a duration of life; for those ancients were beloved of God and [lately] made by God himself; and because their food was then fitter for the prolongation of life, might well live so great a number of years: and besides, God afforded them a longer time of life on account of their virtue and the good use they made of it in astronomical and geometrical discoveries, which would not have afforded the time of foretelling [the periods of the stars] unless they had lived six hundred years; for the Great Year is completed in that interval. Now I have for witnesses to what I have said, all those that have written Antiquities, both among the Greeks and barbarians; for even Manetho, who wrote the Egyptian History, and Berosus, who collected the Chaldean Monuments, and Mochu, and Hestieus, and besides these, Hieronymus the Egyptian, and those who composed the Phoenician History, agree to what I here say: Hesiod also, and Hecataeus, Hellanicus, and Acusilaus; and besides these, Ephorus and Nicolaus relate that the ancients lived a thousand years; but as to these matters let every one look upon them as he thinks fit* (*Antiquities*, 1:3:9).

From this we can conclude that even in the first century A.D., when Josephus lived, he felt somewhat leery and defensive regarding his readers' willingness to accept the idea that the patriarchs lived such long lives (Methuselah holding the record at 969 years). He draws some interesting conclusions as to why this longevity occurred, the most defensible perhaps being that the ancients were "beloved of God."

In this day many scientists have presented their own theories of why human beings age and die. Many of these theories revolve around "somatic mutation," which is basically the belief that random changes in the structure of our body cells cause our bodies to break down, thereby limiting the number of years that we can live, no matter how healthy our lifestyle. Radiation is generally believed to cause these mutations. Some Christian scientists have suggested that before the Flood there may have been a canopy of water surrounding the earth that blocked ultra-violet radiation, thereby preventing human body cells from breaking down. These theorists use Genesis 1:7 and 2:6 ("mist in the firmament") to support the idea of a water canopy and suggest that it was the dissolution of that water veil that caused the Great Flood (see D.W. Patton *The Biblical Flood and the Ice Epoch*, Meridian Publishing, 1966).

However, LDS scientist Eric N. Skousen refutes the idea of a water canopy, calling it inconsistent with modern revelation. He reminds us that the Genesis account is incomplete and may refer strictly to the spiritual (nonphysical) creation phase of the earth. He writes that a water canopy would not have allowed for a clear view of the sun, moon, and stars, which were given to man specifically as a reckoning for seasons, days, and years (Abr. 4:14–17; Moses 2:14–18). He also points out that modern revelation mentions rain in the antediluvian world (Moses 7:28), as well as excessive heat (Moses 7:8), both of which would not have occurred with a water canopy. Finally, he presents other scientific explanations for the Great Flood that would not have required this canopy (Eric N. Skousen Ph.D., *Earth: In the Beginning*, Verity Publishing, 1997, 320–24).

What all of this means is that a scientific explanation for the increased lifespan of man in the early history of the earth may still be forthcoming.

The statistics for the possible size and breadth of the Tower of Babel are taken from various apocryphal sources, including the Book of Jasher, Jubilees, and 3 Baruch. In addition, Jasher wrote that it had a circumference that required a three-day walk, which could mean that it was twenty or thirty miles in diameter—an incredible structure indeed! The idea that such a tower may have actually existed strains the imagination and leads a rational person to wonder if the ancient writers were exaggerating for dramatic effect. These old books are not scripture, and we have been told that they contain many interpolations of men (see D&C 91). Therefore, we must be cautious.

Nevertheless, the fact that the building was described as being massive in size is quite consistent.

Other details about this period of time, including Nimrod's efforts to kill young Abraham, the slaying of the infants, the family reunion of all Noah's posterity, and the conspiracy of Nimrod to take control of the world, are also found in the various apocryphal accounts, as well as in the histories recorded by Philo and Josephus.

The circumstances of Ham stealing the garment of Noah and passing it along to his posterity as a symbol of priesthood authority is alluded to in Genesis 9: 21–24 and Abraham 1:27. For more details regarding this garment, including the notion that it was the same garment that the Lord gave Adam in the Garden, and that Ham gave it to Cush, who in turn gave it to Nimrod, one must again turn to ancient writings and traditions. The significance of the garment as a symbol of authority and power is a recurrent theme in numerous apocryphal manuscripts. *The Book of Jasher,* The Hebrew Midrash, *The Apocalypse of Abraham,* and many other texts all report that this garment was the source of Nimrod's strength and power. If he possessed it this would have justified his claim to ultimate authority over the people and may explain why he was able to gather enough support to conquer the world.

CHAPTER SEVEN

Mary

"We have to go faster!" Joshua urged.

I ran wildly through the woods with young Abram in my arms. I, Mary Symeon, vowed within my heart that nothing would happen to this child—this Father of Nations, this hope for the world. Becky and Joshua had both passed me, though they remained mindful of my awkward pace as I ran with wet garments, the infant in my arms, and the sword of Akish strapped to my back.

We knew these woods were still filled with the purple-cloaked trackers—the myrmidons of King Nimrod. The two men who had toppled over the waterfall had most assuredly recovered by now and resumed their pursuit. The forest was thick, and for that we were grateful, but our reckless flight was unquestionably leaving a trail that the most inexperienced of trackers could have followed. Our prospects still looked grave. It seemed only a matter of time before we were cornered and attacked.

On top of all this, my lungs were straining for breath. Little Abraham continued to cling to my neck, still distressed from all the excitement. And yet he wasn't crying. I feared it was because his small heart was excessively traumatized.

"We must find a place to rest and hide," I announced.

The way that Becky heaved for oxygen, I was sure that she would agree. Joshua, however, looked determined to go on.

"We can't rest," he said. "Mary, at least let me take the sword."

I shook my head firmly and gave him a sharp glare that I hoped would communicate that he was never to ask me this again. The intensity *of emotion that I felt toward Joshua surprised even me. I tried to press it down.*

Yes, I had succumbed to the sword. But only for the briefest instant. Only to get out of a predicament that the sword had gotten us into. At least that was the justification that I told myself. But was it justified? I didn't know! I felt frustrated and confused.

"Over here," said Becky.

She'd found a fallen tree that afforded a small pocket of protection behind which we might find sanctuary. Becky slipped into it first, followed by me and Abram, and finally Joshua. Josh poked his head up to see if there was evidence of anyone pursuing. As of yet, there was none.

As we panted and wheezed for breath, Becky looked at the baby. "How is Shem?"

"I don't know," I said.

Just then he raised his head and looked around. His tiny mouth drooped into a frown and I thought he was about to cry. But instead it looked more like an expression of reprimand. He was telling us emphatically that he did not approve of all this rousting about. But just as quickly, his tiny expression changed again—this time into one of relief. He curled more tightly into my chest, closing his eyes. Abram was hoping that at last the excitement might have abated long enough to fall asleep.

"We should no longer call him Shem," I whispered to the others. "We must call him Abram, for that is his name."

"Abram?" said Joshua. "How do you know?"

"It's because of things the tracker said, isn't it?" asked Becky.

"Yes," I confirmed, and again I looked at the child in wonder. "He is the son of Terah. The woman we met, his nursemaid, was named Amthelo."

"Abram," Josh repeated thoughtfully. "You mean Abraham?*"*

I nodded, unable to suppress a smile. "It all fits together. The fact that Nimrod seeks the child's life. The fact that Terah is his father and that Terah is also Nimrod's chancellor. This baby is the great prophet and patriarch of the Jewish nation. Or rather, this is the person who this child will become."

Josh was still trying to keep his prophets straight. "You mean the same guy who later tries to sacrifice Isaac? The guy who tries to convince the Lord not to destroy Sodom and Gomorrah?"

"The very same," I said quietly, and I tenderly kissed the sleeping infant's forehead.

"Then why did the woman from the caravan—Amthelo—call him Shem?" Becky whispered back.

"She didn't call him that," said Joshua. "She only said the word. But she didn't specifically say that it was the baby's name."

"When Amthelo said the word 'great,'" I continued softly, "I am certain now that she was referring to Abram."

"But he's just a baby," said Joshua. He continued to watch the woods. "How would she have known that?"

"My father taught us that the old manuscripts said much about Abram's early life," I explained. "How Nimrod's soothsayers saw signs in the heavens that told how Abram would one day overthrow King Nimrod. The nursemaid sacrificed her life for him. I can only assume that she had some premonition of the child's destiny."

"Abram is going to defeat Nimrod?" asked Joshua, bemused.

I shook my head. "The soothsayers did not understand. Abraham's kingdom will be greater than Nimrod's, but not because of his armies. Because of his covenant with God. His children will number as the sands of the sea. One day they will inherit the whole earth. You and Becky are part of that covenant, and so am I."

"So what about Shem?" Becky asked.

"Shem is the person she wanted us to take him to," said Josh.

"I believe Joshua is right," I said. "Shem is the son of Noah. He is one of the three branches from whom sprouted all of the children of men."

"You've gotta be kidding," said Josh. "You think this Shem guy is still alive?"

"Yes, I believe he is," I responded.

"Maybe she meant another *Shem*," Becky suggested.

I shook my head. "No. It fits perfectly. I think Amthelo would have wanted to take this child to a place where his safety was assured. Where better than the righteous realm of the son of Noah?"

"Where is this 'realm?'" asked Becky. "How do we find him?"

But at that instant we heard the whinny of a horse. It was some distance through the trees, but it was not from the direction that I would have expected. It had come from the woods ahead of us, not the woods behind. Had the riders managed to bring their horses over the ridge? Had they managed to circle around in front of us?

We pressed low to the ground and peered through the branches of the fallen tree. Weeds and brambles had grown through and around them. This offered us a marvelous camouflage, but still provided a clear view of the open space beyond. We continued to hear the hooves approaching, slowly and cautiously. Again, we held our breaths. Gratefully, the baby remained fast asleep.

A moment later the legs of a great brown stallion stepped into the clearing. The rider was a large man, clad in leather and furs. Plainly, he was not a soldier of Nimrod. He appeared to be a man of the wilderness. He gripped a long, weather-beaten javelin. Also strapped to the horse was a fur-lined sheath with a heavy steel sword. A wilderness of beard covered his face, and his skin was cut with deep wrinkles. But the eyes were keen, and carefully scanning the area. I feared that he may have heard us. He was most thoroughly scanning the brushy area where we were hiding.

Then suddenly his eyes jumped straight ahead. He'd heard something else. I could hear it too. It was the approach of several purple-cloaked trackers, moving swiftly through the trees. The king's soldiers were almost upon us. The bearded man waited and listened for several more seconds. It was at this pivotal juncture that the baby decided to yawn.

He drew in a deep, sleepy breath and let it out with a melodious sigh. The horseman's eyes jumped again, this time to the precise spot where we were secluded. His hand leaped to the hilt of his sword. I decided to take a terrible risk. I folded the baby into my arms and stood up straight.

As he saw me, his shoulders relaxed, but his eyes were no less curious. The two children also stood.

I made sure I had the tracker's attention, then I nodded toward the woods and said, "Soldiers are coming. Will you help us?"

He didn't move. He just watched me. My eyes were filled with pleading. And yet I felt foolish. I'm not sure what I expected him to do. His horse might have supported two additional riders, but not four. From the sounds in the woods, I could tell that at least three, perhaps four, of the king's soldiers were drawing near.

All at once the man grabbed at the reins, turned his mount, and spurred his horse in the ribs. The beast galloped back into the forest. He rode away without having spoken a single word.

The children looked at me, but made no comment. They were clearly of the opinion that it had been an addleheaded idea to ask for the stranger's assistance in the first place. Perhaps they were right. The king's trackers would be upon us at any instant. Josh motioned vehemently for us to follow him. So after our brief reprieve, we were again on the move, but now it seemed that the woods all about us were alive with bodies and voices.

"There!" I heard someone shout.

We'd been sighted! We altered our direction, running away from the voice, but it was plain that the men were coming toward us from several angles. We reached an incline and began scrambling down the slope. I covered the baby's head with my arms as we fought our way through a nest of briars. To our right I saw a flash of purple and gold—a tracker was running parallel with us, drawing nearer.

Suddenly I heard a whir overhead. An arrow! *The arrow disappeared somewhere in the bushes, but it had plainly been meant for us. What was the use of fleeing? Why go any farther? But Josh would not give up. We broke clear of the brambles and reentered a forest of high-canopied trees. Now I could see our pursuers distinctly. There were seven of them—no, there were* nine! *They were tightening the noose!*

Becky tripped. She lost her footing and fell flat on her chest. I reached down to raise her up, still clutching the groggy infant in my other arm. When I raised my gaze, I saw the face of the swordsman who'd fallen into the pool, his chin bleeding, still looking damp and more furious than ever. Two other men were surrounding Josh. This time my attacker was not wasting time. He stalked forward, raising back his blade to cut me down. Becky screamed.

Again, something inside me snapped. I don't know whether it was my desire to save the children, or an uncontrollable impulse to save the Father of Nations, or a combination of everything crushing down on me at once. My mind went blind with indignation. I don't even remember giving the child to Rebecca. But I remember drawing the sword from the cloth. As the soldier's blade was careening toward my head, I swung back. I felt a terrible strength in my limbs. And then the sword of Akish struck.

The soldier let out a wail. My blade had impacted his sword near the hilt. Not only that, it had severed several fingers. As his blade went flying end over end, Joshua ducked to avoid being hit. The soldier collapsed to his knees, pressing his bleeding hand, now shy of three digits, underneath his other arm. The other eight warriors of the king had stopped. They were gawking at me, thunderstruck. All at once I heard a bowstring snap. I turned, raised up the sword and twisted it to the right. Or was it that the sword raised itself and twisted me? But as I twisted it, I heard a sharp ping and twang. The sword had stopped the arrow in midflight. It had clipped it and misdirected its path before it could pierce my flesh.

Now my fury was unrelenting. I gritted my teeth, drew back the blade and rushed at the two men surrounding Josh. With both of my hands gripping the hilt, I made another wild swing, and again I heard the loud peal of steel striking steel. This time the soldier's weapon shattered in two. The man ducked, and the blade of my silver sword barely missed swiping off his head. My mind felt like it was caught in a whirlwind. I was consumed with violence. The second man tried to take advantage of my distraction and brought his sword forward, but I raised up my own weapon and met him in midstrike. Our blades pressed against one another in a duel of strength and will. He tried to push me back, but I didn't budge. I'd never felt such power in my tiny body. As I stared into his eyes, I watched his face slowly change from anger to terror. At last, with a mighty heave, I thrust him back. He fell against several more soldiers rushing to his aid. The lot of them stumbled back and fell onto their tails. But I wasn't finished. I marched forward to finish them all while they were most vulnerable.

At that instant, I saw several brown and white steeds burst forth from the trees, throwing their necks as their riders drew back the reins. Among them was the bearded man of the mountains, his hands now filled with his javelin and sword. The other men were younger, hair long, faces fair and strong. At least two of them were armed with bows, each of which looked as long as the men were tall. The arrowheads were aimed at the soldiers, but like the men in purple cloaks, they were gaping at me with intense surprise.

I stopped where I stood. My thoughts started to whirl as the reality of what I had done—and of what I was about to do—hit me with the force of a battering ram. I saw one of the archers on horseback fire his bowstring. The arrow flew just over my head. It struck a soldier who had been creeping up on me from behind. I turned and saw the arrow protruding from the man's shoulder. He dropped his sword and collapsed like the others.

All at once I felt sickened to my inmost depths. My limb—the one that still held the silver blade—was trembling. I let the weapon fall, clattering on top of the sword belonging to the soldier whose fingers I had severed. I, too, dropped to my knees. I started to retch.

The horsemen drew closer. As the first archer reloaded, the other pulled back his bowstring, prepared to fire again upon the king's men if necessary. There were four horsemen in all to contend with the nine men of Nimrod, although two of them had been wounded.

One of the horsemen spoke—a middle-aged man with eyes like a lion. He, too, had a beard, but it was not as unkempt as the older man, and it was trimmed so that it left the top of his cheekbones bare. "What compels nine soldiers of Shinar to attack a young maiden, two small children, and a babe?"

Another of the trackers, the man with a face like Titus of Rome whom I had seen on the ridge, replied, "I am Githim, commander of the king's guard. We are on the special errand of Nimrod, son of Cush. You have attacked the king's cavalry and interfered with his sacred command."

"This is the forest of Joktan," said the horseman. "Nimrod of Shinar has no authority here."

Githim looked like he was sizzling within. I had the impression that he wouldn't have felt that there was any land or territory outside of his king's authority. "This woman has kidnapped the son of Nimrod's chancellor. We are under orders to return this child to Shinar."

"He's lying!" screeched Rebecca. "They're trying to kill him! They already killed the baby's nursemaid. They've been trying to kill us!"

"Is this true?" the horseman asked the soldier.

The soldier was red with fury. "This is the king's business! Nimrod will send his armies to destroy the inhabitants of these woods if you prevent us from fulfilling our command."

The horseman leaned forward, his eyes cutting Githim right to the soul. "We are loyal only to Melchizedek of Salem. Not to Nimrod the butcher."

Githim fumed another few seconds. His men looked taut, waiting for a signal that would tell them to spring to action. Finally, the commander of the guard asked, "Whose name will I give when I tell Nimrod that a forest dweller has interfered with his most sacred command?"

The older horseman with the grizzled beard decided to answer. He spurred his horse to ride up directly beside Githim, then replied, "You may say—if you live long enough to say it—that Ophir, the son of Joktan, of the lineage of Shem, has interfered."

Githim stewed over this, then replied carefully, "Are you threatening to kill me? You are four men. We are nine."

"Then you shall be the first to die," said one of the archers on horseback, aiming his arrow directly at Githim's heart. This one appeared to be the youngest horseman of all. By my estimates, he was only twenty. He had eyes like shining amber and his long hair was as blonde as flowing wheat.

"What you do not know," said Nimrod's soldier, "is that ten more soldiers are in the woods behind us."

"What you do not know," said the horseman who had first spoken, "is that another of my sons, five of my cousins and friends, and fourteen of their sons are right behind us, arriving presently."

As I looked through the trees, I could see the additional men. They were taking up strategic positions around the soldiers of the king, bows armed and javelins ready. Githim had seen them too. He sank at the shoulders.

"There will be another day, Ophir, son of Joktan," he seethed.

One of the other soldiers helped the man who'd been shot in the shoulder to stand on his feet. The purple-robed guardsmen began to retreat into the forest. Githim gave Ophir the benefit of his vengeful stare as long as possible before he turned and followed after them. The soldier who had lost his fingers gave me a last frightened look and stumbled off behind the rest. Again I felt repulsed and sickened by my actions.

The cousins, friends, and sons began to come forward. Joshua and Becky crowded closer to me, still uncertain if we were any better off with these men than we had been with the trackers. Little Abram in Becky's arms amazingly had remained fast asleep through the entire confrontation.

The middle-aged man with the trimmed beard was the first to dismount and approach us. He smiled warmly, sympathetically, and said, "I am Jared, the son of Moriancumr. My grandfather, Ophir, has already introduced himself." He pointed to another of the horsemen. "This is my oldest son, Jacom." He then pointed to the blonde man with amber eyes. "And this is Pagag, the oldest son of my brother, Mahonri."

Pagag climbed off his horse, his blonde hair settling around his shoulders. He said to his uncle, "We should not have let them go. They will cause us trouble."

"*It is always better—when possible—to leave the slaying of men to God,*" said Jared.

"*But they will surely return,*" said Jared's son, Jacom.

"*Perhaps,*" his father replied. "*But probably not until they have mustered reinforcements. By then their lust for the little one's blood may have subsided.*"

Pagag stepped up to me, his eyes studying me carefully. He reached down and hefted the sword of Akish. He tested the weight of it, his gaze drawn to its surface. I reached out, seized the hilt, and yanked it from his grip. He looked over at me, amazed at my boldness. But at last he smiled disarmingly.

"*You defended yourself admirably,*" he said. "*Where would a woman like you learn how to wield a sword like this?*"

I didn't answer him. Instead I reached back to open the wrappings behind my shoulder, and then I slid the sword smoothly inside.

"*What is your name, maiden?*" asked Jared.

"*Mary,*" I said.

"*I'm Rebbeca,*" said Becky. "*And this is my brother, Joshua.*"

Josh's eyes were swimming with wonder. "*You said your name was* Jared?"

"*Yes,*" he confirmed.

"*And your brother is* Mahonri?"

Jared drew together his dark eyebrows. "*Do you know us?*"

"*Do we* know *you?*" *Josh looked ready to combust. He looked at me, then at Becky.* "*Don't you get it?* Jared *and the* brother of Jared?"

"*We get it,*" said Becky. "*We get it. Now don't embarrass yourself.*"

"*What is your lineage?*" Jared asked me.

"*I'm . . . a Shemite,*" I replied.

"*Are these your siblings?*"

"*They might as well be. I'm their guardian.*"

"*Do you often rescue infants from the soldiers of the king and travel in the wilderness with children?*" asked Pagag.

"*No,*" I said humbly. "*But this . . . is a special child. We are to take him to Shem.*"

"*Whose infant is this?*" asked Jared's grandfather, Ophir.

"*He is the son of Terah,*" I replied.

Jared's eyes widened. He and the rest looked at one another with astonishment, and then smiled with satisfaction. My own thoughts were brimming with wonder.

"She has confirmed the words of the King of Salem to the last detail," Ophir declared. "The descendant of my grandfather, Peleg, and my great grandfather, Eber, has returned. Melchizedek's prophecy is fulfilled."

NOTES TO CHAPTER 7:

There have been occasional efforts to try and tie the ancestors of the Jaredites to specific individuals or genealogical lines mentioned in the Old Testament. One suggestion, as noted in Reynolds and Sjodahl's *Commentary on the Book of Mormon* (Deseret Book, 1961) is to tie Jared to a son of the Hebrew patriarch, Joktan, the son of Eber (or Heber). Eber is, of course, the source name for the Hebrews. Eber had two sons—Peleg and Joktan. The Bible offers considerable information about the descendants of Peleg, including Abraham, Isaac, Jacob, etc. But on the line of Joktan—one-half of the Hebrew lineage—it names twelve sons, and stops. The line comes abruptly to an end. By tradition this group is purported to have settled in southern Arabia, the same location where it has been suggested that the Jaredites embarked on the first leg of their journey to the New World (see Ether 2:6–7).

Among these twelve sons of Joktan is Jerah. "Jared" is proposed by Reynolds and Sjodahl as an alternate pronunciation of Jerah. If this is true, then one of Jerah's brothers would have to be Mahonri Moriancumr. None of the twelve sons of Joktan has a name that even remotely resembles Mahonri or Moriancumr. However some interesting things have been proposed about a son of Joktan named Ophir.

The land of Ophir is mentioned several times in the days of King Solomon as a place where ships were sent to obtain large amounts of gold, gems, and a precious wood called "almug." These items were then used in constructing the pillars and other sections of Solomon's holy temple. Almug wood was also used in making fine musical instruments. There was said to have been no wood like it seen in Israel prior to that time (1 Kgs. 10:11–12).

Scholars are unsure of the location of Ophir. There is a vague reference from a sixteenth-century Spanish invader named Bochart, which proclaims that the land of Ophir is in the New World, specifically Peru. This may have been a pet theory of Bochart that accounted for Peru's vast gold treasuries, or it may mean that the first generation of conquistadors had information connecting Ophir and the New World that has since been lost. A twelfth-century Peruvian glyph has also been translated by explorer Gene Savoy as "Ophir" (Gene Savoy, *The Explorer's Club of New York*, vol. 76, no. 4, winter 1998/99).

Other wild speculations have been that the name Yucatan is related to Joktan and that since the Vikings came to America to get wood, why not the ancient Israelites?

A more reasonable suggestion may be that Ophir was located in India and that almug wood is sandalwood, which is still used to make fine instruments to this day (Bible Dictionary: *Almug*).

Some have speculated that Mahonri Moriancumr is a title, and that Ophir was the actual name of the Brother of Jared. This inference seems a bit of a stretch. But even if the land of Ophir is part of India, this still doesn't discount the possibility that the name is related to the Jaredites. India could easily have been the land from which the Jaredites embarked for the *second* leg of their journey to the New World. (Many forget that the Book of Mormon speaks of two separate water crossings for the Jaredites. See Ether 2:16, 6:4–12.)

In this novel the author has retained the idea that Joktan is an ancestor of Jared because of the strong connection between Joktan's descendants and the region of southern Arabia. He has ignored the correlation between Jerah and Jared only because Jerah *seems* to be associated with a period somewhat earlier than the Tower of Babel. He has also suggested that Ophir is indeed a name associated with the Jaredites by proposing that Ophir was Jared's grandfather, but such speculations carry no more weight than other speculations. More research may be done in the future to strengthen this link between Jared and the patriarchs of the Bible.

CHAPTER EIGHT

Harry

"Harry, he took our family picture!" Steffanie raged after the two of us were securely locked back into our places inside the paddy wagon. My sister was, of course, referring to the portrait in the hands of Shika the Syrian.

"How did he get it?" she continued. "What has he done to Dad and Sabrina?"

We were both reeling with panic. We tried to keep our voices down, but Boath and Partholan listened from across the cage, doubtless not understanding a single word.

I shook my head. "If we just knew who he was, we might have a better understanding."

"He thinks Mary, Joshua, and Rebecca have stolen his sword. What sword is he talking about? Does he mean the sword of Coriantumr?"

"I don't know of any *other* swords that would cause a man to chase three people across the spectrum of time."

"But Dad destroyed it. How could it be in the hands of Mary and the children?"

"I can only think of one way," I said. "That's if they managed to travel back to a century before the sword was destroyed."

Steffanie shut her eyes and pinched the bridge of her nose, as if trying to stave off a migraine. "It's all so crazy."

"What did you think of that helmet?" I asked her. "Or the gold mask that he used to pay Mardon?"

"You don't want to know what I think," said Steffanie. "It's probably ridiculous."

"I *do* want to know," I said, "because I was probably thinking the same thing. Do you remember the helmets worn by the Pochteca traders who tried to kidnap us all those years ago?"

"That's *it!*" she declared. "I *knew* they reminded me of things I'd seen among the Nephites and Lamanites. I just couldn't place it. Do you think Shika might be a Nephite?"

I shook my head. "I'm not sure. But if not a Nephite, he's gotta be part of another civilization from ancient America."

"Jaredite?" asked Steffanie.

She'd just tossed the name out. I was thinking more like Aztec or Mayan, but Steffanie's suggestion sent my mind in a whole new direction. "Who made the sword of Coriantumr in the first place?"

Steffanie shut her eyes tightly. "It was a Jaredite. I can see the name, I just can't quite—"

"Akish!" I blurted out.

"Right!" said Steffanie. "He was the guy who dredged up all the secret combinations that had been handed down since the days of Cain—probably the same oaths and rites at work here in Shinar."

"*Shika*," I whispered to myself. "*Akish*."

Steffanie worked it around in her own mind. "That's weird. It's the same exact name, only pronounced backwards. Goodness, Harry. Do you think he did something that simple and stupid?"

"It makes sense," I said. "If Todd Finlay had wanted to find the sword of Akish, it seems to me that he would try to locate the maker himself."

"Then you think it's possible?" said Steffanie with alarm. "You think Shika is really the Jaredite sorcerer, Akish?"

Boath could no longer contain himself. "Swords. Sorcerers. Secret combinations. What is all this talk? Who are you? If not angels, what then?"

Steff and I glanced at each other.

"Time travelers," I finally said.

Steff looked at the ceiling and shook her head. "Oh, brother. Here we go again."

"What is that?" asked Boath. His tone wasn't scoffing. He seriously wanted to know.

"We've come here from a different century," I said. "A century thousands of years in the future."

"Then you *are* angels," said Partholan wondrously.

"No," I insisted. "We're no different than you. We just know of certain ways to travel in time."

"Time is not a place," said Boath. "It is not a desert or a mountain range. How can one *travel* in *time?*"

"With difficulty," said Steffanie.

"I know it's hard to believe," I said. "I probably shouldn't have said it."

But Boath was going with it. "And you say this man whom you met in the tent of Mardon is *also* a 'time traveler'?"

"It seems that way," I said.

"Can your magic summon other time travelers?" Boath asked. "Men who can help us to defeat King Nimrod? Men who know magic that can free us from our chains?"

I shook my head. "I'm afraid not. I don't know that kind of magic. I really don't know *any* magic. The only thing that can help us now is faith in God. Faith is stronger than magic anyway."

"They are different?" asked Boath, as if he'd never separated the two concepts in his mind.

I nodded. "Faith recognizes that all power comes from God. I think magic would rather convince you that the power is all yours."

Boath scoffed. "The source doesn't matter, so long as the power works to my benefit. I would gladly ascribe all power to God, if only He would bring down Nimrod."

"Wait and see," I said. "I think you'll be happy with the way the future unfolds. Just remember, faith in God is not magic. And it's the only real source of power and blessings."

"In my youth I prayed to the One God for power and blessings," said Boath. "Sometimes He gave it, sometimes He did not. I feel the One God betrayed my faith."

"Faith," I said, "is the belief that God knows what our needs are better than we do."

"You think that explains why my lands were burned and my wife and sons enslaved?" Boath challenged.

I leaned forward. "Faith is also the belief that with God, everything will turn out all right in the end. There will be justice."

Boath leaned forward too. "Sometimes faith just takes too long."

"In this case," I said, smiling, "it may not take as long as you think."

Suddenly Partholan pointed through the bars of the cage. "Look! Faith is at work already."

I raised my eyebrows. That was a little quicker than I'd expected. I sat up to try and see what Partholan was pointing at. Boath's grandson seemed to be indicating the fifteen or so soldiers who'd been placed to guard our cage. It occurred to me that I hadn't heard them muttering to each other for several minutes. I looked out into the darkness.

At first I thought the guards had slipped off somewhere. Their campfire had burned down considerably. But then I saw them lying on the ground. Some were draped over the wooden crates they'd been using as furniture. One was sitting straight up, but his chin was on his chest. Were they asleep? No, they were *not* asleep. I saw one with his head leaning back, mouth open. His eyes were wide open. *Dead?* Was it possible that all fifteen of our guards had been killed?

I saw a drinking cup upside down on the ground, and another one sitting sideways beside the hand of one of the corpses.

"They've been *poisoned!*" I declared.

"It's the work of my men!" Boath said excitedly. "They're *here!* Just as I was assured!"

But if that was true, where were they? If our rescuers didn't act quickly, the other Shinarian soldiers who I could still hear around the other tents would discover the bodies and be up in arms.

At that instant I saw the shadows coming from the east, approaching swiftly. In the dimness of the firelight I perceived the shape of their silhouettes—in particular their helmets. These were not the warriors of Japheth. They were Shika's assassins!

I drew a breath, prepared to shout. What was worse? To be in the hands of Mardon or the Jaredite sorcerer, Akish? I could hardly believe I was asking myself that. Under the circumstances the answer was obviously that we'd rather be in the hands of Mardon. But I hesitated too long. From the opposite side of the wagon, a pair of hands reached through the bars and seized Steffanie around the neck. The tip of a knife was pressed against her throat. It was the ghoul himself—Akish. His pale flesh reflected the moonlight. He seemed to sense what I was about to do.

"Be silent!" he hissed. "If you cry out, I'll sever her head clean off her shoulders."

Steffanie's eyes were wide with fear. The other three men of Shika—that is, of Akish—had reached the wagon.

"These are not my men," said Boath, apparently the last to realize it.

Shika called out to one of the others. "Open the cage." The ghoul tossed one of the helmeted men a set of metal keys. I assumed these keys had already been scavenged off one of the dead guards.

The man in the helmet proceeded to open the rear of the wagon.

Shika said to us, "You two are coming with me. You will help me to locate the thieves who have taken my sword."

Neither of us said a word as Shika's warrior began to unlock the chains around my wrists and ankles. Boath and Partholan were also silent, but looked on in anxious fascination.

"Hurry!" said Shika urgently as his man moved from me to Steffanie. Another helmeted warrior at the rear of the wagon motioned for me to climb out, his blade ready in case I tried anything.

"Who are you really?" Steffanie finally demanded of the man holding her neck.

Shika curled up a corner of his mouth. "You don't believe that I'm Shika the Syrian, eh?"

"We think you're from another time," said Steff. "A Jaredite named Akish."

Shika looked surprised. "I'm impressed. You divined all this on your own?"

"You've gotta admit," said Steffanie, "saying your name backwards is pretty lame."

I feared my sister's cheekiness would get her throat cut right there. But at that instant I began to hear a ruckus to the west. The clash of swords—the shouting of voices.

"Hurry, Nimrah, you fool!" Akish repeated to the man still unlocking Steffanie's ankles.

I finished climbing down from the cage, my eyes warily searching for any opportunity to fight or escape. The man outside had another set of shackles ready to put around my wrists. The last of Akish's cronies stood beside him. He aimed a sword at my stomach to ensure my cooperation. Upon hearing the ruckus, Boath looked more alert and hopeful than ever, peering off toward the source of the disturbance. It appeared that his expectations of an attack from the second division of the Japethite army had not been in vain. Akish had simply reached us first.

Nimrah unlocked the last chain on Steffanie's ankle. Akish pulled the knife away from her neck, directing her to get out of the wagon. At that instant an arrow whizzed out of the gloom. It struck the man who held the sword to my stomach. He arched his back in agony. I took immediate advantage of the diversion. The other helmeted warrior had placed the first half of the manacle around my wrist, but he hadn't yet secured it. I yanked it from him; then I swung the iron at his face, whacking the side of the head. Steffanie leaped out of the rear of the cage.

Akish came around the side of the wagon and tried to grab Steffanie again around the neck, no doubt to use her a second time as incentive for me to submit. But he'd chosen the wrong girl. Steffanie ducked. Then she brought up her leg and planted the ankle directly into the sorcerer's navel. Akish made a windy grunt and fell back.

"Run!" I cried to Steff.

Nimrah tried to leap from the back of the cage and tackle her, but he missed, falling on his face. Steffanie followed me as I bolted northward. A host of warriors were rushing toward the wagon from the south. I didn't know if they were Japethites or the soldiers of Shinar—and frankly I didn't care. Here in the dark they were all equally dangerous. Another arrow flew over my head.

"Where are we going?" Steff asked me.

"I don't know! Just run!"

My vague objective was to reach the buildings of the city—blend into the populace. Then I realized Prince Mardon had sounded an alarm. Men with swords and other weapons were coming to life all around us.

We veered east, toward the place where the captives from the previous day's battle had been quartered. But this area looked the most riotous of all. Many of the slaves were rising up in revolt. The guards were cutting them down left and right.

"This way!" I yelled.

We ran southeast, toward the full moon. Suddenly a massive silhouette appeared in front of us. *Jupiter!* It was an *elephant!* One of Mardon's war tanks had broken loose, stirred up by all the commotion. We threw on the brakes and watched it plow right through a large tent and wagon, stripping off the canvas and overturning the wagon's contents. Several men—probably guards to the tent—scattered. I was about to continue running when Steffanie grabbed my arm.

"Wait!" She rushed over to the spilled contents of the wagon. It looked like booty collected during the campaign—Japhethite swords and shields, gold and silver vessels, etc. But what had caught Steffanie's eye was something that belonged to *us*. It was one of the backpacks! *Steffanie's* pack, to be exact. I was amazed. It was still full of stuff! It was pretty rare that we ever got one of these things *back*. She snagged one of the straps and threw it over her shoulder. I didn't see my own pack, and there was no time to look. The guards hadn't scattered as far as I'd hoped. Two soldiers were rushing toward us with their swords drawn.

"Halt!" one of them cried.

Instead, we ran directly into the area where the rest of the war elephants had been assembled. The majority of these animals had awakened and were making great screeches and howls of protest. Several more soldiers were among them, trying to calm things down, but for the most part the soldiers were keeping their distance to avoid getting flattened. It was into this chaos of swinging tusks and crushing legs that Steffanie and I ran.

A large bull elephant yanked up the stake chained to its back leg and started charging right at us. We dove out of the way. The animal continued forward, plowing through another tent. I helped Steffanie to stand. We started running again, but then veered right to avoid an elephant that was angrily spinning in circles. Another elephant was just ahead, still down on its belly. There was a basket for a single driver on the elephant's back. Suddenly I had a "brilliant" idea. I put that in quotes for a reason. I was overcome by a flash of nostalgia that went back to the land of Desolation and a wooly mammoth named Rachel. The beast had proven to be a magnificent asset in our escape from Jacobugath. I naively believed that if I could drive and steer a mammoth that was twice as large, I could certainly manage an elephant.

"Come on!" I called to Steffanie.

I yanked its stake out of the ground.

"What are you doing?"

"We're gonna try to ride it!" I was already scrambling up the rope ladder. The elephant let out a wail and started to rise.

"But Harry—!"

"Don't think! *Climb!*"

I threw myself into the basket just as the elephant straightened its front legs. Steffanie had tossed up her backpack, but her body was still clinging to the top rung of the ladder. She cried my name again—this time for help. I reached around her neck and under one arm, doing all I could to pin her in place. The elephant threw its trunk and started to spin. I looked around for some kind of reins, but there were none. As I recalled, the mahouts who'd used the elephants in the battle with the Japhethites had controlled them with long sticks, but there was nothing like that in the basket.

I began to realize just how uninspired my idea was as the elephant started charging back in the same direction that we'd just come from. Even if I'd *had* a stick, I still had no idea what the commands were. Not that it would have made any difference, because the animal was now in a panic.

"Hang on!" I shouted to Steffanie.

To the west some of the tents of Mardon's army had been set aflame. I could see hundreds of men fighting with swords and lances. The elephant turned again and the scenery abruptly changed. It was now charging headlong toward the tent of the prince. I tried to pull Steffanie into the basket, but my position was so awkward and the jerks and motions of the elephant were so violent that it was all I could do just to maintain my grip.

"I'm falling!" cried Steffanie.

"No, you're not!" I assured her.

The elephant stormed right into a nest of soldiers. The men parted like the Red Sea, but several of them were pointing at us and shouting, "It's the angels! The angels are on the elephant!"

Among those in the crowd I recognized several of Mardon's top lieutenants, including Lasha, Mash, Arvad, and several others whom I'd seen in Mardon's tent.

Mardon's voice pierced the night, though I wasn't quite sure where it had come from. "Stop them! Don't let them get away!"

Some of these men were no better than robots, and Mardon's command was like an "on" switch. Three soldiers moved in front of the elephant's path, though it did nothing to slow the creature down. They were forced to dive out of the way. Arvad and a second officer attempted the gutsiest move of all—literally rushing to the side of the elephant and leaping up to grab Steffanie's waist. The second officer missed. He slipped under the elephant's rear legs. One of its three-toed feet tromped right in the middle of the officer's chest, surely killing him instantly. Arvad was clinging to Steffanie's waist, as well as the rope ladder. With my free arm I tried to punch Arvad's face, but his hold on my sister was unyielding.

"Don't let go!" I yelled to Steff, but the truth was that I was losing my grip. She was falling!

Arvad raised up his legs and pushed against the elephant's side. Steffanie was wrenched from my arms. Arvad was still clutching her around the waist as they dropped. His push-off had kept them from falling beneath the elephant's legs, but I heard the crack of his back as he landed. Steffanie had landed on top of him.

For a moment my mind was swimming in disbelief. Steffanie was *gone!* The elephant continued its charge, now entering a residential district of the city of Calneh. I saw the soldiers of Mardon surrounding my sister. She'd be recaptured for sure. While I remained on this stampeding pachyderm there was nothing I could do to help her. *How could I have let her go? What was I going to do?* My mind was pulsing with desperation.

I had no idea where this crazy elephant thought it was headed. It seemed determined to get as far away from its handlers as possible. I had no way to stop it. I wondered if my gift of tongues might apply to animals and cried, "Halt!" Whether it understood or not, it refused to obey. The beast seemed to know exactly where it was going, and nothing would prevent it from reaching its destination.

The street began to slope downward. I saw the reflection of the moon on a watery surface. It was the Euphrates. The elephant appeared to be headed for the river. The only thing to do was hang on until it decided to stop. All I knew was that it was taking me farther away from the encampment of Mardon, farther away from my sister.

In exasperation I called out again, "*Halt* you stupid thing!"

The elephant threw its head. I suspected now that it *did* understand me. It just didn't care. It utterly refused to slow down until it reached the riverbank. Fearlessly, it entered the water.

This was my moment to escape. I grabbed up Steffanie's pack, stepped one foot out of the basket, and leaped over the side. I splashed into waist-deep water, doing my best to keep the backpack high and dry. I quickly scrambled away before the elephant tried to drown me. When I turned to look back, the creature was contentedly filling its trunk with water and draining the trunk into its mouth, completely ignoring me.

I stepped out onto the stony shore. In the distance I could hear the sounds of battle. My mind was still reeling with the loss of my sister. *What should I do?* I couldn't escape without her. I couldn't leave her here. If the choice was turning myself in, continuing on with her to the court of Nimrod, or becoming separated from her forever, I'd have given myself back over to Mardon's custody in a heartbeat. If only I'd been able to hang onto her!

That's it, I thought. *I've got to go back.*

And then a greater wisdom settled over me. I felt my pocket. *Yes!* The seerstone was still there. I decided to ask the Lord what to do. I'd ask through the stone. I found a place that looked moderately secluded by brush and boulders, dropped the pack, and knelt on the ground. I pulled the stone out of my pocket and cupped it in my hands. Then I peered into the luminous white surface.

What can I do? How can I rescue her? How can I keep searching for Mary and the children without her? What must I do!?

My questions were probably coming faster than the stone could effectively answer. My heart hammered against my ribcage. I tried to calm myself. I tried to listen.

In spite of all the chaos and confusion, a tiny bolt of inspiration broke through. But the message was very strange—and it wasn't at all what I wanted to hear. The message was to let Steffanie go—not to try and rescue her at this time. Immediately my heart started to rebel.

How could I abandon her? There was no way! Then a second part of the message appeared in the stone. The thought came to me that I should not try and rescue her *without help*.

Without help? Without *help!?* What did that *mean?* Where was I supposed to find help? It was 3000 B.C.! Who was I supposed to ask? I continued to peer into the stone. I concentrated hard—maybe harder than ever before. Surely if the stone was giving me this advice, it must have had some ideas about how to accomplish it. There had to be someone whom I was supposed to find and ask.

I waited. I watched the pearled surface. At last, an image began to coalesce from the mist inside the white expanse. But then my heart sank. It was the same image that I'd seen before—and it was no less disturbing.

The face of the Scythian emerged from the dark stairwell, his bowstring still taut, the arrow still aimed straight at my heart. I groaned in frustration.

"I don't understand!" I cried out loud. "What does this *mean?*"

The Scythian's arrow released. Instantly I saw another face—the face of my beloved friend. This image was the most disturbing of all. Gidgiddonihah's expression contorted in pain as the arrow struck him in the abdomen, spinning him around. It was the first of three arrows that would pierce him that night. But despite his fatal wounds, this giant of a warrior had still managed to expend his last breath in a final glorious effort to save my life and to save the lives of Mary and Jesse.

Why did the stone persist in showing me this? Was it to warn me of what would happen to me or Steffanie if I attempted a rescue? Was it to tell me that I should seek help from someone with the stamina of Gidgiddonihah? Why would the stone tell me *that?* I'd have given my eyeteeth to find someone like Gid. There *was* no one like Gid!

I pulled the stone away as I began to hear voices near the river. I peeked over the boulder that I was hiding behind and saw a cluster of twenty or thirty soldiers rushing down to the bank. Among them was the prince's right-hand man, Lasha. He was pointing at the elephant as it continued happily dousing itself with water twenty feet out from shore.

"That's it!" Lasha shouted. "He must be near. *Find him!*"

Even in the face of a midnight attack by the army of Japheth, Mardon was still determined to prevent my escape. This was my exit cue. I hoisted the pack onto my shoulders. Keeping low, I crept through the brush, following the river southward.

I found a path that led into a grove of tall grass running along the bank. I continued this course for several minutes before stopping to rest and listen. The grass and reeds around me were so tall that it was almost claustrophobic. If not for the light of the moon I would have been totally encompassed in blackness. I wasn't even certain if I was keeping to the trail. But the voices of Lasha and the others seemed to have fallen far behind. Still, I wasn't taking any chances, so I continued even deeper into the reeds.

All the while I kept holding the seerstone. I guess I was hoping that if I kept it tightly gripped in my palm that the Lord might help me make the correct choice about which direction to run. I was anxious to find another place where I could kneel down, pray, and ask for additional guidance.

The trail seemed to be sloping upward, but the reeds didn't become any less congested. Again, I felt thankful for the moonlight. Then I realized that other lights were also guiding me. The first time I saw these lights, I think I ignored them, believing they were just particularly bright stars. Then I did a double take. The sight struck me as so peculiar that I stopped in my tracks. Much of the vision remained obscured by the tall grasses and reeds, but I saw enough to conclude that these lights were definitely not stars. By degrees I became more and more astonished.

"What *is* that?" I whispered out loud.

There was something up there. Something in the night sky. I'm not quite sure how to describe it. The lights were arranged in a long string in the northern horizon. They were very different from the twinkling white specks of Orion or the Big Dipper. They were bright yellow and gold. And mingled among them were lights of turquoise blue and ruby red. It appeared as if, directly beneath this string of lights, there was a black shadow that blocked out the starlight in the northern expanse. I fear I'm not describing this very well. Let me just say that this thing was huge! It was *massive!* Miles and miles wide. The lights seemed to be winking inside a veil of clouds.

All at once I was gripped by a primeval fear—that same fear that I'm sure had gripped many of the ancients whenever they saw a comet or a total eclipse. Or perhaps it was the same fear that anyone of limited experience felt as they witnessed a miracle of God. I'd seen my share of miracles. I'd also seen more than my share of miraculous phenomenon. I'd seen the Rainbow Room and Galaxy Room. I'd seen the magnificent swirling pillar. But this was an altogether different kind of phenomenon. By size alone it was easily the grandest-scale miracle I'd ever witnessed. It was almost like looking at the state of Delaware floating in the sky. Well, hey, let's not be modest. It might have been as large as *Nebraska*. After staring at it for a few minutes I also realized it was *moving*. The massive shadow was steadily and slowly creeping across the horizon at a speed slightly faster than the moon.

I recalled the question that the guard had put to me that morning: *"Did you see your city last night? It lit up the whole sky."*

Could this have been what he meant? Of *course* it was what he meant! What *else* could he have meant?

He'd gone on to say: *"You'll see it again tonight, I'll wager. In a few days we'll see it in daytime. It's that season of the year."*

My whole body was tingling with wonder. It was a floating city! A City in the Clouds. But how was that possible? It defied the laws of nature. Didn't it? It was science fiction. Certainly not science. It violated gravity and physics and every other principle I'd ever been taught. What was keeping it up there?

It could only have been supported and suspended by God's power. The guard had called it *my* city. A city of angels. And why not? What other conclusion was there except to believe it was inhabited by a different class of beings?

I realized I needed to rethink everything that I'd been told over the last two or three days. The meanings of words like "City in the Clouds," or "heaven," or "angels" obviously needed entirely different interpretations than the ones I'd given them. My interpretations had been based on twentieth-century understandings. I needed to rethink the Tower of Babel *itself!* I had to rethink all the motives that Nimrod had for building such a thing. *Holy cow!* A tower to reach heaven! The literalness hit home like a sledgehammer. The Tower of Babel wasn't just some monstrosity designed to reach an abstract place beyond the stars. The builders had had a definite goal all along. They wanted to reach the source of those lights! They'd wanted to reach *heaven!*

But where had the city come from? What was the explanation for its existence? I'd only heard of one city in all of human history that was lifted off the earth. *Oh, my.* I was becoming dizzy. Was it possible that I was staring at the city of Enoch? At the actual realm of Zion that was translated by the power of God?

Rapidly I went over everything that I knew about this legendary place. The sum total of my knowledge was surprisingly scant. I knew that the city of Zion had been taken up into heaven in the days before the Great Flood. I knew that the leader of that city was Enoch, and that the only reason Enoch's son, Methuselah, had remained behind was so that through his loins the righteous prophet, Noah, would be born to save mankind from utter destruction. Finally, I knew that the city of Zion was supposed to return to the earth during the Millennium. Beyond that, I hadn't really thought about it. I hadn't even bothered to seriously ask where this city was. I'd never wondered about the mechanics of exactly how it had lifted off the earth. But *nobody* ever seriously asks those things, do they? They're all matters of faith and trust in the miracles of God—the same faith and trust that I'd been describing to Boath. The faith that leads us to believe in the Great Flood itself.

But the Great Flood supposedly had scientists who supported it— scientists who had provided evidence. As far as I knew *no one* had ever searched for evidence to indicate that a major section of the earth's crust had been removed from the planet. But there it was—looming overhead like one of those spaceships from the movie *Independence Day.* Except that it was not directly overhead. It was still to the north. Would it shortly eclipse the light of the moon and stars? The guard had said that it would soon be visible in daylight. How long before it eclipsed the *sun?* Wouldn't such a phenomenon cause incredible weather changes? Tidal shifts? Then again, was the material of that city the same as the material of the earth? Indeed, it was translated material. But what did that mean?

I remained there in that spot for a long time, musing and pondering the mysteries of God. I felt very small. More insignificant than I had ever imagined. I felt certain that my knowledge about the universe amounted to less than a grain of cosmic dust.

I must have watched that shadow moving across the sky for a good twenty minutes before I was hit by a bright recollection of my immediate problems. It seemed amazing that something like this had so completely distracted me, yet it was also very comforting. Just as *I* was insignificant, for a moment my problems seemed the same.

Some of that exhilaration was still inside me as I opened my palm and looked at the stone. It was time to try again. Time to ask for clarification from the Lord. My mind felt totally open and receptive. I could accept anything. Better yet, I could *do* anything.

In the darkness of that reed jungle it was hardly necessary to cup my hands around it. I could see into the stone's depths as it lay in my open palm. So I sat cross-legged on the damp earth and asked again, "What is it that I should do?"

At last I received a clear and precise answer. I thought I was prepared for it. I'd been convinced that nothing would surprise me. But the answer shook me to the core. It shattered my perceptions of the universe. It wasn't a command. It wasn't even a promise that I would succeed. But a *possibility* entered my thoughts—a possibility beyond the very limits of my imagination. After I received it, I felt astounded that it hadn't occurred to me before. With all that I'd learned over the past few days—all of the possibilities presented by the stone and the silvery pillar inside Frost Cave—I'm surprised it wasn't the first idea to enter my mind.

I realized I had one chance to change the outcome of one of the most terrible events that I'd ever experienced—an opportunity to make right something that seemed totally and completely wrong. As the idea struck me, I started to hyperventilate. Such a rush of excitement came over me that I could hardly contain it. The excitement caused me to stand. Not just stand. It propelled me to my feet, lifted me like a rocket. My veins were boiling. I was on fire. I was burning with the energy of a nuclear reactor.

Father in Heaven, was it really possible? Was there truly a chance that I could succeed?

But the stone was silent. I could not see the conclusion. Only the possibility. And that was enough.

I was about to make another journey through time. I knew exactly where to go, exactly where to find a conduit to reenter the eternal stream. The stone had showed me. It was south, then west—an opening in the earth. A fissure among a hundred other fissures in the side of a cliff. I could see it in my mind, but some of the other details remained vague. As did so many details of how I could actually pull this off.

It didn't matter. It was clear enough for now. I wasn't going to sleep tonight. I couldn't have slept if I had tried. I almost wondered if I'd ever sleep again. At least not until I'd completed my ultimate designs. I was off to change the outcome of history.

I was off to save the life of Gidgiddonihah.

NOTES TO CHAPTER 8:

The astonishing supposition presented that Zion, or the holy city of Enoch, may have still been visible to the earth's inhabitants until the days of the Tower of Babel is based on statements attributed to Joseph Smith by several Church leaders of the nineteenth and early twentieth centuries. In 1921 Apostle Orson F. Whitney wrote:

> *The people who built the Tower of Babel are said to have done so in order that its top might 'reach unto heaven.' It was to prevent them from accomplishing this purpose that the Lord confounded their language. Tradition credits Joseph Smith with the statement that the 'heaven' they had in view was the translated city (of Enoch)* (Orson F. Whitney, *Saturday Night Thoughts* [Deseret Book Co.], 101).

As mindboggling as such a statement is, it seems no more extraordinary than other Old Testament ideas more familiar to us; i.e., the Great Flood, the parting of the Red Sea by Moses, the dividing of the continents in the days of Peleg, or the disappearance of the ten tribes of Israel. However, since we have no firsthand statement from Joseph Smith himself, the remark must be considered apocryphal.

And yet there is an undeniable logic behind the concept. The abstract ambition of the people of Shinar to build a tower to reach "heaven" becomes a conceivable goal when we consider that Nimrod might have been trying to reach a visible object. But if this is true, where is the city of Zion today, and why can we no longer see it?

The scriptures suggest that the lifting of Zion from the earth's crust was a gradual process. In Moses 7:21 it reads: *"And it came to pass that the Lord showed unto Enoch all the inhabitants of the earth; and he beheld, and lo, Zion,* in process of time, *was taken up into heaven."* This is sometimes interpreted to mean that becoming a Zion people is a slow and steady transformation. The interpretation is certainly applicable, but a more literal interpretation supports the concept of a visible floating city that eventually rose beyond the naked eyesight of the earth's inhabitants.

We are not told in the scriptures exactly where the city of Enoch is today, but we *are* told that it will return to the earth when it is translated to a terrestrial state during the Millennium. The JST of Genesis 9:21 reads: *"And the bow shall be in the cloud; and I will look upon it, that I may remember the everlasting covenant, which I made unto thy father Enoch; that, when men should keep all my commandments, Zion should again come on the earth, the city of Enoch which I have caught up unto myself."*

This raises other questions. The physics are astonishing in and of themselves. The explanation is likely to be understood only by comprehending the nature of "translated" or terrestrial matter. In addition, if a landmass was once visible from the earth, did it rotate around the globe? Was it more visible at certain times or seasons (as speculated in this novel)? Did it affect the earth's weather or other geological conditions? How large was this city? And what part of the earth did it first break away from?

These last two questions were partially answered by Brigham Young who, again, claimed that he learned it from Joseph Smith. On March 30, 1873, Wilford Woodruff made the following entry in his journal:

> *Again President Young said Joseph the Prophet told me that the garden of Eden was in Jackson Co., Missouri, and when Adam was driven out of the garden of Eden he went about 40 miles to the place which we named Adam-ondi-Ahman, and there built an altar of stone and offered Sacrifice. That altar remains to this day. I saw it as Adam left it, as did many others, and through all the revolutions of the world that altar had not been disturbed. Joseph also said that when the city of Enoch fled and was translated it was where the Gulf of Mexico now is. It left that gulf a body of water.*

It would be marvelous if we had a more detailed, firsthand transcript of what Joseph Smith actually taught, but we are dependent upon secondhand reports. Did the area of the city or land of Enoch encompass the entire Gulf of Mexico (approx. 630,000 square miles) or just a portion of it? Wilford Woodruff's statement suggests that it was large enough that water rushed in to fill the void, but could other geological processes over the last five thousand years have *also* contributed to its present parameters—processes which would allow for an initial area that was considerably smaller?

Keep in mind that the division of the earth in the days of Peleg was an event that apparently took place several centuries after the city was translated.

Many have interpreted this "division" in Genesis 10:25 as a territorial division between the various tribes. This may also be true, but according to several modern prophets and other inspired sources, it primarily refers to a literal dividing of the continents (see D&C 133:23–24, also Joseph Fielding Smith, *Answers to Gospel Questions,* 5:73–75).

Regarding a more detailed geological history of the earth, we are again faced with the prospect that such understandings may not be forthcoming until the Lord reveals it to His prophets, and possibly not until after the Second Coming. Until then the perspectives of this novel must be viewed only as speculation and the fruits of the author's imagination.

PART II

REEMERGENCE OF THE WARRIOR

CHAPTER NINE

Mary

The two young men, Pagag and Jacom, kindly granted to us the use of their horses while they walked just ahead, leading the animals by the reins. There was a feeling of jubilation among the men of Jared's clan—a celebration of our safe arrival and the arrival of Abram. The advent of a descendant of Peleg and Eber had apparently been a matter of expectation for some years. Ophir, Jared, and the rest acted highly honored that the privilege of helping us to deliver him to the patriarchs of Salem may have fallen to them.

For much of the ride toward Jared's encampment, I remained severely distraught. Something had entered my soul. It entered as I had wielded Akish's blade. It gnawed at me still. I could not believe what I'd done. A part of me felt as if it had withered. My head was black with clouds. There were also wretched and disturbing voices in my mind. I heard the laughter again, and I realized why it had seemed so familiar before. It was the laughter of all the voices that I knew best—my sisters, my father and mother, the children of Pella. But somehow the voices had become warped and twisted, as if the most uplifting, comforting sounds of my life had transformed into something demonic and vulgar. I tried to pray for relief, but I couldn't make myself concentrate. What I needed was a private place to pour out my soul to God. I had to find a way to purge this infection— this unwanted intruder who had taken up residence in my heart.

Joshua asked Pagag, "Are we going to meet your father today?"

Pagag shook his head. "My father has gone to the land of Salem with my grandfather, Moriancumr, to bring grain and supplies. They should return in a few days, though I'm certain that when he hears about the babe, he will immediately want to start back as your escort. He will certainly wish to be present when you present the child to Melchizedek."

"Shem," corrected Becky. "Not Melchizedek. The woman in the desert said to take the baby to Shem.*"*

Pagag gave her a strange look. "They are one and the same person."

"No kidding?" said Joshua. "I always thought they were two separate prophets."

"They are only one," Jacom confirmed. "He is Shem, the son of Noah, but his title is Melchizedek—the King of Righteousness over the Land of Peace."

"How old is he?" asked Becky.

"He has lived three hundred and ninety years," said Jacom.

"Holy mackerel!*" cried Josh. "What does he* look *like?"*

"More fit than you might imagine," said Pagag, "He looks as well as my grandfather, Ophir, and Ophir is only one hundred and twenty-four."

"Only?" declared Becky.

Jacom added, "My father has declared that the days of men have been shortened. It has been coming on since the time of Joktan. Today many of the old patriarchs reside in Salem."

"That's incredible!*" Josh exclaimed. "Can we meet all these guys?"*

"If you are bringing to Salem the descendant of Eber, then I expect that you will be honored with many *such opportunities."*

The idea dispelled some of the darkness in my head. I felt a shiver of wonder and fascination. So many emotions for a single day. I felt myself tottering with exhaustion. For an instant my mind faded. Pagag grabbed my wrist and gently shook me back to alertness.

"Are you all right, Mary?" he asked.

I looked into his concerned, steady eyes. This close I could see the amber glowing inside them brighter than ever. "Yes," I said. "Yes, I am."

It wasn't true. My heart was beating faster. I might have fallen off the horse! I might have dropped the baby!

"You don't appear all right. I think I will ride with you to make sure of it."

"That's not necessary," I protested.

But before the words had even escaped my lips, he swung up and seated himself behind me on the stallion, his blonde hair brushing my face. His arms came around me on either side as he took hold of the reins.

"I said I was all right," I repeated.

He ignored me and said, "The hilt of your sword is poking me in the chin. May I hang it by the bridle?"

I was so flustered that I almost didn't respond. At last I said, "I will do it." I slipped the bundle from around my shoulder and tied it in place.

"An impressive weapon," he noted. "Where did you get it?"

"I . . . came by it by accident."

He leaned around to try and judge the expression on my face. "What kind of accident would earn a sword?"

I turned away, still ruffled by his brusque manner. "I don't wish to discuss it."

"Have I offended you? I certainly didn't mean to."

He sounded sincere. I replied, "No, I just . . . You're making me a little uncomfortable."

"Uncomfortable how?"

Abram had awakened. He looked over my shoulder at Pagag's face and smiled. Abram made a genuine coo.

"Ah, he seems to like me," Pagag declared. "May I hold him?"

I thought about this, then I said succinctly, "Yes, you may."

I handed him over. This gave me the chance that I needed to slip down from the horse.

"Where are you going?" Pagag asked regretfully, bouncing the baby in his arms.

"I wish to walk."

As I turned away I heard Jacom reprove his cousin. "Pagag, Pagag. The girl has been through a terrible ordeal."

"I was only trying to help her," said Pagag innocently.

Jacom chuckled. Pagag made the best of his situation and began talking sweetly to the child.

I walked ahead, grateful to stretch my legs. I also wanted to clear my mind. But immediately the nausea enveloped me again. I spun back as I realized why. Quickly, I returned and snatched my sword off the bridle. Pagag and Jacom gave me an odd look, but I ignored them.

I ended up walking beside Jared. He, too, was leading his horse by the reins. The men of his clan had been hunting. His mare carried portions of a deer and a gazelle, cut into quarters. Some of his cousins had also been setting snares for fowl. Many of them carried cages with birds flapping *inside. Two of them looked remarkably like the American bird that the Hawkins family had served at Thanksgiving—the turkey.*

"How are you feeling?" Jared asked me.

"I don't know," I said. But then I revised my answer. "Better. A little."

His eyes continued to study me. At last he said, "You have a great deal of courage, Mary."

"I don't feel very courageous," I said.

Jared smiled at me with fatherly warmth. I did not know as much about this man as perhaps I should have. I knew that he was an important figure in the history of the Book of Mormon, but I'd not yet read up to the point where his tale had entered into the story. I'd obtained a Hebrew translation of the Book of Mormon shortly after I'd come to live in the Hawkinses' home, but mostly I'd used it along with an English copy so that I might learn to read English more proficiently. I wished now that I'd focused greater attention on simply consuming the scriptures. I knew only that Jared was one day destined for a great voyage across the ocean where he and his brother would build up a powerful nation.

"I think you and the children will sleep tonight in the tent of Jahareh, the wife of my brother, Mahonri. There are only she and the children until Mahonri's return. How long has it been since you slept with a fine canvas over your head?"

"Only a few nights," I said.

"I think she will take special care of you," said Jared. "She may also offer you clean garments, if you desire it."

"I would desire it very much. Though I might do just as well to wash the garments that I have."

"You may do that too." Jared looked at my shoes. "We have all noticed the unusual footwear on your feet, and on the feet of the young ones. Is this a new style that they have adopted in Shinar?"

"I . . . couldn't say what others are wearing," I replied hesitantly.

"What animal or plant was used to make the soles?"

I hedged again and replied, "I'm not certain."

He faced forward. "I'd heard that they produced wondrous things in Shinar, but I still cannot imagine that there are as many extraordinary things as in Salem. It is truly a city of miracles."

"Oh?" I said. "What kind of miracles do they produce in Salem?"

"More than I can count," said Jared. "Lights that burn without flame, music that plays without human hands, counting instruments that can calculate the movement of the earth and sun. There are also many tools for watching the stars, and other implements that improve eyesight, amplify sounds, or create ice from warm water. And medicines! There is no ailment that cannot be cured in Salem."

I looked at him in amazement. "They have all these things?"

"And much more. The blessings of heaven abound among the patriarchs. For them there is no challenge that cannot be met by the prayer of faith, and no problem that cannot be resolved through the power of the high priesthood."

I might have concluded that Salem was a miniature example of the knowledge and learning of the twenty-first century. I had always been taught the citizens of Salem were taken to heaven like the city of Enoch. That was why Jerusalem, or "New Salem," had been so named. It was curious that so much had been forgotten by the time of my own generation, and so much remembered in the last days of the earth. This was the curse, it seemed, of a world like mine where the followers of Christ would not unite and remain constant in their faith. The world of Harry and Meagan had maintained followers of the gospel for almost two centuries. Great knowledge seemed the natural consequence of a world where the Saints remained fixed and determined in their devotion. On the other hand, Shinar and its infamous tower seemed to me an example of great knowledge and learning gone awry.

"How far is it to your clan's encampment?" I asked.

"Just beyond these woods," Jared answered. "Another hour, at most."

Pagag rode up beside me. "Would you like me to return little Abram?"

"Have you grown weary of holding him?" I asked.

"Not at all," he said. "I have many younger brothers and sisters. But I think he is growing weary of me."

As he'd stated, the child was starting to fuss. Not badly, especially considering all that he'd been through, but it was apparent that he was probably hungry.

Pagag reached his hand toward me. "Come. I will pull you up."

"And where will you sit?" I asked.

He frowned. "There is room for all three of us. Is there not?"

"I would be more comfortable with two."

He feigned that he was deeply pained by this, but said resignedly, "Agreed."

I let him pull me up. After I took Abram into my arms, he climbed down as promised, but after a moment he said, "You can hardly blame me."

"What for?"

"For wanting to make your better acquaintance. I am still astonished at how well you fended off Nimrod's soldiers this morning. It was inspiring swordsmanship, either for a woman or a man. Perhaps you will allow me to try out your sword sometime."

I turned away and said coldly, "I would prefer it if you didn't ask."

He looked stymied, but he did not pursue it farther. Instead he said, "There is another reason that I cannot be blamed. I find you . . . quite beautiful."

My, but this character did not waste much time. "I'm flattered, but I would ask for your kindness and nothing more."

He considered this thoughtfully, and replied, "If what you require is kindness, I will do my best to express such sentiments as often as I can." He smiled boldly, and a little mischievously.

I rolled my eyes and did my best to occupy myself with the needs of the baby for the remainder of our journey. To my astonishment, Abram's goat milk still tasted fresh. Some of the knowledge of Shinar was apparently devoted to the manufacture of preservatives.

At last we emerged from the trees and came upon a wide meadow with many fields and vegetable gardens. A stream ran through the area and there were scattered clusters of brush and trees. The encampment consisted of about twenty families and thirty tents. Dozens of small children came running toward us as we arrived. As I looked at the women waiting to greet us, their hands occupied with sewing and cooking, I reminisced on the encampment of the Nazarenes at Pella. It was a pleasant feeling, and it did more than any other factor to quell the chaos in my head. I deeply needed to experience the strong sense of community and camaraderie that had existed among the women at Pella.

To my delight, I was not disappointed. Just as Jared had promised, Jahareh, the benevolent wife of Mahonri, took the four of us in. She pampered and coddled us with good food, including sweet meats, breads, and fresh wine (not to be confused with fermented wine—a point for which the Saints of the latter-days would undoubtedly like to be reassured). She was a kindhearted and gracious woman, and quite comely for someone who had given birth to eleven children, Pagag being the eldest. There were several girls among them who were in their early adolescence and who wanted immediately to befriend Rebecca. The eldest boys, including Pagag, slept in tents of their own just beyond the main tent of the family. Judging by the eagerness of Pagag, I suspected they were anxious to occupy these tents with wives.

Joshua must have felt that he was in paradise. At last he had found companions his own age with all the same interests as himself—hunting, making tools and weapons, and conquering the outdoors. The following day he went with several of the boys to help tend the clan's flocks and herds. He particularly "hit it off" (to borrow the term) with Jared's youngest son whose name was Orihah. It comforted me that he finally seemed to have lost interest in the sword of Akish—or so I hoped.

Abram, perhaps, was the best cared for of all. He was the object of unlimited attention from young and old. There were several wet-nurses among the clan who were more than willing to offer nourishment and comfort.

The clan tended a menagerie of animals. There were different kinds of goats, a small, tame deer with large brown eyes, and some various furry creatures of a type that I recalled seeing at the zoo in Salt Lake City. (I believe the tiny maps outside the zoo's cages identified them as having come from the more tropical regions of Central America.) Among the Jaredites there were also small monkeys in cages, and several logs with caps on either end for keeping honeybees, or, as they called them, deseret.

The most interesting contraption may have been a wagon they had built. It had large wooden wheels. Several enormous oxen with curled manes were kept on hand to pull it. On the back of this wagon was a tank sealed with resin and tar. Inside of the tank were several kinds of fish. The tank appeared to have been designed for overland transport. Judging by this wagon, as well as from the abundance of supplies and animals, I had every impression that the families of Jared, Mahonri, and their friends were planning an extended journey.

We sojourned with Jared's clan for several days awaiting the return of Jared's brother. The sword continued to be a source of conversation and speculation, particularly among the younger clansmen. My persistence at carrying it with me everywhere I went did not help matters. In my mind

I was convinced that if I ever left it unattended, even for a moment, it would be taken and I would never see it again.

But was I merely trying to protect others from its influence, or was I becoming dependent? I thought of the gout-stricken wives of Roman statesmen whom I had seen in the Decapolis. Many could not get through the day without their daily dose of mandragora. There was always a puffy, vacant look in their eyes. Was I destined to become like one of them? Was the sword to become my own narcotic?

Jared seemed the most uneasy about the sword, and he did his best to discourage discussions whenever they arose. I could tell he sensed that something was not quite right about it, yet after three days he had still not asked me about its origin. I wished he would broach the subject soon. Perhaps he might have offered effective ideas on how to dispose of it. I settled on the idea that the person most qualified to provide such advice was Melchizedek himself.

But was a part of me dreading the idea of relinquishing the sword to others? Was I starting to resist the notion of seeing the sword destroyed? I tried to fight these feelings. They were not natural or normal. And yet I was having these thoughts more and more frequently.

I wasn't the only one whose interest in the sword was mounting. Curiously, it was also growing in Pagag, almost as much as his interest in me. Then again, I wasn't quite sure which of us attracted him most. For the past two mornings I'd awakened to discover that he'd sneaked into our tent during the night, tiptoed over the sleeping bodies of Joshua, Rebecca, and his younger brothers and sisters, and laid a bundle of wildflowers above my head. I will admit that it was not an unpleasant odor to wake up to, but the giggling of Pagag's sisters, and the warm, approving smile from Pagag's mother convinced me that it was time to set this young man straight.

This opportunity arrived when he found me later that morning washing my clothes. The men of Jared's clan had dammed up a section of the stream to make a small pool deep enough for washing and bathing. I was just in the process of laying my garments out on the stones to dry when Pagag approached me from behind.

"Good morning."

His voice startled me.

"Did I frighten you?" he asked.

"Yes," I said curtly. "You should make your presence known before you come upon a woman. It's only good manners."

"Sorry," he said. "Forgive me." He sat on one of the stones. "I seem to be making a wide range of mistakes when it comes to you." He hung his head, looking pitiable.

"You haven't been making that many mistakes. You are quite thoughtful and considerate, Pagag. But the truth is . . ." I struggled to word it in a way that might sound the least harsh. ". . . my heart belongs to someone else."

His eyes lifted. "Who?" he challenged.

"A man whom I have loved since I was sixteen years old."

"How old are you now?" he asked directly.

I contemplated not answering, but I changed my mind and declared, "I am nearly twenty-two."

"Why has this man not married you already?"

"Because he has been on a mission, preaching repentance and faith in the true gospel."

"Preaching it where?"

"In . . . a distant land," I replied.

"You must know that Nimrod has outlawed what he calls the 'religion of the Shemites,'" said Pagag. "How long has this man been gone?"

"Two years, but—"

"Two years! Has he sent you a message? How do you know that he hasn't been . . . ?"

I knew what he was about to say. He was about to say "killed" or "executed," but he stopped himself—a rare example of his use of tact.

"I just know it," I said unconvincingly.

Pagag's eyes clouded over with pity. "Sweet Mary. Here you are in the wilderness of Joktan, an enemy of King Nimrod, and you still believe that this man will find you and marry you?"

I found the sincerity of his pessimism immensely irritating. "Yes," I said stiffly. "I do."

"Well then, why don't you tell me about this man? Is he the head of his clan?"

"He . . . I suppose he might be considered—"

"Is he a warrior? Could he protect you?"

"He's not a warrior exactly. But yes, I think he will protect me—"

"Is he handsome?"

"Very handsome."

"Intelligent?"

"Yes."

"Firm in the faith?"

"Yes."

Pagag seemed stumped. The corners of his mouth drooped heavily. Then his eyes lit up and he said, "Ah, but can he do this? *"*

Pagag crossed his eyes, and caused one pupil to move back and forth while the other remained fixed. It was so juvenile and out of character for this gruff and brawny young man that I couldn't help but laugh out loud.

"I knew *it!" he said proudly, pleased as can be that he had drawn laughter from me. "He can't do it, can he! Well, that settles it. I'm clearly the best man for you."*

I laughed several more times, then I stopped and smiled at him sympathetically. "I'm sorry, Pagag. You're a charming and handsome man. I'm sure you will soon capture some young maiden's heart and she will be yours forever. But my heart, unfortunately, is taken."

"You must forgive me if I don't take this as a final statement on the matter. What if you learn that something has prevented your man from ever marrying you? What if he becomes so deluded as to believe that he should marry someone else? Would I be such a terrible alternative?"

"You hardly know me, Pagag. Surely there are women in your clan whom you have known all of your life. Some of them may have loved you from their earliest years. Would you break the heart of a girl who has devoted so much energy and faith to her dreams of becoming your eternal companion?"

"But what about my own heart? There is not a woman in this clan, or in any of the clans of Salem, whom I feel as strongly toward as I feel toward you. There are none whom I find nearly as exciting and mysterious. And surely none who are as capable with a sword."

He looked down at the sword lying beside me on the bank, acting as if it was the first time he'd noticed it. Suddenly he seemed no less mesmerized studying the silver blade as he had been studying me. He had not held it since that day in the woods—had not even tried. But I saw the memory of it in his eyes. Even that brief moment seemed to have made a lasting impression. He reached toward it, but before his fingers could touch it, I moved my own hand into the way and gripped the golden hilt. He looked up at me with a jolt. I narrowed my gaze and shook my head slowly.

He relaxed and leaned back, his gaze now far away. "I'll tell you another reason that you should marry me. One day this people—the descendants of Moriancumr, the children of Jared and Mahonri, will become a great nation. My father has prophesied it. And when that day comes, I will be its king."

I raised my eyebrows. "Your ambition surprises me, Pagag."

He snapped out of his brief trance and looked at me again. "You disapprove?"

"It's not my place to approve or disapprove of you."

"But I value your opinion, and I can tell that you have a strong one. Will you share it?"

I withdrew my hand from the sword and said a little uneasily, "I think it's wrong to desire such a thing. A king should never see himself as anything except a servant of the people, and therefore a servant of God."

"Well, of course," said Pagag. "Did I intimate otherwise?"

"Men who desire to be king for its own sake will, more often than not, turn out to be tyrants."

"That is a strong opinion," said Pagag. "Perhaps that's why I need you most, Mary. You would always give me the proper perspective."

I shook my head. "A woman can do many things, but she cannot satisfy a man's yearning for power. In the end it will always consume him unless he is able to recognize this weakness within himself."

"That surprises me," he grinned. "I thought it was a woman's duty to point out all of her husband's weaknesses—and several times daily."

I continued, undeterred. "I think you should ask yourself, Pagag, why it is that you desire to be king, and if you feel unsure of your motives—if you fear that it may be out of vanity—I would advise you to reject it with all the energy of your being."

He pulled in his chin. "But what if the people want me to be king? What if they demand it of me?"

I sighed and said, "I have witnessed firsthand the misery and devastation that comes when a king is blinded by pride. He ignores the grievances of his subjects. Thousands upon thousands can suffer and die. And all because an unrighteous king worries more about preserving his kingdom than preserving his people or preserving their right to worship and serve their God. If you doubt the purity of your motives in the least, don't take the risk. It is better to sacrifice your kingly rights than to lose your soul."

Pagag was looking at me dreamily. "I find you . . . absolutely fascinating."

I exhaled in aggravation. This wasn't the reaction that I'd been hoping for.

"Where did you witness all this misery and devastation?" he asked abruptly. "There has only been one unrighteous king since the Great Flood, and that is Nimrod. Have you witnessed all this in Shinar?"

I fidgeted, feeling perturbed that he would continue to ask such pointed questions. I had, of course, been referring to the caesars of Rome, but I couldn't have explained this to him. Fortunately, I was saved by the shout of a child announcing, "Father is here! Father is here!"

Mahonri had returned. Pagag and I arose and went to greet him. I was privileged to set eyes on him just as he was climbing off his horse. There was another man driving a wagon beside him who I assumed was his father, Moriancumr. Mahroni soon had a daughter in one arm, and a son in the other. Additional children—his own and those of other clansmen—swarmed around him as he entered the encampment.

I do not think that I had ever seen a more majestic-looking human being. The brother of Jared was extraordinarily large, standing almost four cubits (or by English measurements, six and a half feet.) He wore a beard like his grandfather, Ophir, only more comely and neat. Moriancumr was also bearded and had a striking appearance in his own right, but it wasn't quite the same as that of his firstborn son. It wasn't only Mahonri's physical presence. His very countenance shone from within. And his eyes—! The emotion that radiated from them was pure joy. The joy of eternity, of faith in things to come. The joy of God.

I asked Jared's oldest son, Jacom, if he would go and fetch Becky and Joshua. They were tending the sheep in the upper part of the meadow with two of Jacom's brothers, Mahah and Orihah, as well as two of Jared's younger daughters. I knew that Joshua especially would treasure his chance to meet this man. He and Becky might have stood in greater awe than myself. They were, after all, more familiar with the details of Mahonri's future life.

As Mahonri's eyes connected with mine, he said, "Who have we here?"

Jared proceeded to tell his father and brother the story of how they'd found us in the forest. He told them of Abram and the soldiers of the king. Mahonri listened with fervent interest and afterward asked that the baby be brought to him. It was the most wonderful thing to see such a mighty man so tenderly holding such a small baby. And the reaction of Abram was remarkable! The baby squealed in delight, as if these two personalities had known one another in their former existence and were rejoicing in the reunion.

"So the prophecy of Shem has come to pass," Moriancumr declared.

Mahonri nodded, then he held the baby higher. "Peleg and Eber and Salah will sing praises to heaven. I hold in my hands the fountain from which blessings will flow and fill the earth to the end of time."

My heart leaped to hear the ease with which Mahroni could declare such a prophecy. A tear ran down my cheek. Again Mahonri looked at me. Suddenly his luminous eyes got an unexpected look. I felt as transparent as glass, as if he'd seen everything in my heart in a single instant— who I was, where I'd come from, and even a glimpse of my mortal destiny. It made me feel intensely conspicuous, but at the same time, it was emancipating. How wonderful to think that he knew all my secrets, and that his eyes had not dimmed a whit in their expression of joy and love.

"You have traveled far, Mary," he said. "I am most grateful that you have come among us, and I will be most pleased to escort you and the baby to Salem."

"Thank you," I said, and yearned to say something more, but instead I could only shed another tear.

Again I looked around for Becky and Joshua. Where were they? I was starting to feel nervous about their absence. Then, to my relief, Becky emerged from the brush with two of the daughters of Jared. A moment later, Jacom appeared with Mahonri's two youngest sons. A moment later, Joshua also appeared, running to catch up. I greeted Becky and Joshua with a wide smile. By the looks on their faces I could tell that they recognized the Brother of Jared without anyone having to introduce him.

Oddly, I still felt uneasy. Then, like a blast of freezing wind, I realized the cause of my distress.

The sword!

In all of the excitement of Mahonri and Moriancumr's return I had left it on the bank of the stream. How could I have been so careless? I *couldn't believe my stupidity! The washing pool was on the way to the upper meadow—just south and east of where Jacom and the others had emerged from the brush. Becky and Joshua noticed my look of alarm. Pagag could also see the panic on my face and asked, "Mary, what is it?"*

Without answering, I started to run. I crossed the field between the encampment and the stream, my legs spinning in blind desperation. I entered the small cluster of trees and rushed down to the water's edge. Then I stopped suddenly. I could feel my heart beating in my throat. My body was trembling violently. I just stood there and stared at the bank in disbelief. After a moment Pagag arrived, looking deeply worried.

"Mary, you're as pale as winter," he declared. "What—?"

"It's not here," I muttered. "Someone has taken it."

The sword of Akish had been stolen.

NOTES TO CHAPTER 11:

It is often suggested that Melchizedek, who received the tithes of Abraham, and Shem are the same person. The reasons for this are outlined in volume 1 of the *Old Testament Student Manual*, 67–68. Jewish tradition often names Melchizedek and Shem as one and the same. However, even if they were separate people, they would certainly have been contemporaries. (The Bible says Shem outlived Abraham by more than thirty years.)

Some of the reasons for considering that they are one and the same include the following: The land of Salem was given to Shem for his inheritance, so it would be reasonable to believe that he settled there. Shem was the great high priest of his day. Melchizedek, we are told, reigned in righteousness. The name Melchizedek actually means "king of righteousness." Because of his righteousness, his very name or title is used to identify the High Priesthood after the Order of the Son of God. The scriptures tell us that this was to avoid a too-frequent repetition of the name of the Savior (D&C 107:4).

Curiously, in Joseph F. Smith's remarkable vision of the great patriarchs who stood in the Grand Councils of heaven, Shem is mentioned, but Melchizedek is not. Also, the Nauvoo periodical *Times and Seasons* dated December 15, 1844, edited by John Taylor, speaks of "Shem, who was Melchizedek."

One argument *against* the correlation may be Doctrine and Covenants 84:14: "*. . . which Abraham received the priesthood from Melchizedek, who received it through the lineage of his fathers, even till Noah.*" This seems to suggest that there are several generations between Shem and Melchizedek. However, the scripture could also be interpreted to mean that priesthood authority commenced with Adam and came through the fathers, even till Noah, and then to Shem (Alma E. Gygi, "Is It Possible That Shem and Melchizedek Are the Same Person?" *Ensign*, Nov. 1973, 15–16).

The suggestion that Salem (or Shinar) may have been the seat of miraculous technology in ancient days is strictly speculation on the part of the author. The possibility that such advances in science and learning may have existed anciently, particularly in the days prior to the Flood, is a common topic of discussion among those who study this early period. Some have proposed that since the scriptures tell us that all things are to be restored in the last days, technology may be one of those things (see D&C 27:6). However, very little has been found archaeologically to support this proposal. This may strengthen the argument that such technology only existed in isolated locations like Shinar, Salem, or Zion. Since Babel was destroyed, and since both of the other cities and/or their citizens were translated to heaven, we might not expect to find much evidence of their advanced cultures.

Then again, we might also take a second look at the definition of the word "technology." Are the technologies of today—computers, electricity, combustion engines, medical science, atomic energy, etc.—the *only* ways to define higher learning? What about heretofore-unrevealed technologies in organic chemistry, genetics, or biology? For example, Noah's ability to feed and care for potentially thousands of animal species in the ark described by the Bible for an entire year may well be an example of technology that we could not duplicate today. As well, some have speculated that after the Flood there may have been a proliferation of plant and animal species across the globe. If this process was orchestrated and overseen by Noah and his children, it would be another example of technology that has since been lost. Again, the matter may be deserving of more pondering and study.

CHAPTER TEN

Steffanie

As soon as I fell from the elephant—that is to say, as soon as I was *yanked* from the elephant by that incorrigible weasel, Arvad—I was immediately besieged by soldiers. I was so mad I could have spit nails. I wanted to tear the faces off anyone who came near me. I blackened two eyes and broke at least one nose—the schnoz of that Shemite traitor, Mash—before they bound me hand and foot and carried me like a carpet into the tent of Mardon. That's where they dumped me, guards surrounding the tent on all sides.

"You'd better be worth the trouble, angel," Mardon growled at me as he departed.

Mash, his nose red and bleeding, lingered another moment to give me a dirty look.

"Glad I could give you a face to match your name," I seethed.

I wouldn't have thought that the statement would translate, but Mash clenched his fists in rage. I think he had to exert all his willpower to keep from pouncing and breaking my neck. Finally he turned and followed the prince. I was left alone in the dark while the soldiers and officers of Mardon went to deal with the surprise attack of the Japhethites.

I was petrified for Harry. I heard Mardon command Lasha to take twenty men and bring him back. His precise words were, "If you can't bring him back alive, bring him back dead. Do you understand me, Lasha? If he escapes I'll have you flogged and beaten like an unruly ass!"

I listened to the sounds of fighting for at least an hour before the frenzy died down. The smell of smoke was thick. It was clear that the Japhethite attack had been a complete surprise and that it had exacted a big toll. However, as I began to hear officers' voices outside the tent again, it was also evident that the attack had been thwarted. The Japhethites had been driven back, though I heard mention that the war general, Boath, and his grandson, Partholan, had both escaped. They'd been rescued by their kinsmen. Many other prisoners had also been set free, though from what they were saying, a far greater number had been slaughtered by the Shinarians.

Mardon was furious. Apparently he'd promised his father that the rebellions of the Japhethites would be put to an end, and that he would bring to Babel a fresh crop of slaves to labor on the nearly completed tower. The army's return would now be postponed for another day as they sent several thousand men to pursue the fleeing Japhethites. Mardon, however, would not be marching with them.

"Prepare a caravan with two hundred men and horses!" I heard him shout. "Put the angel, Steffanie, in my carriage! As soon as they recapture the other one, bring him as well—but with his legs broken and his eyes gouged out. He doesn't need eyes to tell what he knows to the king. I will depart for Babel at sunrise."

I pulled at my bonds, convinced that hatred alone might break the ropes, but to no avail. Hot tears ran down my face. I was deathly afraid that the next time I saw my brother he'd be blind and crippled. But what would they do to *me?* Were they going to break *my* legs? Would they gouge out *my* eyes?

Mardon's buffoons arrived a few minutes later and carried me, fighting and spitting, to Mardon's wagon. I head-butted the first man who tried to lift me. This only caused him to drop me, badly bruising my hip; but if they were going to inflict some kind of permanent damage on my body, I wanted to inflict as much damage of my own as possible.

They tossed me into the back of the prince's plush traveling accommodations. His carriage was quite spacious—six large wheels, and a good seventy-five square feet of space. It was almost more like a motor home than a carriage. Like his tent, it also had plenty of pillows and rugs. This sadistic namby-pamby just couldn't seem to get enough pillows and rugs. The only thing that kept me going through the long night as I anguished over Harry's life was to imagine myself pressing Mardon's well-chiseled face into one of those pillows and suffocating the life out of him. Oh, I'm sorry! Is that not a ladylike thing to think? Well, tonight I was no lady. If I hadn't been hobbled by these ropes, I felt sure I could have torn someone limb from limb.

Harry never arrived, crippled or otherwise. In fact, toward morning I heard twenty cracks of the whip. Mardon's bootlicking secretary, Lasha, was receiving his lashes. My heart filled with delight. I gritted my teeth and pinched off a pair of grateful tears. Harry hadn't been caught. He'd gotten away. I suppose I shouldn't have been surprised. Harry was obviously too smart for them. What could I say? He was related to *me*.

I was able to sleep a little after that—not soundly, but sufficiently. I was awakened just as the wagon started to pull out. I lay there for a moment, listening. Someone was inside the carriage with me. From the breathing alone I could tell that it was Mardon. I could also tell that he was standing right behind me. I kept my eyes shut and pretended to still be asleep. It surprised me to realize that my feet were loose. The rope had been cut. Just as I registered this, my hands behind my back were also cut loose. I'd been set free. What in blazes was Mardon thinking? Still, I didn't open my eyes. I just adjusted slightly, as if getting more comfortable, and continued to feign unconsciousness. Inside, however, my adrenaline was percolating. I might have attacked him right then and there, but my hands were numb and tingling from a lack of circulation. I needed to wait a minute for them to fill with blood.

I heard Mardon move toward the other end of the carriage. I braved opening my eyes just a slit and saw him laying aside his sword and some of his armor. He looked a mess—caked in dirt and sweat. His face was also covered in soot from all the smoke created when the Japhethites burned the tents. There was blood on his hands. Beside him was a pot, probably a wash basin, and several towels. His back was partially turned to me as he proceeded to wash the grime from his face and arms.

I wouldn't get a better chance than this. He was unarmed. His sword was actually a little closer to me than it was to him. Was he really this stupid? But despite its convenient position, I wasn't going for the sword. It would take too long to get it out of the sheath. When I finally sprang, I would throw myself directly at him. I'd lunge at him with my claws bared, push him to the ground, and smash that pot right over his head. *Then* I'd go for the sword. I'd take it with me as I leaped from the carriage and made a break for it. I worked the actions carefully through my mind one more time—then my muscles went taut.

Just as the prince draped a wet towel completely over his head, I sprang into action. I wanted to farther energize myself by screaming, but I held it in. If my silence gained an extra second before he could react, all the better. I was on my feet, lunging in all my fury—when suddenly my leg caught! The next thing I knew I was face down on the carriage floor. Of course I smashed down on the only spot where there was no rug. *Dag-nab, confound, and doggone it!* I'd been lying so still that I hadn't even realized it. I *wasn't* free. There was a lousy manacle around my pant leg, fastened near the ankle, attached to a two-foot chain. Mardon wasn't quite as stupid as I'd hoped.

He raised up a corner of the towel and looked at me curiously. "Awake are you? I'm glad to see it. But if it's all right with you, I'm going to sleep."

"What do you want? Why am I in here?" My voice brimmed over with hatred.

"You're in here because I can't trust the fools in my command to keep you put. The fifteen men I'd assigned to watch over you earlier are all dead. But I'm sure you knew that. The dungheads couldn't even smell the aconite in their own brew. But I guess only the nose of a prince is trained to recognize such odors."

"Where is Harry?" I demanded.

He gave me a sideways look, then continued to dab his face with the towel. "Missing still. But we'll rectify that situation soon enough."

"Then you'll break his legs and put out his eyes, right?"

He continued his towel bath without any reaction. "You overheard that, did you? Did you also overhear when I revised that order?"

"No."

"My current command is that he be killed. No questions. No hesitation. I've sent my best assassins to accomplish it. My first report was that they'd found his trail. I'm no longer interested in bringing him to my father's palace. I think your presence will be more than enough."

"So what are you gonna do to me? Break my legs? Gouge out my eyes?"

He smiled crookedly. "That would be lovely. I probably should. And maybe I will yet. But for the moment . . . I like your legs. And I like your eyes."

"If I could, I'd *kill* you," I snapped.

"I know that you would," said Mardon, hardly skipping a beat. "That's one of the reasons I find you so captivating. I think I'd have been disappointed if you hadn't tried just now."

"You're sick," I spat. "And you're a pig."

He arose and stepped closer to me, using a bar along the ceiling for support and balance. He stopped just out of reach, but leaned closer. "Call me what you will. Because make no mistake, my pretty angel. When my father is finished with you, you will be mine. I will keep you for my own will and pleasure. You may never learn to like me. And I will certainly never learn to trust you. But you *will* learn to respect me. Also to fear me. In time, you may even find that you enjoy my attentions. But if not, I can accept that. One day I will be king, and I'm determined that my own heir will be half man, half angel."

I lunged again, lashing at him with my hands. I got a piece of his face, leaving a scratch under his eye, but in the effort he managed to grab one of my hands. Mardon yanked my arm to the side and walloped me hard on the left temple. I went down, sugarplums dancing.

As I lay there at his feet, half-delirious, he said, "Don't think that you will gain advantage of me again, Steffanie. I had fun with you the other day. But it would be unwise for you to underestimate me."

My head was pulsing. I continued lying there, waiting to recover. Mardon turned away. He found a place at the front of the carriage and went to sleep.

Several hours later I pulled myself up again and raised back the curtain over the window. I could only see out of a small corner because of the chain, but what I saw was incredible enough. The tower was so high now that I almost got a kink in my neck trying to see the top. It was ominous looking. A man-made mountain of brick and mortar. There were dozens of stairways crisscrossing and spiraling to the summit. All along the climb were various buildings and platforms, especially toward the bottom.

The land of Shinar seemed like one endless city—as if the population of all the earth had crammed into this one valley. All across the landscape I could see canals and reservoirs, bridges and dikes. The buildings were dingy and worn, but the architecture itself was remarkable. The streets were laid out meticulously with cobbled stones. Many of the structures displayed complicated woodwork and filigree, but this couldn't make up for the thick layer of pollution and filth.

People were bustling everywhere with carts and goods. Both men and women wore jewelry—silver earrings, gold necklaces, and jeweled wristbands. Like the concubines who hung around the prince's tent, the women were usually quite gorgeous. Many of them wore elaborate headpieces festooned with ribbons and semiprecious stones. The women's gowns were long and were designed so that the women's right arms and shoulders were left uncovered. Many of the men were bare-chested, with colorful skirts tied around their waist. Still, it was strange that despite the expensive trappings and bright-colored makeup, the people themselves were rather unkempt. I don't think they'd invented bathhouses yet in Shinar. The smell of body odor was almost as prevalent as the smell of grease and soot. It seemed a strange dichotomy to see so much wealth and decoration among such filthy people.

As I looked off at the river I could see dozens of sailboats and rafts. More buildings stretched in all directions on the opposite shore. The citizens of Babel greeted the prince's caravan, but at the same time they seemed a bit surprised. I heard one man ask what had become of the army. I think they'd been expecting the prince's return to be accompanied by a bit more fanfare. Mardon slept through all of it. I think he even found the crowd noise irritating and pressed a pillow over his head to block it out.

Around midday some servants entered the carriage and set down a feast of fruits, breads, and cheese. The prince *still* did not wake up.

It took a little work, but I managed to reach the bread tray and the bowl of white cheese curds. Then I ate the whole thing.

At last the caravan came to what seemed like a final stop. As I looked out the window, there appeared to be a large gathering atop a massive stone platform. It stood ten feet off the ground and was accessed by a wide stairway. The platform itself was about half the size of a football field. Elaborate buildings surrounded it and there were many carved pillars and arches. The central structure behind us was the largest of all, but because of the angle I couldn't see all of it. I assumed this was the palace of Nimrod. Or at least it was *one* of his palaces. From everything that had been said, I'd come to assume that the primary residence of the king was destined to be at the summit of the tower.

There was a knock on the carriage door. "Prince Mardon. You must come forth."

The prince sat up, still looking exhausted and disheveled. He glanced at me, but only in passing. I don't think he was especially looking forward to this afternoon's events. At last he reluctantly arose and answered the door.

"Have my cape brought to my room in the palace," he told his stewards wearily. "Put the angel in chains. I want her standing beside me when my father arrives. Paint her up a little. But don't change her clothes."

"But Prince," said the steward nervously, "your father is said to be anxious. He awaits the signal—"

"I'm going to *change* first," Mardon snarled. "Do you understand?"

The steward backed off. "Yes, noble Prince."

Mardon looked straight ahead and let out a miserable sigh. As he stepped off the carriage, he said, "While you're at it, bring me a pitcher of strong ale."

Soon enough I was surrounded by orderlies and several buff soldiers. My hands were again locked in shackles. My wrists were becoming so chafed I was afraid the skin would start to bleed.

I was led from the carriage and taken toward a building to the right of the main palace. The king's residence was a gaudy-looking thing. It sort of reminded me of the Kremlin in Russia with all the various teardrop-shaped turrets, except that here in Babel they weren't as round on top. No matter what Nimrod built, he liked it big and he liked it loud.

They took me to a stable of sorts with pipes that had flowing water. I was shut into a room with no roof to be groomed for the occasion. But I'm afraid I didn't cooperate very well. Since I was apparently the prince's main homecoming gift to his father, I knew that no one would have dared to hurt me. I took solid advantage of this and kicked and punched and elbowed anyone who got too close. Finally, they wrapped me in strips of cloth like a mummy and proceeded to arrange my hair. Several women also tried to apply makeup, but I smeared it against my shoulder every chance I got. When they tried to put on cherry red lipstick, or lip paint, or whatever it was, I licked it off and spit it into the face of one of the guards. Even while I was wrapped up like a mummy, it took two people to hold my head so that they could finish. The instant they unwrapped me, I immediately tore off the headpiece they tried to tangle in my hair and smeared the makeup *again*.

This only inspired them to lock the shackles behind my back. I was rewrapped in cloth. The headpiece and makeup were reapplied. I think if I'd managed to mess it all up again some of those poor orderlies would have committed *hara-kiri*, which wouldn't have been any great tragedy. However, I was growing somewhat tired of the game and decided it would be best if I just got this over with. They still took no chances and left the mummy wrappings in place on the upper half of my body. In this same condition I was led outside and forced to climb the steps of the large stone platform.

If anything, the crowd had grown larger. Of course everybody was gaping at me as if they'd captured Bigfoot. One sentry at the top of the stairs looked so engrossed as he stared at me that I couldn't resist shouting "Boo!" in his face, which nearly caused him to trip over the edge. After that I was carried the rest of the way to the top and returned to the presence of Mardon. The king's son was wearing a bright black and purple cape with gold hems. He, too, was gussied up for the occasion.

Mardon saw the wrappings encircling my torso and said, "Take those off."

"But noble Prince," protested the guard, "she will disarrange herself."

"If she does," said Mardon darkly, "I'll gouge out her eyes here and now."

I gave Mardon a vicious look, but the threat was sufficient to ensure my cooperation. The guards and orderlies smirked at me with pleasure. As the wrappings were removed I took in my surroundings with a little more interest. The number of people actually standing on this platform had been sort of an illusion. In reality, they were tightly crowded around the edges. The very center of the platform—a space of about half an acre—was empty. At the north end of the platform was a large roll of carpet. It was the largest roll of carpet I'd ever seen, and its color was blindingly red. Just by its size, and by the fact that several dozen men were standing along its length, I deduced that it was about to be unrolled to cover the entire central portion of the platform. Mardon and I were standing on the south end, facing the great tower. The sight truly was breathtaking. It loomed over us to the north, its massive base only a mile or two distant. On either side of us stood dignitaries and nobles, all wearing that corny squared-off beard that looked like a braided floor mat.

I looked around to see if there was any sign of a person who might be King Nimrod. I glanced back toward the palace to see if he and his entourage might be walking toward the platform to join us. It all seemed very strange. We were obviously gathered here to meet the king, but His Majesty was nowhere in sight. It was almost as if they expected him to materialize out of thin air. Half of the people seemed to be looking toward the summit of the tower. The other half were looking at Mardon, awaiting his signal.

"So where's Daddy-O?" I asked Mardon.

He completely ignored me and nodded to one of the nearby dignitaries. This man in turn waved his arms toward the men standing along the carpet roll. Another row of men had positioned themselves just beyond the carpet, standing along the northernmost edge. Suddenly these men raised up a chorus of white flags. Each man held two of them—one in each arm. The flags were about ten feet tall. They started waving them toward the Tower of Babel, crossing them and uncrossing them like semaphores.

The other row of men started rolling out the bright red carpet. They did so with incredible speed and efficiency, as if they'd been trained exhaustively for this task. But it was the chain reaction of the white flags that wowed me in particular. As I looked toward the base of the tower, I realized that *another* row of white flags was also waving. Just as I noticed this, I spotted yet another line of white flags a short distance higher. And then another, and another. Row after row of white flags started waving. It was like watching a wave in the bleachers of a football stadium. The lines of white flags climbed higher and higher up the slope of the pyramid until, I must confess, they became harder and harder to see. It might have been the most magnificent display of pageantry I'd ever witnessed.

The men unrolled the carpet until the very end of it lay right at my feet. Displayed across it was a gigantic lion with a flowing golden mane. In fact, I think it *was* gold—or at least gold paint and thread. The way the sun caught it made me think that it would probably be visible all the way to the very summit of the tower, like a buzzing neon sign.

A moment later, I realized this was exactly the intent. The crowd had gone silent. Their eyes were riveted on that summit. I was totally bewildered. What in tarnation was going on? I wanted to ask Mardon, but I held my tongue. I feared that speaking right now might be a mortal offense.

Then all at once the crowd gasped. I squinted into the bright azure sky. Something was floating up there. I could only guess that it had been thrown or launched from the tower's summit. It was too far away to tell what it was. Was it an eagle? This seemed ridiculous. If it was a bird, the thing was the size of a pterodactyl. The tiny floating dot continued to grow larger and larger. As I realized what it was, my heart skipped a beat.

It was a *flying machine!* Well, not a *machine* perhaps, but a glider. Like the carpet, its wings were also bright red. We watched it swooping and cavorting through the air, drawing more gasps and sometimes laughter from the onlookers. We must have watched it floating in the air for fifteen minutes. The closer it got the more like an actual airplane it began to appear. There were tail wings. There were even two sets of front wings, like a biplane. This glider was fairly large. A little closer and I could tell that there was more than one passenger. A dozen men might have been guiding this contraption. Who'd have believed that such a thing had been built five thousand years before Wilbur and Orville Wright? A flying machine in ancient Babylon? But there it was! I was seeing it with my own eyes! King Nimrod had conquered the secrets of flight.

The only one who didn't seem impressed was Mardon. He'd probably seen this airshow more times than he could count and just wanted to get it over with. When it reached a height of about three hundred feet, some of the people on the platform began fidgeting nervously. Others were descending the stairs. The pilots intended to land the craft exactly in the center of the carpet. I might have guessed that on former occasions the landing hadn't gone as planned and some of the onlookers had been run down, possibly knocked off the platform. But the vast majority remained steadfastly in their place.

At two hundred feet the crowd began to applaud and cheer. The glider wasn't coming down quite how I might have expected. I'd been concerned that the runway was too short, but its descent was slow and steady, with a quality that reminded me of a parasail. I could now judge that the span of both wings was about thirty-five feet—about half the width of the platform. The glider had three cribs, or cockpits. Three men stood in the center cockpit, while two more were riding in the cribs under each of the double wings. In all there were five passengers. There was no mistaking which one was the king. Unlike the purple-cloaked men on either side, Nimrod wore a robe the same color as the carpet—the same color as the glider's wings. It might have been an illusion, or maybe he was standing on some kind of dais, but from here he appeared almost two feet taller than the other men. The two individuals in the side cribs controlled much of the aircraft's steering and descent. They were very good at what they did, because the glider was coming in smooth as silk.

At last, with a rapturous roar from the crowd, the biplane touched down. The two passengers under the wings hung their legs out at the last moment and ran the contraption to a halt. Afterward the two passengers in the main crib leaped out to help hold the glider down. There was a notable breeze, and the aircraft clearly wanted to take off again. Other men on the ground began tying the glider in place.

More began folding up part of the upper and lower canvas to eliminate some of the wind's lifting force. The whole affair was splendidly orchestrated.

Finally, Nimrod leaped out of the center crib and landed on the platform. There was no further applause. The crowd proceeded to kneel—that is, all but me and Mardon. I couldn't believe Nimrod's size. His height had been no illusion. *Gracious!* He must have been over seven and a half feet tall. And every inch was rippled with muscles! If I'd thought that Mardon was the epitome of the perfect physical man, it was only because I had not seen his father. This guy was a *giant*. Didn't the scriptures say something about giants once walking the earth? Well, here was one of them. Okay, maybe the scriptures had been talking about something different, but he was definitely the largest man that *I* had ever seen. This was saying something, 'cause I'd met an awful lot of basketball players in my time. Nimrod also had an odd, turned-up beard that twisted into a point, almost like a horn, on his chin. When this horn was combined with a pair of thick, pointy eyebrows that curled up on either side, I might have compared him to a triceratops.

He crossed the platform and came toward his son. Mardon forced himself to smile in greeting, but the prince was clearly intimidated. Who wouldn't be? His father towered over him by a foot and a half. Before he reached us, Nimrod motioned for the onlookers to rise. As the crowd came to their feet, they remained reverently silent, waiting to hear what the king would say to the prince.

Nimrod paid me a single curious glance, but then he ignored my presence for the most part and said to his son, "Have you returned victorious?"

"Yes, Father," said Mardon in a formal tone, but with a slight hesitation. "The armies of Shinar are always victorious."

Again there was an eruption of cheering and applause.

Nimrod looked down into the palace square, his eyes searching. Before the cheering abated, he leaned in and asked Mardon in an aside, "Where is your army?"

"A day behind me," said Mardon. "There were some . . . complications. But everything is well in hand. The last division of Japheth's army is being destroyed even as we speak."

Nimrod's tone became angry. "You abandoned your men?"

"With good reason, Father."

The king leaned in even closer, and said in a threatening whisper. "It had *better* be."

Mardon tried to appear resolute, but I saw him swallow.

"Who is this?" asked Nimrod, indicating me.

"She is the reason that I have come. Ask me formally."

Nimrod's eyes remained angry. With considerable reluctance, he raised a hand to the people. The applause and cheering died. Nimrod stood back a pace and continued speaking for the benefit of the crowd.

"I am pleased with your victory, Prince Mardon," his voice boomed. "You have brought honor to the lineage of Cush and the people of Shinar."

"I have brought more than honor," said Mardon, his voice again formal and affected. "I have brought you the key to victory against the Heavenly City."

The crowd began murmuring with interest. Nimrod's expression changed markedly. I wasn't sure if it was a look of curiosity or if it was a warning. He was probably concerned that his son was about to say something rash.

Mardon continued, "Your Majesty, I present to you a denizen of the clouds. I present to you an *angel*."

The murmuring turned to a shocked gasp, then to louder murmuring. Some of the closest dignitaries backed away a step. Nimrod's surprise was worth a Polaroid. In any other setting I guess I'd have found an introduction like Mardon's to be rather flattering. Who wouldn't enjoy being described as an angel? But in this setting it was just plain weird. This whole *thing* was whacko! However, my biggest worry was that this was just the beginning. I feared things were about to become stranger than ever. A feeling of loneliness spread over me.

Where are you, Harry? I cried in my heart.

Never in my life had I wanted or needed the company of my little brother more than now.

NOTES TO CHAPTER 10:

The idea of a flying machine in the court of Nimrod is a tradition that dates back to some of the early apocryphal works. He is said to have used birds to carry him to heaven for reconnaissance. Also, there is a story of him piloting a flying chariot and experiencing a very "undignified landing" (Nibley, *Abraham In Egypt*, F.A.R.M.S., 573).

Archaeologists have unearthed several interesting objects over the years, and some of these scholars have suggested that these objects might be parts of a kind of ancient aircraft. It was reported that while excavating in Bronze Age deposits near the site of Knossos, Greek archaeologist Aphron Asophos came upon some twisted metal objects which, when restored, had the appearance of small, light-weight wheelless chariots, each with an elongated cone in front and aerodynam-ically sophisticated wings on each side. Additionally, a "birdlike" wooden "toy" was found during excavations in Egypt in 1898. When recreated from balsa wood, this toy has demonstrated the ability to glide through the air (*Flying the Saqqara Bird*, Martin Gregorie, http://www.catchpenny.ord/birdtest.html).

Certain passages in some ancient documents have also been interpreted by some to describe ancient flying machines. In the *Halkatha*, an old manuscript of Babylonian laws, there is purported to be a passage that reads, "*To operate a flying machine is a great privilege. Knowledge of flying is most ancient, a gift of the gods of old for saving lives.*"

A curious inference is also found in a manuscript composed in Sanskrit by King Bhoja in the eleventh century A.D. The work is called *Samarangana Sutradhara* ("Battlefield Commander") and all of chapter 31 is devoted to the construction and operation of a peculiar kind of military aircraft. King Bhoja claimed his knowledge was based on Hindu manuscripts that were ancient even in his time. One passage describing these aircraft reads:

> *Strong and durable must the machine's body be made of light material, having wings joined smoothly with invisible seams. It can carry passengers, it can be made small and compact, it can move in silence. If sound is to be used successfully, there must be great flexibility in the driving mechanism, and all must be put together faultlessly. In order for it to accomplish its intended purpose, it must last a long time, it must be well covered in [this word is not translated], it must not become too hot, too stiff, nor*

too soft, and its sharp-pointed battering ram must also be long lasting. Indeed, the machine's main qualities, which are remembered by one and all, include unending motion, which is to say perpetual motion. Smoothness is one of the machine's supreme qualities, thus, the working of the machines is versatile, complete, not given to expansion, not complaining, and always suitable . . .

In this novel the author chose to portray an ancient glider. However, another passage from this same ancient Sanskrit document describes an unusual engine and means of propulsion:

. . . Thus inside one must place the Mercury-engine, and beneath it the iron heating apparatus properly mounted. Men thusly set the dual-winged, driving whirlwind in motion. The concealed pilot, by means of the mercury-power, may travel a great distance in the sky.

An extremely swift and nimble vimana *(aerial machine) can be built, as large as the temple of the God in motion. Into the interior structure four strong mercury containers must be installed. When these have been heated by a controlled fire from iron containers, the flying machine develops thunder-power through the mercury, becoming a machine much to be desired. Moreover, if this iron engine with properly welded joints be filled with fluid (mercury?), when ascending or descending over land it develops power with the roar of a lion . . .*

It should be noted that no evidence of a vehicle that fits this description exists in any other documents of the ancient world. Mercury certainly does not qualify as a combustible material, although in the ancient world it was often thought to have mysterious magical qualities. However, in this same document, another type of combustion is also described which might be closer to gasoline:

The conquering yantra's *manufacturing details is greatly desired . . . using light-weight wood to build a great air-going machine of a strong-bodied type. In the central container is the liquid consumed by the engine, which gradually burns away during complete combustion. . .*

. . . Fully renowned is the conquering of the following motions: Vertical ascent; Vertical descent; Forward; Backward; Normal ascent; Normal descent; Slanting; Progressing over long distances, through proper adjustment of the working parts . . . And its musical sound and throbbing thunder can easily drown out the trumpeting of the elephant in panic. It can be moved by musical tones.

Shining in every direction, their machine (yantra) could travel wherever the imagination dictated. From their great height they saw stimulating dances, drama plays, and pristine dance ceremonies. The machine gained renown among Royal dynasties and various nations. In such a manner the High-Souled ones flew, while the lower classes walked. All those friends succeeded in their much-deserved acquisition of a yantra, by means of which human beings can fly in the air, and non-earthling, Celestial Beings can come down to mortals in their visits to Earth.

The basic manufacturing techniques of these *yantras* or *vimanas* are said to have been used by British and American aircraft companies since World War I, and have been found to be based on sound aeronautical principles. The complete design, however, is not offered in the ancient text because, as it says, "elements of these machines would be wrongly used" (R. Cedric Leonard, *An Ancient Airplane*, Apr. 2002).

Although this information is interesting, at present no conclusion can be drawn with regard to the existence of ancient flying machines. But again it highlights the possibility that there may have been technologies that existed prior to the Flood, or shortly after the Flood, which were lost at the time of the confusion of tongues.

CHAPTER ELEVEN

Harry

At first light I finally stopped to find out if there was anything edible in my sister's backpack. I knew that my own backpack had plenty of army rations, candy bars, and trail mixes. Surely Steff would have packed her own food, though she'd never really mentioned it. Normally, we had very different tastes. Back home she was kind of a health nut—crunching wheat germ and guzzling high-energy liver-and-whey-shake types of things. Fortunately, at the moment I didn't feel very picky.

I'd been walking for about seven hours now and I was still inside the jungle of reeds. However, some cliffs to the west helped me orient my bearings, and now and then I also caught glimpses of the Euphrates River to the east. I felt certain that I was going in exactly the direction that the stone had instructed me.

As I might have expected, my sister had remained true to form. There were dozens of little freeze-dried packets—*gourmet* no less: *Lentil Curry Couscous, Organic Kettle Chili, Chicken Primavera, Skillet Foccacia, Buttered Pasta and Herbs* . . . Man, it was a good thing I was hungry. She also had a nice full canteen, and a convenient aluminum bowl, so I quickly stirred up a concoction of *Corn and Black Bean Chowder*, blessed it, and proceeded to inhale. It was a little crunchy since I couldn't boil the water, but it filled the pit.

I decided I should travel a little closer to the cliffline in hopes of getting out of these claustrophobic reeds. All I knew about the place where I would find the time conduit was that it was downstream and

I would recognize it when I saw it. I had a strange notion that I would have to access the cave, or crevasse, by water, but I figured that this would explain itself when I got closer.

Right at the base of the cliffs ran a small stream, little more than a trickle. It was flowing south. I assumed that eventually it would drain into the river, so I decided to follow it. A few minutes after I started along this trail, I spotted something very disturbing in the sky.

Actually, I *heard* it first—an ominously familiar squawk. It was that lousy falcon that had been used to spot the escaping stragglers on the battlefield. As I looked up into the sun, I could see the red leather band dangling off its leg. Curse that bird! Undoubtedly it had been sent to try and find me. It continued to hover overhead, squawking and screeching, making sure to pinpoint my exact location to whoever was stalking me.

Unfortunately for the bird, I'd honed a few choice skills during my years on Lincoln Island. One that had proven particularly useful was my ability to pick off seabirds with a single stone. This had come in quite handy on certain evenings when we needed to fill our cooking pots. I don't think this falcon had ever come across someone with such skills, because it was flying awfully low, almost as if it were daring me.

I casually reached down, snatched up a stone, drew back my arm, took careful aim, and fired. Suddenly the squawk took on a different tone—more like a strangled rooster. The spy falcon began spiraling to the earth. It landed in a heap of feathers about twenty feet in front of me, right at the edge of the little stream.

Problem solved.

But shooting down the falcon didn't change the fact that my location had been revealed—and now I had the additional complication of the owner's temper. Finding his dead bird would undoubtedly send him into a tizzy fit.

However, as I prepared to flee, I realized that the falcon was *not* dead. It fluttered around a bit, and then tucked its wings against its body, trying to shake off its disorientation. I lifted another rock and approached it. My motives for what I was about to do were two-fold. If it recovered it would only go back to its job of tracking innocent men. If it was mortally wounded, it would be best to put it out of its misery. Finishing the job might be the most humane thing that I could do.

And yet I hesitated. It looked up at me, its dark eyes full of fear, but also capitulation. It seemed to know that it was about to die and had resigned itself to the fact, but there was also a plea for mercy. That's what got to me. After all, it really was a beautiful bird—a nicely spotted peregrine, if I remembered my falcons correctly, with a black mask for a face and a fluffy white breast (a little ruffled at the moment from its landing.)

I groaned audibly. The stupid thing was probably going to die anyway, but I reached down and picked it up. It was too stunned to even attempt to bite me. I slipped the backpack off my shoulder, opened it up, and laid the bird carefully inside. It would sit right on top of my sister's sweat pants and the freeze-dried food. As an after-thought, I tied its leather band to one of the straps, just in case it recovered enough to escape. Then I hoisted Steffanie's pack onto my shoulders and hightailed it out of there.

I no longer felt it was wise to follow the stream. That's just what the tracker would *expect* me to do, right? At this point it was impera-tive that I not be predictable. I decided to climb the cliffs. Perhaps I could get high enough to spot the tracker before he spotted me. About twenty yards downstream I found a place where I could ascend without much difficulty. I continued until I reached the top of the ridge. Then I wandered along the ridgeline for several minutes until I found an overlook of the river valley.

Almost immediately I saw one of the men who'd been following me. It was the dude with the eyepatch—the man whom I'd first seen outside the prince's tent. Even then I'd wondered if his injury was the handiwork of one of his birds, though I sincerely doubted it was *this* one. If a bird had done that to me, I think my first impulse would have been to break its feathery neck.

The man had found the place where I'd shot down his bird. He was examining the scattering of loose feathers along the bank. Just as I'd anticipated, he looked as mad as a hatter. Eyes full of hate, he scanned the surrounding area, eventually following along the cliffline. I remained very still. Another man soon emerged from the reeds and joined him. He studied the ground for footprints. A third man also emerged. They were armed to the teeth—bows, spears, swords, and probably an assortment of knife blades. These men were professional assassins. I felt sure of it. And I had a strong feeling that they were not here to take me back alive.

I scooted away from the edge until I could stand. Then I made my way across country. The ridge led up to a sandy plateau that seemed to go on for miles. I maintained a southward course. Eventually I knew I'd have to turn back toward the river. I depended on my inner compass—and the seerstone—to tell me exactly when.

An hour later there was a violent fluttering behind my head. The falcon was attempting to take off. The leather strap kept it in place, but its wings and free leg were scratching and slapping my neck. I took off the backpack and laid it aside. If Steff's pack had been any lighter I think the bird would have taken off with it. The falcon obviously wasn't seriously injured. I crouched down and watched it. The bird glared back, flapping and fluttering every time I attempted to move closer.

After I felt it had sufficiently exhausted itself, I said in a steady voice, "So what am I going to do with you, eh? If I let you go, you'll try to get me killed. If I kill you, I'll feel guilty. Not *too* guilty, mind you, but . . . a little. Still, I'd hate to do it. Not your fault that you got hitched up with an assassin for an owner. Any chance that you and I can make an arrangement?"

The bird continued to watch me, almost as if it were listening.

"Here's the deal," I continued. "You come with me quietly, not trying to bite or scratch my head off, and after I get to where I'm going, I'll set you free. You don't have to be owned by *anybody*. You can hunt mice and squirrels—do anything you want. What do you think?"

It made no reaction. I decided to try a different tack. I pulled down my sleeve, and held up my forearm. Then I stepped a little closer and said in a sugarcoated voice, "Hey pretty bird. Are you a nice bird? Yes, you're a *very* nice bird, aren't you? Would you like to sit on my arm?"

It remained still, watching me thoughtfully. After it decided that I'd moved close enough, it went nuts, shrieking like a banshee, trying one last time to fly away. It even managed to drag the backpack a few inches. I backed off and sighed heavily.

"Enough of *this*," I muttered in frustration.

I took off my shirt, made it into a net of sorts, waited for just the right instant, and threw it over the bird's head. After some struggling, I got the falcon more or less pinned inside of the top the backpack. To make room for its body I pulled out Steffanie's sweatpants and one of her T-shirts. The zipper came up to its neck on both sides. Finally, I maneuvered its head inside the long sleeve of my shirt, which allowed for its beak to show, but covered its eyes. Actually, it sort of looked like the periscope on a submarine. Afterward, I grabbed up the sweatpants and T-shirt. My own shirt was smelling pretty rank. I decided to exchange it for Steffanie's. It wasn't the most fashionable of T-shirts. But who in 3000 B.C. was going to care if I wore something that read *Hunter High School Girls' Basketball—Wolverines Rule!* Next I tied the sweatpants around my head, which must have looked ridiculous, but I hoped it would keep the back of my head from getting pecked.

I walked south for another hour, at last veering toward the east and back toward the river valley. I felt sure that my pace was faster than the trackers. After all, they had to stop and check for signs, right? Maybe they were thinking they could outlast me, but with Steffanie's gourmet vittles, I could have easily gone on for days.

However, I didn't think this was going to be necessary. My senses told me that the time conduit was getting quite close. I climbed back down the cliffline and again located the trickling stream. I moved swiftly along its course and soon arrived at the banks of the mighty Euphrates. It was a slow and lazy river the color of pea soup. What's more, it *smelled* like a lazy river—swampy and fetid. The opposite shore was nearly a half-mile away. Along the western bank there were cliffs that crawled along for several miles. It was here, I realized, that I needed to look for a crevasse.

I took out the seerstone and cupped it into my hands. Was I supposed to climb overland a ways and drop down from above or . . .?

No. I felt strongly this was *not* the plan. The answer was clear, and a little strange. It seemed the Spirit wanted me to travel *upstream* for a short distance. I knew better than to question such things, so I started walking north, up the riverbank, back in the same basic direction that I'd come from, except that I wasn't following the tiny stream. I didn't have to go far before I felt impressed to approach a tangle of bushes near the water's edge. As I got closer, I realized they *weren't* bushes. That is to say, the bushes had been piled there. I began dragging them away until the thing they'd been hiding was revealed.

It was a *boat!* Or at least a boat of sorts. Animal skins had been shellacked with some kind of sealant and tied around a double frame of sticks. Along the lower part of the frame more skins circled the craft's length. These skins were sewed over some kind of floatable material, almost like one of those cushion things inside a life jacket. All in all, it looked more like a floating bathtub than a boat, but there was a single round oar lying in the bottom. The paddle's shape reminded me of a dental mirror. The boat didn't look too encrusted with mud yet, leading me to believe that it had only been hidden here a short time.

After making sure that I wasn't being watched, I slipped off the backpack and placed it in the bottom. The falcon gave a couple of squawks, almost as if it realized what I was about to do and felt that it should be a voice of protest. Carefully, I lifted the wooden frame out of the mud and dragged it down to the water. I pushed it out about five feet, until the river's depth was about a foot and a half, and climbed inside. There really wasn't a bottom to the boat—just skins. It was sort of like floating in a gunnysack. I used the oar to push the rest of the way out into the water, then I let the current carry me away from shore.

The falcon made another squawk. I decided to show some compassion and pulled down the zippers on either side of its neck. Then I pulled the shirt off its head. It flapped its wings a few times to loosen up, then contented itself to perch there and look out at the water. It didn't try to fly off. It seemed to have given up on the idea of escape. Only one problem: I was getting kinda thirsty, and the canteen was underneath it in the pack.

"You gonna let me get that canteen?" I asked. "Eh? Gonna let me get a drink?"

I wrapped the sweatpants around my hand and floated my arm a little closer. The bird made no move to attack me. It also didn't flap around and go nuts. I eased the arm close enough that it could have torn the flesh of my upper arm if it had wanted, but instead, the bird just watched me. When I got so close that it might have also nipped my shoulder, it nervously flapped its wings once, and walked down the edge of the backpack as far as the strap would allow. If I didn't know any better, I'd have thought it was politely making room for me to do what I wanted.

Still keeping one eye on the bird, I reached in and took out the canteen. As I sat back and took a long drink, the bird continued to observe my behavior. After wiping my mouth, I asked it, "Are you thirsty?"

It squawked—just one single sound.

"Thirsty?" I repeated.

Again, it made a single squawk.

"You understand that? Water? Would you like some water?"

It squawked two more times, as if was saying, *Yes, you nitwit. I just told you twice!* I took out Steff's aluminum cup, poured a little into it, and eased it toward the falcon's head. Its eyes were no longer watching me—they were watching that cup. When it was close enough, it happily dipped its beak and started drinking.

"Good girl," I said. "Or boy." How did one tell with a falcon? Rather than call the bird "it" all the time, I decided he looked like a male.

As soon as he finished drinking, the falcon looked up at me and made another squawk.

"Hungry?"

He squawked again, this time with a great deal of excitement. Whatever word his owner had used for food or water, my gift of tongues seemed to have translated it.

I rifled through the contents of the backpack again, still wary of getting nipped. The bird made no such attempt. I was fortunate to find a package labeled *Chocolate Chip Cookie.*

"Amazing," I said to the bird. "Sis actually packed a cookie."

I tore open the packaging. Then I poured out the aluminum cup and crumbled the cookie into it. I pushed it close to the falcon's head. It took one look, then gaped back at me as if I was a total moron.

"Sorry," I said. "I guess you're not a seagull. So what is it that you eat? I'm all out of field mice at the moment. *Hey*, I got an idea."

I reached into the pack and found the freeze-dried *Chicken Primavera.* I ate the crumbled cookie myself (no sense wasting it) and poured the contents of the *Primavera* into the cup. I found a total of twelve pieces that I assumed were chicken. Altogether there might have been enough meat to equal the size of a mouse. I saved the rest of the primavera on another plate, then doused the meat nuggets with water, stirring with my finger. I glanced at the bird, feeling a little embarrassed. He'd probably been raised on fresh raw meat. If *I* didn't find this stuff appetizing, I could only imagine how the bird must have felt.

After the pieces felt soft, I eased the plate forward. "It's chicken. I know it's slightly cannibalistic, but it's the best I can offer right now."

The falcon stared at it a long time, sniffing and studying the Styrofoam-looking morsels. I was afraid he was going to turn up his beak in disgust, but then he snatched up one of the pieces and swallowed it down. The bird looked at me and made a chirp. Miracle of miracles. He *liked* it!

I balanced the plate on top of the backpack and let him finish. Then I took up the oar and began steering the bathtub farther downriver. I tried to steer it closer to the cliffs. My eyes carefully searched all the crevasses and grooves in the rock. I was looking for something specific. I'm not sure if it was an image or just an idea, but when I saw it, I felt sure a bell would sound in my head.

Dozens of crevasses opened right at the level of the water, but nothing appeared quite right. I half-paddled and half let the current carry me for another five minutes. I was just about to ask the Lord for clarification through the stone when *bingo*—there it was—a narrow crevasse just ten feet down from a larger crevasse. My boat might have rowed into the larger crevasse or cavern with room to spare. But it wasn't the right one. I had to enter the narrower crevasse. It was a little tricky at first getting the boat inside. I had to paddle the nose directly through the opening. The current didn't want to cooperate, but with some ambitious paddling, and after grabbing the stone wall with my hands, I managed it fine.

The bird saw that we were going into a dark place and fluttered his wings. I tried to comfort him.

"It's all right. Everything's cool. You'll be just fine."

The space was so narrow that I could put my hands on both stone walls and push my way along. Finally the outside light became dim enough that I decided to use Steffanie's flashlight.

She had a nice one, waterproof—with four long, size-D batteries. Its light made a powerful beacon into the gloom. The watery cavern seemed to go on forever. I pushed my way through the tunnel, fearful that the space would soon grow so narrow that I'd get stuck. But after another thirty feet it opened up into a wider room. There were copper-colored stalactites hanging down from the ceiling and water dripping everywhere. This place was actually pretty dang awesome. I thought back on the dusty tunnels of Frost Cave and told myself this was the way to go. If only all spelunking were a casual canoe ride into the depths of the earth.

But a little farther and the journey stopped being so casual. I spotted a sloping bank on the right side of the boat. Several dry caves appeared to branch off toward the north. (If right still meant north, that is. I was a little confused on my bearings.) The disconcerting part was that there was *another* boat. It was pulled up onto the shore. Someone else was in here! Were the assassins that resourceful and clever? Had they watched me paddling down the river and rowed into this cavern ahead of me, maybe using another tunnel? That seemed unthinkable. Where would they have gotten another boat? Then again, it was quite a fluke that I'd found mine. But even if it *was* them, where were they now? Where was anybody?

I had a half a mind to keep on rowing. The water tunnel definitely went farther on. But somehow this didn't seem right. It was a strange notion, and I had no idea what it meant, but for some reason I felt that I was supposed to learn something here. Or perhaps someone was supposed to learn something from *me*.

I rowed over to the shore, my nerves like bowstrings. The flashlight revealed dozens of footprints. Someone—or many someones—had been using this shore for a long time. As I climbed out and pulled my tub onto the bank, I looked back at the falcon, still tied to the backpack.

Suddenly I remembered my promise—the one about letting him go when I reached my destination. Maybe it was stupid to feel obligated by a promise to a bird. It's not as if he had understood me. Had he? The falcon was presently hiding his beak in his wing feathers. I wasn't sure if this was out of fear or because he was trying to sleep. Maybe the darkness had convinced him that it was bedtime.

A promise is a promise, I decided. I'd spared his life because it seemed too cruel to kill him. It seemed no less cruel to drag him any deeper into this cave. Falcons and caverns just didn't seem to mix.

It occurred to me that he might find his master and lead him to this place, but somehow I wasn't too worried about that. Even if he did, I very much doubted that I'd still be here when the assassins arrived.

I reached over and untied the leather band from the backpack.

"Hey," I said, "Wake up."

He didn't respond.

"Yo. You're free. The exit is that way, in case you missed it while you were asleep."

I probably should have remembered my promise earlier. The exit didn't seem that far—only about a seventy-five yards—but falcons weren't bats. I wasn't sure if it *could* find its way out.

Then the falcon did something I wouldn't have expected. He opened his eyes and stepped onto my shoulder. *Yikes!* This thing had some claws! They dug right into my flesh! From the way he was clenching, I decided he definitely hadn't been sleeping. He was scared to death.

"Okay, okay. Fine. *Aaagh!* But here. Let me do this. I'll tie this around here and you can perch on top of it. Okay?" I took Steffanie's sweatpants and tied them around my opposite shoulder and under my arm. "Here. Move right over here."

I convinced him to climb onto my other shoulder. Afterward, his beak went right back under his wing. If I was going to free him, I realized I'd have to paddle back to the entrance. Just as I thought this, a light flickered behind me.

I turned my head swiftly. It was a torchlight, coming from the passage to the left. The flicker was moving away. Someone had heard me talking to the bird. I turned off my flashlight. With it off, I could see the torchlight more clearly. It continued fading in the other direction.

I started down the tunnel. After a short distance, the torchlight seemed to brighten. It was no longer moving. I decided it must be a different torch. A stationary torch. I walked a little farther and proved my own hunch. But then I stopped.

There were statues all around me in the chamber. Idols! They stood against the chamber walls, like totems designed to frighten off trespassers. One idol had the head of a lion, another a jackal, another was shaped like a crocodile, and the last one had a head like an eagle. Each carving was intense—eyes cruel and jaws snarling. My first impulse was to turn around and get out of there. Someone obviously did not want visitors.

I heard footsteps. Another torch—the original torch—flashed again in the tunnel ahead. The footsteps didn't sound like an adult. They sounded like a child.

"Hello?" I called out.

The torch continued moving away. The realization that it was a child reassured me. I continued on, still keeping my own light switched off.

"Hello!" I called out again more loudly.

I smelled smoke. After another fifty feet, a new chamber opened to my view. At last, I'd come face-to-face with the residents of the cave. The area was fairly well furnished with awnings, bedding, food, and many other comforts, including pots and utensils. It was well lit by torches. There was a neatly stacked pile of wood and a small campfire, the smoke ascending into lofty cavern vaults. Six or seven people pressed close together under a canopy in the background. Among them was the child whose footsteps I'd heard, still holding the torch. It was a boy with short, dark hair. The other people were mostly women. But standing only a few yards in front of me in a defiant posture was a man who looked to be in his early to mid-thirties. He had a roundish face and a pointy chin, accentuated by a short beard. He held another torch—as well as a knife. Just behind him was an older gentleman. His wardrobe rang alarm buzzers inside me. He wore a bright, purple and black cloak with yellow and red seams, just like the officers in Mardon's army, but much fancier. The yellow seams looked like embroidered gold. His whole body was decorated with jewels and rings. Like other men in Nimrod's ranks, he also had a squared-off beard eight inches long that hung down from his face, and his hair was tied back behind his head.

The younger man was my immediate concern. After all, he had the weapon. "Who are you?" the younger man demanded. "Why have you come here?"

"I mean you no harm," I said. "I'm unarmed. My name is Harry. I'm just passing through."

"You passed through the quadrangle of the gods—Elkenah, Libnah, Mahmackrah, and Korash. Do you not realize the curse? Are you not afraid?"

"Uh—I . . . I don't know those gods. And I don't believe in idols."

The younger man looked incensed by this, but the older man stepped forward and asked, "Are you an agent for the king? Surely you followed me here yesterday when I brought provisions to my wife."

I shook my head. "No. I didn't follow anyone."

"No one else knows this cave."

"I came here by unusual means. I swear, I don't know who you are."

"He's lying!" the younger man accused. "*Everyone* in Shinar knows the robes of the king's chancellor, Terah, son of Nahor."

Terah, son of Nahor. The younger man was right. I *did* know who he was. Or at least I'd heard of him. This was an unexpected twist. It was astounding! Was this the chancellor whom Boath had told us about? Could this really be the notorious father of Abraham? Was this the man who'd supposedly betrayed his household by allowing his son to be killed by the king? And yet if he were truly an accessory to murdering his own flesh and blood, why was he hiding his wife in this cave?

"That falcon on your shoulder," said Terah. "I *know* it. I recognize the strap on its leg. It is Rafa, the spy-bird of Casluchim, the king's assassin."

"Then the man is also an assassin!" charged the younger man. "He has come to kill us!"

"No!" I insisted. "It's not true. The king's assassins are actually trying to kill *me!* I threw a rock and knocked this bird out of the air. I promise you, I'm not here to cause you any trouble. I'm only trying to reach a place deeper inside this cavern. If I were an assassin, why would I have come in here unarmed?"

They mulled this over, then Terah asked, "Why would the king's assassins be hunting *you?*"

"Because I was their prisoner," I replied. "I escaped last night."

"Then you are Nimrod's enemy?" asked Terah.

I wondered how I should answer this. He was the king's chancellor, and yet he was obviously hiding from the king—or least hiding his wife, part of his family, and perhaps a few of his servants. It seemed to me that I could get burned either way, so I settled on the truth.

"I wasn't his enemy three days ago," I explained. "But I guess I am now. His son, Prince Mardon, kidnapped my sister. He's taking her with him to Babel."

Terah grunted. "That sounds like Mardon. One day he will be far more dangerous than Nimrod. By what means were you brought to this cave?"

I hesitated, then I decided to confess all. "I was brought by the Spirit of the Lord—through this." I brought the stone out of my pocket.

Terah came forward a little and looked at the stone in my hand. He then looked up at me. "A Urim?"

I nodded. "Or a Thummim. I'm not really sure. Maybe it's just a plain seerstone."

He studied me a moment longer, then said, "I believe you, Harry."

The younger man scoffed in protest. "You *believe* him, Father?"

"Yes, Haran," said Terah. "You can tell by looking at him that he is no assassin."

"But we cannot let him go," said Haran. "He will tell them that he has seen us. He will give us away to spare his own life!"

"I have no desire to cause you harm," I repeated. "I don't care who you are or why you're here—"

"We are here because some say my father betrayed the king," Haran explained. "There is a great reward for telling what you have seen. You expect us to believe that you are not tempted?"

"If I wanted a reward, I'd have run back to my boat the second I saw you. I assure you, I just want to do what I came here to do."

"You're overreacting, Haran," said Terah, sounding conciliatory. "No reward has been issued for us. The king has sent no assassins. I did not betray him. I fulfilled his request. Soon he will accept this, and so will the entire world. Those who have spoken against me will repent. This misunderstanding will be cleared up for always."

I looked into Terah's eyes. Was he confessing to the awful crime that Boath had accused him of committing? "But . . . you didn't kill him, did you?" I asked. "Your son is still alive, right?"

They gawked at me. *Oh, boy.* I wish I could have learned when to keep my mouth shut. The statement also drew the attention of one of the women at the back. She arose and started walking slowly forward, her eyes full of hope.

Haran took one step closer to me, the knife still firmly in his grip. "I thought you said you didn't *know* my father."

"I—I don't," I said. "I mean, I wouldn't have known him on sight. But I heard the story—"

"What did you hear?" Terah demanded.

"Just that you . . . that the king wanted to kill your son, and that you . . . that you took gold and did as Nimrod requested. It was just a story I overheard while I was imprisoned."

"Who told you that my son still lived?"

"I just . . . find it impossible to believe that any man could allow the murder of his own infant child."

"He knows more than he's saying," said Haran. "He's been lying all along! He's Nimrod's spy!"

This was getting out of hand. If I were them, I'd have probably thought the same thing. There had to be a way out of this. Maybe my idea about turning tail and running wasn't so bad.

The woman, now standing beside Terah, spoke next, her eyes pleading. "Do you know where my son is?"

Terah grabbed the woman's shoulder. "Emetelai, no!"

I realized Terah had tried to deceive me. He'd wanted me to believe, like everyone else, that his son had been murdered. But the jig was up. The mother suspected that I knew something, and nothing could have kept her silent.

"Four months ago my son was born here, in this cave," said Emetelai. "But twelve days ago I sent him off with my nursemaid to the city of Shem. Have you seen him?"

"Now we *have* to kill him," said Haran. "He knows the truth."

"He knew it already," said Emetelai, still looking at my face. "He knows where Abram is. He knows his destiny. I can sense it. Please tell us. You are a stranger, but I feel strongly that God has brought you to me."

"Is it true?" asked Terah, finally giving in. "Do you know the whereabouts of our son?"

Wow, I thought. Maybe the woman was right. I felt a strange, but consoling feeling inside me. Maybe the Lord *had* brought me here.

"I don't know his whereabouts," I said. "But I know that he lives. And I know that he'll be fine."

"How do you know this?" asked Terah.

"Did you speak to my nursemaid, Amthelo?" Emetelai pleaded. "Did you meet her caravan?"

"No," I said. "It was nothing like that. I only know that God is watching over him. Abram   will be a great man. A great prophet."

"Who are you *really?*" asked Terah mysteriously. "You say that you do not believe in the gods of the four winds. What *do* you believe? Your appearance . . . the way you are dressed. Are you . . . ?"

Not again, I thought. "I'm not an angel, if that's what you're wondering." Then I became thoughtful and added, "But I think . . . I may be . . . a *messenger.*"

It was starting to make sense. I'd felt prompted to follow that torchlight. Maybe I'd been brought here just so that I could speak comfort to a mother's heart. Terah and Haran didn't give me particularly good feelings. But Emetelai was different. God loved Abraham's mother very much. I sensed that Abraham's survival was not Terah's doing; it was the actions of this humble woman. She accepted my words, and her eyes were moist.

"Then Abram will arrive safely in Salem," she said confidently. "He will reach the house of Father Shem."

"We are grateful to you," said Terah, sounding a little uncertain. "When I arrived yesterday, I did not know that my wife had sent my son away. Soon I hope that he can return, but until Nimrod is convinced that the child he killed was mine, his heart will not be softened. Abram will have to remain with the patriarchs."

I felt sickened. A child had died? *Whose* child? This I felt, was Terah's part of the scheme. He'd sacrificed *another* child—someone else's infant boy—to save his own neck. Somewhere a poor servant or peasant woman was grieving to the depths of her soul. This was how Terah had fooled the king.

"I'm sure you will see him again," I told the mother. But my emotions were mixed. I'd read the book of Abraham several times. One day I knew that Terah would try again to have his son killed.

Haran still looked distrusting and irritated. But Terah said to me, "We will remember your visit here. In honor of your reassuring words to my wife, I will make an offering to the gods of the four winds. I will see to it that from this day forward the falcon on your shoulder becomes a symbol of eternal messengers from Shagreel. He is the true god of the sun, not Nimrod, son of Cush."

I shook my head. "No. It wasn't any sun god that sent me. It was the God of Noah. The God of Enoch. It was our Father in Heaven."

Terah looked at me blankly, then he nodded. "So it was."

He didn't understand, but Emetelai understood, and a pained smile climbed her cheeks.

Terah continued, "You said that you were passing through on your way to the deeper part of the cavern. Is there anything that I can offer you?"

"Perhaps you can tell me which way to go," I said. "I have to find a certain chamber—a chamber that emits lights."

The boy at the back blurted out, "*I* know the way."

"Be silent, Nahor," said one of the other women.

"No, Lahazib," said Terah. "Let our son speak. Tell the messenger what you know."

Apparently Emetelai wasn't Terah's only wife. He'd also brought *another* wife to this dank place.

Nahor, who I presumed was seven or eight, came forward and asked, "Are you seeking to row beyond the lair of the dragon?"

My eyes widened. "The lair of *what?*"

"The dragon who lives in the cavern lake. I have rowed there in my father's boat. I have seen the golden light that shines from the tunnel beyond. But I did not dare to go there. The lake was disturbed. The dragon was in the water."

"What does this dragon look like?" I asked apprehensively.

The boy shrugged. "Like any other dragon."

What was next, I wondered? Was I going to have to battle space aliens?

Terah interjected, "You must excuse my son. The child has been here four months. His imagination is vivid. You need not fear dragons in these caves. Dragons are only found in the great deep." He turned to Nahor. "And even if there *were* dragons, this man is a messenger of the gods. He has nothing to fear from man or beasts."

Apparently these people really believed in dragons.

Terah continued, "One of the reasons that I had my son, Haran, hide my wife's boat farther upriver was to keep Nahor from pursuing any other dangerous adventures."

That answered the question of whose boat I'd found. Still, I suspected that the *main* reason Terah had taken Emetelai's boat away was to keep his family imprisoned.

Nahor became insistent. "But there *is* a dragon living in there. I heard his roar. He is there."

I couldn't worry about this. I had to reach my destination. I asked Nahor, "Will you tell me how to reach this lake with the golden light?"

Nahor looked at his father, who finally nodded his consent.

I bid farewell. Little Nahor took his torch and led the way back through the tunnel. The bird—Rafa—fluttered a little as I started to walk, but then he stuck his beak back into his feathers.

When we arrived back at the boat, Nahor pointed up the dark channel.

"You must row through there," he explained. "There is a tunnel where the ceiling is very low. You may think that you cannot fit. But if you lay down in your boat, you will. After a while, it will open up. The stones on the walls will start to glow. You can follow those stones all the way to the lake. If you are seeking the golden light, you will see it from there."

I was starting to think I was in a Sinbad movie. Glowing walls, golden light, sea dragons. The boy's description seemed sincere, especially considering my experiences with Frost Cave. The stones on the walls sounded a lot like the Rainbow Room, and the golden light might have easily been a swirling pillar of energy. It sounded exactly like what I was looking for.

"Thank you," I said to Nahor.

I said good-bye to the half brother of Abraham and continued on. My sleep deprivation for the last thirty-six hours was starting to wear on me. I convinced Rafa to reclaim his perch on top of the backpack.

I decided not to release the falcon yet. For the sake of Emetelai and the others, I couldn't risk that he might lead the trackers here. I had no idea what I would do with the bird when I reached my destination. Then again, what was I going to do with *myself*? What would this mission entail once I passed through the time conduit?

I preferred not to think about it. I feared my little mind would start to implode. I still couldn't believe I was attempting this. There were so many questions still remaining. Questions that seemed unanswerable.

I could only hope the Lord would continue to help me every step of the way through my use of the stone. If it failed—that is, if *I* failed—I feared it might create an uncontainable breach, a catastrophic ripple, or an irreversible paradox. I sincerely feared that I might destroy the fabric of time.

NOTES TO CHAPTER 12:

The story of Terah switching his child with the child of a servant is found in Jasher 8:33–34. Other statements about Nimrod's effort to slay the infant according to the prophecy of his soothsayers are alluded to in other texts. Scripture revealed by modern revelation also attests to Terah's chronic idolatry and his additional efforts to have Abraham killed (see Abr. 1:7, 16–17, 30). Such facts are not mentioned in the Bible, but *are* supported by numerous apocryphal works. (Terah's idolatry is mentioned in the *Book of Jasher*, *Book of the Bee*, *Book of the Rolls*, *Book of the Cave of Treasures*, *Syriac Commentary on Genesis*, *Jubilees*, *Pirqe de Rabbi Eliezer*, and many others.) A vague reference to Abraham's fathers serving other gods is given in Joshua 24.2, but without details or specifics. Terah's attempts to kill Abraham are mentioned in *Book of Jasher*, Falasha Story, Rahsi: Regarding Genesis, *Story of Abraham . . . with Nimrod*, and others, as well as in the Moslem Koran.

The concept of Abraham being born in a cave is a common theme of many apocryphal texts. This was purported to be part of the strategy of saving him from Nimrod. Other traditions mention Abraham being tutored or nurtured in his early years in the house of Noah or Shem.

The exact composition of the family of Terah, including the names of his wives, varies from manuscript to manuscript. The tradition is quite consistent, however, that Haran was a young man by the time Abraham was born, which may be in contradiction to the account in the Bible, which states that *"Terah lived seventy years, and begat Abram, Nahor, and Haran"* (Gen. 11:26). Unless we propose that these three brothers are triplets (which is never attested in any apocryphal work) we can probably assume that the correct rendering of this verse would be that by the time Terah was seventy years old, he had begat all of his sons, Abram, Nahor, and Haran. It is probably also reasonable to assume that Abram was the youngest brother and that this pivotal seventieth year of Terah's life is Abram's birthdate. Several sources report that at the time of Abram's birth, Haran was thirty-two.

Numerous apocryphal works claim that Terah's sons were born of different mothers. As already mentioned in the notes to chapter 5, Abram's mother is given a variety of names. There is no specific reference to the fact that Terah practiced polygamy, but since we know that many of the other patriarchs did, it seems reasonable that he also practiced it. It's also possible that an earlier wife or wives passed away and Terah remarried. Possible names given to Terah's other wives include Lahazib, Tahuitha, and Juna.

CHAPTER TWELVE

Mary

Even hours after I had discovered that the sword of Akish was missing, my mind continued to be tormented with anxiety. While Mahonri, Jared, and Moriancumr tended to the provisions brought from Salem, Pagag and Jacom, along with many others, including Joshua and Rebecca, helped to scour the area around the pool and stream for any sign of the silver blade. Even Jared's grandfather, Ophir, helped in the search. But despite all our efforts, absolutely no clues were discovered.

I looked at everyone with suspicion. If Pagag had not been beside me the entire time when I went to greet Mahonri, I would have immediately suspected him. Even knowing that he'd remained with me, I wondered if somehow he'd found a way to move it while my back was turned. I tried to remember who had led the way as we departed from the pool. Could he have tossed it into the water? That seemed impossible. I would have heard the splash. Besides, several of the young men had searched the water thoroughly. Could Pagag have conspired with another of his brothers? Oh, this was excruciating! It was awful to feel such suspicion and mistrust.

"We must question every last person in the clan," I told Ophir. "We must search the entire encampment."

"We will do so," said Ophir, his wrinkled forehead furrowed and perplexed. "But I cannot believe that anyone in my kinship would steal something like that. We have no need of gold or silver here. The Lord provides us with all that we require."

"You don't understand," I said to him. "They wouldn't steal it to sell it. They would steal it to own it. They'd steal it for—"

I was about to say "power." But how would I have explained what I meant? He was already looking at me with deep-felt concern. Even pity. I felt ashamed. I was trembling every few minutes. Was this what it felt like to suffer a withdrawal from narcotics?

I considered all the possibilities. I even wondered if Joshua or Rebecca had taken it. Particularly Joshua. I wondered if somehow he had sneaked away from the others in the meadow. The pool was between the meadow and the encampment. But Joshua vehemently denied it. Everyone denied it. It was almost as if a stranger had taken it—someone not of this clan. Could it have been stolen by one of the king's soldiers? Might one of them have backtracked and followed us here? No one claimed to have seen strangers about, so I had to reject this idea. The thief was in our midst. I felt sure of it. But who?

I overcame my reluctance and decided to tell Mahonri and Jared about the sword. I wasn't quite sure why I felt any resistance at all. Was the sword still influencing me? Was this part of the withdrawal? I pushed such anxieties aside and confronted Jared, Mahonri, and their father, Moriancumr, that night in front of Mahonri's tent. Jahareh was there. Becky and Joshua were also present, along with Pagag. Little Abram was inside the tent in the care of Jahareh's oldest daughter, Setra.

"It's an evil sword," I explained.

They looked at me strangely, almost blankly.

I added, "It was cursed by a powerful sorcerer."

"A sorcerer?" Jared repeated. He looked over at his father and brother.

"What is this sorcerer's name?" asked Mahonri.

"Is he one of the magicians of Nimrod?" asked Moriancumr.

"I—I don't know," I said. "But his name is Akish. And I know he wants to use the power of the sword to conquer and kill. I saw him use it to murder a man in cold blood. I heard him utter evil words."

Mahonri was thoughtful, his finger caressing his beard. "Why would you be carrying such a thing?" he asked.

Joshua answered, "We wanted to keep it away from him. We wanted to keep anyone wicked from finding it and being able to use it."

"We wanted to destroy it," added Rebecca. "We hoped we could throw it into the depths of the sea."

"But I saw you using it to fight the soldiers," Pagag said to me.

I lowered my head in shame. "I know it. But don't you see? That's proof of its powers. I'm no warrior. I have never learned how to use a sword to fight. It endowed me with the ability to do what I did."

Mahonri remained thoughtful, each word spoken only after great consideration. "I am sure that the father of lies can work great sorceries among the children of men. But such things are the tools of the wicked against the wicked. They cannot harm the righteous, not unless they succumb to its temptation."

"I'm afraid . . . I may have done so," I said, my eyes filling with tears of remorse. "I was only trying to protect the children. Protect little Abram. It found my weakness, and I believe it influenced the circumstances in ways that made it more likely that I would give in."

"It is no flaw to protect innocent life," said Jahareh sympathetically.

"But I made a choice. There was a moment—a terrifying moment—when I chose to rely upon it, rather than relying upon my faith in God. And ever since that moment . . . things have been growing more and more . . . confused." I started trembling again. Jahareh came closer to offer comfort.

"I should've never given it over to you," said Joshua, sounding critical.

Everyone looked at him curiously.

"You also carried this sword?" asked Moriancumr.

"Only for a day," I said in his defense.

Mahonri asked him, "Did you give in to its voice?"

"No," said Josh vigorously. "Never. I didn't make any 'choice' like Mary. I never relied on it."

"What about the attack of the lions and tigers?" said Becky.

"That was different," said Josh. "They were animals. I never wanted to hurt anyone. I never wanted to hurt a person."

"How many animals were killed?" asked Jared.

"Two or three," said Josh.

"Try six or seven," said Rebecca.

Josh looked a little embarrassed, but he continued to express discontent. "I just should have kept carrying it. I sure wouldn't have lost it. I wouldn't have let it out of my sight for anything."

Mahonri's eyes seemed to be searching Joshua's heart. At last he said, "I think this sword may have taken hold of you more than you know, young one."

Joshua's shoulders sank. I think he revered Mahonri a great deal. Such words were painful for him to hear. Joshua made no reply.

"I hope it's gone for good," said Rebecca. "I never wanted to bring it with us in the first place."

"You may search for it again tomorrow," said Jared. "But the day after tomorrow, we will leave for Salem with little Abram. In the morning my son, Jacom, and several of his cousins are riding to Salem ahead of us to announce our coming. I hope that this joyous occasion is not tarnished by such an evil thing."

"If we find it, I suggest that it be delivered to Melchizedek," said Moriancumr. "He will keep it in his house in Salem, or he will destroy it, according to his wisdom and according to God's will."

I nodded, though a part of me was repulsed by the idea of seeing it destroyed.

"Very well then," said Mahonri, rising to go into the tent with Jahareh. "In a few moments we will call for prayer."

Jared squeezed Joshua's shoulder—a gesture of friendship and support. Then he and his father also departed, leaving us alone with Pagag.

"Tomorrow I will help you again to look for it," Pagag told me. "But I'm starting to believe that a wanderer may have taken it. Or perhaps it was taken by God Himself. Has this occurred to you?"

I mulled over Pagag's suggestion for about three seconds, then dismissed it with a shake of my head. The sword was still near. I could feel it.

I stared Joshua straight in the eye and asked again, "Did you take it?"

"No!" he retorted. "Mary, how would I have—?"

"All right," I interrupted. "I'm sorry." I sighed wearily and shuddered once more. "I'm just . . . just so tired.

It was a long night of tossing and turning. I felt that I could still hear the voices of my loved ones, only now they were full of hatred. All those who I cared for most in this world despised my very presence. Harry was among them. He despised me most of all.

Thank heaven for the dawn. By morning I was starting to feel somewhat improved. Even relieved. I felt the spell of the sword might have been starting to abate. Like the last two mornings, the smell of wildflowers wafted over my face. Pagag had come again in the night. Today's bouquet was particularly ambitious. It contained every color of the sunrise—*reds and violets and yellows. I sat up and smelled the petals close to my face. Whether or not Pagag had intended for these flowers to represent a new beginning for me, that was how I took them. I believed everything was going to be all right.*

The search for the sword continued while Jared and the others prepared to return to Salem. I must admit, I did not search as vigorously as I had intended. Something within me began to fear that I might actually find it. Instead, I was more inclined to spend time with little Abram and the women of the clan. Tomorrow I was going to Salem, and four days later I would present this child to Melchizedek. The pangs of separation were setting in already. Odd how attached I'd become to this tiny bundle of energy over the past few days. The happiness of having come so recently from the presence of Heavenly Father was always upon his face. It radiated in his little eyes, and in his indomitable smile, and in the sound of his cooing.

Pagag found me late that afternoon and announced that the day's search had been unsuccessful. His hair was wet. He wore only some dripping trousers and a coarse towel around his shoulders.

"I searched the pool again with my brother, Ethem," he said. "We still found nothing. Do you continue to dismiss the idea that God may have taken it to spare us all from its influence?"

I was barely paying attention. I didn't want to think about the sword anymore. Abram seemed fascinated with my lips and took great pleasure in trying to pull them off my face. With each attempt I made a surprised face and caused him to make a delightful squeal. At last I focused on Pagag's question and said, "I don't know. I'm not sure of anything." Then I said, "But I still feel God leaves men to deal with the evil that they have created."

"Have you already forgotten the Flood?" said Pagag. "In this case God dealt with it quite directly. My father feels that the kingdom of Nimrod is just as ripe for destruction as the old kingdoms before the Flood. He says that the Lord will act swiftly, and there will be an upheaval unlike any that has ever been manifest on the land. The tongues of men will be confounded. No longer will they be able to understand one another's speech. I do not understand how it will happen, but according to my father, the Lord has decreed it."

"Has the Lord also told him when *it will happen?" I asked.*

"All that my father will say is that it will be soon. My father and uncle have prayed earnestly that our kinship might be spared from this confusion of tongues, and they believe that their prayer has been heard. Nimrod has kept the people from settling in all parts of the world, according to the Lord's command. Nearly all of the children of Noah are presently gathered in Shinar, but the Lord will scatter them far and wide. This is why my father has been preparing our people for departure. That is why my father and grandfather have brought seeds of every kind of grain and fruit from Salem. We have been commanded to journey into the valley northward where the Lord will give us farther instruction."

"Do you know where it is that you are going?" I asked.

He shook his head. *"Only that it will be a choice land above all the lands of the earth. And that the Lord will make us a mighty nation—greater than any other nation that has ever been. Even greater than the kingdom of Nimrod. That is the Lord's promise because of the faith of my father and uncle."*

I smiled at Pagag warmly. He seemed delightfully caught up in the events of the future. *"It sounds like a wonderful destiny. A great adventure."*

Pagag sat in front of me, now looking sullen and vulnerable. He seemed unable to look into my eyes as he said, *"It will be far more wonderful if you are with me, Mary. If you would become . . . my wife."*

Slowly, he looked up to see my face. There were tears in the corners of my eyes. I turned away, no longer able to look at him.

"I could make you very happy, Mary," he persisted. *"I would not rest until you were the happiest woman on earth. We could have many children, and they would all have dark eyes, full lips, and flowing dark hair like you."*

"I can't," I whispered.

His countenance darkened. *"Is it still him?"* he asked gruffly. *"This man who preaches the gospel in distant lands?"*

"Of course *it's him,"* I said. *"I already told you. I love* him, *Pagag. I gave my heart to him."*

"But I give my heart to you!*"* he insisted. *"And I love* you.*"*

I was shaking my head. A tear carved a path down my cheeks. I could think of no reply.

Suddenly Pagag rose up. He said abruptly, "He's dead, Mary! You must face it! And even if he were alive, how would he ever find you? Even if he lives, do you think you will ever see him again?"

This last question cut deepest of all. It felt as if he had reached in and torn my heart from my chest. I couldn't listen anymore. I couldn't sit here. Pagag's sister, Setra, came out of the main tent. I arose and placed Abram in her arms. She took him, her face full of curiosity and confusion.

"Mary, wait——!" said Pagag.

I fled through the tents.

"Mary!" he continued. "I'm sorry! Forgive me!"

I ran beyond the limits of the encampment. I didn't stop until I'd reached the stream and the pool. I dropped to my knees, my sobs choking in my throat. It hurt so badly. Was Pagag right? Was Harry dead? Would I never see him? I couldn't conceive it. I refused to believe it.

I was twenty-two years old. I was beyond the years that most women in Pella, or indeed anywhere in Judea, would have married. I was far beyond the ages of my sisters when they had married.

Pagag was the son of Mahonri Moriancumr, the brother of Jared. Many might have wondered if a girl could ever hope to do better. But one fact remained. I didn't love him! I absolutely did not love him! I loved Harry! Oh, how I loved him. How I missed him.

A part of me wanted to curl up and expire. It crossed my mind to plead with the Lord, but I rejected it. This was a prayer that the Lord apparently refused to hear. But what was I saying? Prayer was all I had! I'd never had such thoughts before. Where were they coming from? *My Father in Heaven was the only one who would listen. Again I felt desperately ashamed. I was kin to my Lord and Savior. People should have expected better of me. I expected better of myself.*

"I'm sorry, Heavenly Father," I wept. "I do *want to pray. Please tell me, Father—where is he? Will I see him again? Is he seeking to find me even now?" With greater apprehension, I prayed, "Does he really want me, Heavenly Father? Does he* love *me?"*

No answers came into my mind. I suppose I might have expected this. Not long ago my faith had faltered—if only for that one brief instant. Now I was reaping the fruits of that failed moment.

Why should I be complaining? I was just a frivolous female. In my world of Judea in 70 A.D. *a girl did not decide in matters of love.*

Husbands were chosen for *her. Parents, relatives, and those much older and wiser decided issues of matrimony. For a hasty moment I despised the modern world of Harry Hawkins. Modern sentiments had seduced me into believing that love was a matter decided by the heart. In 70 A.D. the system had been far superior. After all, the heart faced enough pain and agony in mortality. Why compound it with the heartbreak of love? In my world a girl knew her* responsibility. *Responsibility was more important than love. In fact, love was the* reward *of meeting one's responsibilities.*

Again I felt the temptation to stop praying. But I didn't listen. I would never listen to that temptation again. Instead, I prayed with even greater fervency. But I no longer prayed for what I *desired. I prayed to know what the Lord desired* for *me. And I didn't stop. I was still praying long after the sun had gone into the west. I wasn't sure if I had received an answer to my question, but eventually I felt that wonderful, familiar feeling. It pierced my heart and spoke comfort to my aching soul. This only made me sob more. Again, I felt that love that had sustained me for every day of my life. Through so much sorrow and so many trials.*

And perhaps I did *receive an answer. It didn't come to me in words, but it simmered warmly in my thoughts. I felt that I should wait to make any decisions regarding my destiny. I believed that the Lord would reveal to me at a future moment the critical course of my life. At least I hoped I was interpreting it correctly. Yes, I was sure. This was what Heavenly Father wanted me to do.*

Tomorrow we would travel to Salem with baby Abram. In a few days I would meet the King of Salem. Maybe Shem would have additional answers for me. This notion filled me with an even brighter ray of hope. Perhaps Melchizedek would tell us how we might return home, and how I might reunite with my love.

I would not have the sword to protect me on this journey, but for the first time in days, I felt that this would be preferable. I didn't miss it. The Lord had purged almost all of my desire for it. I felt free. Only one problem remained, and one preponderant question. Who had really taken it?

And what evil did this person have planned?

NOTES TO CHAPTER 12:

The Book of Mormon tells us that "Jared came forth with his brother and their families, with some others and their families, from the great tower, at the time the Lord confounded the language of the people" (Ether 1:33).

It's unclear whether they began their journey before or after the languages were actually confounded, although it should be pointed out that the exact *process* by which the Adamic language was confounded is unknown. If it was a gradual process, then this confounding may have been well underway before the brother of Jared prayed to the Lord asking Him to spare them from its effects. If it was a singular event, then we must presume that Jared and his brother were forewarned by revelation and thus prayed for the Lord's mercy beforehand. It would also be interesting to learn if this confounding of languages meant that every single person on earth was confounded, or whether it only applied to various families or kinships. However, the Book of Mormon may answer this. Jared's fear that his family might find themselves not understanding one another implies that this phenomenon affected every individual, or at least very small groups.

The Lord commanded Jared to "gather together thy flocks, both male and female, of every kind; and also of the seed of the earth of every kind" (Ether 1:41). We know that as a result of this command Jared and his family and friends laid snares to catch fowls, prepared a vessel for transporting fish, and also took with them swarms of honey bees or "descret" (see Ether 2:2–3). Some have speculated that it became Jared's responsibility to entirely populate the New World with animal life, almost as if he were a lesser equivalent of Noah. However, this may not have been necessary. We know that at least a century elapsed after the Flood before the lands were divided. In that period of time many different animals—and certainly all kinds of birds and insects—could have made the necessary migrations across the super continent. We know for instance that in the New World the Jaredites had elephants, along with horses, asses, and of course cureloms and cumoms (Ether 9:19). No mention is made of Jared transporting elephants, or other large species, such as elk or buffalo, and certainly there is no mention of dangerous predators or reptiles. These species, it seems, were already there.

However, because the Lord commanded them to transport so many animals and seeds, the Jaredites probably did introduce at least some new species and crops to the New World. It's incredible to think that all of these animals, seeds, food, supplies, and people (Jared, Mahonri, their families, and twenty-two others), fit into eight sealed barges with only two stones apiece for light. Such a feat staggers the mind. It also serves to remind us that if we seek to accomplish an extraordinary task, our first reliance, above all else, should be on the Lord.

CHAPTER THIRTEEN

Harry

"Okay, Harry," I said to myself, breathing deeply. *"Get a grip."*

Just as the boy, Nahor, had described it, two or three hundred yards after I started rowing I found a tight passageway that branched off the main channel. The ceiling was only about three feet higher than the water level, and according to my flashlight it became even narrower farther in. My worst fear since childhood had always been the fear of being buried alive. The phobia had taken root when I was trapped by a collapsed wall in Jacobugath at the age of ten. So be it. This was another chance to conquer it.

I rowed right up to the entrance and started to pull myself inside. Rafa, who'd pretended he was asleep during most of our journey through the watery cavern, made a squawk. He climbed down off the backpack and perched in the bottom of the boat. A moment later there were only a few inches between myself and the stone overhead. I was forced to lie on my back, pulling the boat along by finding hand-grips on the ceiling. At one point the roof was so low that the rim of the boat scraped. I took several deep breaths to calm my nerves.

To bypass the lowest point I actually had to push on the ceiling and press the boat down deeper into the water. I did this several times before I was able to scrape past. It was like being trapped inside a coffin. Maybe I should have climbed into the water, but then there wouldn't have been enough weight in the boat to get under the low points. I continued on, having faith in Nahor's assurance that the channel would soon open up.

A moment later the height of the ceiling increased. I was able to sit up and use the oar again to propel myself along. The falcon climbed back onto my backpack. After I'd gone a short distance farther, the stones along the walls and ceiling began to glow with a phosphorescent whiteness. The colors changed the farther I went. One tunnel was almost blue and another bright orange. Finally the colors began to mingle, like the walls of the Rainbow Room. The last long passage was like rowing through a train tunnel illuminated by Christmas lights. Steffanie's flashlight was no longer necessary. Even Rafa became excited, flapping his wings as if he greatly desired to take flight.

Beyond the passage the cave opened up into a large lake, maybe twice the size of my high school gym. Water was dripping everywhere. The ceiling was a labyrinth of shafts and vaults. A rainbow-like glow continued to illuminate the area, but not as brightly as the tunnel. I hesitated before entering the lake and peered across the water. There was the golden light, just as Nahor had promised. It emitted from a thin shaft at the water's edge. This shaft curved around and entered an unseen chamber. The golden light had a hypnotizing quality to it. I felt certain that inside that chamber was a phenomenon very similar to the swirling pillar in Frost Cave. I'd almost reached it at last—my transportation to Gidgiddonihah and the key to rescuing my loved ones.

Yet I procrastinated, carefully studying the surface of the water. I could see several feet into its depths. The wall of the cave curled back underneath, revealing a dark and murky universe. It surprised me to see a school of white-colored fish swimming past the boat—the first evidence of subterranean life. It was impossible to tell how deep the water was.

I stared again at the golden glow. I couldn't shake the feeling that somehow Rafa and I were not alone. Was it my imagination, or was the surface of the lake a little choppier than before? Maybe the arrival of my boat had added to the general choppiness that was created by all the dripping water. Still, this hardly seemed to justify the strange series of waves lapping against my canvas tub. The feeling here was very spooky. I understood why Nahor had been reluctant to row over to that golden tunnel.

As if taunting me for my fears, Rafa took flight. He flapped around in the open space. I think the falcon was hoping one of those shafts in the ceiling might offer it a passageway to daylight, but none of the vaults appeared to go up that high. Nevertheless, my confidence increased. *If the bird isn't worried,* I told myself, *then why should I be worried?* Stupid logic, I know. Being in the water wasn't exactly the equivalent of flying around in the air.

Despite my confidence, my muscles remained tense with anticipation. I paddled steadily, doing my best not to make any great disturbance in the water. If anything, the bird was making more ruckus than I was, fluttering around the ceiling, diving and swooping over my head. It finally found a perch about fifty feet above and paused to groom its feathers.

As I reached the center of the lake, something unusual occurred. About thirty feet off my port side a ripple appeared in the lake's surface. The wave caused my boat to wobble. Adrenaline gushed into my bloodstream. Whatever had made that ripple, it was *big*. My first impulse was to freeze—stop rowing, stop agitating the water. My second impulse—a much *wiser* impulse—was to start rowing like a madman.

After I'd made it about three-fourths of the way across, another ripple appeared fifteen feet off starboard. Whatever this thing was, it was circling me. *It was getting ready to strike!* My mind went blank with terror. There was a *dragon* in the water. But there were no such things as dragons, right? Then again, I wouldn't have thought that there were mammoths in ancient America either.

The tunnel with the golden light loomed just ten yards ahead. Just inside of it was a ledge where I could climb ashore—if I made it that far. A third ripple disturbed the surface just ahead. It was between me and the tunnel. Something broke the water. A fin? The top of a head? I couldn't tell. But it swam on, leaving the way clear.

Still paddling like crazy on both sides of this awful tub, I entered the narrow channel and rammed the front end of my boat into the rocky shore, knocking me forward. I turned back and looked. The surface about twenty feet out into the lake rippled again. Then there was a small blip in the water created by a tail or a fin. The unseen creature seemed to dive into the abyss. My heart and lungs were working at full capacity. I'd made it! I'd survived. Whatever was out there, it had delayed its attack just long enough to let me escape. Not a very efficient predator, I thought. If this was a movie, I might've felt gypped. Instead, I heaved a sigh of eternal thanks.

Through the narrow opening that led out into the lake I could still see the falcon up on his perch in the ceiling, watching me. I feared this might be the end of our short-lived relationship. But there was no reason to give up quite yet. I wrapped Steff's sweatpants around my forearm. Then I balanced one foot on shore, stuck two fingers in my mouth and let out a high-pitched whistle. I raised up my forearm the way I'd seen them do it on television. The falcon waited a moment, then spread his wings and swooped down off the ceiling. He started flying right toward my arm.

"Whadda ya know," I said to myself. It looked like I had me a bird for a companion.

Just then the lake surface erupted. An enormous reptilian head, its jaws agape and bristling with fangs, surged upward to snatch the falcon in mid-flight. My heart exploded like shattered crystal. A roar filled the cavern, a scream like a train hitting its breaks. In all the splashing I wasn't sure if Rafa had survived, but then he flew out of the chaos. However, the beast was *pursuing* him! Using its pendulous tail, it rocketed forward, snapping in three quick successions as Rafa flapped his wings. The bird entered the gap, but so did the creature's head! Its bright yellow eyes with red pupils were coming *right at me!* My blood froze. As the bird's wings flapped into my face, the dragon's shoulders (if you could call them shoulders) collided with either side of the opening. But was it a dragon? To me it looked more like a dinosaur—a *Mosasaur* to be exact—a thirty-foot monster with the head of a T-Rex, the body of a fish, and a flat, undulating tail like an eel.

The dinosaur chomped down on the back end of my boat. One of my feet was still inside it—as was my backpack! I fell backward as the boat was yanked away from shore. In a last-ditch effort, I lunged for the pack, seizing one of the straps. My chest slipped into the water. The whole floating bathtub was ripped to shreds by those teeth. It lunged again at my head, but again its size prevented it from squeezing into the gap. I scrambled backwards, hugging the pack.

Rafa was flapping on the ground behind me, squawking to high heaven.

In a final lunge, the monster came at me like a crocodile, offering me a full display of all its teeth, and curling my nose hairs with a blast of its foul, fishy breath. My heartbeat rose to a final crescendo. Then, as suddenly as it had appeared, the dragon sank below the surface and made a flip turn, splashing us with its tail and retreating into the murky blackness. My boat looked like a torpedo had hit it. It, too, sank into the gloom.

I took a moment to recover from the shock, then my mind filled with exhilaration. A *dinosaur!* I'd seen a *living dinosaur!* The bird was still going nuts. I think poor Rafa felt he'd had enough psychological trauma for one day. I offered him my arm again, but he acted as if he wanted nothing more to do with me. After I spent several minutes speaking soothing words to him, the falcon at last climbed onto my shoulder. I stroked the back of his neck.

"Now see?" I told him. "That's *two* adventures we've gone through together. I think we're gonna get along just fine."

Without a boat, there was no direction to go but forward. This was perfectly fine, because the golden light was glowing more brightly than ever. My adrenaline was still percolating as I carried my feathered companion and Steffanie's backpack deeper into the tunnel. The golden light grew more intense. I wondered if I might soon feel a pulse of energy, much like the pulses that had struck every seven and a half minutes in Frost Cave, but nothing like that ever occurred. I walked down a long, ascending corridor until I arrived at the source of the light.

The sight was gorgeous, not only for its appearance, but for what it represented. I was here—the point of no return, the final threshold between myself and the unexpected. The light source was a swirling wall of energy—or maybe it was more like a window. If I could have seen the whole thing, it might have looked exactly like the Frost Cave pillar, but at the moment it was hard to tell since it was encased in rock. Its color was a warm, reddish gold, like a treasure chest filled with bullion. To reach the window I had to endure a tight squeeze through a triangular-shaped gap. I wouldn't be able to jump into it, like in Frost Cave. I'd have to crawl to its surface, then sort of "inch-worm" into the energy field. Now the question was when.

But this was only the *first* question. There were so many more. *One thing at a time.* I reached into my pocket and found the stone.

I still hadn't fully recovered from my encounter with the dinosaur. I sat back against the wall of the cave and tried to settle my mind. The bird climbed off my shoulder and onto the ground. It continued watching me with great interest, no doubt wondering what in Jupiter's name we were doing here.

I cupped the stone in my hands and sealed my palms around both eyes to block out the light. *When?* I asked in my mind. When should I go?

The answer came immediately. That was also the instruction— *immediately!* This answer startled me. Was I almost late? I'd been hoping to wait a while, gather my wits, maybe rest. I still had so many questions: What would I be facing? What would I do? But such questions would have to be postponed until I reached my destination.

"Okay, Rafa," I said. "Let's go."

The bird tilted his head. *Go where?* he seemed to be asking. I held out my arm. He climbed aboard. I wondered if bringing Rafa was such a smart idea. Last time I'd been shot out of a geyser. At other times I'd been sent over waterfalls. Such a journey could prove fatal to a bird. But he'd made up his mind. Rafa was going along. With the pack's strap around one shoulder, and the falcon perched behind my head, I began crawling toward the golden window.

Inches away from the swirling surface, I said to Rafa, "Ready?"

He made a squawk.

I reached over my head as if to stroke the falcon's neck, then I snatched him around his body and pulled him in tight. He made another squawk, this one much less enthusiastic, and he nipped at my hand. With my other arm I reached into the sparkling light.

My hand seemed to liquefy inside the window. The energy began dragging me in. My molecules made blurry brown lines, candy-striping their way up the window. I heard one last squawk from the bird before my head was drawn inside the swirling energy. The next journey through time had begun.

And what a short journey it was! I was violently thrown, like getting tossed out of a revolving door. My back impacted against a stone wall. The bird fell out of my grasp. He lost a few more tail feathers as he flapped to get away from me. I felt dizzy; there was a reverberation in my ears, and my eyes saw double vision. But after a few seconds everything stabilized.

I took in my surroundings. I was sitting on a damp sheet of stone that sloped slightly downward. It was a cave of some sort, with a ceiling about four feet overhead. The only light source was the swirling energy. Like in ancient Mesopotamia, the pillar was mostly encased in solid rock. But its color was quite different—a purplish hue, like watered-down grape Kool-Aid. The character of this cave was much different from the last one. The air was stodgy and humid; the stones seemed to be perspiring. The falcon was already walking down the tunnel. He looked like he'd finally had enough of me. Life had obviously been much less complicated when he was Mardon's spy.

I started to follow the falcon. I had a strange feeling throughout my body. I knew I hadn't slept in almost forty hours. My adrenaline was pretty much exhausted, but this feeling was different. I couldn't pinpoint it. I felt terribly lightheaded, yet it wasn't the kind of lightheadedness that accompanied sleep deprivation. Then again, I couldn't recall ever staying awake quite this long. I decided to brush off the feeling as a kind of jet lag from passing through the time conduit.

I caught up to the bird and convinced him to climb back onto my arm. I think he did so more out of habit than loyalty. We descended the passageway until we could hear the sound of water. The sound grew in volume until I realized it represented a fairly substantial waterfall. The purplish light from the pillar faded behind us. I took out the flashlight and flicked it on. After another half-minute we arrived at the source of the sound.

The flashlight revealed the waterfall and nothing else. It appeared to be a dead end. The falls rushed down into what looked like a hole in the earth. But as I drew closer, the flashlight beam seemed to penetrate the rushing cascade, shining through to a chamber beyond. This left me little choice. I'd have to go through it. Right now the whole idea of getting wet was about as appealing as eating sand. *Man,* I felt weird! This backpack was dragging on my shoulders like a ton of bricks. I slipped it off and plopped it on the ground.

Food, I told myself. *That* was the problem. My body needed some extra energy. Before plowing through that waterfall, I decided to rustle up a little more of Steffanie's gourmet grub. I knew time was running short, but I also knew that if I didn't find some energy, I might utterly fail at what I'd come here to accomplish. I also found another meat dish for Rafa—*Chicken and Rice Divan*. The bird became my friend again almost immediately. I downed a bowl of *Organic Kettle Chili* and fed the bird another seven morsels of spongy meat. Neither of us were especially satisfied, but it would have taken four more minutes to soften another bowl of that stupid food, and I didn't think we had another four minutes to spare.

I looked at Steffanie's pack. I was afraid it had reached the end of the line. I wasn't carrying it any farther. It would take all the energy I had just to carry the flashlight. A little snap, like on a dog chain, allowed me to hook the flashlight to my belt loop. I didn't figure the pack was going anywhere, but before I left it, I pulled out my old shirt.

"C'mere Rafa," I said. "Time for you and me to take a swim."

He approached me innocently enough, and for his trust he got another shirt thrown over his head. Before he could even react to this final act of indignity, I charged through the waterfall like an NFL noseguard. As we burst clear of the water on the other side, I released the falcon. I was wet, and the old shirt was wet, but Rafa was reasonably dry. The view on the other side of the waterfall surprised me. I was standing in a stream. I was *outside!* The surrounding trees and hillside were bathed in moonlight. If it had been daytime, I'd have surely seen the sun through the cascade. But at this hour I couldn't have possibly anticipated that I would be emerging from the cave's mouth.

Rafa's reaction to all his ill treatment wasn't unexpected. He took to the sky and disappeared into the twinkling stars. I really didn't expect to ever see him again. *Oh well.* Hadn't it been my intention from the beginning to set him free? Besides, here in this place and time he'd never again assist the armies of Shinar. Still, I was going to miss my feathered companion.

The creek was eight feet wide. I was in knee-deep water at the base of the waterfall. I sloshed over to the bank and half-sat, half-fell onto the stones. Here in the moonlight, with the falls roaring in my ears, I assessed my present situation.

The obvious question was, *Where was I?* But I felt that I knew that one without farther help. I'd known my destination since last night. It was 73 A.D. I was back in Greece. The beech and fir trees surrounding the stream, as well as the general lay of the land confirmed it. After spending the last two years in this country, particularly in the region around Athens, I almost felt as much at home here as I did in Utah. But what direction was I supposed to travel?

And this was just the beginning. There were so many other questions. But something was wrong with me. For the first time I began to sense that it had something to do with the place itself. For more insight I needed the seerstone. I cupped it in my hands and tried to clear my head.

Concentrate. It seemed harder now than ever before. I think the Spirit helped me. My mind suddenly opened wider than I think I could have managed on my own. In the course of three or four minutes, I understood what I needed to do—not the details, but the essence. And more importantly, I understood the extraordinary challenges I was facing.

The strange weakness that had engulfed my body was like nothing I'd ever experienced. How can I describe it? It was sort of like a person with a transplanted lung or kidney or heart. Sometimes the human body rejected such transplants, right? The cells, or antibodies, or whatever else, go on the offensive and try to destroy the foreign organism. I felt like this was happening to me. But instead of just one organ, my entire *body* was being rejected. I was being rejected by the very century into which I had been thrust. I was being rejected by time.

There was only one explanation for this. It was because I was *already here!* Man, that's gotta sound bizarre. Simply put, my body was already in this world. I was crossing paths with a segment of time where I stood the chance of coming face to face with *myself!* Somewhere out there in this Athenian night was an eighteen-year-old kid living through one of the most traumatic days of his life. At this very moment, about eight miles from this exact spot, my younger self was being rescued from an Athenian prison—rescued by Gidgiddonihah and a band of twenty Nephite warriors. It was all happening *right now!* Gid's tragic death was due to take place in a few short hours.

The concept horrified and exhilarated me all at once. But wasn't this what I had wished for? Wasn't this the event over which I had agonized for so long? Wasn't this the night that I had relived time and again and dreamed that somehow I could change? This was it!—my chance to do things differently. My chance to make it right. The opportunity was before me. But as it turned out, the risks were far greater than I'd anticipated.

My very life had become a fragile thing. Time itself had become fragile. I was living a paradox. There were now *two* of me in the same realm. This fact contradicted every shred of logic. But here I was, living the reality. And yet every molecule in my body was screaming in rebellion. It wasn't right. It was not how things were supposed to be.

But how could that be true? There must have been *some* reason that I was allowed to be here, and I thought I knew what it was. It was because Gid should not have died that night. He was not *meant* to die in Greece in 73 A.D. At least that's how I chose to interpret it. Anything else was beyond my comprehension.

But in spite of my noble aspirations, I was facing serious complications. If I tried to linger here any longer than it would take to complete my objective, I was sure to die. I was already intensely uncomfortable. Two things would farther intensify that discomfort. First, the length of time that I remained. Second, the distance that I maintained with my other self. The closer I got to my body's actual position in this place and time, the more difficult the physical challenge would become. I wasn't quite sure what all the ramifications would entail—what effects I would suffer—but I knew it was coming.

There was one other rule that could not be broken—and this was the most critical of all. I could not, under any circumstances, be revealed to my other self. The stone had made this quite clear. If there was a moment when I found myself looking directly at myself—that is, if ever we found ourselves looking at each *other*—the effects would be instantly fatal for both of us. If I saw him it might be okay, but if we saw each *other*, it was over. A shockwave would reverberate through the fabric of reality. Not only would I die—but I feared it would become as if I had never *lived*. This may have been the trickiest operation I'd ever attempted—and the chance remained very real that I could fail.

But for the moment, the biggest challenge I faced was the complete enervation of my body. I was tired in a way that I had never been tired before. All I wanted to do was curl up right here on these rocks and go to sleep. But if I did this, I wasn't sure I'd have the strength to reawaken. The mission would be doomed.

I pulled myself to my feet and started walking to the southwest. I was high up in some foothills. Every now and then I caught snatches of the countryside below. Shortly I felt sure that I would see the estate of Epigonus. Epigonus was the fat, corrupt, and sleazy councilman who had kidnapped Mary. He would kidnap Jesse, the young Jewish orphan, too. Epigonus was also the man who owned the two Scythian bodyguards who were responsible for Gidgiddonihah's murder.

Tonight Epigonus was dying. He'd had a heart attack earlier this afternoon, shortly after we'd confronted each other in the city council of Athens. His servants had brought him back to his estate and laid him in his bedchamber. The megalomaniac's final wish was that he wanted to die like a Scythian king. Not only would *he* die, but he would also insist that each of his servants die with him. In addition, his last surviving servants—the Scythian bodyguards—would set his estate on fire. His mansion would become his funeral pyre.

Every step felt like I was walking against a repelling magnet. Within ten or fifteen minutes I could see the shadow of an oddly designed mansion in the valley below, surrounded on three sides by a moonlit lake. This was it—the unholy ground where Gid had perished. The sight sent a shudder through my frame. Within a few hours flames would engulf every structure inside those outer walls, lighting up the sky.

My thoughts also turned to Mary. I realized she was inside the tower of that mansion at this very moment. She'd been there for several weeks, terrified for her life. Suddenly a familiar emotion welled up inside me—the very emotions that had driven me to act that night. It was the memory of my Jewish princess. Her face had hovered in my thoughts for three long years as a castaway on Lincoln Island. I wondered if I would see her tonight. Somehow I had to resist the urge. If I saw Mary, I'd only risk being seen by myself.

I made my way down the hillside and soon entered the woods that surrounded the property's perimeter. At this point I flicked the flashlight off and crept very slowly through the undergrowth. There was no hurry yet, and I needed to maintain my focus. I felt I could feel every blood cell as it scraped its way through my veins, almost like a million little shards of broken glass. A headache was throbbing behind my temples. My lightheadedness persisted. I feared the dizziness would make me sloppy. I might make a fatal mistake just by not recognizing signs of danger in time.

A moment later I heard noises in the forest. They were sounds of violence. I got down on the ground and started to crawl. What was going on? For the life of me I couldn't remember. Had it been so long ago, or was my lightheadedness impairing my memory? I could see the silhouetted walls of the estate looming on my left. Then, through the trees, I saw the source of the noise.

My heart tightened like a fist. It was one of the Scythian warriors. The movement was still some distance away, but there was no mistaking the outline of that greasy crop of black hair. I even knew which one he was. This was the man with two striking serpents tattooed on his cheeks. It was not the one whose arrows would kill Gidgiddonihah, but it was the same man who Gidgiddonihah would slay with his last breath of strength. It would mark the final time that Gid saved our lives.

I heard a scream—but it wasn't the Scythian. I knew that scream. It was Jesse! The memory came rushing back. I knew what moment this was. I crawled a little closer. The Scythian was fighting with someone in the darkness. I saw his knife blade strike down and I heard an awful grunt as life seeped out of a man's belly. Two other bodies were lying on the forest floor. They were the bodies of the men that Gid had sent to stake out the area until the rest of us arrived from the prison. Jesse had led them here. A few moments from now, when the rest of us finally arrived, it would only be to behold the aftermath of the Scythian's butchery.

Unbelievable. If I'd arrived a few minutes earlier, I might have prevented this tragedy as well. The Scythian was now struggling with Jesse. The boy escaped his grasp. He tried to run away. *Jupiter!* He was running directly toward *me!* If he continued on this same path, the boy would step right on my head. But then I saw the Scythian raise his arm and fling something—a chain connected by two iron balls. It was the same instrument that he'd used on me beside the canals at the port of Piraeus. The chain had brought me down like a mountain goat, and it did the same to poor Jesse.

With his legs tangled, Jesse tripped onto his chest, knocking the wind from his lungs. As he raised his eyes, something *else* took his breath away—it was the sight of *me!* He gaped at my face in bewilderment as I lay in the underbrush, as if I shouldn't have been here. I think my appearance also confused him. After all, how was it that I'd suddenly aged three years? And where did I get these unusual clothes?

Fortunately, Jesse had the presence of mind to lunge to the right, kicking and clawing to try and get away. The Scythian swooped down on top of him. I held my breath in dread, but Jesse had managed to crawl far enough away to divert attention from my position.

"Get off me, you pig!" Jesse yelled. "Let go!"

The Scythian grabbed Jesse's hair and began dragging him off. The boy looked terrified. His eyes glanced toward me. I could read his mind. He was no doubt wondering why no one was trying to save him. If I was here, surely Gid and the other Nephite warriors were here as well. *Why wasn't anyone attacking?* My conscience burned with guilt. I was unarmed. What could I do? *Just hang on for another hour, Jesse,* I said in my mind. *You will be rescued—and by* me. This is to say, by the *younger* me.

The Scythian laughed at him. "Maybe I'll spill your guts, like them?"

It was the first sentence I'd actually heard one of the Scythians utter. Each time I'd been in their presence, they'd never said a word. In my nightmares I could sometimes hear their voices—creepy, guttural voices that scraped like sandpaper. I couldn't have explained it, but this was precisely how it sounded. It was just as I'd imagined.

He hauled Jesse away and they disappeared in the forest darkness. Soon they'd enter the estate's main gate. Jesse would be tossed into the tower with Mary while the two Scythians prepared for Epigonus's death by barricading the doors to every mansion entrance and slaying every living person within it.

I grabbed the trunk of a nearby tree and pulled myself up. This was ridiculous. What was I supposed to do? I barely had enough strength to walk. How was I supposed to prevent Gid's assassination? A weapon. I needed some kind of weapon. I approached the bodies of the slain Nephites. One of them had a dagger clutched in his grip. I reached down and pried it away. Then I stood again, balancing against another tree.

My headache was pounding like a sledgehammer! I'd never felt anything like it. I needed to sit down. I needed to wait. But not here. I staggered off to the right a short distance. Then I sank down behind a large tree trunk, pinching my eyes shut to drive out the pain. *Rest.* There was nothing else I could do right now. If I could just sleep for five minutes. That's all I felt I needed. Then I'd have the strength to keep going, to finish the mission. Yes . . . sleep.

It was the deepest, yet the most excruciating sleep I'd ever endured. Nothing about it was refreshing. And the dreams were so schizophrenic. I felt like I was constantly being squished, crushed, or smothered. All of my phobias were magnified a hundredfold. I was pinned between walls, buried alive under a mountain of cement, crushed by steamrollers, and trapped within blocks of ice. I felt myself swirling inside the pillar of energy, the centrifugal force pinning each of my molecules against the inner shell, rendering me unable to move or think or escape. Worst of all, I *could not wake up!* I know because I made a conscious effort to try. My eyelids were like anvils. I couldn't raise them!

Yet I could hear voices now—familiar echoes, people I knew, events that I had lived. I gritted my teeth. I forced myself to wake up—forced my eyelids to lift. My vision was blurry. The headache was worse than ever. But at last I could distinguish the voices.

"*Who did this?*" someone asked, his voice hot with fury.

I knew that voice. It couldn't belong to anyone else. *It was my old friend! It was Gid!* Even hearing his reborn voice was like a lightning rod to my soul. And yet he wasn't speaking to me. He was behind me, about twenty yards through the trees. I bent my neck and tried to see around the tree trunk. My body was so stiff, as if stricken with rigor mortis. It felt as if moving would tear my flesh and crack my bones.

Then I heard another voice. "The Scythians."

It was *me!* It was my voice! I could see them now. I could see myself and Gidgiddonihah, and sixteen or seventeen more men, all of them Nephites, all of them here to help me stage the bold rescue of Mary. I also saw my old friend Micah, the former Essene, my fellow survivor from Lincoln Island.

"Two men did *this?*" raged Gidgiddonihah, indicating the mutilated bodies of the three slain Nephites.

I continued observing from the darkness of the trees—watching an event that I had lived. I was witnessing a replay of events from three years ago.

Another Nephite named Jashon approached Gidgiddonihah. "The boy isn't among them."

They were talking about Jesse. I looked at the expression on my own face. I knew what I was thinking. From that statement I had concluded that Jesse was still alive. He'd been taken inside the estate.

"How do we get over the wall?" asked Jashon.

I saw the wheels spinning in Gidgiddonihah's military mind. I'd almost forgotten how noble he looked, how unconquerable.

He asked me, "What opens that gate?"

"It raises up," I replied. "There's some sort of mechanism that lifts it with chains."

I looked so young, and yet so lean. I knew it had only been a few weeks since my rescue from Lincoln Island. I still had the skin-and-bones look of a castaway. Thankfully, the mounds of Greek pasta that I'd eaten during my mission had put some meat back on my skeleton.

"Are these Scythians his only warriors?" Gid asked.

"He has a lot of servants," I said. "They might also give us some trouble. Then there's the tigerhounds. Five of them."

Tigerhounds. I'd almost forgotten. They were the biggest, meanest dogs I'd ever laid eyes on. As I thought about what lay ahead for those courageous souls, I realized that it was a miracle that *any* of them had come out alive.

"I'm not worried about dogs," said Gid, grasping his bow. "In fact, we'll *need* the dogs. At least in the beginning. We'll need them as a distraction . . ."

Gid went on, explaining his plan of building a human pyramid to climb over the wall. It was one of Gid's cleverer ideas. Gidgiddonihah was a warrior beyond compare. Nothing should have been able to defeat him. Nothing except the dumb luck, the awful stroke of fate, that awaited him. I felt a tremor of helplessness. If only I could have called out—warned him of what lay ahead. If only I could reveal all that I knew about the Scythian who would be waiting in the darkened stairwell. If Gid had known, he could have fired into that darkness just a split second sooner and saved himself. I wanted to call out so badly, but I had to suppress the urge. It would mean the end of everything. When I saved Gid, I had to do it without his knowledge. I had to do it without anyone seeing me or knowing that I was there. I shivered at the prospect. It seemed impossible—more difficult than the entire operation now facing these extraordinary men.

The conversation continued. Gid expressed his chilling opinion that Epigonus and the Scythians already knew that we were here—or at least that we were coming. I watched myself and the others move toward the edge of the moat. Gid was the first to leap into the water. The rest followed, lining up along the wall. The human pyramid was formed. Gidgiddonihah, Micah, Antipus, Jashon, and I began climbing the arms and legs of the other men, reaching toward the top of the wall.

For the first time I dared to move a little closer. I pressed my back against the trunk and struggled to stand. My breath felt strained, as if I wasn't getting enough oxygen. I staggered to the next tree and got a better look at the men climbing the wall.

I had to have a plan. *What was my plan?* It was hard to organize my thoughts. I realized that somehow I had to get inside the estate. I had to follow Gidgiddonihah and myself into that secret passage under the lake—the passage that would lead into the museum room of Epigonus's mansion. And again, I had to do it all without being seen. In my condition, however, there was no way I could have climbed that wall. I had to go through the front gate. Gid's plan was to create a diversion while we stood atop the wall. He and I would head to the left while the others would walk along the same tightrope of stones toward the gate. Four tigerhounds would be killed by our arrows. As I recalled, an arrow would graze Jashon's arm. He would fall into the moat. Micah and Antipus would leap down and land on the inside. They would wait in hiding until the Scythians retreated into the house to accomplish their final evil acts.

All I could think to do was wait until Micah opened the gate from the inside. Then I'd have to sneak past them, cross the estate, and find the passageway under the lake. But would that give me enough time? By then the house might already be consuming in flames. By the time I reached the stairwell, Gid might already be dead! I shook off the thought and moved quietly through the woods toward a place where I could watch the gate.

The hounds started barking. I heard Gid's voice announce the command to "Separate!" Two figures began running left along the top of the wall; four figures began running right. The Nephites who had created the pyramid were climbing out of the moat, moving in the same direction as the four men, toward the gate. I stopped and crouched in the undergrowth. I couldn't afford to be seen now. I didn't like to stop. It seemed more painful to start moving again. My muscles and joints stiffened up immediately. However, my shortness of breath was improving. I think it was because Gid and my younger self were moving farther away. The closer we were to each other, the more impaired my physical and mental capacities seemed to be. I wondered if my other self was experiencing similar effects. Apparently not. After all, he'd gotten here first. He'd been part of this reality for over three years. *I* was the entity that didn't belong.

I could hear tigerhounds yelping as arrows struck them. Shortly, I heard Jashon cry out in pain. There was a splash as he fell into the moat. Then another splash. I knew it was the Nephite named Uzziah. He too had fallen on this side of the wall. Their fellow Nephites jumped into the water to help them.

"Are you all right?" I heard someone ask.

"Just grazed me," said Jason.

"Where are Antipus and Micah?"

"They jumped down on the other side," said Uzziah. "Rotten fate! I lost my footing!"

"Shhh!" snapped someone else.

For several moments everything went quiet. Even the men in the moat went perfectly motionless. I heard horses galloping inside the walls, but I couldn't tell what was happening. I remembered that one of the Scythians would ride over to investigate the archway leading up to the front gate. The other would stalk very close to the place where

Gid and I were hiding. But even though Gid and I had felt certain that the Scythian knew we were there, he didn't approach. He seemed to know that he would be in a better position to take care of us later.

Micah and Antipus had obviously found an excellent hiding place inside the walls, because in a few minutes the two Scythian warriors would ride back toward the mansion with the last surviving tiger-hound running behind them. They would then go inside with no intention of ever coming out.

After a while the company of Nephite warriors made their way closer to the main gate. I watched anxiously from my place in the trees. How long before Micah dared come out of hiding to let them in? I was growing more impatient by the minute. I needed to keep moving. I needed to keep my muscles from becoming rigid.

Five minutes passed. *Ten* minutes passed. Gid was only a few minutes from death! The Nephites outside the gate looked anxious as well. Several speculated that Micah and Antipus might have been killed or captured. Jashon suggested they build the human pyramid again and try once more to get someone safely over the other side. But just as he said this, a chain started cranking. A space appeared at the bottom of the gate. It was lifting. Micah had arrived at last!

Even before the gate was fully raised, the Nephites slipped inside and disappeared. Within seconds, they were all gone. Then the most horrifying thing started to happen. The chain started cranking *again!* The gate was closing!

I staggered out of my hiding place, limping, agonizing, dragging my enervated limbs. *No!* I screamed in my mind. *Don't close it!* The space was only three or four feet wide as I began crossing the stone bridge. I unsnapped the flashlight from my belt loop. With excruciating pain, I dove toward that falling gate. I held the flashlight out front. As I landed it felt as if my body shattered into a thousand pieces, but the gate had stopped falling. The only thing holding it up was the steel canister of Steffanie's four-battery flashlight.

My head was ringing, echoing. I barely had the presence of mind to roll underneath the narrow space. Afterwards, I lay there in the shadows, certain that I was about to be surrounded by Nephites, who would all be stunned to speechlessness. Maybe they wouldn't recognize me. I was sure I looked like death warmed over—so white and pale I probably had the appearance of a ghost.

But no one surrounded me. I turned my neck and peered out through the archway toward the mansion's eccentric-looking towers and uneven levels. Several Nephites were still visible, fanning out across the premises. They would try to fight their way inside. Soon they'd discover that the place was so strongly barricaded that it was impossible to breach. Shortly thereafter the flames would start to ascend the mansion walls. The fire might have started already. I needed to keep moving. I almost didn't care anymore if someone saw me. Time was running out.

I yanked on the flashlight. I wasn't even sure it would still work, but I felt I needed it. It wouldn't budge. The heavy gate had pinned it in place. I made one final attempt to dislodge it by kicking it with my leg. At last, the canister jarred loose. The gate fell closed. I barely pulled my leg out in time to keep it from getting crushed.

None of the Nephites seemed to have heard, or else they no longer cared. I grabbed the flashlight. The glass over the bulb was smashed, but amazingly the bulb itself looked intact. My sister had good taste in flashlights. I wanted to switch it on, see if the bulb would still ignite, but this wasn't the time or place.

Again, I struggled to my feet. With the flashlight and dagger still in hand, I emerged from the archway and entered the darkened grounds of the estate. I tried to keep close to the wall, doing my best to keep from being noticed. I circled around the reeds of a marshy area to the right of the gate—the area Micah and Antipus had probably used as their place of hiding. I wasn't sure I remembered this area from before, but the only time that I would have seen it was as I exited the grounds. I was so consumed with grief at that moment that I wouldn't have remembered anything.

I'd followed along the inside perimeter wall for some distance, then I crossed toward some tall grass near a line of cypress trees—the same area where Gid and I had been hiding when we were almost discovered by the Scythian. All of this was like an ultimate déjà vu. I could see the surface of the lake reflecting the glow of the moon. Just ahead was the grassy mound. At the edge of this mound sank a stone stairway, much like the stairs to a root cellar. I crept along the cypress grove. As I was about to cross the final distance to the mound, a shadow leaped from behind one of the cypresses.

My reflexes were too slow. The dagger was knocked from my hand. I was tackled to the ground. A knife blade was pressed against my stomach. As my vision cleared, I was looking up into the face of my old friend, Micah.

His eyes widened in astonishment. "Harry?"

He climbed off me quickly. I continued to lay there in a hurricane of nausea and dizziness. I rolled onto my side and vomited the remains of my *Organic Kettle Chili*.

Micah watched me in consternation. "I'm so sorry. I didn't recognize you. Harry, what are you *doing* here? Where is Gidgiddonihah?"

"Micah," I said, wiping my mouth, my lungs wheezing for oxygen. "Micah, help me stand."

He reached under my arms and started to lift. "Did I hurt you badly? What have I done? Harry what's *happened* to you? You look *terrible*."

"Don't let anyone see us," I wheezed.

I tried to lead Micah behind the cypress branches, outside the view of the other Nephites who were scouring the area around the mansion.

"What's wrong? Why are you dressed in—?" As he studied Steffanie's T-shirt with its Hunter High School insignia, his expression suddenly changed. He looked at me closely in the moonlight. His eyes narrowed. "You are not Harry Hawkins—"

I reached out and grabbed the collar of Micah's tunic. "I *am* Harry. Micah, we've known each other for . . ." I had to think a second. " . . . for three years. I want you to listen to me. I want you to trust me. You need to forget that you ever saw me here."

He looked totally perplexed. "Forget that I—?"

I shook his collar. The action accelerated my own dizziness.

He drew me upright. "You're not well, Harry. I better get you—"

"No!" I screeched. "Micah *please*. You and I have been friends through the hardest of times. Are you still my friend?"

"Of course—"

"Then believe me now. Please, I pray that you'll believe me. You need to walk away from me, Micah. If you try to stop me, someone will die."

"Who?"

"Gidgiddonihah."

"Gidgiddonihah? But where *is* he? Where are Jesse and Mary?"

"Jesse and Mary will be all right. It's *Gidgiddonihah* who's going to die tonight. Micah, I know what I'm saying. You have to let me go, and then tell no one you ever saw me or spoke to me in this place."

He still looked terribly bewildered, but he was finally listening. It must have been the desperation in my voice. "But Harry, I don't understand."

"And I can't explain it," I said, "except to say that you were right."

"Right about what?"

"When you said that I wasn't Harry Hawkins. I mean, I *am* Harry Hawkins. But I'm not the person inside that house. I'm not the person with Gidgiddonihah."

I had no idea what constantly compelled me to try and explain the most incomprehensible concepts to people who had no hope of understanding. Yet Micah continued to listen calmly. I'd almost forgotten the closeness and loyalty that we'd felt toward each other at this time in our lives. After all of our plights and trials together, we had grown to trust one another in a way that few friends ever did. Yes, Micah was listening closely. He may not have comprehended my words, but somehow he *believed* me.

"What is it that you want me to do?" he asked.

"Nothing," I said. "Keep doing exactly what you're doing. Don't alter *anything*. Go to the mansion. Keep trying to get inside. In a few minutes this whole place will go up in flames. Don't try to follow me, Micah. If you do, Gidgiddonihah will die. Other people might die too."

"But Harry, you're sick. You're not well enough to . . ." Again he studied the awful sincerity in my face. At last, he gave up all resistance. "All right, Harry. I will do as you say."

He released me. I started to walk away. Another wave of dizziness overcame me. I started to collapse. Micah stepped over quickly to keep me from falling. He let me recover, then reached down and retrieved my flashlight and dagger. I took them, my hands shaking. Micah looked at me gravely. I tried to reassure him with a smile. It was so good to see my old friend.

"Now let me go," I said hoarsely.

I continued to stagger through the darkness until I reached the grassy mound. I didn't look back. It took all of my concentration to keep from falling as I descended the muddy stairs. The lock at the bottom entryway was broken. I'd broken it myself only ten minutes ago.

I entered the tunnel, my feet dragging, my jaw set with determination. Tears of frustration filled my eyes. What was I *doing*? How could I possibly change the outcome of impending events in my condition? Yet I trudged on, around the corner, past the iron wheel that would shortly release water into the tunnel. I ambled down the next flight of stairs. It was becoming too dark to continue. Time to see if this flashlight still worked. I switched it on.

There was no light beam. I was wrong. The gate *had* destroyed it. Just for good measure I slapped it against my leg. The beam flickered, then went out again. As I shook the canister, the light flickered on and off. To keep it working, I had to hold it very steady, which in my condition was next to impossible.

I finally reached the long corridor with six inches of standing water and began sloshing my way toward the other end. Again, I was sorely tempted to rest. I resisted the temptation. In five minutes, Gid would be mortally wounded. I struggled up the stairs at the opposite end, lifting one leg after the other. A minute later, I arrived at the doorway that led into the museum. I switched off the flashlight and clipped it to my beltloop. There was plenty of torchlight inside this antique-filled room, but I was still finding it difficult to see. My right eye was somewhat weak anyway from an injury that I'd sustained in ancient Caesarea many years ago. But this was different. Things weren't blurry exactly. More like washed out—as if half of what my eyes normally perceived wasn't there.

I already smelled smoke coming from other parts of the house. Any second one of the Scythians would enter this room and set it ablaze. He would try to burn the sacred scrolls that were piled atop a red table to my right, but Mary—my wonderful Mary—would arrive to save eleven vital manuscripts. Should I help her to save them? There was no time. I'd have to leave it to her. My body was still fighting the repelling magnet. Yet I was maintaining a steady pace. I just had to keep moving.

I reached the stairs that led up to Epigonus's room. Now things were becoming tricky. I realized Gid and I might be inside that room right at this very instant, carrying on our final conversation with the dying councilman. I proceeded with extreme caution. If ever there was a chance that I might come face to face with myself, it was now. As I reached the top, I carefully peered through the doorway. No one else was in the room. No one except Epigonus himself. He was lying amidst the six spiral pillars that surrounded his circular bed, his breathing erratic. Here finally was someone sicker than I was. Epigonus was at the very brink of death. I looked beyond him toward the doorway to the stairwell. There it was—the dark chamber from my nightmares. I heard voices within. This gave me hope. I wasn't too late. One of the voices was mine.

As I crossed the room, the body lying on the bed cracked open his eyes. Epigonus looked at me, trying to focus. I glared back at him with contempt. Here lay the *real* reason for all of this—the real reason for Gid's death.

In a voice that was barely a peep, he asked, "Wh—who are you?"

I took a deep breath to steady my voice, then replied, "Don't you recognize me?"

He looked confused. "But I saw you . . ." He raised a finger toward the stairwell.

I leaned closer to him. "Then I guess I'm Harry's guardian angel. Don't you believe in angels, Epigonus?"

This elicited one last look of surprise. Afterward, Epigonus started to choke. His eyes glossed over and the last gasp of air seeped from his lungs. His body went still. Epigonus was dead. I looked at him sadly. Few were as unprepared for this moment as he was.

I continued toward the stairwell. It felt as if I were pushing against all the forces of the universe. As I arrived, I looked up the steps. The stairway curved around as it climbed to the tower. I couldn't see Gid or myself, but I could clearly hear our voices.

"The chains are new!" Gid declared in frustration. "I can't break them!"

I remembered this scene perfectly. We were trying to breach the doorway. Gid was about to ask me for my sword.

Sure enough, I heard him say, "Give me your sword."

As Gid started hacking at the bolt, I looked toward the bottom of the stairs. This was it, the lair of the Scythian, the place where he would launch his fatal attack. The sight of it entered my soul like a cold wind. As before, I couldn't see a thing down in that darkness. Something told me that no one was there. But wasn't that obvious? If he'd already been in place, he'd have already fired an arrow into my ribs. The Scythian hadn't yet arrived.

I started to descend the stairs, like descending into a vortex of blackness—a place of pure evil. A few steps from the bottom, I felt my legs give out. I hugged the dagger to my chest and held the flashlight with my other hand. I couldn't let them clatter! But this also kept me from being able to put out my arms to brace against the landing. I rolled once on the hard steps and smashed against the far wall. I gritted my teeth to keep from crying out. I realized I'd accidentally cut the flesh between my thumb and finger with the dagger. I could feel the sticky warmth on my palm.

I held perfectly still. Gid had ears like a wolf—I was sure he'd heard. But up the stairs I could hear the sound of hacking. No one responded. The smell of smoke was growing heavier. My dizziness had reached an apex. It actually surprised me that I was conscious at all. My mind was fading in and out. I tried to sit up. My muscles no longer wanted to obey my commands. If I remained here, I'd be killed in a matter of seconds.

I looked toward my right. There was a foyer and another heavy wooden door. Underneath it was a thin sliver of smoky light. This was where the Scythian would enter. Using every ounce of remaining strength in my body, I dragged myself across the floor and into the foyer. It felt like I was dragging against a hundred cords. After I'd gone about three yards, I began to hear footsteps. Someone was approaching the wooden door.

With a last mighty effort I pulled myself into the dark corner to the right of the doorway. I'd drawn my legs up toward my chest just as the door began to open.

The foyer filled with a harsh, crimson light. I could hear the flames, and I perceived the light of a torch. A cloud of smoke wafted into the foyer. The door opened halfway, stopping just short of colliding with my knee. The beat of my heart was like a crashing echo in my brain. I watched the man's profile edge slowly forward. His face stopped just before I could see his eyes. He listened. The voices at the top of the stairs were still audible. I could now hear Mary's tears of joy.

Suddenly, from behind the door, I heard something that I hadn't remembered. It was the pant of a dog. Of course! The Scythian had not been alone in the stairwell. Just after Gid had been shot—just after he'd fired his arrow in return—the tigerhound had leaped out of the darkness. It was finally slain by the broken sword blade in Jesse's hand. From behind the door the hound made a low, sinister growl. Its padded feet took several steps into the foyer.

I didn't budge a muscle. I didn't breathe. The dog was just standing there, staring straight ahead. Didn't it smell me in the corner? Obviously the smoke had confused its senses. I gripped my dagger more tightly.

This was my moment to strike. This was the moment I'd been waiting for. The Scythian needed only to come forward another step, then I could raise my blade and slay him where he stood. It was my chance to change the future—to save the life of Gidgiddonihah! The moment was now.

But I couldn't *do it.* I barely had the strength to lift my hand, let alone leap to my feet and deliver a fatal blow. Gidgiddonihah's murderer was four feet away—he hadn't yet seen me—*but there was nothing I could do!* The Scythian moved ahead a little farther. He took his torch and tossed it back into the other room. Then he shut the door. The room again became as black as pitch. I continued to lie perfectly still as the Scythian and the tigerhound moved toward the landing at the bottom of the stairs.

From this angle the faint glow shining down from Epigonus's room offered me a vague outline of the Scythian and his dog. They gazed toward the top of the stairs in silence. The tigerhound made another low growl, but the Scythian grabbed his collar.

"Be still," he whispered. "Not yet."

The dog was itching to attack, but it obeyed its master and waited. Tears sprang from my eyes. My body was wracked with pain, but it was nothing compared to the agony of being unable to act at this critical moment.

I could hear Gid's voice at the top of the stairs. "The house is burning. Let's move! Let's move!"

I watched the Scythian draw an arrow from his quiver. He loaded it stealthily into his bow. This was the arrow that would pierce Gid's abdomen. It would take two more arrows to actually slay him, but this first one may have been the most critical. If only Gid could have seen it coming! If only—

My heart stopped. *I knew what I had to do!* I heard their footsteps starting to descend. I saw the Scythian take aim.

At that instant I flipped on the flashlight. It didn't ignite. I struck it against my hip. The beam shot across the foyer, illuminating the Scythian and his dog. The Scythian turned and looked at me in alarm. The tigerhound turned as well. And that was enough.

In that brief instant of hesitation, I heard the twang of a bowstring from up the stairs. The missile struck the Scythian's chest. No longer was Gid firing blindly into the darkness. He'd fired at a clear and visible target. As a result, it was a bull's-eye directly into the Scythian's heart. The Scythian's bow discharged, but it was a wild shot. The arrow shattered against the stone wall and ricocheted back toward me. The Scythian collapsed. In his last few seconds of life, he did not look up those stairs toward the man who had killed him. He gaped at me. That is to say, he looked into the flashlight beam. Then he fell forward, dead.

The dog looked confused. It wasn't sure who to attack. In the end it flew up the stairway exactly as it had done before. A few seconds later I heard the awful yelp as it was stabbed in the throat, just as it had happened the first time. But then I heard something new.

It was my own voice: "That's a flashlight beam! Somebody's shining a flashlight!"

I stiffened in horror. Harry was coming! I knew myself, and I knew that I would be desperately curious to discover the source of that light beam. *You idiot!* I cried in my mind. *Don't do it!*

I had only a few precious seconds to act. I reached underneath the wooden door and pulled it open. With my last ebb of strength I started dragging myself into the room beyond—a room glowing with flames. I left the dagger and flashlight behind. Footsteps were rushing down the stairs. They were *my* footsteps!

"Wait!" cried Gid. "Don't be a fool!"

Thank heaven for Gidgiddonihah. Before anyone had reached the landing where the Scythian lay dead, I was able to pull the door closed. But how could I bolt it? I knew that Harry would try to push through; I didn't have the strength to resist him. There was a board leaning against the paneling. I looked up at the door. Two steel brackets were bolted in place about halfway up. The door was designed to be barricaded from this side. I grabbed that board and tried to raise it up. It felt like a block of lead. I slid it higher up the door, pushing with all my might.

Just as I let that board fall into place between those steel brackets, someone from the other side of the door started yanking.

"Give me a hand!" I heard myself call out.

Everyone on the other side of the door—me, Jesse, perhaps even Mary and Gidgiddonihah—yanked and pulled and strained at that door, but the board held firm. I sank to the floor in relief.

"That's enough!" I heard Gid shout. "We can't get out this way. Let's go back!"

That voice was so full of power. It seemed to me the sweetest sound I'd ever heard. Gid was alive. He wasn't wounded. No arrow had pierced his stomach. The life of my hero had been saved.

Or had it? The people on the other side of that door still had some terrible moments ahead. The second Scythian warrior would try and kill Mary as she rushed forward to recover the sacred scrolls from the fire. I would thwart his efforts by leaping on him from the banister. Gid would then fire an arrow between his shoulder blades. A burning shelf would tip over on top of him. But in spite of it, the wretched old cuss would make his way back through the tunnel and turn the iron wheel. The waters from the lake would spill down on our heads, nearly drowning us. Gid would deliver the final deathblow to the Scythian, but it would be the last act of a mortally wounded man. Would it all play out differently now? Or much the same? Maybe Gid was destined to die tonight no matter what happened. Was it possible that I'd misinterpreted the message through the seer-stone? Could this all be some grand lesson to prove to me that I had no power against fate? I refused to believe it. I'd *changed* fate. I'd changed it because it was *meant* to be changed.

But at what cost? My energy was depleted. The room around me was blazing—the furniture, the curtains. There seemed to be no escape. But then my thoughts turned to the face of the girl Harry and Gid had rescued only moments before—a face filled with so much courage and love. Suddenly I realized why I was doing this. Yes, it was for Gid, my eternal friend. But it was also for *Mary*. After all, I'd rescued Gid in the hope that he might help me to find her again. Just as it wasn't meant for Gid to die, it also wasn't meant for me to be burned alive. The ceilings were high. As a result, smoke wasn't yet choking my lungs. I perceived a clear pathway through the flames. But could I rise to my feet? Could I walk?

I realized I *did* feel stronger. Perhaps because my younger self had moved farther away. My vision had not improved. Rather than walk, I decided to try and crawl. Every part of my body felt welded together and rusted, but somehow I managed to reach the opposite side of the room. There I found a doorway lined by pillars that led into another section of the house. The adjoining room was also in flames, but the fire was centered more toward a single corner where furniture had been piled against the wall, possibly to block a rear entrance. There were bodies within that pile of furniture—servants of Epigonus—charred and blackened.

A rafter fell from above, splattering sparks across the floor. I continued crawling toward a massive wooden door. I was sure this was the primary entrance to the house. I realized I wasn't the only one who'd tried to use this route of escape. The body of another servant lay on the floor, slain while trying to remove the wooden planks that barred it shut. I squinted to try and see the barricades. The servant had succeeded in removing the highest of the three planks. He'd been in the process of removing the middle barricade when a Scythian sword had apparently struck him down. The middle barricade appeared to be hanging diagonally, caught on one side.

I dragged myself past the dead servant and seized the hanging barricade. If I'd possessed my normal strength, lifting those planks would have been a cinch, but in my present condition it was like moving a mountain. They were twice as heavy as the board that I'd used to bar the door to the stairwell. I pulled myself higher until I could reach the bracket that held the left half of the middle plank. I heaved upward, groaning within, straining with all my might. The plank fell loose. As a reward for my efforts, it fell on my arm. Not that it mattered. I hardly felt it. My body was already so wracked with pain that additional pain made no difference.

All that remained was the lowest barricade. I latched onto it and tried to lift. It was wedged inside both brackets. I couldn't budge it! Another burning rafter collapsed in the middle of the room. In a matter of seconds the entire ceiling would come down. I remembered watching this very event as I mourned over Gidgiddonihah. Most of the roof would come down all at once.

Suddenly an idea illuminated my thoughts. *Leverage!* I grabbed the plank that I'd already removed and slid the end of it underneath the lowest barricade. Then I laid the middle part of it over the body of the dead servant. I laid my full body weight across the other end of the plank and pressed down.

The lowest barricade raised up out of the brackets and clunked onto the floor. The large wooden door fell open several inches. Heaving for breath, I pried it open another foot and a half and crawled outside. I could smell fresh air. I could see the horse stable burning across the way. I couldn't see any people, but this may have been because my vision was dim. I pulled myself down several stone steps. Then I crawled a short distance from the house.

As I reached one of the cypress trees at the edge of the lake, my body finally gave out. My muscles went completely rigid. As I opened my eyes and gazed across the water, I thought I could see several people on the other side, near the grassy mound. It didn't seem to me that any lake water was being sucked into the subterranean tunnel. Either this event hadn't yet occurred, or because of what I'd done, the second Scythian had not managed to turn the iron wheel. Or maybe there'd been a much darker conclusion. There was no way to know, and I wasn't sure I would *ever* know.

I looked past the walls of the estate toward the rising foothills. My cave was up there—the cave beneath the waterfall. But reaching it was out of the question. I'd gone as far as I could go. Hadn't I been warned that I could only exist in this world for a short time before my body completely deteriorated? Apparently that time had arrived. At least I didn't feel any more pain. My thoughts had become so jumbled. Mary's face appeared again, hovering over me like a wisp of smoke. I'm not even sure I realized that I was dying. All I wanted to do was sleep.

The next voice I heard sounded quite ethereal. The volume rose and fell, and the echo made it almost incomprehensible.

"*What can I do?*" I thought it said. "*Where can I take you?*"

Something about it sounded vaguely like Micah. But I was unable to open my eyes.

"*Point,*" said the voice. "*Do* anything! *Tell me how I can save your life!*"

I tried to move my tongue. I think I managed to whisper four words: "Stream. Waterfall. Cave . . . behind."

I felt myself being lifted. The sensation was almost like my spirit rising out of my body.

"*You have to help me, Harry. Try to stand. Grab onto the horse's mane.*"

My hand was guided to something. I did my best to grab on, but I think what saved me was a burst of inhuman strength from Micah. He laid me over the horse, then climbed up behind me.

"*Where is the stream?*" he asked. "*Just nod. Is it north?*"

I must have nodded, because the horse started to move. I managed only one more word. "Gid?"

"*Gid is alive,*" said Micah. "*Everyone made it—you, Mary, Jesse. We also saved eleven old scrolls. The others have all gone to Piraeus to meet the ship. I told them I'd catch up later. I just had a feeling—a 'hunch,' as you used to call it—that I might find you.*"

My mind filled with joy. I'd done it. I'd succeeded in my quest.

The next thing I remembered was a cold douse of water as Micah carried me through the waterfall. How he'd managed to locate the cave from my utterance of four short words was a miracle by itself. From there he must have followed the dim glow of purplish light and laid me at the foot of swirling pillar.

"*What should I do, Harry?*" he asked. "*Tell me what I should do.*"

Still lacking the strength to open my eyes, I could only point at my pocket. Micah reached inside and found the seerstone.

"*A stone?*" he asked. "*You want the stone?*"

I opened my hand. Micah placed it in my palm. Then he helped me close my fingers around it. My body filled with warmth. Suddenly

I had the strength to utter a few more words. Micah's voice also resounded a little more clearly.

"My arm," I said. "Place my arm . . . into the light."

"What?" he asked incredulously.

"But not yet."

"Not yet? When?"

"Wait," I said. "I will say when. But careful. Don't touch the light yourself. Just . . . my arm."

"Harry, tell me what will happen to you."

I couldn't answer. It would take too many words. But I knew the answer in my heart. I knew *precisely* what would happen, and where the pillar would take me.

At that instant I heard a strange squawk.

"Go away!" snapped Micah.

"No," I whispered. "The bird . . . is with me."

I felt the falcon climb onto my stomach and perch there. The bird was wet. Somehow I found the strength to smile. Rafa hadn't grown tired of me yet. The silly creature was devoted enough that it found a way to cross through that waterfall on its own. Or maybe he'd recognized that this world was definitely not his own and concluded that I was the only way to get back to where he belonged.

Micah also placed a strap of Steffanie's backpack over my other shoulder. I couldn't say if the wait was a minute or several hours. But when the moment arrived, my fist was still gripping the seerstone. I couldn't even have said for sure if Micah was still there, but when I uttered the word "Now," he must have heard.

I didn't have a chance to say good-bye to my friend, or a chance to thank him. The energy field carried me once again into the river of time. At last I fell asleep—a pure, healing, blissful sleep that my body needed so badly.

How long I slept is a bit of a mystery. All I know is that when at last I opened my eyes it was daylight. The sky was as blue as turquoise. A man-made canopy of palm fronds was shading my face. I was lying on a cushion of cotton blankets. Another face was looming above me—a face I knew so well. The hard lines on the warrior's brow had hardly changed. Neither had the crooked grin that had been his trademark as long as I can remember.

"Harryhawkins," he said. "Glad to see you're finally awake."

"Gidgiddonihah?" I replied, almost in a whisper. My eyesight was back to normal again. Only tears blurred my vision.

"Hey, now. Do I look that bad?"

"Is it really you?" I asked, still disbelieving.

He nodded. I heard a squawk. Perched on a nearby post was Rafa, the falcon. But the faces I saw behind Gid's shoulder were equally astonishing. *It was Micah!* And beside him was *Jesse!* They were both several years older than when we'd parted in the tunnels of Frost Cave. As I'd prayed, the stone had brought me back to Nephite times. It was official. Gid's destiny *had* changed. He'd survived the journey and had gone back home with Micah, Jesse, and the other Nephite soldiers.

Gidgiddonihah spoke. "It's about time you came here. I was getting rather soft. I told myself, there's only one reason Harryhawkins would come looking for me. At least I *hope* there's only one reason. You need me for another adventure."

I embraced my old friend. "That's right, Gid. Another adventure."

Notes to Chapter 13:

In this chapter the main character confronts a "dragon" which is subsequently identified as a dinosaur. Creationists who dismiss modern theories of evolution frequently suggest that dinosaurs and men may have existed simultaneously upon the earth. Some Latter-day Saint scientists have proposed that dinosaurs and other prehistoric life-forms were part of a preparatory phase that made the earth chemically and biologically suitable for mankind (see Eric N. Skousen, *Earth: In the Beginning,* 134–39). However, is it possible that some creatures that are today called "dinosaurs" survived into Old Testament or even modern times?

It should be remembered that naturalist Richard Owen coined the word "dinosaur" (Greek for "terrible lizard") in 1841. Prior to that time the strange animals associated with fossil remains were known by other names. The word used most frequently seems to be "dragon."

Dragons have been a part of the lore of numerous ancient civilizations from the Chinese to the Greeks, to the Norse, and to the Mayans. Such lore, represented both in writing and pictures, will often depict men and dragons living side by side. Ancient heroes like Gilgamish, Beowulf, and Saint George are said to have slain such dreaded beasts, while conquerors like Alexander the Great and historians like Herodotus reported the existence of such creatures in the diaries of their travels. Artifacts from Incan burial tombs show rock carvings of beasts that closely resemble Tyrannosaurs, Sauropods, Triceratops, and Pterosaurs, while a rock painting in White Rock Canyon near Blanding, Utah, shows men alongside a long-necked creature that closely resembles an Apatasaurus. Many other examples could also be cited.

The Bible uses the word "dragon" forty-eight times. In many of these references the scripture seems to represent a real living creature. Not all of these may be referring to a dinosaur, but some references like Psalms 91:13 and Jeremiah 51:37 appear to be talking about a true animal that was familiar to the ancient writers. The most dramatic biblical references are in the book of Job, chapters 40 and 41. Here the Lord describes two creatures (behemoth and leviathan) and declares Himself to be mightier than both. In 40:15–18 it reads:

> *Behold now behemoth, which I made with thee; he eateth grass as an ox. Lo now, his strength is in his loins, and his force is in the navel of his belly. He moveth his tail like a cedar: the*

sinews of his stones are wrapped together. His bones are as strong pieces of brass; his bones are like bars of iron.

Some Bible commentators suggest that this large grass-eating creature was an elephant or a hippo, but this would not explain a tail that moves like a cedar tree.

Job chapter 41 describes an even more dramatic creature that dwells in the oceans and cannot be slain by spears, darts, or arrows: *"Out of his nostrils goeth smoke, as out of a seething pot or caldron. His breath kindleth coals, and a flame goeth out of his mouth"* (vv. 20–21) and *"He maketh the deep to boil like a pot* (v. 31)" and *"Upon the earth there is not his like, who is made without fear"* (v. 33). Some have felt that these verses are describing a crocodile, but this conclusion hardly seems adequate.

The idea of a water dinosaur having survived the Great Flood seems plausible and might account for such modern phenomenon as the Loch Ness monster of Scotland, or Mokele-mbembe of Lake Tele in the Congo, or the discovery of an unidentified animal carcass that was caught in the nets of Japanese fisherman near New Zealand in 1977. Many will pass off both modern and ancient dinosaur and dragon stories as the products of human imagination. Such accounts may well have been embellished over time, but they may also be based on a core of historical truth. It seems natural for people to be attracted to the idea that dinosaurs and sea monsters might still exist. But whether they exist or not, the fact that such creatures did once roam the earth is uncontested. We await only the light of modern revelation to tell us more about such creatures and their role in the eternal plan.

PART III

THE ANGELS
OF BABEL

CHAPTER FOURTEEN

Steffanie

Who'd have thought that I would ever be the center of attention in the meeting hall of a king? Maybe the center court of the Delta Center (as I was awarded the MVP for the WNBA) but not the throne room of the royal hosts of Shinar.

In fact, as I gazed upon the throne of Nimrod I wondered if this whole setting—elevated thrones, jeweled crowns, etc.—was a setting that Nimrod had actually invented, a pattern that would be copied by almost every king throughout the history of the world. His crown hung low on his brow and had five golden points. Like everything else, it was chunked up with diamonds and rubies and whatever else could make it as gaudy as possible. I'd have wagered that the whole idea of kneeling in the presence of another human being also belonged to Nimrod. Every custom of royalty—as well as the whole notion that one man could lord himself over another—could probably be traced back to the seven-and-a-half-foot giant who sat before me now.

But Nimrod's wasn't the only throne in this hall—it was just the highest. There were thirty different seats at the front of the chamber, all very different and every one occupied by a dignitary of Nimrod's court. Well, I take that back. One of the seats on the lowest dais, directly under the king, was conspicuously empty, but I couldn't have said who should have been sitting there.

Possibly the most interesting throne was the one that sat directly beside the king, though it was slightly less elevated. This was the throne of a woman. In a way, it looked even more distinguished than Nimrod's. It may not have been as high, but it jutted out toward the center of the chamber, almost like a diving platform, and definitely demanded its own attention. But it wasn't so much the throne as the woman herself who evoked the greatest fascination. This, I felt certain, was the Queen of Shinar.

I don't think I can adequately describe all the thoughts in my head as I gazed at her. I'd already seen so many beautiful people in this country that it was sort of becoming redundant. After all, beauty really only exists when there's something ugly to compare it to. Well, in comparison to this woman, I might have said that every other woman in Shinar was rather plain. Her body and face had perfect symmetry, so much so that her every gesture, whether sitting or standing, was womanly, dignified, and graceful. I swear it was poetry to look at her, like a passage of unforgettable music. The instant that I saw this person, I felt afraid of her, as if her image alone were like a truth serum. Could I lie to such a woman? And let me remind you, I was a *woman!* I couldn't imagine what effect she'd have upon a man. I think any one of them would have melted into a pool of drool at her feet.

Her royal robe was white, but with a shimmering blue tint. She wore a golden headpiece with a dazzling tiara, but there was also a natural luster in her golden blonde hair. On her chest was a red and silver amulet in the shape of a dove. Or was it an arrow? It might have been either. Despite the king's seven-and-a-half foot physique and unconquerable presence, I still wondered if this woman was somehow the secret to his power.

On further observation, I began to sense something else about her—something darker. As her hypnotizing blue eyes watched me, I began to sense a cold calculation. In her exquisitely chiseled face, I could almost feel that her whole heart was devoted to the submission of every living creature. Behind the full curves of that rosy mouth and prominent chin, I sensed a terrible impatience, one that could inflict unspeakable cruelty. Was I reading too much into it? I didn't think so. Just her body language communicated that she believed this was just as much her empire as it was Nimrod's, and if Nimrod had tried to deny it to her, I swear she'd have eaten him for lunch.

And believe it or not, it wasn't just the queen who stirred my imagination. She just demanded the most attention from anyone on the floor, which at the moment was only me. There were other distinguished persons in that royal gallery—some very old, but all of them had a look in their eyes as malevolent as the most hateful and evil people I'd ever met.

Unlike the platform outside where the glider had landed, this was not a public gathering. The hall could have fit several thousand onlookers, but right now I was the only object upon that shining marble floor. Well, unless you counted Mardon, but he was looking more and more like a squirming piece of larvae every moment. He knew his place—I'll say that much for him. And it was significantly below that of most of the other people in this room. I was starting to think that his little expedition to wipe out the last remnants of the Japhethite rebels was sort of Mardon's first big opportunity to spread his wings and do something significant. By the frequent swallows and nervous ticks in Mardon's manner, I suspected that he was afraid he'd blown it completely and was about to face a great deal of wrath. I think he felt his presentation of me was the best chance he had of finding redemption.

I was made to stand there in shackles before the royal gathering until every person was comfortably in their seats. I suppose I was glad that at least my hands were locked in front instead of behind. In truth, I felt a little like Abinadi standing before the throne of King Noah—just like in that one painting. Even the atmosphere seemed similar. The place stank of incense—don't ask me what kind. (It reminded me of Glade bathroom freshener.) The guys seated along the bottom row were all wearing tall hats—like dunce caps—with tassels hanging down behind. Their intricately braided beards hung as low as their belly buttons. It was very smoky, hot, and stuffy, and despite the glow of several dozen lamps, it was also annoyingly dark and full of shadows.

As soon as Nimrod's rear end was planted on his throne, he began the interrogation. The first question was directed at Mardon.

"So where did you find this creature?" he asked.

"At the edge of the wilderness of Joktan," said Mardon. "She and another . . ." He stopped himself rather abruptly, but then he realized he'd stuck his foot in it and would have to continue. "She and *another* angel were captured as spies by our cavalry while they were observing our victorious battle."

"*Another* angel?" Nimrod repeated.

Mardon swallowed again. "Yes. Last night he attempted to escape, but I sent Casluchim and several other assassins to slay him."

"You wished to *kill* him?" The question had been asked by the woman, and with marked disapproval.

"Yes, Queen Semiramis," said Mardon. Then hastily, "As an act of boldness to show the men how weak and vulnerable these creatures really are. My command was that the angel's corpse be brought immediately to Babel for your inspection."

"Forgive me if I remain skeptical of your recovery efforts," huffed Nimrod. "But of course I have only your failure to find Chancellor Terah and his infant child—the abomination of his loins—as examples of your miscalculation."

Mardon squirmed. I wasn't sure who these people were that Nimrod was talking about, but it was obviously a very sore point between Mardon and the king.

The queen's gaze fell on me again, and the corners of her mouth turned into a pout. "What is her name?"

"Steffanie," said Mardon, a formal ring in his voice, like he was introducing a circus act.

An older man spoke next. He sat on the opposite side of the queen in a throne adorned with exotic animal furs, and armrests of pearl and ivory. "This is not an *angel*," he grunted insultingly. "The prince is deceived. I had angels described to me by my grandfather on several occasions, and although Noah was senile even then, his description was certainly accurate enough to dismiss this 'Steffanie' as a fraud."

Mardon said in desperation, "Forgive me, noble Cush, but you are mistaken. She proclaimed with her own tongue that she fell from the City in the Clouds."

That wasn't exactly accurate. *Harry* had proclaimed it, not me.

Nimrod sat there pontificating. "I will admit that she has a beauty that I have not seen before. A very rare and exotic variation of the usual female characteristics. But what other evidence have you that she is an angel?"

"You need only speak to her for a few moments," said Mardon. "She is very cunning, but not intelligent enough to hide her origin. Also, she brought with her a travel bag filled with magic. This bag will arrive tomorrow. But it is her physical prowess that truly confirms her identity. Her strength and stamina are beyond the powers of mortal women." He glanced at me slyly. "Though not of mortal men."

"What says the girl?" asked Queen Semiramis. She leaned forward, her crystal blue eyes stabbing into me. "Are you an angel from the Heavenly City?"

I'd shaken off some of the trance that she'd put me under, but by no means all of it. I shook my head and said in a subdued voice, "No. I'm not an angel, and I don't know what city you're talking about."

Mardon huffed. "See what I mean? Her attempts at deception are slow-witted, lacking both logic and creativity. Who would ever proclaim that they are unaware of the Heavenly City?"

Nimrod was becoming more interested. He said to me, "Do you expect us to believe that you have never seen the City in the Clouds?"

I cocked an eyebrow and shook my head. This was so darn weird. He sounded like this was something that he'd gazed upon many times. A city floating in the clouds? Didn't they have something like that in *Empire Strikes Back?* For a second I wondered if I was in a sci-fi movie.

Another distinguished man, perhaps as old as Nimrod, spoke from the gallery. "If you are not an angel, then why do you tell such an insipid lie?"

Mardon answered, "Because, Noble Havilah, it is as your brother the king has always stated—the heavenly beings are deceitful and cunning by their very nature. She cannot *help* but lie. She is a mindless sycophant of the God we seek to conquer."

I took in the gallery of thrones, my head shaking in disbelief. "You guys are out of your minds," I said, only half aware that I'd said it out loud.

"What was that?" demanded Nimrod.

"She called us 'out of our minds,'" said Queen Semiramis.

"Why do you call us crazy?" demanded Nimrod.

I shut my eyes and gave my head a quick joggle. "Oh, man. I don't even know where to begin. I can't believe the things you're saying. You actually think you can *conquer God?*"

"You see?" said Mardon with all the vigor of an attorney making a point to a jury. "Even while she lies she would try to frighten us at the prospects of our conquest. She would try to undermine our confidence in more than a century of planning and labor. She *is* an angel, Father, just as I—"

Nimrod raised his hand. Mardon instantly clammed up. The king now seemed to be taking this whole matter a little more seriously. It appeared that he was really starting to believe Mardon's claims of my "angelhood." Oh, brother! How was I supposed to respond? They really *were* wacko. It was no joke. They were as loony as jaybirds.

"Why do you feel that heaven's God cannot be conquered?" Nimrod asked me calmly. He firmly set his gaze, as if to concentrate hard on my answer. I realized that he was trying to pick my brain, somehow hoping I might give away some secret strategy.

I was beside myself with incredulity. "Is this a real question? What am I supposed to . . . ? The question itself is so . . . so *nuts!* What's with you people? Do you know what you're saying? This is *God* you're talking about! You think you can defeat the Being who created the universe? The one who framed the stars and made the sun and every planet? You're talking about attacking the Father of your spirit? How could *anyone*—? What in a *million years* would make you think this was remotely possible?"

The queen replied, "Apparently, Steffanie, you are not only a deceiver. You are also *deceived*. Who told you the God of Heaven was also its framer? Who told you that He conceived the universe?"

"Excuse me? Are you trying to tell me that He didn't?"

Another man spoke up. "That is precisely what she is telling you." He was older, like many of the others, but he had a dark complexion and piercing gray eyes. "Were you a witness to these events?"

"What do you mean?" I asked.

"What my brother Caanan is trying to ask," said yet another man with a long, leathery face, "is whether you saw such events with your own eyes. Did you see the God of Heaven create these things?"

I thought carefully and said, "Actually, I think I *did*. I'm *sure* I did. I just don't remember it. I would have witnessed it before I was born."

"Do you mean before you became an angel?" asked the queen.

"I told you, I'm not an angel."

"This is proof!" blurted another man, completely ignoring my statement. "The same spell of forgetfulness that was cast upon mortals has also been cast upon the angels."

"Of course, Philistim," said Nimrod. "I've tried to tell you this many times. Without such spells do you think that heaven's God could ever perpetuate such vicious lies?"

"Nevertheless," said Queen Semiramis, "what the angel says is quite true. She *did* witness the universe's creation. We were all there. But only after the veil is removed from her eyes, as it has been removed from Nimrod's and mine, will she finally see the truth. Only then will she know the depth of heaven's premeditated subterfuge. And at last she will see who it was that framed the earth and stars."

"Just who do you think framed it?" I asked in frustration.

The queen smiled, and then said plainly, "I did."

My jaw dropped. This was La-la Land. Plant a flag, post a sign. These people were in total La-la Land.

"I, Semiramis, framed the stars," she farther declared.

"And I, Cush," said Nimrod's father, "set the planets."

"And I, Calah, created the moon."

"And I, Caanan, built up the mountains and deserts."

"And I, Sidon, created the rivers and seas."

"And I, Havilah, created the clouds and rain."

"And I, Zemar, created fire and wind."

"And *I*," declared the king in a voice to silence all others, "as the mighty creator of the sun, sanctioned and commissioned it all."

I gaped at him, still too stunned to reply.

"Didn't you realize," asked Nimrod in perfect soberness, "that I was a god?"

I laughed, but it was a strange, exhausted-sounding laugh, overwhelmed with the utter ridiculousness of what I was hearing. Immediately there was an eruption of murmurs among the people in tasseled hats. One was bold enough to stand and cry, "*She has expressed blasphemy!*"

Again, Nimrod raised his hand. The gathering muttered for a few more seconds, then went quiet. The king was still awaiting my answer. I did my best to straighten up. I assessed the faces of everyone present. Nimrod and the others had sounded completely serious, so I decided to respond with equal seriousness.

"No," I said. "I don't believe you are a god. I worship only one God, and He is my Father in Heaven."

The old man, Cush, rose out of his seat. "You would give your devotions to a Being who once destroyed all life on earth? A God so full of envy that He would drown the very creatures whom He commanded to worship Him? The God to whom you pay homage is a God of *hate!* He spared my grandfather, but cursed my father! His blessings and cursings are the whims of a diseased and festering heart. My son wears the holy garments that once glorified Father Adam. With these garments he has become a mighty hunter of all corruption and iniquity. With these garments Nimrod *is* a god—a greater god than any who reign among the clouds and stars! He reigns over the earth itself. He is great because he seeks to glorify all mankind above the jealous, vengeful God of Heaven. Can there be a more righteous and benevolent ambition than to conquer and destroy such a perverse and evil kingdom?"

The resonance of Cush's words seemed to echo through the hall long after he'd finished talking. I felt the weight of everyone's enmity upon me, and I began to feel a little shaky. Tears were starting to form in my eyes. I raised up my chains and pressed one of my hands to my brow to try and fend off the dizziness.

"*Wow*," I said. "You people are so screwed up. I don't know what to say. I really don't know what to say."

In fact, I was mumbling even now. I no longer felt much of an affinity to Abinadi. When Abinadi had stood before the priests of Noah, hadn't the Spirit filled his mouth with great and stirring words? My mind was a blank. I felt like I had an ultimate stupor of thought. It was almost as if the Lord didn't *want* me to speak to them—didn't want me to bear my testimony. This disappointed me terribly. With all the stress that was weighing on me, I would have at least liked to vent my fury with a little righteous indignation. Was it because I wasn't a prophet that my mouth was stopped? Was it because I wasn't worthy? Or did the Spirit just not want me to cast my pearls before swine? Maybe it was just that when Abinadi had delivered his words, there was actually somebody in the audience who would listen. *Alma* had been in the audience. He was one of Noah's priests; he'd even recorded Abinadi's words. I began to wonder if there was anybody here who could possibly hear or comprehend any message that I might deliver. It seemed doubtful. What was I saying? It was *certain!* These folks were about as far out in the ozone as anyone could possibly be.

My stupor of thought seemed to please Nimrod. He said to his son, "Our angel appears to have lost her tongue. This is good. It gives me great assurance. I commend you, Prince Mardon. You have done a wise thing to bring her to us just two days before the commencement of our wondrous campaign." He said to the whole gathering, "What have I always taught regarding the moment that earth meets heaven?"

Caanan answered, "It has been revealed that in this moment the spell of forgetfulness that veils the minds of men will disappear."

"Yes," said Nimrod. "And just as this is true for all men who cross such a threshold, so it will also be true for an angel. Tonight the Heavenly City will be visible at dusk, and in two days it will pass close enough to the tower that our soldiers will finally be able to launch their long-awaited invasion. Let me ask you, Steffanie: if at this moment of truth your clouded memory is restored—if the erroneousness of your devotions is revealed—will you join us then? Will you become an ally in the cause of defeating the tyrant God? At this moment I have five thousand men converging to meet at the tower's summit. They will be joined by the five thousand men of Prince Mardon as soon as they arrive in the city. Tomorrow I will begin the final ascent myself. As I have promised from the very beginning, I will join them in their sacred cause. We will enter the Heavenly City with fire and judgement. Your knowledge, Steffanie, of the ethereal realm could prove invaluable to my armies. But I do not ask your loyalty until the very moment that this threshold is crossed—not until the veil is lifted and the smoke is cleared from your mind. Is this not a just and merciful offer? You have nothing to lose. Nothing except an eternity of falsehood and corruption. And in return you will gain all the glories of the Kingdom of Shinar."

I shook my head. "I don't want to be anywhere near you when you cross any thresholds. If I could manage it, I wouldn't be within a hundred miles of this place. I don't know what all you people have been smokin', but you've obviously been smokin' it for hundreds of years. Didn't you learn anything from Noah and Shem? How could any of you have forgotten the power and might of God?"

At last, I could feel something stirring inside me. This was the moment. My tongue was loose. At last, I would bear my testimony.

"I've *seen* God," I continued. "That is to say, I've seen His Son. I've touched the hand of Jehovah. And He is the God who created this earth. I've witnessed His power, but more importantly, I've felt His love. I've seen His might stretched out across the land. I've watched the sky ignite with fire and I've felt the earth tremble after He unleashed the fullness of His wrath. I know what He can do to something like that tower of yours—the one that you think will help you to reach the clouds. He could blast the whole thing with one sweep of His hand. One breath of His mouth. And worst of all, I suspect that He's about to do it. So I'm begging all of you—*any* of you who have the slightest glimmer of the Spirit still inside you— turn back to the God of Heaven. Turn away from your wickedness, and the wickedness of Nimrod. Turn away from *anyone* who would proclaim himself a god on earth while he's still in the flesh. Repent and plead for Heavenly Father's mercy. Plead for the salvation of His Son. It's . . . your only hope."

That was it. I'd said it. The speech wasn't exactly on par with Abinadi or Alma or Jeremiah, but I swore that I could feel every word of it flowing through me. I even wondered if somewhere among the ranks of these thirty men there might have been someone who was really listening—someone who the words were actually penetrating. At least I had their attention—every last person. They were gazing at me and then glancing nervously at their king.

As I might have expected, King Nimrod hadn't been moved in the least. He gave a little laugh. After that, several more of the men began laughing. The queen also laughed. What was it that I'd said about casting my pearls before swine? Oh, well. Maybe the testimony was more for me. How many times in a person's life can they bear a testimony like that? It felt so good. Maybe they could take it with them to the next world. Something told me that this was a journey many of them would be making very soon.

"Well spoken!" Nimrod declared. "One of the most eloquent speeches in behalf of your God that I've heard in a long while—perhaps since the days when Shem's missionaries were sent here from Salem. Since I had these deceivers executed long ago, perhaps it's only fitting that we should hear such words again so close to the eve of our triumph. Remember what she has said, nobles of Shinar! The day after tomorrow I will have her speak again. I will have her address us from the clouds of heaven. You will compare what she has uttered now to what she will utter then, after the fires of truth have seared her heart." He turned to his son. "Prince Mardon."

"Yes, my Lord Father."

"Arrange a litter that will carry her to the summit—No, on second thought, let her walk. You say that she has strength and stamina beyond the capacity of mortal women? Then let her climb the steps herself. Let her feel the ache in her angelic joints as she strives for that lofty height. After all, I won't allow anyone to carry *me*. I will also be ascending on foot."

"It will be done, King Nimrod," said Mardon. "I will escort her personally."

Nimrod turned again to me, his pointy beard aimed between my eyes. "After all these years, to think that we will make this magnificent assault with an angel in our midst! A denizen from the heavenly realm as our guide!" He sighed in great satisfaction. "Your arrival is a great omen, Steffanie. A sure sign of our impending victory."

I said smugly, "I wouldn't have thought that a god was worried about signs. I thought a god could manufacture his own omens."

The smile fled his face for an instant, but only an instant. Again I was heckled with the sound of his stomach-turning laugh. It occurred to me again that I wanted to be a hundred miles from this place. Actually, when Nimrod launched his crazed attack, I wished I could have been a thousand *light years* from here. But it looked like I was going to be right in the middle of it—right at the very summit of the Tower of Babel. A chill, like freezing acid, ran down my spine. I had no idea what was going to happen two days from now. Again I pondered the details of everything I'd heard: floating cities in the clouds, ten thousand warriors converging against heaven. My mind just couldn't seem to grasp it. But there were a few things I *did* know. I knew the ultimate fate of Nimrod's empire, and I knew that the people of the earth were about to be scattered and their language confounded. I had a queer feeling—a very black premonition—that this process was about to begin. In two days I feared I was going to witness something extraordinary—one of the most singularly unusual events in the history of the world. Yet in spite of it, only one thought kept pounding in my head.

I wished I could have been somewhere else.

Notes to Chapter 14:

Some have attributed the concept of polytheism—the idea that multiple gods or deities represented different aspects of nature (sun, moon, sea, rain, fire, childbirth, etc.)—to ancient Chaldea (Babylon). If so, then the party guilty of composing the original structure of this religion could well have been Nimrod. As the people of the earth were scattered, such a premise was apparently modified and adapted to other polytheistic cultures, including that of Egypt, Greece, Rome, Scandinavia, and India.

In fact, concepts that came out of ancient Babylon can be compared to virtually every polytheistic society. The most telling comparison may be the role that Nimrod may have claimed for himself. Many ancient manuscripts state that Nimrod, or Bel-Nimrod, was the original sun god. This would suggest that the sun gods of other cultures—Ra, Shamash, Moloch, Apollo, Chemosh and others—are basically a derivation of Nimrod's original model.

This legacy of establishing a corrupt pattern of worship is also associated with Nimrod's wife, Queen Semiramis. After Nimrod's death, it is written that Semiramis continued to perpetuate his idolization. Legend has it that she conceived through adultery and gave birth to an illegitimate son whom she named Tammuz. After claiming the child had been conceived supernaturally, she told the people that he was Nimrod reborn. But in the end, it was not so much the son who was worshiped as the mother. Semiramis became the mother of heaven, or the mother of the gods.

Many different ideas from the ancient religions of Babylon appear to have come down through the centuries. A key doctrine that has been twisted by the adversary is the idea of a divine mother-son relationship. As the populations of the earth were scattered, the concept of Semiramis's miraculous conception and birthing of a reincarnated sun god was apparently carried with them. Thus, in many parts of the world, the people began to worship a divine mother and god-child long before the birth of Christ. No doubt the practical purpose of this would have been to confuse, circumvent, and distort the actual miracle when it finally occurred.

The divine mother of heaven appears in different ways and is called by different names, but she has the same basic characteristics: beauty, fertility, and the ability to grant blessings and cursings. The model applies to Isis in Egypt, Indrani in India, Cybelle in Asia, Hera in Greece, Shing Moo in China, Hertha in Germany, Sisa in Scandanavia, etc. Many have also closely associated her with Ishtar, a name that is said to be the philological origin of the word "Easter." Even Israel, when it fell into apostasy, worshipped Ashteroth, who was known to the Jews as the "Queen of Heaven" (Jer. 44:17–19). But the origin of the mother-God icon seems to be Semiramis, the queen of Babylon (George F. Foryan, *Semiramis: Legendary Mysterious Queen of Assyria;* Yisrayl Hawkins, *The Original Goddess: Semiramis of Babylon*).

CHAPTER FIFTEEN

Harry

The four of us—Gidgiddonihah, Micah, Jesse, and I—stood at the edge of the cenote in the middle of the jungle. It was like a dark well, about seven feet across, leading down and down into nothingness. The stone had directed me to come here; otherwise, I doubted if this hole had ever been seen by human eyes. Perhaps a few animals had found it, and perhaps some had even become its victim by falling over the precipice. Brush had grown up thickly around its edges. Gid used his Roman sword—a souvenir that he'd kept from Greece—to cut his way through, while Jesse and Micah used their heavy saw-toothed obsidian blades. Gid had actually brought three swords home with him from Judea. One he'd left in his hut, and one he'd given to me. I hadn't held a piece of fine steel in my hands for almost three years. I must admit, it felt good.

The limestone edge of the cenote had appeared so suddenly that Jesse had almost fallen in. I'd reached out and grabbed the boy's arm. Calling him a "boy" wasn't exactly accurate anymore. He was fifteen now and nearly as large as me. He wore his hair a little longer than I remembered it, and his olive complexion was darker than ever. Micah was also looking more like a man than a teenager. His sandy hair had thickened, and his defiant-looking eyes were combined with a steady, determined jawline.

But it was the sight of Gidgiddonihah that continued to overwhelm me. It was really him—my old friend and hero. His appearance was as rough-and-tumble as ever. The bumps in his nose—broken several times over the years—and the scars on his face still gave him that look of unparalleled dignity. They were the wounds of a righteous warrior. In his eyes still burned the fire that I had known for most of my life, though I must admit that it looked a little more tame than usual. Maybe he was right about starting to grow soft while living in this peaceful and prosperous Nephite era. I think the prospect of another adventure reignited all his passions for life.

Yesterday Gid had revealed that he and Jesse had found me in the depths of the forest, almost as if I'd fallen out of the sky. Rafa, the falcon, had remained near me the whole time. Gid and Jesse had been hunting a mountain lion in the highlands of Zarahemla when they'd heard someone groaning in the underbrush. They carried me back to their camp where I remained unconscious for another eleven hours.

Apparently the pillar of energy had deposited my body a little more accurately than I could have imagined. I'd landed in Zarahemla in approximately 76 A.D. For Gid and the others it had been almost three years since we'd last laid eyes on each other in the tunnels of Frost Cave—the same passage of time that I had experienced. It was as if the tragic events of ancient Athens had never taken place—as if the grief and mourning that had oppressed my mind for three long years were a total waste of energy. Maybe there was something extraordinary to learn from this. The emotions were probably comparable to what we will feel with any of the reunions with departed loved ones that we will one day experience in the life to come. All of our memories of grief and pain will evaporate like a puff of steam, leading us to wonder why we had ever felt so tormented.

The Nephite warrior, Jewish orphan, and former Essene had actually gone into business together, gathering exotic furs and feathers in Zarahemla's misty mountains. Nevertheless, it took very little persuasion to entice them to join me in my quest to rescue Steffanie and to find my beloved Mary, Joshua, and Rebecca. Their eagerness bolstered my heart and reminded me again that there are few blessings on this earth more glorious than true and loyal friends.

It had taken a day and a half to arrive at this place in the jungle. We continued to peer into the foreboding pit. Rafa, who had been flying overhead throughout our journey, landed on a tree limb overlooking the cenote. Micah leaned over and dropped a stone into the blackness. We waited to hear a splash. There was nothing.

"Does it have a bottom?" Gid inquired.

"I'm sure it does," I replied, "but not the kind of bottom that you might expect. It's a time portal. It will transport us back to the place where I can help my family."

"A time portal?" asked Jesse.

"Yes, like the tunnels in Frost Cave—the same tunnels that brought you here."

This was still somewhat difficult for Jesse and Micah to grasp. After all, Zarahemla was a different place than Judea or Greece, but not a different *time*. The concept of "time travel" was still a little fuzzy to them.

"Let me see if I understand this," said Micah. "You're telling us that this pit—this cenote—will transport us back to ancient Babylon?"

"I think so," I said.

"Why aren't you sure?" asked Gid. "What exactly did you see in the stone?"

I sighed. "It wasn't an image really. Just a moment. I've simply asked the Lord to send us to the place where we are needed most critically. You have to understand, my whole family is caught up in a whirlwind right now—Meagan, Marcos, my Uncle Garth. I'm not even sure of the situation with my father and Sabrina. I don't care what moment we're transported to. I'll leave that to God. The most important thing is that we leap into the pit at precisely the right instant."

"When is that?" asked Micah.

"Soon. When it comes, I'll know it." I tightened my fist around the seerstone.

Jesse leaned over the edge and shuddered. "We're just supposed to leap *blindly*, not knowing where we will go or what will happen?"

I nodded.

Jesse blew a sigh. "You already had to go back to save the life of Gidgiddonihah. I hope that you won't have to go back to save the rest of us if we're smashed on a rock bed below."

"That can't happen," I replied. "I mean, I'm not sure I could survive another attempt like the last. The next time . . . I think it would kill me."

The feeling was actually a little stronger than "I think." The stone had communicated this message very clearly to my mind. If I ever made another attempt to enter a field of time where my body already existed, I would wither and crumble in a matter of minutes. One paradox per lifetime—that's how I chose to look at it. Even now my stamina wasn't fully recovered. There was a tingling in my flesh that hadn't entirely gone away. But none of this mattered. Gidgiddonihah was alive. Even looking at him right now I had to restrain myself from shouting for joy. I think Gid was getting a little tired of seeing the wonderstruck grin on my mug. I couldn't help it.

Gid was still having a hard time accepting my story. He shook his head and said, "I remember those events in Athens as well as anyone. Nobody needed to save my life. We defeated both of those miserable Scythians without complications. No arrow fired from their bows ever came *close* to piercing my flesh."

"Don't you remember the flashlight beam that illuminated the Scythian in the stairwell?" I asked him. "Don't you remember banging on that door to try and get through to the other side? I was right there—just on the other side."

"*I* remember it," said Jesse. "I also remember finding the flashlight at the bottom of the stairs. I've kept it for the past three years, even though it stopped working shortly after we arrived in Zarahemla."

"I might have an extra set of batteries in Steffanie's pack," I said. "But what did you think when you found it? What did *I* say about it?"

"You didn't know *what* to think," said Micah. "None of us did. Except me, of course. I knew exactly where it had come from."

"Didn't you ever tell them about riding back to the burning house and finding me?" I asked Micah.

He shook his head.

I found this astonishing. "You mean you never explained how you carried my body to that cave behind the waterfall?"

"You told me *not* to," said Micah. "Don't you remember? You said it quite emphatically."

That's right. It was just before I'd entered the tunnel that went under the lake. I'd told him to forget that he'd ever seen me. As usual,

Micah had been true to his word. I should have recalled this characteristic from my years with him on Lincoln Island.

"Micah never explained to us why he rode back," said Gid. "But I remember that when he returned, you chided him sharply for being gone so long. The ship had almost sailed without him."

"*I* chided him?" I asked.

"Of course," said Gid. "You were *there*."

"I'm just glad to know that I'm not crazy," said Jesse. "I *knew* that I had seen you in the woods before I was taken captive by the Scythian. But when I tried to ask you about it, you emphatically denied it."

"I denied it?"

"You tried to convince me that I was hallucinating."

I squeezed my eyes shut and shook them open again. This was all so confusing. I remembered *none* of this! All that I recalled about that night in Athens was the horrible grief. Micah, Jesse, and Gid had completely different memories of what had occurred. Yesterday Gid had even reminisced about the events of Apollus's baptism and meeting John the Beloved. It made me dizzy to think of it. And yet . . .

Somehow I *did* have a blurry recollection of the events that they were describing. I couldn't explain it, but in my head there was a strange image of watching Micah ride back toward Epigonus's estate, almost as if some secret chamber of my mind was slowly releasing an entirely different perspective of what had occurred. I had a dim recollection of arguing with Jesse over the very event that he was describing. I also saw flashes—quite vague—of Gid on the ship as we journeyed home, and flashes of the moment when I embraced him and said good-bye. The images were so ethereal, like trying to remember a dream from my boyhood. Was I creating these images in my imagination? I wasn't entirely certain.

We waited at the edge of that cenote for another hour. As the time drew near, I looked around for Rafa and held out my arm. The falcon had flown off again, but even if I couldn't see *him*, he had never stopped watching *me*. Just before he swooped down and landed on my forearm (which was still protected by a triple wrapping of Steffanie's sweatpants) he dropped a half-eaten, large rodent at our feet. At least Rafa would be well fed before undertaking this journey.

I'd asked Gid to bring along a small wooden box with air holes, about the size of a mailbox. Its purpose was to protect the bird during the unpredictable voyage through time. I realized it wasn't going to be easy to coax Rafa to get inside. He still didn't seem to trust me entirely, but by first putting the dead peccary inside the box, we were able to entice him to enter. Then Jesse distracted him long enough for me to get the lid on. The falcon made a racket, again utterly incensed, but he was otherwise unharmed.

I think Gid was more enamoured of the bird than anyone else. "I once knew some Ammonites who used falcons to hunt," he said. "If your bird is trained in the same manner, you'll never hunger in the wilderness."

"I'm really not sure why he stays with me at all," I said. "I've hit him with a rock, dragged him into a cavern, nearly gotten him eaten by a dragon, and drenched him under a waterfall. In return all he's gotten out of it is a couple morsels of dehydrated chicken."

"He is meant as a blessing to you," said Gid. "Someday he may save your life."

"No more than you, I'm sure," I replied.

Gid huffed at this. "I don't think I've saved your life any more than you have saved mine, Harryhawkins. I suppose it's time that I thanked you for what you did for me in Greece. I may not fully understand it, but . . . I believe it happened." Hesitantly, he asked, "Tell me something. On that night that I . . . died . . . what were my last words?"

I replied solemnly, "You spoke of your late wife and little girl."

Gid nodded. This made sense to him.

"If I hadn't changed things," I said guiltily, "you'd be with them now."

"Not if I wasn't *meant* to be there," he replied emphatically. "Isn't that why you felt you were told to go back?"

I nodded, my confidence returning. "Yes, I felt that very strongly."

"There you are," said Gid succinctly. "I suspect they'll still be waiting when my time comes. But not until I'm old and gray, maybe with another brood of young ones circling around me, and another strong woman at my side."

"That'll be the day," Jesse teased.

Gid puffed up his chest, feigning offense. "You don't think I'll find one who'll have me?"

"Oh, certainly," said Micah. "I'm sure we can rustle up some old, toothless widow if we look hard enough." He winked at me.

Gid scoffed. "Tell me, Harry. Why do I put up with these two pirates?"

"I have a feeling you were meant for each other," I replied.

Jesse looked into the pit again. "How much longer will we wait?"

"It's almost time," I said. "Let's get ready."

The four of us stood at the edge of the precipice. I could feel the renewed tension and nervousness. You'd have to trust somebody a great deal to agree to jump into a bottomless pit with him. Jesse was having the hardest time of all.

He asked, "Are you certain there isn't another way?"

"This is the closest conduit," I said. "I haven't inquired, but the next portal may be hundreds of miles away."

"Are we all going to jump at once?" asked Micah.

"I suggest two at a time," I said. "But don't let more than seven or eight seconds pass between jumps, or you might end up in the middle of the Mediterranean Sea during the Peloponnesian War."

"I'll jump first," said Gid.

"I'll go with you," said Micah.

I looked at Jesse. "That leaves you and me for the second wave."

He nodded and swallowed.

I waited another minute, then I grinned at everyone. "Just like old times?"

Gid grinned back. "Like old times."

"Now!" I cried. "Jump!"

Gid and Micah leaped into the blackness. I clutched the box with Rafa inside. My free hand grabbed the strap of Steffanie's pack.

"Go!" I said to Jesse.

We leaped together into the void. The jagged walls of the cenote flew past my eyes. But then the light flickered out. Suddenly, I could no longer see Jesse falling with me. There were flashes, like blue streaks of lightning, and an instant later I sensed that I was engulfed by water. It wasn't like I'd landed in a river or lake, but as if the water had simply coalesced around my body. Next I felt as if a force like a firehose was whipping, sloshing, and slapping against me. It was like being caught in a waterspout. Everything was still pitch black. Churning water raged in my ears.

All at once I was thrust into the air, like being shot out of a cannon. I landed in a rapidly moving stream. The weight of the pack pressed me right to the bottom, but the depth was only a few feet—and quickly receding. I pushed up with one hand. My other arm still clutched the wooden box with Rafa inside. The bird let out a squawk of complaint, but at least I knew that he'd survived.

My body came to rest unexpectedly on the stony surface. The water continued rushing around me until it was only an inch deep. Then it seemed to trickle away into almost nothing. Clearly we'd arrived at our destination—wherever that destination might have been.

"Gid!" I cried into the darkness, coughing a few times to get the water out of my lungs. "Jesse!"

"I'm here," Gid said.

"So am I," said Jesse.

"Micah?"

"Yes," he said, coughing violently. "But I think I swallowed the Sea of Galilee."

Surprisingly, Rafa was fairly quiet. I wondered if he'd gone to sleep, like all the other times we'd ended up in a cave.

"Jesse!" I called out. "Do you have that flashlight?"

"Here."

I felt the canister nudge my ribs. I unzipped the pack and dug down to the bottom until I'd found what felt like two separate packages of size-D batteries. There in the dark I tore open the packages, opened the flashlight, and fumbled until I'd gotten it all back together. The hardest part was feeling for the "plus" bumps on the end of the batteries. The old dead batteries that Jesse had left inside were pretty corroded. This old flashlight had been through the grind-mill. I'd have certainly understood if it no longer worked. I screwed the top back in place and pressed the button.

And there was light! I shined it around until I'd accounted for my three companions, all of them looking wet and disheveled. Then I looked over our location. It was quite unusual. At first I couldn't figure it out. Was it a cave? I wasn't quite sure. We were inside a tunnel of some sort. It was shaped like a perfect arch. The ceiling was about five feet overhead, except for the far end, where it looped upward. At the top of the loop was a three-foot diameter hole. Apparently this was where the water had shot us out. Looking the other way, the tunnel curved around and disappeared.

I immediately opened the box and dumped out the falcon, along with the carcass of the peccary and a pint of water that had seeped through the airholes. Rafa shook off his wings.

Gid got to his feet and looked around. "This is man-made," he observed. He felt along the wall, which was composed of large hewn stones, cemented together.

"Is it a sewer?" asked Jesse.

"I'm not sure," I said quizzically.

Micah turned to me. "I thought you said that this 'time portal' was always associated with natural phenomenon. Didn't you say that it expelled you out of a geyser?"

"That's what it did the *last* time I arrived here," I said. "I have a feeling that some of the conduits that connect the fields of time and space move around."

Gid crinkled his forehead. "Explain that in plain Nephite."

I shrugged. "I'm not sure I can describe it any clearer. I don't understand it myself. What I mean is that sometimes the portals are associated with very specific locations—like the Galaxy Room—and sometimes the portals appear and disappear, almost like a wrinkle in the fabric of space, like when you found me unconscious on the jungle floor."

"So what are you saying?" asked Micah.

"He's saying that we could be just about anywhere," said Jesse.

"No," I replied. "The Lord wouldn't have sent us just anywhere. Wherever it is, it's where we're supposed to be."

"Then let's start moving," said Gid. "I suggest we follow the falcon."

Rafa was already walking down the tunnel, perhaps drawn by the smell of fresh air. We arched our backs to accommodate the low ceiling and followed the bird around the bend. The tunnel had a slightly downward grade. We seemed to be going deeper, which wasn't very comforting. I'd have assumed that any exit would have been above us. I wondered if we should have ventured the other way, perhaps crawled through that three-foot hole. But if there were another blast of water, we'd have gotten washed right back out.

The bend continued for some distance, until we arrived at a fork. It consisted of another three-foot-diameter hole. I shined my light inside. The surface inside was dry, unlike the floor under our feet, which was still slick with runoff. The main tunnel made a sharp turn to the left. Then there was a rounded cliff with a nine- or ten-foot drop.

"What is this labyrinth?" asked Micah.

"I think I see daylight," Jesse announced.

There was a faint glow just over the edge of the drop, shining in from the tunnel beyond. Rafa spread his wings and flew down to the next level. Then he continued walking toward the source of sunlight. The drop-off wasn't particularly high, but the rounded cliff made it difficult to maneuver.

"Grab my wrist," Gid said to Jesse. "I'll lower you down."

I did the same for Micah. Both of them landed squarely on the floor below.

I turned to Gid. "You first."

I took his wrist and did my best to lower him over the drop-off. After he'd landed at the bottom, I tossed the flashlight to Jesse. Then I got down on my belly and slid over the rounded edge, landing firmly on both feet.

As we turned toward the opposite end of the tunnel, our faces were illuminated by sunlight. There was definitely an exit about seventy-five yards beyond us. We could perceive a patch of the blue sky. The quality of the light was somewhat subdued, as if it was close to the end of the day.

We could see Rafa. The bird continued making his way toward the opening. As he finally reached the lip of the exit, I had a strange feeling. Maybe it was just the bird's excitement. He squawked delight-edly as he gazed out at the wide world, almost as if he recognized it. It occurred to me that if Rafa felt at home here, I might never see him again.

But if this moment was good-bye, the falcon didn't make any effort to express it. Without turning back, he opened his wings and launched into the open air, gliding outward. But then I felt sure that he floated *down*. When he disappeared, it was *below* the level of the opening. Apparently the exit was some distance above the ground. I started to feel nervous inside. I had the awful impression that I knew exactly where we were.

Just as this thought struck me, I heard an odd rumbling, growing louder. Micah was the first to interpret it.

"Water," he announced. "It's headed this way!"

Terror rippled through me. There was no telling how high above the ground that exit was. We could be washed over a thousand-foot cliff.

"Quickly!" said Gidgiddonihah. "Stand back to back! Lock elbows!"

"Huh?" asked Jesse in befuddlement.

"Just do it!" I called out.

I knew what was on Gid's mind. I threw off my backpack. Gid and I stood back to back, pressing our shoulder blades together. We locked elbows. Before Jesse and Micah could mimic the action, they had to pull their obsidian blades around from behind so that the weapons hung against their breasts. Afterwards, they got into the same position.

"Press your feet against the walls." Gid commanded. "Make your legs wide for balance. Push with all your might!"

The roar was almost upon us. Gid and I pressed so hard that we were suspended in midair. The water would hit Micah and Jesse first. I gritted my teeth and braced for impact.

The water not only blasted from the hole just above the nine-foot drop, but it was also rolling down the main tunnel. The two torrents merged. A liquid wall crashed into our bodies and rolled over the top of us. Gidgiddonihah and I held firm, but the force of the impact was too much for Micah and Jesse. I felt Jesse's body collide into mine. Micah latched onto Gidgiddonihah. Gid and I locked our legs and dug our heels. Jesse didn't make it any easier. He grabbed onto my face, looking for a grip. He stuck two fingers into my mouth and tried to find a grip using the inside of my cheek. His other arm latched onto my torso.

The worst of it lasted only ten seconds, and then the current began to subside. And not a moment too soon, because there was no strength left in my legs. They finally buckled, but by then the force of the wave had decreased dramatically. We'd survived another potential disaster. Nevertheless, we were swept along with the current for about forty yards, tumbling and sliding toward the sunlight. Finally the torrent was reduced to a mere trickle. The tunnel opening was only about a hundred feet farther. I realized the current had carried Steffanie's backpack right over the edge.

"Do we still have the flashlight?" Jesse asked.

"No," I said. "That was washed away too."

"Doggone-it!" he said—a euphemism that he must have originally learned from me. "And we just got it working too."

We got up and sloshed the rest of the way to the end of the tunnel. As we reached the lip of the exit, the impression that I'd received a moment earlier was verified. The sight was absolutely spectacular. We were in the middle of the sky! The sloping edge of the tower must have descended for three or four thousand feet before it reached the valley floor. The base was surrounded by hundreds of buildings, and in the far distance I could see several ugly black lakes. No doubt these were the major source of bitumen slime used to hold this monstrosity together. I also noted some massive scars on the landscape—sand and rock quarries that might have once been high hills before their substance was molded into bricks and transported here. These quarries, as well as the black lakes, were surrounded by tightly knit networks of buildings that looked considerably less attractive than the rest of the city of Babel. I could only conclude that these were the shantytowns of the count-less slaves who'd helped Nimrod construct this tower. In the nearer distance, perhaps a mile from the base of the tower, stretched a wide platform covered by a bright red carpet. There were several men standing on the near end of this platform waving flags. Beside the platform were several lofty structures. The tallest must have stood four or five stories, and it sort of resembled that one building in Russia with the teardrop-shaped turrets. I strongly suspected it was one of Nimrod's palaces.

"Where *are* we?" asked Micah, his eyes wide.

"Haven't you guessed it?" I replied. "We're inside the Tower of Babel."

Directly below us about a hundred feet was a level balcony—just one of the many balconies, or terraces, that encircled the tower at various levels. The water from the tunnel had poured into a cement cistern, nearly the size of a swimming pool. But how had Nimrod gotten so much water this high? Then it occurred to me: maybe the majority of it had been collected during rainstorms, like the fortress of Masada. There was plenty of surface area on this tower to catch vast amounts of rain.

The terrace below us was covered with tents—at least three dozen—supported by ropes and poles. The occupants of those tents were soldiers. I easily distinguished the blue and red uniforms of foot soldiers, and the shimmering purple and gold robes of officers. Presently many of the men were crouching along the bank of the cistern, drinking heartily and gathering buckets of water. At the edge of the balcony another man was waving a pair of bright red flags. He seemed to be communicating with someone higher up the tower. That explained the sudden deluge of water. He must have asked someone above us to release water from a higher cistern.

All along the various platforms and terraces I could see more tent cities and thousands of soldiers. Hundreds more soldiers hadn't yet settled into camp. Long rows of men—divided into units of about a hundred soldiers each—continued ascending the various stairways and sloping pathways, all pushing toward the summit. They looked like dozens of blue and red centipedes, squirming determinedly to a higher elevation. More and more of the units were settling in for the evening. The sun was a brilliant scarlet fireball, sitting right at the edge of the western horizon.

But why in the name of Jupiter were thousands of soldiers assembling on the slopes of the Tower of Babel? The same question was percolating in Gidgiddonihah's military mind.

"It almost appears as if they're making ready to launch an attack," he observed. "Or a vigorous defense."

"Are they expecting someone to attack the tower?" asked Jesse.

"If I didn't know any better," said Gid thoughtfully, "I'd say they were expecting to find an adversary at the summit."

"At the *summit?*" I said in surprise. Was it possible that the army of Japheth had taken up a defensive position at the top? But how would they have gotten past Nimrod's armies in Babel and reached the stairways of the tower in the first place?

Micah suggested a solution to the riddle. "They're mounting an assault against heaven."

We gawked at him in bewilderment. We realized that he was serious.

"Say *again?*" asked Jesse.

"Haven't any of you read the ancient manuscripts?" asked Micah petulantly. "I committed many of them to memory in my youth, and they recount quite plainly that Nimrod's primary reason for constructing this massive tower was to defeat the armies of God and lay claim to the kingdom of heaven." He looked at me. "I thought you told me that in your century these manuscripts are still read and scrutinized."

"I was talking about the *Bible*. But I think the total discussion of Babel in the book of Genesis is four or five verses—at least in *our* version."

All at once I remembered the City in the Clouds—the extraordinary sight that I had witnessed from the reeds on the night that I had escaped from Mardon's encampment.

A little absently I said, "I think Micah is right."

Gid raised an eyebrow. "These men truly think they can wage war against heaven?"

"Not against *heaven*," I corrected. "But definitely against *something*."

They looked at me queerly.

"I'm not sure if I can explain," I said. "You'll just have to see it for yourselves. You should be able to very soon."

I scanned the horizon. There was nothing in the evening sky that even remotely resembled the cloud with the glowing lights that I had seen that night. Thinking back, it had seemed to me that the floating city was *beyond* the Tower of Babel. That would have placed it *behind* us. The massive tower might have been blocking our view. We needed to climb around to the other side.

"Look," said Jesse, pointing at the cistern below.

Several men were making their way out into the water to fetch something. I leaned out as far as I dared. They were going after Steffanie's pack. The waterproof pack was floating right next to the wall.

"That's the last we'll see of *that*," said Micah.

"They might not find the light," said Jesse. "Surely it sank to the bottom."

I continued to watch the soldiers in the water. One waited in the shallower water while the other swam out the last few yards to finally fish the backpack out. I wanted to see what they would do with it, but I was also curious for another reason.

"Careful, Harry," said Gidgiddonihah. "Don't let them see you."

"I want to see how deep that water is," I said.

"What are you thinking?" asked Micah hesitantly.

"The same thing we're *all* thinking," said Gid. "There's only one way down from here. And it's a hundred-foot leap."

"There may be another way down," I said. "But it would have the same result. If there's another wave of water, we might just let it wash us over the edge."

"What about going back the other way and crawling upward through one of those narrow tunnels?" asked Jesse.

I shook my head. "We'd never be able to climb back up that nine-foot ledge. Especially while it's wet."

"You'd rather splash down in the middle of several hundred soldiers?" asked Micah.

"We'll wait until dark," said Gid, "when the army is asleep."

"Even if the fall doesn't break our legs," said Jesse, "our splash will wake the dead."

"I don't think we have any other option," I said. "The stone wouldn't have brought us here unless Steffanie or Mary were in the area. I have a strong suspicion that it's Steffanie."

"Why would they make her climb the tower?" asked Micah.

"I told you. They think she's an angel. They probably think she can stand up there and convince the Lord to surrender. Or maybe they think she'll provide some critical military advice. Who can say with someone as deranged as Nimrod?"

"So where would we search for her?" asked Jesse.

I looked down again at the cistern. "We may be about to find out."

The men had finished retrieving the pack. As I might have expected, they were showing it to one of the purple-cloaked officers.

"Keep your eyes on that pack," I said. "If my instincts are correct, they'll carry it precisely to the place that we need to go."

"I still don't understand the plan," said Jesse. "Even if we find her—even if we *rescue* her—how will we get down from this tower?"

We looked to Gidgiddonihah for a possible answer, but the Nephite warrior only shrugged.

"I wouldn't worry about details," he said, grinning crookedly. "It makes you grow old before your time."

Jesse and Micah looked confused, but to me the statement had great wisdom. Details were for God. In a mission like this, we did best to take things one moment at a time.

The men below carried on a discussion about the pack for several minutes. The superior officer examined the contents, which only seemed to baffle him dramatically. Finally, he appeared to draw the conclusion that I'd been hoping for. This was obviously a matter for higher authorities. He ordered that the pack be taken elsewhere. My secret hope was that it would also be the place where they were keeping Steffanie.

A detachment of runners departed from the terrace with the backpack in hand. I followed them with my eyes as far as I could. Daylight was fading fast. I could hardly distinguish one knot of men from another. And then, to my great regret, I lost them altogether. They went behind a kind of stone facade still under construction at the edge of a large landing to the east. The men were still climbing. Their final destination seemed to be farther up the tower. At least we knew the general direction that we needed to follow. That is, if we ever got down from this ridiculous height.

We sat and waited for several hours. Gidgiddonihah remained at the lip of the opening, closely observing any developments. Finally he turned to us and announced, "I think we should do it now."

My heartbeat quickened. I looked over the edge. There was no movement. Just dozens of silent tents, the canvases flapping in the stiff breeze. The entire face of the tower was still. Only a few torches or lanterns were glowing—but none of them were burning directly below us. I couldn't even see any sentries. The army was apparently under orders to get a good night's rest. The stars were bright. The moon glowed like a white opal, with flecks of blue and green. The night wind was rather cold at this altitude. Fortunately, my clothes were pretty well dry. But that was about to change.

"We should try and leap all at once," said Gid. "No need to create more than one splash. Afterward, we'll swim quickly toward the east end of the cistern."

"Tuck your legs," I suggested. "It'll make your splash bigger, but it may spare your legs if it turns out to be shallower than I think."

"And if we're attacked?" asked Jesse.

Gid nodded toward Jesse's obsidian-edged sword, still wrapped in leather behind his shoulder. "Then I suggest you remember all that I taught you."

I looked down at the target again. Funny how this jump seemed twice as frightening as jumping blindly into the cenote. It was almost better not knowing what was at the bottom. We lined up along the edge. After a curt nod from Gidgiddonihah, I began the count.

"One. Two. *Three*."

We jumped. Since I was on the far right, I tried to jump out a little farther to keep from knocking anyone as I landed. I think Gid, on the other end, did the same. The cold wind ripped into my flesh. As I fell, I tucked my knees. A hundred feet slipped by in an instant.

I felt the slap of water, like a swat from a paddle. Despite tucking my legs, I went right to the bottom. The pool was only about seven feet deep. If anyone had failed to take my advice, there were sure to be broken limbs. The explosion as four bodies cannonballed into the cistern must have been tremendous. It may have even splashed some of the tents.

My head broke the surface. The others were a short distance away. Micah and Gid were already swimming toward the east wall. Jesse swam over to make sure I was all right.

"I'm fine!" I whispered. "Follow Gid! Let's go!"

Gid's advice was inspired. There was a tunnel on the east end of the pool with about six inches of headroom. It was undoubtedly designed as a kind of canal to send water to a cistern farther down the tower. Just as Jesse and I swam under the ceiling, several silhouettes appeared along the banks of the cistern, talking excitedly.

"A missile from heaven!" one of them exclaimed.

I thought at first he was suggesting it was a meteor, but apparently he meant something more specific. The splash had been interpreted as a divine attack. No one seemed to have heard us swimming into the tunnel. We waited and watched. After a few minutes a dozen more men assembled, still speculating about the cause of the splash. A few lamps were ignited. We pressed under the ceiling a little farther. None of the soldiers dared enter the water. Someone even suggested that it might be poisoned.

An officer in a purple cloak announced, "The angels must know we're coming. They are aroused with the fear of Nimrod. Praise to our King!"

"Praise Lord Nimrod!" several chanted in response.

Gid motioned that we keep moving. The tunnel was pitch dark. I could barely see my hand in front of my face. The water level was up to our necks.

"Where do you think it leads?" I whispered.

"It must lead to a gate that releases the water," said Gid.

"Then it might be a dead end," said Micah.

But at just that moment we began to perceive a blue beam of moonlight up ahead. We soon arrived at the gate that Gid had anticipated. It looked as if it was hoisted by a mechanism of pulleys and chains somewhere up above. There was an access corridor leading to the surface. We exited the water and climbed the stairway. Suddenly Jesse stopped.

"My *sword!*" he exclaimed. "I've lost it! It must have fallen off when I landed in the water."

"And you've only just realized it?" scolded Micah.

"I've got to go back," said Jesse.

"No," I said sternly. "We'll have to go on without it."

"I *can't!*" He'd already jumped back into the water.

"*Jesse!* Are you crazy?" I went back down the stairs to prevent him from leaving.

"Wait for me up top," he said and swam into the darkness.

I felt Gid's hand on my shoulder. "Don't try and go after him. When Jesse gets something in his head, there's no stopping him."

"But he'll be killed!" I protested.

"The boy is more clever than you think—a trait he honed as an orphan."

"Even if he can swim back out into the cistern without being discovered," said Micah, "what are his chances of finding that weapon in the dark?"

"Don't underestimate him," said Gid. "Let's go up top and wait."

The access corridor took us out into the night air. I was shivering violently. We huddled together near the cement structure that housed the mechanisms that controlled the cistern gate. One of the tower's many stairways blocked our view of the platform where the soldiers had made their camp. This also prevented us from seeing Jesse.

A half hour later I was going berserk with worry. "I have to go back and find him."

Gid stopped me again. "Wait a little longer. He likes to take his time."

"Gid's right about that," said Micah. "It took a lot of patience to capture a live jaguar."

"Jesse caught a live jaguar?" I asked in amazement.

"Juvenile," said Gid. "Still, it nearly took his head off. Earned us a nice trade in the markets of Gideon."

"Markets?" I asked. "I thought everything was held in common in Zarahemla in 76 A.D."

"*Common* markets," clarified Micah. "Everyone is still expected to provide their share. That day we provided a live jaguar."

A shadow appeared on the terrace below us, moving quickly. It was Jesse. His arms were loaded down with something. He crossed behind one of the archways that supported some stairs leading toward the summit and approached us briskly.

"Did you find it?" Micah called to him.

"Of course," said Jesse cockily. "But I left it there."

"You *left it?*" I asked.

"I took this stuff instead." He unloaded his arms. An array of soldier's uniforms and weapons landed at our feet. "Some of the soldiers must have washed their clothes. They left them out to dry."

"You stole their clothes?" asked Micah, grinning.

It was hard to suppress a laugh. "I apologize, Jesse, for ever underestimating you."

Gid examined the weapons. "I'd have my men flogged if they ever allowed their weapons to be stolen."

"I only took the two bronze swords," said Jesse. "I thought they might make Micah and me less conspicuous than carrying those bulky obsidian clubs. But you still haven't seen the best part." Jesse kicked through the clothing and revealed the purple and yellow cloak of an officer.

"Jesse, you're a genius!" I exclaimed. "That's for you, Gid."

The salty old warrior declined. "You wear it, Harry. This is your mission, and I'm proud to serve under you."

I smiled, my confidence surging. "Then here's the plan. At first light we blend in with the other soldiers. We climb with the rest and keep an eye out for Prince Mardon or the entourage of King Nimrod. That's where we'll find Steffanie. I'm also hoping that rescuing Steffanie may lead us to finding Mary and the others."

Gid and Jesse nodded, but Micah still looked troubled.

"What's wrong?" I asked him.

"I'm still worried that if we find Steffanie, we'll never make it off this tower."

"I have that figured out too," I said. "She'll become *our* prisoner. We'll claim that the king commanded us to take her down."

Micah shook his head. "That's not what I meant. I'm worried that we'll never make it off in *time*."

We let this sink in. I understood far better than I cared to admit. A war was about to commence—man versus God. The concept filled my heart with an icy chill. But it was God's side of the campaign that caused me the deepest concern. Nowhere in the modern world was there a tower like this. Yet it should have stood longer than the pyramids. Something was going to happen to it, and like Micah, I didn't want to be anywhere near when it did. The urgency to finish our mission burned more intensely than ever. Tomorrow was a day of judgment—a day of reckoning.

Tomorrow, for the second time in my life, I expected to see the fullness of the wrath of God.

CHAPTER SIXTEEN

Mary

Salem.

It was a name of reverence and wonder even in the time of my father, Symeon Cleophas, in first-century Judea. Many of us had been taught that the old city of Jerusalem (before the Romans had destroyed it) was only a rebuilt citadel on the landscape of a mysterious and magnificent city whose residents had disappeared without a trace from the face of the earth. Since Abram was presently a very small child, I knew that it would still be a few years before its citizens would be exalted in a manner like unto those of the city of Enoch, but the aspirations of Salem were evidently the same—to build a perfect community, a landmark of devotion and dedication to the gospel of the Messiah.

Many times during our four-day journey to its gates, I felt keen feelings of unworthiness to be visiting such a place, but every time I held little Abram in my arms such feelings subsided. I realized that as long as I repented of my sins—as long as I continued to strive to live according to the example of my Savior—I was as clean and innocent as this little babe. Simply put, I would be at home in this place. I would belong.

But if this land that we were crossing was Judea, it had hardly any resemblance to the Judea where I had been raised. The region was lush and fertile, abounding with forests and plenty of water and drainage. On the fourth day we passed through a valley that Mahonri called the plain of Jordan. We also crossed a river of the same name, but if this was the River Jordan where I had bathed and drawn water as a young girl—the same river where my Lord and Savior was baptized—then clearly there had been a dramatic transfiguration of the country. Instead of a barren wilderness full of scorpions and thieves, it was now the very image of the Garden of Eden. Rather than a dead, salty sea between the hills of Judea and Moab, I could see a beautiful gulf, a crystal blue lake whose surface glistened in the morning light with a luminescence like beryllium. As well, the Jordan River did not meet its death in this desiccated valley. According to Mahonri and Pagag, it flowed on to the Red Sea.

Try as I might to name the landmarks and hills that I should have known so well—the valleys of the plain, the hills of Jericho, or the Mount of Olives—they all seemed only vaguely familiar. Perhaps I should not have underestimated the geographical changes that can take place in three thousand years.

Salem was a walled city in the midst of a panorama of rolling hills. Even from a distance the sight of it stirred my soul. Its size was immense, but not because it was congested with people. The dwelling houses—all of them immaculate—were spaced out evenly on large plots of land. The city's wall did not seem any great barrier of defense. It stood to the height of a man, and it seemed to me more of a boundary than a barricade. This place was defended by something far more powerful than walls or weapons, and I could feel this more palpably the closer we rode.

In the very center I saw a gleaming building that I felt sure was a temple of God. Unlike that monstrosity in Shinar, this appeared to be an edifice of elegance and simplicity. The fields surrounding Salem abounded with crops and livestock—sheep and cattle and goats, all healthy and flourishing. I had never seen a community so well tended, so free of dilapidation. The artisans and builders were meticulous in their detail, all of them servants of a master plan that was surely orchestrated by Salem's king.

Our approach must have been seen from afar, because as we neared the city gate, there already awaited a welcome party of about a hundred people to greet us. Jacom and the others were among them, having fulfilled their assignment to inform the residents of our coming.

"Who are they all?" inquired Becky, her imagination stimulated, as was mine, at the prospect of who we might meet this day.

"You think you're going to know all of their names?" teased Joshua.

"I'm ignoring you," said Becky.

"Don't worry," I told her. "I'll help you to know the lineage and accomplishments of everyone we meet—if I can remember them all myself."

Joshua had been moody and restless for much of the trip, but particularly so this afternoon. He seemed torn between a desire to meet so many venerated prophets and fulfilling some other task or responsibility. But of course, he rebuffed any effort that I made to ask him why he was so restless, insisting that he was just anxious to see Salem.

I had made a concerted effort since our departure to avoid thinking about the sword. I still did not feel wholly immune from its influence. I decided if I kept it from my mind, I might grow strong enough to resist it in every particular. Yet a part of me continued to wonder about Joshua. I knew that the sword had affected him. Mahonri and others had also recognized it and stated so. But I did not quite know the level of his dependence—whether he merely suffered a mild yearning left over from the day that he had borne it, or whether the sword could entice him toward something more insidious. After all, it was Joshua! *Sweet, rambunctious, good-hearted Joshua. My love for him may have blinded my judgement.*

Pagag helped me down from the wagon with the baby in my arms. There were sighs of admiration and expressions of delight from the surrounding crowd. We were finally about to deliver the Father of Nations into safe and righteous hands. Pagag, too, was smiling at me with great warmth. As usual, his smile made me feel awkward. For the last few nights I'd had to endure his friendly advances as he persisted in trying to win my heart. But am I being truthful when I say that I had to "endure" his advances? I think I was enjoying it far more than I should have. But what girl would not take pleasure in the attentions of such a strong and attractive young man? What is the modern term? I was surely "lapping it up." I usually found that I could clear my head by concentrating on the face of Harry Hawkins: on the kindness of his smile and the love that radiated in his eyes on the day we bid farewell at the port for airplanes in Salt Lake City. But would his face always remain as focused in my mind as it was now?

Mahonri and Jared, along with Pagag, Ophir, and Moriancumr all surrounded me as we approached a venerable man who appeared to represent the whole gathering. All eyes, of course, were on me and the baby—mostly the baby.

"Welcome to Salem," said the man in a low and resonant tone. "I am Arphaxad. I have been sent to bring you and the infant child, my descendant, to the house of Shem."

Becky looked at me questioningly.

I whispered to her, "Arphaxad is Shem's son."

"How old is he?" she asked.

But Arphaxad overheard and answered pleasantly, "I am nearly three hundred and fifty. And how old are you little one?"

Becky thought a second, then said, "About one-thirty-fifth of that."

Jared's father, Moriancumr, embraced another man with age lines as deep as his own.

"Who is that?" asked Joshua.

Mahonri answered, "That is my great-grandfather, Joktan."

"Criminy!" said Joshua. Then aside to Becky, he asked, "Hasn't anybody since the Flood ever died?"

An austere-looking man with curled gray hair and clear brown eyes came up for a closer inspection of the baby and said, "So this is my grandson of the sixth generation. Plainly he takes after me."

"Nonsense Eber," said another man affably. "His eyes are blue. Surely he takes after me."

"We'll see if they remain *blue, Father," said Eber.*

"You're both *mistaken," said a woman. She was old, but still had a shining complexion and bright eyes. "A child's beauty comes from his grandmothers. Weren't you aware? I'm sure your father, Salah, would agree."*

"Nicely put, Azurad," said Eber. "As your husband, I must concede."

"As your father," said Salah, "I think that's wise."

Abram squealed, quite enjoying the attention. There were so many grandmothers and grandfathers ogling over him that I could hardly keep track of them all. I was overwhelmed with emotion. In most cases I couldn't have said who among these grandparents was younger or older. If an extra hundred years had brought on a few additional wrinkles, it wasn't enough to help me judge their ages.

"I don't know any *of these names," whispered Joshua, somewhat perplexed.*

Another older man with a cleft chin came up behind the boy. "I'm afraid we don't know your name either, young one."

Joshua turned. "I'm—uh—Joshua."

"An honor to meet you, Uh-joshua," he said. "I am Peleg."

"Peleg!" said Josh excitedly. "I know you! In your days the earth was divided, right?"

"*That's why I was so named,*" *he said succinctly.* "*Now let me have a look at my great, great, great grandson.*"

Joshua stopped him. "*Wait. I've always wanted to ask—What was it like when the continents broke apart? Were there a lot of earthquakes? A lot of tidal waves?*"

Peleg looked at him a little strangely. "*I'm afraid I wasn't there. I was only an infant. But as with any miracle, you can be certain of one thing.*"

"*What's that?*"

"*God was there.*"

Joshua pulled a face. I think he'd been hoping for something a little more substantial. But Peleg only winked.

Arphaxad got the crowd's attention again. "*It's time! My father is waiting. Let us journey to the palace of the king.*"

If I had thought that Salem from a distance was extraordinary, it paled in comparison to walking in its midst. Indeed the architecture was fascinating—two- and three-story dwelling houses with glass windows of every shape, stained and colored in reds, emeralds, and blues. The homes were situated on large plots with burgeoning flower gardens—orchids and irises, tulips and roses, jasmine and violets—and fruit trees of all kinds, many varieties that I never thought would have grown in Jerusalem! There were no animals on the streets of Salem. These remained in the fields surrounding the city. Our own wagons and beasts were stabled outside the city gates. In Salem the people walked wherever they traveled, although in one instance I saw a vehicle that looked very much like a bicycle, but with three oversized wheels. A tricycle?

I saw people wearing eyeglasses, and as we neared the center of the community there was a column with a clock—not a sundial, mind you, but a timepiece with various dials and hands—a mechanism that must have operated in a manner similar to clocks in Harry's day. The buildings in the temple district had magnificent marble, metalwork, and stone facades, and the streets were paved with patterned stones. There were beautiful little waterways with arched bridges. Everything seemed so practical and yet so charmingly attractive, including and perhaps especially the garments of the people. There were simple gowns and lovely tunics of exquisite manufacture. There were no poor in Salem, and no one hawking wares in a stifled market. Goods and services were delivered freely, and exchanged for the goods and services of others.

The people lined the streets and leaned over their balustrades and open windows to watch our arrival. There was much hand waving and joyful communion between the patriarchs and the people. Many more gathered to our company as we walked, including delightful children with sprightly faces, no less excited at the tidings of Abram's coming than the venerable grandparents themselves.

The biggest surprise was perhaps the "palace" of Shem. It certainly was not the grandiose structure that I might have anticipated for the palace of a king. The only characteristic that might have distinguished it from any other abode in the community was its placement very near the temple of God.

Have I failed to describe the temple? I must do so immediately! I had seen the temple of Solomon in all its glory after the extensive refurbishment begun by King Herod. This renovation was completed in the year I was born. Though in size I would have to say that the two buildings were comparable, in materials this one seemed much more elegant. If there was any palace in Salem, this was it, and it was a monument designed not to glorify man, but God. Nothing was spared in gold and silver, fine marble, and bronze, loving workmanship, and vigorous upkeep. Most uniquely, a light emanated from a tower beyond its gates. The light of day was waning and I saw this temple beacon as plainly as any light that ever illumined the golden statue of Moroni in the latter days. It did not flicker like a lamp flame. I could not have defined its source of power, but in purity it seemed almost like a light ignited by God.

The courtyard of Shem's dwelling house had been transformed into a place of feasting and celebration, and many more distinguished men and women were waiting for us there. As we entered, the person first to step forward to greet us was a man in a white and blue robe. A lengthy, but well-trimmed beard touched his chest, and deep creases of age reached from the corners of his eyes. He first approached Mahonri and Jared.

"Forgive me," he said, "for not greeting you at the city gate with the others. We were informed that you had arrived, and there were still some preparations—"

Mahonri took his hands. "No need to apologize, King Melchizedek. We come to honor you, and to honor your seed, as well as to fulfill the promise of the Lord."

An elderly woman, but strong and graceful of face, was beside the dignified Shem. She came to me, put her hand on my shoulder and gazed into the face of tiny Abram.

"Is this the child? Are you the noble young woman who has brought him to us?"

I nodded. "My name is Mary. This is Joshua and Rebecca."

I found this woman no less captivating than Melchizedek.

"I am Sedeqetelebab," she continued. "My husband and I are eternally grateful for your service and sacrifice."

I was at a loss for words. "I . . . I am moved . . . am honored that . . . Thank you."

The grandeur, the fullness of this moment seemed to rush in on me all at once. I thought I had readied myself both mentally and spiritually for this—I truly did not want to feel overwhelmed. But to meet the wife of Melchizedek was an experience for which I was not prepared. So little was written on the women of the early ages, but in the face of Sedeqetelebab I felt I was given a glimpse of the greatness of the role such women had played. She'd been aboard the ark of Noah; she was one of the eight survivors who had repopulated the earth. I'd already known that I would be astonished at the presence of Shem, but the touch of his wife upon my shoulder somehow brought it all to a zenith, and I was trembling with emotion.

Sedeqetelebab smiled at me with a warmth that seemed to brim with prescient understanding. "Now, if you will permit, I will hold my great grandson."

She'd left off a considerable number of greats. Next Shem, the revered King of Salem, clasped my hands.

"As my wife has stated, we are overjoyed at what you have accomplished," he said. "The Lord is with you, Mary. I sense that He is close to you in spirit and . . . in generations."

There was a slight question in his voice as he said this. He seemed somewhat perplexed—something that I don't think a person with four hundred and fifty years of spiritual experience felt very often. A light ignited in his eyes, and he sent me a look that reminded me of the moment when I had met Mahonri—all-knowing, accepting, and teeming with love. I think Shem knew without any introduction or explanation that I was the Savior's grandniece.

Becky and Joshua also seemed at a loss for words. Well, I suppose I shouldn't include Joshua. He mustered the courage to ask Shem another unusual question. "I heard somewhere that as a child you stopped the mouths of lions and quenched the violence of fire. Is it true?"

Shem raised his bushy gray eyebrows in mild surprise, then answered in all sincerity, "It is true. But not by my own power. Never by my own—but by the power of God."

Joshua pursed his lips and nodded. "That's cool."

"Come," *said Shem.* "Before the festivities are underway, you must meet someone else. I told him of your coming and he is looking very forward to it."

Shem and Sedeqetelebab led the children and me into the interior of the house. Mahonri and Jared, along with the rest of their clansmen, remained outside to associate with relatives and friends. As we entered the doorway, Becky nudged Joshua and whispered teasingly, "'That's cool?'"

After crossing through a gallery we entered a garden area that was situated in the central part of the house. It had an open roof, rather like the villas of the Romans. There was an apple tree in this garden, the branches heavy with fruit, and to our surprise there was also a baby zebra. That's right. A zebra! *But it was the man feeding an apple to this zebra who captivated our attention in particular. He was seated on a stone bench. Beside him was a cane. At long last, here was someone who looked genuinely and irrefutably* old—*as ancient as the mountains themselves. Yet it was touching how tenderly he stroked the baby zebra behind its neck and leaned forward to kiss its striped forehead.*

My heart sent a warm rush of blood through my veins. I knew the man's identity before Shem had made his introduction.

"Father," *he said to him.*

The old man was a little hard of hearing and noticed us for the first time. A smile crossed his features and it seemed that his eyes and all of his wrinkles smiled with him.

Shem went to his side and spoke to him gently, referring to the baby in his wife's arms, "I have brought to you the son of your tenth generation. He is called Abram."

Becky tugged excitedly on my hem and whispered, "That's Noah, isn't it? That's Noah!"

I nodded, and tears—wonderful, sweet-flowing tears—came to my eyes.

"Abram," Noah repeated. "Well, then let me see him."

Sedeqetelebab brought him forward. She laid him in Noah's arms, but continued to support part of the child's weight until she was sure that her feeble father-in-law had him well in hand. The baby zebra moved to the end of the bench and fed upon another apple in a pottery bowl.

"Abram," Noah said a second time, and gazed deeply into the child's countenance. For the first time, even little Abram's face seemed to be filled with reverence and wonder.

"Ah, yes," Noah continued. "He is 'exalted father.' But he shall soon be the 'father of nations.' For the Lord will proclaim him thus when the time is at hand. He will sojourn with us only briefly, until shortly after the time of judgement and the confusion of tongues, and until the children of men have begun to fulfill God's command to scatter abroad in all parts of the earth. Then he must be returned to his family in Ur of Chaldea."

I was astounded. The prophecies gushed from his mouth like water from a spring. I felt convinced that this old man's mind resided as much in the past and future as it did in the present, as if all three were continually before his eyes. In truth, I believe he had one foot—and perhaps considerably more of his body than this—firmly established in the eternal world.

"Father," said Shem, "I would also like you to meet the three young heroes who saved the child's life."

"Yes," said Noah. "I will meet them. Bring them forward."

Shem completed the introduction, though it was hardly necessary. "May I present my father, Noah, who is also the father of us all."

Noah returned the baby to Sedeqetelebab. Then he reached his hand toward us. I perceived that he was also dim of sight, and yet I also knew that few people in history had ever seen things so clearly.

Here he was—the prophet who had witnessed the great deluge of the world! How it must have broken his heart to see so many of his posterity now in a similar condition as when the Lord had baptized the earth. Here was the man who had spent 120 years building an ark according to the Lord's command, who had gathered in all of the animals, male and female, and cared for them until the waters had receded. Here was the progenitor of the human race! His blood flowed in my veins and every other man, woman, or child I had ever seen and known! Though I was looking straight into his countenance, and though my emotions were spilling over like a great fountain, I still felt certain I did not appreciate this moment for what it was. I could not comprehend it!

"Come here, my child," he said, and I realized he was speaking to me.

I stepped forward and let him take both of my hands into his own. I needed one of my hands to wipe my eyes, but he held them firmly. His palms were wrinkled and rough, but they were still inexplicably warm, and the warmth spread through me. His eyes closed halfway.

"Yes," he said again in a whispering, almost sibilating voice. "You are a woman of many centuries. But the time you have chosen is in the last days . . ."

I glanced at Shem and his wife. I wondered what they would think of such a declaration, but their faces were calm and full of understanding, as if they already knew many of the things that Noah was proclaiming.

Noah continued, "Let your heavy heart be lightened, young one. You are highly blessed of the Lord, and your destiny is in the hollow of His hands. You needn't worry over those you love. They too are in God's care, and they are here, and they will come to you quite soon . . ."

I wiped my eyes on each of my shoulders and asked with a sniffle, "They are here?"

He nodded. "You will make some important choices soon, and I wish to assure you that your choices will indeed make you happy. Be glad of heart. Few are so favored as you, Mary Symeon, and your generations will bless your name forever. You will yet see many great and glorious things, all in the good time of the Lord."

I continued to weep, my head bowed. He released my hands and then I felt one of his palms touch my cheek. He leaned forward and kissed my forehead. When I looked up, his eyes were aqua blue and sparkling with wonder. I could not resist, and I kissed his cheek in return. Then I politely moved aside for Rebecca.

Becky's small hands disappeared inside Noah's long, aged fingers. His approach was a little different with Becky. He said to her, "Your gifts are great, Rebecca, but you try to carry the world on your shoulders."

She gave a little-girl shrug, trying hard to keep from smiling so wide that her face would split. "I guess . . . because I love everybody."

The patriarch's eyes filled with empathy. "I know how that feels. You have already saved so many."

The smile abated a little, and she said weakly, "I . . . I don't feel like I saved anyone."

"Ah, if only you could see their circumstances without you! Not a pleasant vision. Your heart is pure, little one. Purity of heart is a rare and exceptional thing. You wield great power for one so small. But you must know, to feel great love is to also know great pain. Have you already discovered this?"

Undoubtedly no one had experienced this truth more poignantly than Noah.

Rebecca nodded.

"It is not often that someone can preserve that love in the midst of such pain. You mustn't let it overwhelm you. For there will be some, Rebecca, who you cannot save. Or so it will seem for a time. But do not despair. Inevitably you will triumph."

She pondered this. It was all so weighty and deep for a young girl. At last she said, "Can I ask you something?"

"You may," said Noah.

Shyly, she inquired, "Which animal is your favorite?"

His wrinkled brow wrinkled all the more as he pondered the question quite seriously. It was delightful to see a ten-year-old girl stump a nine-hundred-year-old man. Then he grinned and said to Rebecca, "The horse. My favorite is the horse." He reached over, scratched the zebra on the ear, and added, "With or without stripes."

Now it was Joshua's turn, and I sensed that he was quite apprehensive. In fact, for an instant I feared he would not step forward at all. But Noah's hand was extended, and Joshua could not refuse it. He edged forward slowly, then with a sigh of resignation, puffed up his chest and gave his hands to the great prophet.

Almost immediately Noah's expression changed. "You have a troubled mind, young Joshua."

"I do?" said Josh, swallowing.

"Your heart is not right. Your objectives are noble, and your will is as strong as an ocean gale. But first you must make your heart right before the Lord."

Joshua jerked as if he might pull away, but then he seemed to melt, and a tear escaped his eyes. "How can I do that?"

"By repentance," said Noah.

"I'm sorry," said Joshua.

"You did not sin against me.*"*

Joshua was trembling now. We watched the scene with intense concentration. This was the moment that I knew for certain that Joshua had taken the sword. And I deeply feared that a great part of it now controlled him.

Noah continued, "There are many ways that you can achieve that which you desire. But without the support of God, you proceed at the risk of your own soul. Though it may be possible in part to succeed in your objectives, the cost may be too great to bear."

"But," said Joshua, still shaking, "I might succeed?"

"Joshua," I snapped, and fought an impulse to step forward. Somebody desperately had to slap some sense into this child.

"Yes," Noah said to Joshua, "but it may also destroy you, along with many others whom you love."

Joshua peered into Noah's face, the prophet's eyes burning with vivacity. Suddenly Joshua broke away. Without looking at anyone, he fled past Shem and Sedeqetelebab. He flew through the garden's entranceway.

"Joshua!" I cried.

Rebecca cried his name as well. Melchizedek and his wife looked surprised, but not Noah. In him I saw complete understanding, and a hint of sadness. I quickly apologized and thanked them, and then Rebecca and I pursued Joshua to the doorway of the house. But as we emerged onto the threshold of the terrace, the large flowering hedges on the walkway hindered our view. I moved beyond them, continuing to call Joshua's name.

It was almost dark, and the courtyard was so crowded with new celebrants arriving for the feast that I did not immediately see him. My eyes scanned the grounds, the foliage and fountain, and beyond to the pillared arches at the edge of the property. Rebecca's eyes were also searching. She continued deeper into the crowd.

I saw Peleg, son of Eber, leaning beside the fountain and approached him.

"Did you see Joshua?" I asked him. "The boy who asked you about the earthquakes?"

"Why, yes," said Peleg. "He just passed by here and went . . ." Now his eyes, too, were searching.

Moriancumr, the father of Jared, also saw my distress.

"What's wrong, Mary?" he asked me.

"It's Joshua. He ran away."

The longer I searched, the more frustrated I became. But besides the frustration, a palpable dread was swelling inside me. Where could he have gotten to so fast? The boy seemed to have entirely disappeared. And what were these objectives that Noah spoke of? What was the great and terrible thing that Joshua wanted to accomplish? My dread intensified as I realized that whatever it was, he would seek to do it with the sword's aid. But the sword was nowhere near here. If Joshua had taken it, he surely would have hidden it somewhere in the encampment of Jared. Wouldn't he have? Unless somehow he had brought it with us, but that seemed . . .

My dread was transforming into panic. And now not only was Joshua missing, but Rebecca us well.

"Mary!" said Pagag, approaching me in haste at the edge of the courtyard. "My grandfather says that Joshua is missing."

"Yes, and now Becky too," I said, my frustration at its apex.

"Don't worry yourself so much," said Pagag. "I'm sure we will resolve this quite easily. Come. We'll search the main thoroughfare back toward our wagons."

Pagag took my hand. We started back toward the city gates. All at once the beauty of Salem had become a blur of colors. Again the responsibility that I felt for these children's lives weighed oppressively on my heart. Had Noah really said that the world was on Becky's shoulders? It was no less on mine. I would not fail to bring Garth and Jenny's children safely home, no matter what it took, even if such efforts brought me to the very brink of catastrophe.

NOTES TO CHAPTER 16:

The description of the valley between Judea and Moab, where now sits the body of water known as the Dead Sea, as a lush and well-watered "Eden-like" region during the time of this novel is based on descriptions offered in the book of Genesis. In chapter 13 it reads:

> *And Lot lifted up his eyes, and beheld all the plain of Jordan, that it was well watered every where, before the Lord destroyed Sodom and Gomorrah, even as the garden of the Lord, like the land of Egypt, as thou comest unto Zoar* (v. 10).

Therefore, we are left to conclude that the destruction of Sodom and Gomorrah literally transformed this area into the desolate landscape that it is today. This may cause us to wonder about scientific texts that teach us that such events occurred hundreds of thousands, or even millions, of years ago.

Educational textbooks are rife with dates about the age of fossils, geological strata, and other phenomenon associated with the formation of the earth. These dates are almost exclusively drawn from radiometric dating methods that were developed during the twentieth century, the most common being carbon-14 and uranium-234. Such methods measure the rate of radioactive decay for sub-nuclear isotopes. For these dating methods to be considered accurate with regard to a true picture of earth history, scientists are dependent upon a long list of assumptions. Foremost, they must assume that the rate at which radioactive elements decay has been constant since the earth's formation. In other words, they must assume that the environment of the earth—particularly its radioactive environment—has never changed. This scientific perspective is called uniformitarianism. Science generally assumes that the earth, along with the sun and the rest of the solar system, condensed from a huge nebulae of interstellar gas and dust. It also assumes that the earth has been part of this solar system since it was created, meaning that the basic "nature" of physical matter and cosmic radiation has remained unchanged. Uniformitarianism assumes that there has been no alteration (contamination) of the chemical elements in earth or atmosphere in all of the millions of years since the earth was formed.

Modern prophets have refuted each of these assumptions. We have been taught that the earth was not created here in this solar system, but "fell" here after Adam's transgression. Brigham Young said:

When the earth was framed and brought into existence and man was placed upon it, it was near the throne of our Father in heaven. And when man fell . . . the earth fell into space, and took up its abode in the planetary system, and the sun became our light (Brigham Young, *JD*, 17:143, July 19, 1874).

Also, the effects of such events as the Great Flood, along with other chemical alterations perpetuated by physical and spiritual phenomenon, could radically alter the results of radiocarbon methods. For an accurate measurement of such data, a scientist would have to personally observe such phenomenon throughout the entire history of the world and make adjustments to account for all of the variables. Since no scientist has ever been permitted to observe the earth's history through all its epochs of preparation and man's occupation of its surface, we remain dependent upon revelation from our Heavenly Father. He has promised us that information about the earth's history and other mysteries of its formation are forthcoming (D&C 101:32–34).

We learn from the Joseph Smith Translation of Genesis that the people of Salem where Melchizedek was king "wrought righteousness, and obtained heaven, and sought for the city of Enoch which God had before taken, separating it from the earth . . ." (JST, Gen 14:34). It has been suggested that Salem was taken up into heaven and reserved to come back to the earth at the end of the world, much like the city of Enoch. However, most believe that only the citizens themselves were translated, and the real estate remained.

The descriptions provided herein about the layout of Salem, the palace of Shem, the existence of a temple, along with other suggestions, are purely the author's speculations, but are based on the layout and design of Zion or the New Jerusalem for Jackson County, Missouri, during the nineteenth century. The layout of "Zion" communities may closely resemble one another throughout the world's history. According to the *History of the Church*, the city of Zion in Jackson County was to be divided into blocks of ten acres each, with streets that were 132 feet wide, central blocks being reserved for temples, schools, houses of worship, public buildings, and storehouses. The blocks surrounding the central square were to be divided into lots of about one-half acre each and specifications are even given as to where the home would stand upon that lot. The blueprint also explained how the farms and fields for livestock were to be laid off around the community.

The original city plat was designed to cover only a one-mile square and would accommodate only about fifteen to twenty thousand people. When this square was filled up, the Saints were to "lay off another in the same way, and so fill up the world . . . let every man live in the city, for this is the City of Zion" (*Doctrinal History of the Church*, Vol. 1, 358–59). Many communities where the Saints settled in the nineteenth century followed this same revealed pattern.

LDS educator W. Cleon Skousen points out that with this system the economic, educational, and social advantages of city life would be enjoyed by all, but as the community grew it would be *automatically* decentralized so as to avoid the confusion, congestion, and social irresponsibility that too often typify city life in the average modern metropolis (Skousen, *The First 2000 Years*, Bookcraft, 1953, 171).

This novel makes the point that very little is known of the women who stood beside the great patriarchs of the Bible. Unfortunately, this is true of almost all scriptures, including the Book of Mormon. We too quickly forget such women even in modern Church history. For instance, how many of us could name the first wife of Brigham Young? (His best-known wife was Mary Ann Angel, who was actually the prophet's *second* wife; his first wife, Miriam Works, died in 1832.) Or even more recently, the wife of David O. McKay (Emma Ray Riggs) or Ezra Taft Bensen (Flora Smith Amussen)? The contribution these women made to help these men become such powerful leaders should never be overlooked.

Amazingly enough, we do have most of the names of the patriarch's wives from the Old Testament, that is, if we can rely on *Jasher*, *Jubilees*, and other ancient apocryphal texts regarding such matters. Some of the names are given in this chapter. Others include Emzara, the wife of Noah; Lomna, the wife of Peleg; and Edni, the wife of Enoch. Just as it would be fascinating to personally know the patriarchs, it would undoubtedly be equally fascinating to know their wives.

The Old Testament indicates that Noah lived 950 years, making him the second-longest living person in the scriptural record. As stated before, the idea that Abraham may have met Noah or Shem or any of these other patriarchs is a matter of speculation, but the scriptures do indicate that these people were all contemporaries. The idea that all of these patriarchs may have gathered into the city of Salem at the time of the confusion of tongues is also speculation, but it seems reasonable that in a world where a man like Nimrod rebelled against the Lord and built an empire that persecuted the righteous, anyone choosing to remain faithful would gather into a central location for preservation and protection. During the time of the Tower of Babel, Melchizedek's city of Salem seems like it would have been a natural place of refuge.

CHAPTER SEVENTEEN

Steffanie

I have a confession to make.

I was not in quite the physical shape that I thought I was. After a day of ascending stairway after stairway, switchback after switchback, it felt like someone could have peeled the flesh off my leg bones like a banana. My muscles felt like Dove Bars under a hot sun, melting away until there was nothing left but a bony stick.

It might not have been so bad if my hands hadn't been chained together and then attached to the waist of a soldier with biceps like Mr. Universe. I never realized just how important a person's arms and shoulders were while climbing. Without the full range of motion, it was twice as hard to balance my body weight. Everything focused on the calf muscles. They had to bear almost the entire burden. The chain also added extra weight. Besides that, the steps were considerably higher than modern steps. Add to this the fact that the taskmasters that Mardon had placed in charge of me allowed very few opportunities to rest.

Okay, I better modify that. The dizzying pace might have been directly my fault. Mardon kept himself only a few yards away from me the entire day. I knew he was there to watch me sweat and gasp for breath, but I was determined that I would give him no such satisfaction. I don't know where I got the gene that made me so obsessively competitive, especially when the competition was against guys (and *triply* so when the competition was against jerks like Mardon), but this gene was embedded deep down in my skin cells and there was no getting rid of it.

The pattern that Mardon and the others had wanted to establish from the beginning was to climb for ten or fifteen minutes and then rest for five. But during the first rest stop, I refused to sit down. Mardon lounged regally upon the first wide platform, a cortege of servants wiping his brow and providing him with fruit juice.

I said to him, "Is it too steep for you? Or are you just not feeling well today?"

That got his goat. I felt I had Mardon pegged pretty well. He was the epitome of empty-headed male dolts. Add to that his sadistic depravity and you had about as shallow an individual as fate could produce. I knew what it would do to his ego to be outdone by an angel—particularly a *female* angel. Predictably, he immediately reduced our five-minute rest stop to three.

Throughout the morning he frequently glanced over to see how I was holding up. I rarely returned the look, focusing instead on my feet. It seemed like I was *forever* focusing on my feet. That's what a person does when they climb stone stairways. I tried to breathe only through my nose. If someone wants to appear exhausted, all they have to do is breathe through their mouth.

So far I was feeling pretty good. During the next several rest stops, I remained on my feet like before. Mardon also remained on his feet and refused the proffered refreshments. I, however, drank as much water as they would give me. I may have been determined, but I wasn't stupid. I would let this distinction be reserved for the son of Nimrod.

Toward the end of the morning, as I guzzled from a flask of stale H_2O, he said to me snidely, "Apparently we haven't been giving you enough water over the past few days. Or are you just growing weary of the climb?"

I wiped my mouth. "I'm doing just fine. I might even do a little better if you took off these chains. Just where do you think I'd run off to while we're on this tower?"

"You're an angel," he said. "You might send a signal to your compatriots who will then whisk you back to your City in the Clouds."

"Right," I said, rolling my eyes. "I forgot that you were delusional. If that was gonna happen, don't you think they could still whisk me away in chains?"

"I'm surprised that you can't answer that for yourself," he sneered. "No one will attack so long as we keep you surrounded by armed men. Your particular brand of being are cowards by nature. My father has taught this truth for decades."

"Cowards, eh?" I said calmly. "Is that really how you'd characterize my brother and me?"

The question made him uneasy. I think he worried that if all angels were truly like us, his father might have made some serious miscalculations. But he couldn't confess it. For him to confess such a thing was blasphemy.

"Absolutely," he said darkly, leaning forward. "Cowards to the marrow of your bones." He abruptly called for an end to the rest stop.

As I looked back down the tower, it hardly appeared that we'd gone any distance at all. Even after another two rest stops, we'd only climbed about fifteen hundred feet. Unfortunately, I was feeling some serious strain in my muscles. Still, I refused to sit down. Mardon also refused.

"Getting tired?" I asked him, working hard not to betray any breathlessness in my voice.

He was not quite as successful at masking his own strain. "Of course not. I'm doing . . . quite well."

"I see," I said. "Then why not cancel the next rest stop?"

I don't know what I was doing. I guess I was feeling suicidal.

"My men don't need to be exhausted so early in the climb," he replied.

"Oh, I see," I said sarcastically. "You're only thinking of your men. You're so benevolent and kind, aren't you, Mardon? Why don't you just admit it? You're a wimp. What's the word you like to use? You're a spineless *eel*. Without your father, you couldn't command a rabble of slaves in a slime pit, let alone an army."

That pushed his buttons. He came at me, eyes ferocious, and grabbed my arm, digging in his fingers.

"Careful," I said. "I'm your father's secret weapon. Remember?"

He glared at me, teeth clenched, temper boiling. Finally, he released me with a shove.

"We'll not rest at the next terrace," he announced to his men. "And no more water for the angel. She seems to think she has the stamina to outlast a man. We'll see who falters first."

His eyes were full of enmity and loathing. I could tell he would have preferred to see me trip, tumble to the bottom of the tower, and break every bone in my body, including my neck. What was I trying to prove? As usual in these things, it was nothing of any significance. Just that I could climb these cretins into the ground. Besides, I was defending the dignity of angels.

What was I talking about?

"Don't go loco on yourself, Steffanie," I whispered.

Mardon's squadron of twenty men also seemed to take this challenge to heart. The contest had begun.

My only advantage was that I was considerably lighter than most of these guys—not as much gravity working against me. But I had the added burden of this stupid chain. Honestly, this might have been the most difficult contest I'd ever undertaken. I mean, I was all for fair competition between men and women. But let's face it. The male of the species is usually better designed for these sorts of things.

What am I saying? Scratch that. Forget I ever said it. This was my chance to prove a pet theory of mine. Men may have been stronger overall, but in a contest of endurance, it was absolutely impossible to defeat a determined female. Besides, I had my hatred of Mardon to sustain me.

The first of Mardon's soldiers began to give out after about two hundred more steps. They tried to sit down.

"Up, you maggots!" Mardon commanded.

It was impossible now for me to keep from panting. My mouth hung open, swallowing as much oxygen as possible. Sweat oozed off my brow, the salt stinging my eyes. My sleeve was already drenched and helped very little in wiping my face. *One more step*, I kept telling myself. *Just keep lifting that knee.*

We got some relief when we arrived at one of the slanting switchbacks that crisscrossed the western face of the tower. The pathway had ruts down the center, apparently designed to transport large loads of bricks in a wheeled cart drawn by heavy ropes. After the bricks would arrive at the next steep stairway, there was an ingenious pulley system built into the wall to lift them to the next level. Right now these stations were vacant. Despite the fact that a considerable amount of work remained to complete the tower, its slopes had been abandoned to make way for the soldiers.

The switchback made things a little easier, but my legs were still feeling awfully wobbly. Mardon's men continued panting and gasping, sounding like a chugging locomotive. Each of them glowered at me from time to time, as if *willing* me to give up. Frankly, I wasn't sure what kept me going. I may not have been an angel, but I was convinced that angels were supporting me. Would angels really support me in a contest of pride? I realized this was more than that. I felt I was teaching—representing—something important. Whether it was a lesson for Mardon or for his men, I didn't know. But the thought filled me with courage, and also humility. My anger dissolved a little. Still, the sight of the next steep stairway made me queasy.

Mardon spoke to me, his lungs short of breath. "My, my. More stairs. Sure you wouldn't . . . like to rest? One of my servants . . . brought grapes and oranges. Maybe . . . you'd like some. Is there any water left . . . inside that throat of yours?"

"Come a little closer," I replied, "and I'll see if . . . I can work up some spit." I guess my humility wasn't perfect.

Mardon snorted. I think it was supposed to be a laugh. "You never . . . cease to amaze me . . . with your dim-wittedness. To answer . . . your earlier question: If all angels . . . are like you . . . our victory . . . is assured. Pride alone . . . will be your downfall."

My step faltered. I burst into laughter—so hard it was hurting my chest. The other men were relieved that I had stopped. They leaned over, wheezing for breath. One of them lost his breakfast.

I gaped at Mardon. "You're lecturing *me* . . . about *pride?* I'm afraid . . .you've misjudged me. I'm doing this . . . for the exercise."

Without a pause, I began climbing the next stairway. Several of the men had had enough. They collapsed at the base of the steps. This included the ogre who held my chain. Since the chain was attached to his waist, this did present a challenge to my forward progress.

Mardon unlocked the chain from his waist. He pointed at another man—the one who still looked the strongest. "You! Carry it!"

Begrudgingly, this man took the chain. To show off I took my next several strides two steps at a time. Actually, it nearly broke my back. But I kept going. Mardon shook his head, trying to taunt me. Another pair of soldiers collapsed on the stairs, their lungs heaving.

Finally the new soldier assigned to carry my chain sank to his knees. Mardon was also ready to collapse. I was close to that point as well, but I remained determined not to show it. I continued climbing, one trembling leg at a time, only now I was dragging a ten-foot chain between my feet. We must have climbed a thousand feet during this little contest alone. Yet I refused to turn and look at the landscape. It would only disorient me all the more. I might even fall over backwards. Right now Mardon couldn't have cared less that I was dragging a chain. He was worried more about his own crumbling stamina.

Suddenly it was only Mardon and myself. The rest of his muscle-bound hulks were strewn along the stairway below us, like a multi-car pileup on an interstate. I think the prince was genuinely frightened that angels might prove to be a superior race of beings. Then, as luck would have it, I accidentally stepped on the chain. I tripped, driving my poor knee into the stone. I clutched the bruise with both hands, but I could hardly feel it. My blood was pumping so hard I couldn't really feel anything. Mardon made sure that he'd climbed just one step beyond me, then he too lay on his side and heaved. There was a small hint of a grin on his mug. That did it. I hadn't given up. I'd just tripped. With a final burst of energy I climbed five, six, seven—*ten* more steps!

Then I collapsed, using any strength left in my limbs just to keep from sliding back down the tower. Mardon barely had the strength to look up at me, but oh, what a look it was! A look of utter defeat. *I'd won!* No, let me say that more modestly.

I'D WON!!!

But that wouldn't be entirely honest. I hadn't done this alone. I was sure of that. *We'd* won. Me and the angels.

Mardon and the rest of us sat there recovering for a long time. I fell asleep for a few minutes right there on the steps, so I couldn't have said for sure how long it was before we started dragging ourselves up to the next platform. There was a pool of water at this level. The prince and his men dove right into it. They even allowed *me* to get wet. That is to say, no one stopped me. No one would look at me either, except for Mardon. He said to me in his typical side-ways, derogatory manner, "What I find so amazing is how equal to the strength of men the inhabitants of heaven really are. It contradicts everything that the Shemites try to portray."

"I'd be worried you might find out that I'm not an angel at all," I replied. "In which case you just got your butt kicked by a woman."

He looked at me nervously, but could think of no reply.

For the next few hours the rest stops were rather frequent. We finally reached a kind of city built right into the side of the tower. It was laid out on a wide platform that crossed nearly the entire southern face. There were dozens of buildings and apartments. There was even a stone wall with a gate, though the wall was still incomplete. It appeared that we had climbed approximately three-fourths of the way up the tower. To my surprise there were also flower gardens, and even some vegetables and fruit trees growing in plots the size of boxcars, sort of like oversized garden boxes. And *horses!* This was the most incredible sight of all—a corral with four actual horses! Another corral had a dozen head of cattle.

Mardon must have sensed my amazement, because he explained, boasting, "They were brought here as calves and foals. We hoisted them up the walls in the same manner as any other equipment."

"For goodness sakes *why?*" I asked.

"Because my father commanded it," he replied, closing the subject.

Nimrod had reached the city as well, along with his cohort of nearly two hundred and fifty men. The staff, who were apparently stationed here on a permanent basis, had prepared a typical feast for the arriving royalty. Unfortunately, I wasn't invited, and frankly I didn't give a hoot. All I wanted to do was sleep. They shut me inside a stone apartment of sorts situated right against the edge of the tower. There was a window in my room with about a three-hundred-foot drop on the other side. There was even a kind of toilet with running water. But what I appreciated most was the sight of a feather mattress. For the moment this place looked better than a suite at the Marriott. Mardon's soldiers grudgingly removed my wrist shackles, then slammed the door and locked it from the outside. There was some barley bread and pomegranates on a plate near the bed, along with some mushy stuff in a bowl that smelled sort of like vegemite. I'd tried vegemite once in Mr. Turley's geography class. I was the only one in class who liked it. Thus, I dug in.

I consumed every last morsel and crumb. Then I rolled over on the mattress. I was out in a matter of seconds. But if you think I was headed for a long, blissful night of slumber, think again. It seemed like hardly a minute had passed when I heard someone unlocking my door. Several lamps entered the chamber along with a half-dozen men. Leading the way was King Nimrod. Right behind him was Mardon.

I glanced out the window. It was still vaguely light. I guessed that I'd only been asleep for about an hour, yet my legs felt as stiff as plywood.

"What's going on?" I said. "Why did you wake me up?"

"Because it's morning," said Nimrod. "And because I want an explanation for *this*."

His statement about it being morning was shocking enough. Was that really dawn that I saw outside my window? But what he plopped at the foot of the mattress was far more perplexing.

It was a backpack. *My* backpack. In Mardon's arms was another backpack. This one was Harry's. I must have still been half-asleep, because it took a full three seconds for the information to come together in my head. I remembered that I'd managed to steal back my backpack on the night that my brother had escaped. I'd tossed it up to Harry while he stood inside the elephant's basket. I was sure that he'd taken it with him as he fled. But here it was. This provoked a tremor of fear. Had they captured him? Had he been killed?

"What have you done to my brother?" I demanded. "Where is he?"

They didn't reply for a moment, as if studying me to try and learn some unspoken secret. Father and son glanced at one another, then Mardon said, "Perhaps you should be telling *us?*"

I furrowed my brow. "Huh?"

"Don't be coy," said Nimrod. "This was found yesterday evening floating in a cistern just below here. And this was discovered in the same vicinity."

The thing they displayed next also got my full attention. Or perhaps I should say it evoked serious confusion. It was a club of sorts whose edges were lined with razor-sharp black glass. I hadn't seen a weapon remotely similar to this since . . .

My eyes widened. It was a *Nephite* weapon! An obsidian sword! "Where did you say you found that?" I asked.

But they weren't here to answer questions. They were here to *ask* them. "What do the angels know of our campaign to attack the Heavenly City?" demanded Nimrod. "What have you told them?"

I shook my head in astonishment, my mouth opening and closing like a catfish.

Mardon held the obsidian sword closer to my face and demanded, "Is this one of your weapons? Is this how they have armed heaven's warriors?"

I turned up my palms. "I'm at a total loss, guys. I have no idea what—"

"You will answer our questions!" Nimrod exploded.

"But I don't know any more about it than you do!"

"You're a *liar!* The men who slept near this cistern also reported an attack in the middle of the night. A missile was fired from heaven. It landed in the water."

Mardon added, "They also reported the disappearance of several uniforms and swords."

A flame started glowing in my heart. A flame of hope. Was it possible? Was Harry really here? Had he actually gone back to Nephite times and recruited help? It seemed utterly preposterous. Too good to be true. Yet what other explanation was there?

"It looks like," I began, "you guys are gonna have your hands full."

At that point the seven-and-a-half-foot king of Shinar lost it. He grabbed me with both of his massive hands and hoisted me into the air, shaking me like a rag doll. "*You will answer our questions!*"

My eyes were as wide as trash can lids. I almost went into shock. This giant could have crushed me like a Styrofoam cup right there in his hands. Finally, he dropped me. I crumpled to the floor, still gaping up at him in terror.

He asked again, thundering, "*What does God know of our plans?*"

His hands closed into fists. I was sure he was going to strike me. One strike from a fist like that could shatter my skull. I turned away and raised my arm as a flimsy defense.

"Everything!" I exclaimed, my voice cracking, my mind swimming in fear and rage. "He knows everything!"

"What have you told Him?"

"I haven't told Him anything. I don't *have* to! Don't you get it? *He already knows!* He's known all along. He knew before you were born! How could you not realize these things?"

"*Lies! Nonsense!* If He'd known what I would do, I would not have been born at all! He does not control these things! He is not all-seeing and all-knowing! He may have duped the Shemites. He may have duped the angels. *But He has not duped* me! Why has He infiltrated my ranks with spies? What are His secret plans?" Nimrod raised his fist. "Tell me now or I will strike you dead on this very spot!"

"All right!" I blubbered. "I'll tell you! I'll tell you exactly what's going to happen! But there's nothing you can do about it! It's going to happen no matter what—!"

"*Tell me!*"

I faced him again, my eyes as cold as mercury. "He's going to destroy this tower. He's going to destroy *you*, Nimrod. Then he's going to confound the speech of everyone on the earth. He'll do it because you've come out in open rebellion. Because you've tried to make yourself a god on earth. Because you've taught everybody to defy Him, and ignore Him, and mock His laws and commandments. You've mocked everything—even by the garment you wear. You think you have godly power, but you're about to find out what power really is. You and all—"

"SILENCE!" he boomed. "I'll not listen to propaganda! Give me information that I can *use*. You will tell me how you communicate with your God!"

I gaped at him, flabbergasted. I still couldn't believe this was really happening. I couldn't fathom how people could be so ignorant of the ways of the universe. It was like I was on another planet. I suddenly wondered if I knew part of the reason men's lives had been cut short—why they'd no longer live nine hundred years. For a heart as corrupt as Nimrod's, there seemed to be no limit to the delusions that could infest his mind. That *Satan* could spawn inside it. And no limit to the delusion that Nimrod could heap upon others. If this situation continued, the progress of man would be thwarted. A condition like the one that prevailed just before the Great Flood, when people became so twisted that there was no hope for progression, would take hold every couple of generations. Mankind wouldn't stand a chance. Oh, I don't know! Maybe I *didn't* understand! But one thing was clear. These people were past feeling. Walking zombies. God had no choice but to do what He was about to do. He'd do it because He loved his children.

"Prayer," I replied.

"What?" asked Nimrod.

"That's how I communicate with God. I tell Him everything just by bowing my head, closing my eyes—"

"And He hears your words?" asked Mardon.

"Yes," I replied. "He'd hear your words too. He hears every—"

Nimrod cut me off. "What have you told Him?"

I shook my head. Again, it was like talking to aliens. "I always tell Him everything. Everything that's happening. Everything in my heart. I asked Him to protect me. To protect my brother and family and to bring us home."

Nimrod leaned forward. "You'll arrive sooner than you think. But it won't be by God's hand. It will be by *mine*. Now send this message to your God. Tell Him that today we meet at last. Today the Heavenly City will pass close enough to the pinnacle of my tower that nothing can stop my army from entering His domain. You, Steffanie, will be part of my triumphal entry. And then, my fair angel, you will know that power on earth is far mightier than the power of heaven." He turned to Mardon. "Take her the rest of the way to the summit. We'll meet at midday in the great tower square and assemble the ranks of the army for this evening's attack." He turned to the other men, who must have been his highest-ranking generals. Among them was the apostate Shemite, Mash, whose nose I'd had the privilege of denting, and at least two faces from the throne room—Havilah and Zemar.

"Spread the word among your officers," Nimrod concluded. "There are spies in our ranks—imposters from the City in the Clouds. Root them out. Bring them to me. I will slay them before the eyes of my men and before the eyes of heaven."

Even as Nimrod departed and as Mardon put shackles back around my wrists, my imagination continued to swirl. Harry was here. I felt sure of it. He and his companions were disguised as soldiers of Shinar. Did they realize that Nimrod was on to them? How could I warn them? They were here to save me, yet I almost wished they'd go back the way they'd come—avoid the cataclysm that I felt sure was about to befall this edifice. But another part of me thanked Heavenly Father that I had a brother like Harry.

Somehow I had to get away from these brutes on my own. I didn't care how. If my assessment of this farce was correct, Nimrod would have every breathing person on this tower lined up atop the summit before day's end. That would leave us an open escape route to the valley floor. I felt I was growing more anxious by the moment. *Please, Heavenly Father. Give me inspiration. Let me seize the opportunity when it comes.*

* * *

Our grueling climb recommenced within the hour. My muscles were still stiff and sore, yet it surprised me how quickly I worked it out. Were my guardian angels working overtime on my ankles? I actually felt *stronger* than yesterday. Maybe I was born to be a mountain climber. Look out Mount Everest! I might be the first Mormon girl from Provo, Utah, to reach the summit.

Other groups of soldiers were also starting the last leg of the climb. The stairs leading to the top were crawling with people. There were ten thousand men on this pile of bricks. As the ziggurat became narrower toward the summit, the area became more and more congested. I was constantly scanning men's faces, hoping to see Harry, or perhaps the face of a familiar Nephite. Maybe I'd see Jashon or Heshlon or one of the other warriors who'd helped Harry in Greece. Or even Micah and Jesse. Despite all the faces, no one resembled my brother. I feared that Nimrod and his generals might have already captured them. Mardon's regiment had increased to over a hundred soldiers. I think they may have been anticipating a rescue attempt, and he wasn't taking any chances.

It was midafternoon when we reached the main summit of the Tower of Babel. The architecture up here was amazing, and surprisingly complex. I'll bet it was only a third of a mile square, but it had many platforms and levels, most of them still under construction. The whole thing was designed to be a self-sustaining community. There was a large pool directly in the center, and many ditches and gutters to capture rain water. Then, of course, there was the gangplank.

Calling it a gangplank doesn't really offer a good visual perception, but that's what it reminded me of. It was a long, narrow stairway leading up into . . . well . . . *nothing!* It was almost as if it expected a space ship to dock beside it. Basically, it was this enormous triangle of bricks, one edge sloped and the other sheer. It was about twenty-five feet wide and about a hundred and fifty feet high. This triangle was nestled right up against the northern face of the tower. I said its height was a hundred and fifty feet, but that was just its height from the main platform. To stand on top and look over the side, the drop must have been five hundred feet. Much of the main tower along the northern face had yet to be completed, but this hadn't stopped Nimrod from going forward with today's circus. The middle of the northern face was actually designed into kind of a wedge. The gangplank sat right in the middle of this wedge. I could only guess that this unusual stairway leading to nowhere was intended for one purpose—as an access point so that Nimrod's troops could invade heaven. It was as if Nimrod expected this mysterious Heavenly City to float right up next to the gangplank, just close enough to allow his soldiers to leap aboard. I realize it sounds insane, but that was how it appeared.

I should also mention that at the very top of this gangplank it looked like there was an airplane, much like the one that Nimrod had used to float down to his palace. In fact, below the gangplank, all along the wedge that made up the middle section of the northern face, there were other smaller planes, or gliders. They were tied down with ropes, just waiting for a command to launch. Apparently, it wasn't only a "foot" assault planned against heaven. It was to be an aerial assault as well.

This whole thing just seemed so logical—so meticulously thought out. Was it possible for insanity to also be logical? Nimrod's invasion was focused on an actual physical target—not just the hazy, indefinable heavens. Could there really be a floating city? I couldn't believe I was even asking myself that question. But considering all the other wigged-out stuff that I'd seen and heard, was there any reason that this should be any more shocking?

A stiff breeze blew out of the east, making it much colder than it probably should have been, even for this altitude. I wanted to hug my shoulders, but the shackles prevented that. There looked to be a storm headed this way. I chuckled at the irony.

"Why are you laughing?" demanded Mardon.

I nodded toward the east. "Looks like your father planned for everything—except the weather."

"It will take more than a little wind and rain to stop the armies of Shinar," he said arrogantly.

I smiled at his naivete, but then I shivered again. This shiver had nothing to do with the cold. I realized that my anxiety was mounting like a glacier as I gazed out at that approaching storm. Memories of another approaching storm sprang to mind—one that I'd seen when I was fourteen years old. These clouds were still far away. Nevertheless, my heart was pounding.

We continued walking between some unfinished buildings along the tower's western face. Finally, Mardon commanded the battalion to come to a halt. We hadn't reached the central square, but the spineless Prince of Shinar had something else on his mind. He motioned to one of his officers. The soldier came forward, a pack of sorts strapped to his back.

"Put the other chains on her ankles," Mardon instructed. "Hobble that proud step of hers."

My anger sizzled and crackled as the additional shackles were locked in place. I was sure Mardon had some stupid point to this, but I wasn't quite sure what it was. As we began walking again, my stride was shortened by half. I had to take almost two steps for every one of theirs. If the purpose was to make me appear weakened and ridiculous, I suppose it worked quite well.

We passed through an archway and entered the main square of the summit. The gangplank sat right at the north end of this plaza. The ranks of the army of Shinar were arriving by the hundreds now. The streams of men were lining up in tidy rows, all facing the northern horizon. The officers in their purple and gold cloaks barked commands to make sure the lines were straight and that the men looked ready and able. They became even *more* aggressive in their treatment of the men when they saw the approach of Mardon.

Ten thousand soldiers. It really was incredible. The square was filled to capacity. Nimrod's army might have been larger than this, but this was definitely the limit for how many he could fit effectively on the summit. In any case, he must have felt it was enough to do the job.

As Mardon marched before the first row of soldiers, each of the square-jawed musclemen stood at attention. But they weren't watching the prince. They were gawking at me. After all, I was the reason they were here. That is to say, my "kind." My *"species."* I was the singular representative of the enemy. It occurred to me that my whole entrance had been anticipated and orchestrated. Mardon and Nimrod had *wanted* to parade me around like this. I guess the sight of a captive angel, looking humiliated and led by a chain, was meant to bolster their confidence. And yet I sensed in the men's eyes a strange reverence. Even fear. Maybe it was because I kept a tight smile on my face, as if I knew a deep secret that no one else knew. In reality, my nerves were at the breaking point. I was constantly stealing a glance toward the eastern sky. Was it my imagination, or were the clouds in that direction becoming even blacker? Knowing the final outcome of Nimrod's scheme was hardly comforting to me now. Like having your car break down in the middle of Sodom or Gomorrah, I must confess that I was feeling the first twinges of full-blown panic.

We passed a man in the line of soldiers whom I recognized from our first day here. It was the falcon guy—the man who wore the diamond-shaped eyepatch to cover a disfiguring wound on the left side of his face. The same stupid falcon was still sitting on his arm—the one that had betrayed us to Mardon's horsemen. How I hated that bird. Its airborne spying was the reason we were in this mess in the first place.

The falconer seemed to have a particularly malignant scowl on his face. I'd always suspected that this man had been part of the assassination squad sent after Harry. I sent him a kind of exaggerated frown, like a sad clown, to taunt him for his failure. Then I grinned like the Grinch. He must have understood what I meant, because his eyes got razor thin. The falcon flapped its wings.

The next men were also leering at me. I jumped at them suddenly. The men leaped back and put their hands on their weapons. I laughed heartily. I was still laughing when I happened to notice the face of one of the soldiers in the second row. My laughter ended abruptly.

I shut my eyes and shook them open again. I stopped walking. I couldn't help it. My legs had seized up involuntarily. It was an asinine thing to do. No doubt everyone else had also noticed the break in my stride. They must have also seen my dangling jaw.

I thought I'd worked out this moment in my mind. I'd been telling myself all morning that if I happened to see Harry or another familiar face that I would not react. I might send them a secretive nod, but I would not give away their position. I'd entirely failed. But the face in the second row was so astounding—so perplexing—that I couldn't contain my reaction.

It was Gidgiddonihah.

How was this possible? It *couldn't* be. Gid! My thoughts started to spin. It must have been a mistake. Gid was *dead!* I actually hadn't seen him since that day in Bountiful when I was fifteen, but of course I'd heard all about his amazing exploits in Greece. I'd wept when they told me how he'd died saving Harry, Mary, and Jesse. In the millisecond before everyone noticed my reaction, I vacillated back and forth: Was I really staring at Gidgiddonihah, or a perfect twin—a replica in the form of a soldier? The hint of tension that crossed the soldier's face convinced me otherwise. It *was* Gid! Whatever the explanation, whatever the miracle, I felt sure I was staring directly into the face of a Nephite warrior.

I tried to turn away. I tried to continue forward in a casual manner, as if nothing important had distracted me, but it was too late. Mardon had noticed my reaction and made an immediate interpretation. I think he'd been watching for a reaction like this all day. He'd been patiently waiting for a moment when I might betray the identity of one of the angelic spies by a faltered step or surprised expression. Now he had both, and sprang to action.

"Halt!" he cried to his men. He came to my side. "Who is the spy? Where is he?"

I was in full control again, and I responded without skipping a beat. I stepped up to one of the men in the *first* row—a soldier who stood directly in *front* of Gid.

"Billy Bob!" I yelled excitedly. "What do you think you're doing here? Run, you fool! They know all about you! *Run!*"

The soldier's eyebrows shot up. Was I talking to him? He became flustered, looking around desperately as weapons were drawn. Even his comrades on either side were eyeing him viciously. Because of his surprise, he had a classic look of total guilt.

"Seize this man!" cried Mardon. "He's a spy from the Heavenly City!"

The man opened his mouth to protest, but in the next second, two of the men from Mardon's company leaped on top of him. The accused soldier tried to throw them off. It was instant pandemonium. A hundred men converged to help in the capture. I looked around, but I'd lost sight of Gidgiddonihah. Then my eyes met Mardon's. That weasel was still studying me! He'd seen me looking around. Why did I have to be so obvious? I could tell he felt sure that I had lied. He knew that I'd identified the wrong man.

The prince turned to the soldier who carried the chain to my wrists. "Get her to the palace! *Quickly!*"

Mardon did nothing to help the man at the bottom of the dog pile. His only pressing concern was whisking me away from a possible rescue attempt. He and five other men from his battalion hurried me through the commotion toward a large, unfinished structure at the eastern end of the plaza. I was sure that if I had tripped, they'd have been only too happy to drag me.

We entered an enclosed colonnade with an unfinished roof that circled toward the main palace compound. Mardon marched just ahead of me, as if he wanted to be ready to seize my chain in case of an attack. However, this was his biggest mistake.

I wasn't going to cooperate another moment. Gidgiddonihah was out there. That meant that Harry was also near. It was this thought that inspired my next action. We passed a pillar of the colonnade. The opportunity was too perfect to pass up. I raised my hands, despite the shackles on my ankles, and leaped sharply to the left.

The chain immediately caught Mardon around the neck. I yanked my arms and pinned him against the pillar. Then I twisted around the pillar, tucking underneath the chain, and cast a second loop around the prince's throat. The shackles on my ankles nearly caused me to trip, but the effort to maintain my balance only pulled the chain tighter. Mardon choked out a cry. His hands flew to his neck. The soldier carrying my chain came toward me, hands outstretched, but I grabbed the chain along the exact place where it was strapped around the pillar, raised up both of my feet, and kicked the man in the chest. He fell backwards. The knot tightened on Mardon's throat even more. His efforts to draw a breath caused him to let out another squeal. The other soldiers also started to react, drawing weapons. That's when I made the slickest move of all. I snatched the knife from Mardon's belt and placed it against his bulging Adam's apple. The prince's men stopped cold, assessing the situation gravely.

"Still think we're *equals*, eh?" I said.

The chain carrier whom I'd sent sprawling backward had returned to his feet. He'd let go of the chain and had drawn his sword like the others. I pressed Mardon's blade more firmly against his neck.

"Unlock these shackles or I'll kill him," I threatened.

"What do you think you can accomplish?" Mardon choked out.

"Shut up!" I snapped. I said to man with the keys, "Did you hear what I said?"

He looked at Mardon for a signal. But then he seemed to make a decision on his own. "You can't frighten us with your threats," he seethed. "Do your worst. Our noble prince has expressed often how he would sacrifice his life for the cause."

"What's wrong with you!" Mardon screeched to his soldier. "Unlock the manacles, you idiot!"

Fumbling a little with the keys, the soldier came forward.

"Don't try anything," I warned again.

He began to unlock the shackles on my ankles. The other men held their positions, but they looked thirsty for blood.

Mardon spoke to me again, his voice raspy. "Do you think you can escape? Where would you go? My father will have you killed the instant he finds out what you have done. He's looked forward to this day his entire life. He will not tolerate disruption."

"Then he should have killed me already," I replied. "Disruption is my middle name."

"You still believe your comrades will rescue you?" challenged Mardon.

The question was answered by a totally familiar voice. "I think it's a very real possibility."

Harry! My brother emerged from the shadows at the far end of the colonnade, a Roman sword in hand. At the same moment Gidgiddonihah appeared behind us, *both* hands armed with weapons—a Roman sword and a Nephite hatchet.

They faced the five soldiers who'd accompanied us from the square. Mardon recognized Harry immediately. His face went crimson with anger.

"Kill them!" he cried. "They're angels! They're spies from the Heavenly City! KILL TH—!"

I yanked the chain tighter around Mardon's throat and cut off the last word. But his soldiers had understood. The man with the keys abandoned his efforts to unlock my restraints. Only my feet were free. Two of the soldiers faced off with Harry while the remaining three went after Gidgiddonihah. Harry deflected the first strike of a soldier's weapon. The clash felt like a blow to my own body. My brother was *awesome!* I couldn't believe it! It was as if he'd been *raised* fighting with a sword. Obviously he'd paid attention during all those years he'd lived among the Romans. Still, it was two against one. My nerves remained on edge.

Gidgiddonihah immediately killed one of the men of Shinar by throwing his hatchet. He laid into the two remaining fighters like a grizzly. The clash of swords split the air. I realized it would attract the attention of more soldiers in a matter of seconds. That is, if Mardon's cries hadn't attracted them already.

One of Harry's opponents made a shriek of pain. Harry had dealt a blow to the soldier's arm. The man collapsed against the brick facade at the right of the colonnade, his limb bleeding. One of the last two soldiers fighting against Gid was also struck down.

In my distraction, Mardon seized my arm. He pushed the knife away from his throat and punched at my face with his other hand. However, as I fell backwards, it only choked him worse. I had this guy pinned but good. He tried to pry the sword away from me, but I resorted to a stereotypically female defense and bit down hard on his wrist. He shrieked and grabbed me by the hair, but by then another sword tip was pressed into his belly. The sword belonged to Harry.

Gid and Harry's remaining opponents had turned tail, fleeing back toward the square. Harry's teeth were tightly clenched. I'd never seen him so inflamed with fury. I was sure he'd kill Mardon then and there. Mardon shook his head, terrified for his life. But then Harry turned up the hilt of his sword. He drew back his arm, ready to deliver a nullifying blow.

"No!" I said to Harry. "Let me."

I brought up my own studded sword hilt and knocked him hard. Mardon went limp, out like a light. I slackened the chains and let him slip to the ground.

"The keys!" I called to Gid. "They're in that man's cloak!"

The soldier who'd unlocked my legs was already dead. He was the first man Gid had slain. Gidgiddonihah fished the keys out of his pocket. A swarm of angry faces appeared at the western end of the colonnade. At the same instant, more soldiers arrived from the other direction—part of Nimrod's personal guard from inside the palace. Knocking out the prince might not have been the wisest decision. We now had no hostage.

"Through here!" shouted Harry.

We ran into a narrow channel behind the brick facade on the north side of the colonnade. I wanted desperately to ask Gid why he was here—how it was possible—but this wasn't the time.

"Where's Micah and Jesse?" Gid asked Harry.

"Still among the troops in the plaza," Harry answered. "I asked them to secure one of the gliders."

"*Gliders?*" Gid and I asked simultaneously.

"Can you think of a better way to escape?" Harry inquired.

"Who's gonna fly it?" I asked.

"It's a glider! How hard can it be?"

"I'll not get aboard that contraption," Gid insisted.

"Yes, you will," said Harry. "I'm not gonna lose you again."

The channel came to an abrupt end. As luck would have it, we were at the edge of the tower, a short distance from the northeastern corner. A two-hundred-foot drop loomed before us. To our right stood portions of the unfinished palace of Nimrod. The northeastern face of the tower was crisscrossed with networks of scaffolding. Apparently the king had planned to construct elaborate stone balconies and walkways that jutted out from the edge. The view to the northern river valley and mountains was certainly better than the view to the slime pits and shantytowns to the south. One scaffold crossed right below our feet. I think it was supposed to have been some sort of aqueduct to bring water directly to the palace yard. It ran along the sheer northeastern edge until the last hundred feet or so. Then it veered away from the wall, cutting straight across to the pool west of the square. On either side of this was a dizzying drop of several hundred feet. The good news (if there was any) was that the aqueduct reconnected with the main part of the tower within a stone's throw of the first glider. The bad news was that we could see several thousand soldiers of Shinar from this vantage point. At the moment they were facing northwest, but if any one of them did so much as turn his head, we'd find ourselves overwhelmed by infantry in seconds. Soldiers were also coming toward us from behind.

But despite our enemies drawing nearer, my attention was riveted toward the northwestern sky—not to be confused with the *eastern* sky, which continued to darken. The phenomenon to the north was entirely different. And at the moment considerably more awe-inspiring.

At first glance I might have mistaken it for an enormous cloud. There was certainly a billowing, misty quality around its edges. But there was something else in its midst. It's not easy to describe. There were shapes and colors and lights in that cloud. It was too obscured by tufts of mist to make out anything specifically, but I was sure that there were *buildings* up there. *Floating buildings!* And if that wasn't mind-blowing enough, the cloud was headed *toward* us. The wind was gusting powerfully from the east, but this cloud was actually moving steadily from the *northwest*, oblivious to the weather—oblivious to the flow of every other cloud in the sky! Gid looked no less entranced.

"What *is* that?" I gasped to Harry.

"Heaven," Harry replied with remarkable matter-of-factness. "That's the whole reason Nimrod built this thing. He's trying to reach heaven, and that's the 'heaven' he's trying to reach."

"Is it really a part of heaven?" asked Gid.

Suddenly the answer popped into my mind.

"The city of Enoch!" I declared. "It's the city of Enoch!"

I wasn't sure why I'd blurted that out. But I felt strongly that what I'd declared was right. I'd always heard that the city of Enoch was raised up from the earth, but I'd certainly never thought about it in such literal terms. Yet there it was, totally visible to the world's inhabitants. My heart was glowing. My cells were tingling. *The city of Enoch!* I just stood there and gawked, absolutely mesmerized.

Harry's bark shook me back to reality. "Let's move!"

My trance was instantly replaced with terror. Our only escape route was across that unfinished, unstable aqueduct! It was only two feet wide. Any loss of balance would be positively fatal. I still had these awful shackles on my wrists. Voices began shouting behind us.

We leaped down onto the aqueduct. As I landed I felt myself tripping forward, but Gid's strong arm pulled me back. My eyes bulged out of their sockets as I focused on the jagged face of the unfinished tower two hundred feet below.

Harry led the way across the aqueduct, his feet stepping swiftly and carefully along the flimsy scaffolding that held the top layer of bricks together. As I glanced over Gid's shoulder, I saw two dozen men now standing where we had been standing along the northeastern edge. The scaffolding quivered under our feet as two of those men leaped onto the aqueduct behind us, swords in hand. I recognized them. One was Mash, the apostate Shemite. The other was Zemar, one of the arrogant faces from the throne room—the same guy who'd proclaimed himself the god of fire and wind. They were advancing furiously.

A dizzying drop loomed on either side of us. Gid drew his sword and faced the attackers. There was no room for Harry to assist him. After only two swings, Gid caused Mash to lose his balance. The Shemite officer screamed and whirled his arms in circles, but it wasn't enough to keep him from plunging over the side. Zemar was undaunted. He came at Gid with all his rage. The two men traded blow after blow, fighting to keep their legs within a two-foot perimeter. Gid worked Zemar into a certain pattern of trading blows and then, at the last second, he withdrew his sword. Zemar's weapon skimmed past the Nephite's nose as close as a razor. But as a result, Zemar threw himself right over the edge. There was another terrible scream, cut off after a few brief seconds. The god of the wind had met his end on the jagged bricks below.

Hardly a second passed before the next attack was launched. I looked back toward the northeastern edge and spotted the man with the eyepatch. His dreaded falcon was still perched on his arm. He uttered a curt command.

"Face!" he hissed to the bird, pointing directly at Harry. "*Face!*"

The falcon spread its wing and flew at my brother. I was sure its orders were to scratch and claw at my brother's eyes. Even if Harry raised his arms to fend it off, he'd surely lose his balance! Then Harry did something that surprised the heck out of me.

He raised one arm. That's all. Just raised it and said, "Rafa!" I couldn't believe it. That crazy bird perched right on my brother's arm, grasping its claws into the thick folds of the officer's cloak. Harry even stroked its head! Then Harry sent the falconer a cocky grin.

The falconer was incensed beyond words. He leaped down onto the scaffolding, rushing forward, shaking the aqueduct under his feet. He pulled the long bow off his shoulder and drew an arrow out of his quiver. At that point I may have witnessed the most incredible event of all. The falcon perceived what its master was about to do. It squawked and launched from Harry's forearm. It flew right into its master's face, fiercely flapping its wings. The falconer threw up his arms to protect himself. As a result, he dropped the arrow—then the bow. At last the poor man, in an effort to flee back in the other direction, lost his footing and toppled over the side.

I couldn't stand it anymore—the sight of such terrible deaths. I turned toward my brother, seeking to hide my face. He put his arm around me, but it was only to pull me forward. We still had seventy feet before we reached the opposite end. The wind had picked up considerably.

Suddenly Gidgiddonihah cried, "Get down!"

I caught only a brief glimpse of the thing that had freaked him out. Apparently three or four more archers were ready to fire arrows. We flattened against the top of the aqueduct as arrows whizzed over our heads. I looked back toward the archers. As I saw the sky beyond them, the sight froze in my vision like a brand on the eyes. In the last few minutes—the last thirty *seconds*—the black cloud in the eastern sky had swept upon us like a tidal wave. It completely filled our scope of vision. A curl at the top of the cloud looked literally like magnificent claws, clenching down on the Tower of Babel.

"Do you see it?" I asked Harry.

He nodded. He'd seen it. It wasn't exactly easy to miss. The archers and soldiers had also seen it. Their object to kill us was instantly abandoned. They were pointing frantically at the overwhelming cloud. Not since Jacobugath had I seen a phenomenon that remotely compared to this. I might have thought that all life on earth was about to be snuffed out. Because that's exactly how it appeared.

It looked like the end of the world.

CHAPTER EIGHTEEN

Harry

The massive cloud was closing in all around us, like a great fist preparing to squeeze the life out of Nimrod and his army.

Gid, Steff, and I continued to lay flat against the narrow aqueduct that led to the central plaza on the summit of the tower. The wind was becoming so strong that I felt like we were hanging on for our lives. I shouted back to Gidgiddonihah, "Let's keep moving! We'll crawl if we have to!"

We had to reach those gliders. Somehow we had to commandeer one of them before all hell broke loose upon the Tower of Babel. That is, before all *heaven* broke loose. The powers of Hell were nothing compared to this.

My eyes scanned the swarms of panicking soldiers in the main plaza. I was desperately trying to spot Micah and Jesse. Where could they be? I thought perhaps that I might have seen a pair of soldiers who looked familiar at the base of the triangle-shaped stairway that was situated in the middle of the northern face. But the wind was causing my eyes to water, and I couldn't be sure.

I held my sister's hand as we got back on our feet, crouching low to help ensure our balance. Gidgiddonihah kept one eye on the soldiers behind us, making certain that no one attempted to fire any more arrows. Honestly, I think the entire mass of Nimrod's troops had forgotten about us entirely. Surely they recognized by now that everything they had done, everything that Nimrod had proclaimed, had incited the wrath of the Almighty.

All at once I felt Gid's hand on my shoulder. "Harry, Steffanie, *look!*"

As I turned to see what had captured Gid's attention, the breath rushed out of my lungs. I was filled with awe. Something was emerging from the midst of that terrible black cloud. It was almost impossible to tell where the cloud vapors ended and the emerging shapes began. But I could see them—*thousands* of them—descending from the vapor's fingertips. In fact it appeared as if the shapes *comprised* the fingers of the clenching hand.

I'd only seen heavenly beings twice in my life. Once was among the ashes of the ruins of Jacobugath—an experience that even now seemed so ethereal and mystical that it was hard to place it in reality. The second was at the temple of Bountiful, as the angels of God descended to encircle Joshua and Becky and the other small children whom Jesus had blessed. The character of what I was witnessing now was entirely different. Nevertheless, I was convinced that I was still gazing upon the same class of heavenly beings.

It was an army of angels. In their hands were shields of light and swords of fire. It was absolutely spectacular, and for the longest time I couldn't tear my eyes away. Had the men of Shinar really thought that Steffanie and I were angels? Well, they were about to find out what angels really were. Now they would see the glory firsthand. At least to *us* it was glorious. To them it was undoubtedly horrifying.

Yet as I watched the army of God descend upon the Tower of Babel, I still could not decide if the angelic shapes were actual personages or a vision of gossamer ghosts in the misty clouds. I thought of Moses and the plagues. Was this how it had appeared when the power of God had descended upon Egpyt to take the firstborn sons of Pharaoh's subjects? In any case, the effect was no less spectacular, and the random cries among the ten thousand soldiers turned into screams. As the personages seemed to pour directly into the heart of the congested summit square, I actually saw soldiers run to the edge and leap to their deaths.

Then the fireworks began. An extraordinary bolt of lightning discharged from the center of the clenching hand. It was the thickest actual lightning bolt I'd ever seen—as wide as a redwood tree and blindingly white. A hundred other minor bolts flashed off the main trunk. The thunder was earsplitting, like a collision of planets. The duration of the flash must have been three entire seconds—an eternity for a lightning strike—and when it was done, all the buildings along the southern face of the summit had either exploded or erupted into a raging fireball. It appeared as if the tower had burst into flames for quite some distance down the southern face. After all, the principal element that held this monstrosity together was flammable bitumen tar. Still, I don't think anything except the kind of lightning bolt that we'd just witnessed could have ignited it.

The three of us crouched down on the scaffolding of that narrow aqueduct, feeling as vulnerable as insects before a welding torch. More lightning discharged, more thunder echoed and reverberated, and the buildings on the far western face of the tower also exploded into flames. Our feelings of awe were rapidly transforming into gut-wrenching terror. I could see it in Steffanie's eyes. I don't think I'd ever felt so assuredly in the wrong place at the wrong time. And yet I retained the presence of mind to continue urging Gid and Steff to keep moving.

Then the second phase of nature's wrath unfolded. The bricks and scaffolding beneath our feet began to vibrate. I quickly realized that the entire tower was trembling. An earthquake! Steffanie screamed. The convulsions caused her to trip backwards. She let go of Mardon's sword. She was falling! I dropped to my chest and thrust out my arm. Somehow I managed to catch the chain that bound her wrists. I caught it right in the crook of my elbow and hung on with all my strength. Gid helped me to hoist her back onto the aqueduct. As I glanced back toward Nimrod's palace, I watched that entire corner where stood the unfinished structure crumble and collapse. It disintegrated into a rockslide and tumbled all the way down the northern face. Half of the aqueduct crumbled with it. The wood scaffolding that had held the top layer in place splintered and snapped. The stones fell away only a few yards behind us—right where we'd stood only ten seconds before!

"Go! Go!" shouted Gidgiddonihah.

We crawled the rest of the way across the aqueduct, finally hoisting ourselves onto the central platform of the tower just as the remainder of scaffolding collapsed behind us. But the earthquake continued. Soldiers were running every which way. The various structures around the plaza were teetering over and crushing anyone who stood beside them or sought to go inside for refuge. I heard several high-pitched snaps as the ropes that bound three of the closest gliders broke free. The planes vibrated and bounced like toys on a coffee table, finally toppling over the edge. The sky had become a suffocating swirl of blackness, both from the overarching cloud and the burning tar. The thunder and wind and the rumble of the earthquake forced us to communicate at the top of our lungs.

"Where do we go?" yelled Steffanie.

Gid pointed toward the very pinnacle of the tower—the 150-foot triangle of stones where the largest glider was still situated. "I see them!" Gid shouted. "I see Micah and Jesse!"

Through the smoke and mist we could dimly perceive two lone figures on the stairs of that pinnacle, fighting the awful vibrations to reach the summit. We started running in that direction, dodging the swarms of desperate soldiers, many of whom seemed uncertain which way to flee. Of those still standing, the majority appeared headed back toward the tower's main stairway, despite the fact that flames engulfed that side of the edifice.

As we got within twenty yards from the first steps of the pinnacle, the earthquake's intensity amplified. The ground started to split. A fissure opened up right at our feet, crawling all the way across the center of the plaza. Soldiers fell inside the crack. The Tower of Babel was splitting in half—dividing us from Micah and Jesse!

"Jump!" I cried.

"I can't like this!" shouted Steff, indicating the shackles on her wrists.

"Lay them down on the ground!" yelled Gid.

She did as Gid commanded. The Nephite raised up his Roman sword and smashed down as hard as he could. He struck three times on the exact same link. At last it broke. Steffanie was free. But by now the fissure was almost seven feet wide.

We took it at a run, the broken chain still dangling from Steffanie's wrists. We leaped at once. As I was in midair, I caught a glimpse of the chasm's depth. It seemed to penetrate for miles—all the way to the valley floor. I landed and rolled. I'd made it! Gid and

Steffanie had also made it. I got quickly to my feet and helped Steff to stand. The three of us continued fighting our way to the base of the pinnacle.

Other soldiers had the same idea for escape as ourselves. Most of the gliders were either being consumed in flames or had fallen over the edge, but I saw seven or eight individuals fighting for control of one aircraft just to the left of the pinnacle. Seconds later they tried to launch it, but the glider was too small; there were too many on board. It teetered over the side and dropped like a rock.

I focused again toward the top of the pinnacle. I could still see two figures. One beckoned toward us. It *was* Micah and Jesse! They'd spotted us! By some miracle the glider was still intact. They appeared to be pulling at the ropes, straining to keep the plane from falling over the edge. The stairway was now sitting at a tilt—much like the ground under our feet. The split down the center of the plaza went under the right side of the pinnacle. And yet the triangle itself had not split. However, the far right end was jutting out in midair, as if the entire thing might break off any second, crashing and rolling down the northern face.

Steffanie and Gid led the way. They arrived at the pinnacle's base and began the 150-foot climb. But seconds after I started ascending the steps, someone leaped on my back. I was smashed flat against the stairs. I turned my head and saw the teeth-gnashing grimace of Prince Mardon. Gid and Steff hadn't seen him. They continued climbing.

"I'll kill you!" Mardon raged. "You're not an angel! You're a *man!*"

He had no weapon. Steffanie had taken it. My own sword was still deep in its leather sheath. Mardon drew back his fist to pummel my face. I turned my shoulder, forcing his knuckles to impact the stone stairs. I brought up my elbow and walloped him in the side of the head. Mardon rolled off. I reached for the hilt of my blade, but immediately he lunged at me again, trying to push me into the crevasse.

At last Gid and Steffanie realized I wasn't beside them and turned around. But not before Mardon had barreled into my chest. I landed on my back, my head and neck extended out over the edge. I pressed my palms into the prince's face, trying to dig my fingers into his eyes. Finally, I managed to throw him over. We rolled to the bottom of the steps. Mardon slipped off the edge. He clung to me, one arm around my neck and the other gripping my cloak. Mardon wasn't going to fall without dragging me over with him. I finally managed to pry one of his hands from my cloak, then with a last mighty thrust I drove my knuckles into his chin. The other hand let go. However, the force of my punch caused me to slide forward. Steffanie grabbed me from behind. My six-foot-two-inch frame was pulling us *both* over! Finally, Gid's powerful hands seized us both. He pulled us in from the edge. As I looked down, I realized that Mardon hadn't completely fallen. He was still clinging to some bricks a few feet down the crevasse wall. I might have taken my sword and finished him then and there, but instead I turned away and again started to climb. Steffanie and Gid stayed close beside me.

After we'd ascended about thirty steps, I glanced back again. Mardon had somehow managed to hoist himself back onto the surface of the plaza. He was about to make another attempt to rush us when a voice called to him from the opposite side of the crevasse.

"Mardon, stop!"

As of yet I hadn't seen the face of the madman who had brought about this event, but I felt certain that the colossal figure on the opposite side of the chasm was King Nimrod. He was armed with a tremendous sword. The crevasse was now twenty feet wide. It was impossible—even for him—to make the leap. Mardon looked at him in confusion, as if he recognized his father's voice, but hadn't understood the words.

"Mardon, help me across!" Nimrod yelled. "We'll fight them together!" He pointed to some lumber near a collapsed wall. "There! Lay it across! *Quickly!*"

Mardon turned out his hands and shook his head. "I don't understand! What are you saying?"

Nimrod looked equally confused. "What? Did you hear me? Get someone to help you if you must! We must reach that flying machine—!"

Mardon interrupted. "I can't—I can't understand you!"

"What's wrong, you idiot!" cried Nimrod in frustration. "Why are you babbling?"

It had begun. The great confusion. Because of our gift, we could understand them, but they could no longer understand each other.

Gid and I continued the relentless climb. Father and son kept screaming at one another until the wind and thunder drowned out their voices.

At last Gid, Steffanie, and I reached the top of the pinnacle, struggling to keep our balance in the face of the teetering stairs. Micah and Jesse were still desperately fighting the ropes to keep the glider from blowing away. It was a miracle that the canvas wings hadn't shredded in the squall.

"Get aboard!" I yelled at them.

"Not yet!" cried Jesse. "*You* get aboard! We'll cut the lines!"

There were three baskets for passengers—two under the biplane's wings and one in the center. Micah and Jesse would ride on either side, while the rest of us crammed into the middle. Steff and I climbed inside the basket. Gid hesitated. Even with the tower crumbling under his feet, he remained skeptical that this option was any safer.

"Trust me, my old friend!" I shouted to him.

Gid climbed aboard and took the center position, hanging onto the rim of the basket for dear life. Micah and Jesse sent each other a signal, then their swords came down on the ropes.

Immediately a gust of wind lifted us into the air as easily as a leaf from a sidewalk. I turned and glanced back at the pinnacle. Mardon appeared on the platform. He'd given up trying to understand his father and made a last-ditch effort to save himself. But he was too late. The tail of the glider slipped out of his grasp. He watched us ascend into the turbulent sky. Seconds later a crack appeared at the pinnacle's base. There was a loud crash as it began to fall apart, creating a shattering echo. As it collapsed, it carried with it the Prince of Shinar. The entire northern face, all five thousand cubits of it, was consumed in flames. The pinnacle fell into those flames and disappeared, swallowed up by the tremendous heat.

"Harry! Grab that line!" cried Steffanie.

My sister was desperately trying to control the flight of the glider. The wind was whipping us from side to side. The biplane's canvas frame was stressed to the max. Steff was pulling at a line on the other side—just one of the glider's steering mechanisms. I grabbed the line on the opposite side to help at least stabilize the wings, but I couldn't prevent myself from turning back to see the awful and magnificent destruction of the Tower of Babel.

The whole thing seemed to be ablaze. It was completely split in half. One side was sinking rapidly and toppling to one side, almost as if a volcano were erupting from underneath. But if it can be believed, an even more spectacular sight was taking shape in the eastern sky. The heavens remained dark on every horizon, but it was still light enough to perceive a funnel cloud forming in the smoky blackness. It was unlike any tornado that I'd ever seen—either on newscasts or created by Hollywood. *Jupiter!* This thing was larger than the entire tower! I watched in dreamlike amazement while the funnel contorted and twisted, filling the atmosphere with dust and debris. In a few moments it would swallow the Tower of Babel from top to bottom, overwhelming it with enough kinetic energy to scatter every brick for a hundred miles in every direction. In the course of only a few scant minutes, God would lay to waste the work of five generations of Nimrod's slaves.

I had no idea how fast we were cavorting across the sky, but it was surely at the velocity of a hurricane. We were entirely at the mercy of the wind, and the mercy of God. Surprisingly, I didn't feel afraid. I felt sure Heavenly Father was our pilot. At last I faced away from the tower. But as I looked at my companions, I realized their eyes were glued to another sight just ahead.

The clouds were opening up, just a little. Lights were looming just below the altitude of the glider. But it wasn't the ground. These lights were floating in the air. Wonder and awe spread over me from head to toe. The rumble of the earthquake and the raging of the wind faded. We watched the landscape of Zion in silence, my heart soaring like the glider. Through a vapor of mist I could see marble-white buildings of every shape and symmetry, flawless and balanced, like perfect mathematical equations. The wide streets reflected a golden sheen, while the roofs shone with a luster like mother-of-pearl. I felt sure that I could see people, but whether they were angels or men was unclear from this height. Undoubtedly they were translated beings, caught in the miracle between mortality and exhaltation. I could see trees and illuminated parks and gardens. There were bright patches of flowers, sparkling waterfalls, and turquoise streams and lakes. The lights of the city of Enoch seemed brighter than anything created by electricity, but it wasn't a brightness that made me squint. It was a power that seemed generated by the love of God. I could feel that love so powerfully, like a fortifying field, protecting and purifying this holy realm.

There were tears in my sister's eyes. She smiled at me and took my arm. Gid still gripped the front of the basket, though he couldn't help but gape with enchantment. Also watching in breathless wonder and reverie were Jesse and Micah.

"Have you ever seen anything so beautiful?" Steffanie whispered, as if afraid to disturb the hallowed feeling.

But shortly the mist seemed to thicken; the landscape became foggier and foggier. I felt we'd only seen a portion of the massive phenomenon. But it was enough to stay in my mind forever, until I saw the city of Enoch again when God's hand brought it back to dwell upon a sanctified earth. The sky darkened again and after a few minutes I realized we'd passed beyond Zion's airspace. I saw a few lights still behind us, but a half-minute later we were surrounded again by turbulent skies.

Suddenly I realized that something was flying in the air just off our left wing, soaring like the glider, hardly flapping at all. I heard a familiar cry in the night, the squawk of an unlikely friend. A smile as wide as the riverbend crossed my face. It was Rafa! My precious and faithful falcon was coming with us to our destination, wherever that destination was.

Now that the spectacles of fire and light were behind us, Gidgiddonihah's airsickness was returning.

"A Nephite," he said, looking green, "was never meant to fly."

I felt the seerstone in my pocket. We couldn't know where the wind was carrying us, or where we would finally touch down, but as with other destinations in this adventure, I was sure that I would know it when we got there. I could see mountains in the distance and the thinnest band of dark purple light. Steffanie and I, along with Jesse and Micah, continued to hang onto the various steering lines, trying to get a better feel for how this aircraft was guided. But for the most part the steering remained beyond our control.

Something in the west seemed to be beckoning to us. I sensed this strongly, but at the same time I began to feel an emotion that I wouldn't have expected—an odd tremor of spiritual uneasiness. I wasn't sure what it meant. I almost dismissed it as a flashback of all the stress that we'd already endured. And yet it was almost as if there was one more battle still left to fight this night. The very idea was almost incomprehensible. I was so exhausted I could hardly hold up my chin as it was. However, if this was the Lord's will, I could only pray that I'd be up to the task.

Yet as the glider carried us onward into the limitlessness of night, I sensed that this battle might be different than most others. I sensed that it was more than a struggle for life and limb. The stakes were higher.

This might well be a battle for someone's eternal soul.

NOTES TO CHAPTER 18:

Many of the details regarding the destruction of the Tower of Babel are based upon accounts from several ancient sources. In *The Book of Jubilees* it reports, "The Lord sent a mighty wind against the tower and overthrew it upon the earth" (*Jubilees* 10:26).

From the Sybilline Oracles we have this account:

> *Then the Immortal raised a mighty wind And laid upon -
> them strong necessity; For when the wind threw down the mighty
> tower, Then rose among mankind fierce strife and hate. One
> speech was changed into many dialects, and earth was filled with
> divers tribes and kings* (*The Sibylline Oracles* III, 97–107).

In the *Book of Jasher* it reads:

> *And as to the tower which the sons of men built, the earth
> opened its mouth and swallowed up one third part thereof, and a
> fire also descended from heaven and burned another third, and
> the other third is left to this day, and it is of that part which was
> aloft, and its circumference is three days' walk. And many of the
> sons of men died in that tower, a people without number* (*Jasher*
> 9:38–39).

The Tractate Sanhedrin of the Babylonian *Talmud* also states, "A third of the tower was burnt, a third sank [into the earth] and a third is still standing" (Tractate Sanhedrin XI (fol. 109A) of Seder Nezikin, p. 748).

If a part of the tower was left standing, it may be unlikely that it resembles a man-made structure. We can speculate that its initial destruction, along with five millennia of natural decay, may have reduced it to rubble and covered it with enough topsoil that it now appears only as a large hill. Its location may still be in northern Iraq.

Another tradition reported by a middle-eastern traveler in the twelfth century states, "fire from heaven fell in the midst of the tower and broke it asunder" (Bochart, *Geographia Sacra* I, 13).

Furthermore, we have accounts of its manner of destruction from the New World. One legend recorded by Pedro de los Rios concerns the pyramid of

Cholula in Mexico. He writes that after the waters of the Deluge receded, one of the survivors began to build a large structure. *"It was his purpose to raise the mighty edifice to the clouds, but the gods, offended at his presumption, hurled the fire of heaven down on the pyramid, many of the workmen perished, and the building remained unfinished"* (J. G. Frazer, *Folk Lore in the Old Testament,* Vol. I [London, 1918].) Frazer adds that *"It is said that at the time of the Spanish conquest the inhabitants of Cholula preserved with great veneration a large aerolite, which according to them was the very thunderbolt that fell on the pyramid and set it on fire"* (Cf. E. B. Tylor, *Anahuac,* 277).

Another Mexican tradition, recorded by Diego Duran in 1579 *(Historia de las Indias de Nueva Espana y las Islas de Tierra Firme* I [Mexico, 1867], 6ff.), tells of giants who built a tower that almost reached the heavens, when it was destroyed by a thunderbolt.

Although the accounts may vary in their details, it does appear that the tower met a very violent end and serves as an interesting and powerful testimony to the inevitable consequences of such a blatant affront to God.

CHAPTER NINETEEN

Joshua

My mind was made up. Nobody could tell me, Joshua Plimpton, that I wasn't doing exactly what had to be done. I may not have been doing what was best for me—*Noah had pretty much confirmed that. But what did it matter if one kid perished while saving a whole nation? Wasn't there a scripture like that in the Book of Mormon?*

I knew that I was a total scuzzball—a dishonest, conniving, rotten, good-for-nothing little twerp. And I didn't care. If I managed to do what I intended to do, it would all be worth it—even if it destroyed me in the end.

I ran through the streets of Salem until I reached the city gate. Then I ran toward the stable where we'd parked our wagons. I was going to get the sword. Yes, I had stolen it from Mary. And yes, I had lied to everyone. I felt terrible and gross for what I'd done. But none of them would have understood. How could *they understand? They weren't Nephites. Okay, so neither was I. But in my* heart *I was. I was Nephite more than I was anything else.*

Almost a week ago I'd found the sword after Mary had left it by the stream. I'd felt like the sword was calling to me. Somehow I knew that Mary had left it alone. And I realized something else—the sword didn't want to be with her anymore. It wanted to be with me. The sword was bad for Mary. It was controlling her. She couldn't handle it. The difference with me was that I knew *it would try to control me. I knew its game. Therefore, I could fool the sword while the sword thought it was fooling me. I could be smarter than the sword.*

Seven days ago I'd hidden it in a place where I knew that no one would find it. I was sweating bullets the whole time that everybody was looking. The place I decided to hide it was inside the Jaredite's fish tank—the big one on the back of the wagon. I was sure that nobody would ever think to look at the bottom of the tank. And I was right. That is, the sword was right. I think it was the sword that gave me the idea. I can't remember. In any case, it worked. I left it there until the night before we left for Salem. That night I got it back and hid it in another ingenious place—the place I was headed now.

I crept around behind the yard where we'd left the wagons. There was a caretaker on duty, but only one. Everybody else was inside the city. They were all celebrating the arrival of the baby, Abram. I don't think the caretaker had ever had much problem with unauthorized sneaks, because it was very easy for me to slip past him.

I'd hidden the sword right above the axle that was underneath our supply wagon. I'd tied it there with a rope. As I'd predicted, nobody'd thought of looking there. I'd wrapped it in a rough flaxen blanket. I felt underneath the wagon to see if it was still there. It was. I breathed a sigh of relief and started untying the ropes. Before I pulled it out, I looked around one last time to make sure that nobody'd seen me. I knew that Mary and the others would be searching for me, but so far none of them had come out of the city gate.

My original plan had been to leave the sword right there in the fish tank until we returned, but the night before we left, I changed my mind. And it was a good thing that I did. After what Noah had said, everybody knew that I was guilty—especially Mary. I could tell by the look on her face. This was a complication that I hadn't expected. It would force me to put my plan into action a little earlier than I'd intended. And that was okay. There was no sense putting it off any longer.

I took the sword out from underneath the wagon and held it in my hands. I felt that feeling again—the feeling that had come over me that very first night in the desert when the sword had kept me warm. It was the feeling of being invincible—that no one could stop me. No one on the whole face of the earth.

I didn't have to ask the sword which direction to go. I already knew. I also knew that it was gonna take me all night to get there. I was gonna go find the same exact cave that Harry and Meagan and my dad had used to go back and forth between our century and ancient Judea. The cave most likely wouldn't look the same as it would a couple of thousand years from now, but it would serve the same purpose.

I started walking toward the hills. The night was cloudy. There was no moon or stars. Soon it would probably start to rain. But I wasn't worried. I could have found my way even if I'd been blindfolded. The sword was going to guide my every step. I practically didn't have to do anything. The sword would do it all. It had to. I was controlling it.

So you're really going through with this. I'm proud of you, Joshua. I'm very proud.

Don't talk to me.

Why not?

Just don't talk to me. I don't need you to be proud of me. I'm just using you to accomplish something good.

I understand. I won't speak with you if you insist. But I think you would like to be reassured. I sense that you are having doubts that what you are doing is right.

I'm not having doubts. I'm a Nephite. I know this is right.

Very good. You *are* a Nephite. If not by blood, you are a Nephite in spirit. But even if you felt no kinship whatsoever, it wouldn't make it any less right. You will be a hero to millions, Joshua. You will change the destiny of a nation. You will save an entire race of people from annihilation. I will help you to do it.

You have no choice. I'm making you do it. You have to do what I tell you to do.

Absolutely true. You are the master. I am your servant. But I feel I must warn you. You are being followed.

I turned around and looked back down the hill. The city of Salem was brightly lit, especially the temple and the area around the house of Melchizedek. I ignored that and looked across the hillside between me and the city gate. Sure enough, somebody was coming quickly toward me. I knew right away who it was, and I made a sigh that sounded more like a growl. It was my sister, Becky. Almost the second that I recognized her, she called out to me.

"Joshua!"

Don't wait. She will try to foil your plan.

Yeah, whatever. She's my sister. What do you expect me to do?

Start running. Don't stop until we find a place to hide.

Oh, thanks. Like I couldn't figure that one out on my own.
I started running over the crown of the next hill.
"Joshua, wait!"
I entered a ravine with a babbling brook. Just beyond it were some boulders. There were also trees scattered throughout. I hated to do this. The guilt was tearing me up, but the sword was right. I had to hide from her. She wouldn't understand.
I ran for about ten more minutes. I saw flashes of lightning toward the east, followed by loud cracks of thunder. Quite a storm seemed to be coming this way. At last my wind started to give out. I looked around for a place to hide.

Over there. There's a cavity in that outcropping of boulders. You'll be safe in there.

Seemed like as good a place as any. I ran toward the boulders. The night had become so dark that I could hardly see, but the flashes of lightning kept me on the right track. After a minute I found the cavity that the sword was talking about and climbed inside. As of yet, it wasn't raining. There also wasn't much wind. Just the lightning and thunder in the east. I knew that Becky wasn't too fond of thunderstorms. I expected her to turn around and head back to Salem long before she got this far.

Still, I couldn't wait here long. She'd surely tell Mary and Pagag and the others which direction I'd gone. They'd probably all grab their horses and come riding after me. I decided I'd head south for a while, just to throw everybody off my trail.

You think that's a good idea?

Excellent idea.

You realize I don't have any food. And no water.

Don't worry. I will take care of you, Joshua. You can trust me. I would never misguide you.

At that very instant I heard my sister's voice howling over the thunder.

"Joshua! Please! Where are you?"

I peeked out of the hole and saw Rebecca about fifty yards away, crossing the patch of meadow in front of my hiding place. I only saw her clearly whenever the lightning would strike. She looked like she was wandering around aimlessly, not caring that she might get completely lost in weather like this. I snarled in disgust. Why wouldn't she just go back to Salem? Why was she so gosh darn gung-ho stubborn all the time? My little sister could drive me absolutely crazy!

So what was I supposed to do now? Let her keep wandering around the countryside to get struck by lightning or drowned by the rainstorm? The sword had assured me that she'd never find me here. I was tempted to just wait till she was gone, and whatever direction she went, I'd go the opposite. But I couldn't do it.

Yes, you can.

She's my sister!

She will be fine.

I can't do it! I'm gonna confront her. I'll just tell her how it is and send her back.

It's a mistake, Joshua. You're safe here. I promise you, nothing ill will befall her. Do not leave this cavity.

Then something surprising happened. The next time the lightning flashed, I realized Becky was looking right toward me. She was walking right toward my hiding place! But it couldn't be true. The sword *had brought me here.*

She kept coming closer. What was going on?

She's going to find you.

WHAT?

I warned you not to leave the cavity, even for a moment.

But I didn't *leave the cavity!*

She has seen you.

That's impossible! She couldn't *have! I barely poked my head out. If she'd seen me, she'd be calling my name right now!*

"Joshua!" yelled Rebecca. "Joshua, are you in there?"

It was no use. I stepped out of the cavity and stood before her with a scowl on my face. Rebecca's face brightened with relief. I realized she'd been crying. She ran toward me to embrace me.

"Joshua!" She threw her arms around my neck.

I removed them and stood her back to shout in her face. "What are you doing? Why are you following me?"

She yelled some questions of her own, the tears still streaming down her cheeks. "What's wrong with you? Where do you think you're going?"

"I'm going away, Rebecca. There's nothing wrong *with me. I've never felt so right about something in my whole life."*

Rebecca looked at the sword tied behind my shoulder.

"Yes," I barked, answering her question before she could even ask it. "I stole it. Okay? Now you know. Now everybody knows. I did something terrible. I admit it. I'm sorry."

She decided the tone of my voice sounded anything but sorry. "No, you're not. Why, Joshua? Why are you doing this?"

"I don't want to have to explain myself. You wouldn't understand. No one would understand! Becky, I want you to go back."

She shook her head. "Not until you tell me what's going on."

"I'm going to Nephite times. That's all you need to know."

Don't try to explain it to her.

"Shut up!"

Becky looked at me queerly. "Huh?"

"Not you," I said. "I wasn't talking to you."

"Who were you . . . ? You were talking to the sword, weren't you?"

"Yes. So what? I was talking to the sword. You used to talk to the seer-stone. I'm talking to the sword. What's the difference?"

"Big difference. Every difference. Joshua, the sword is evil. Don't you see that?"

"Everything is evil if you use it in the wrong way. I'm going to use it to accomplish something great. Something spectacular."

"You can't! It doesn't work that way! The sword only takes, Joshua. The stone works on faith. Faith in the Lord. Like the Liahona. The sword is just an imitation. It's evil. It can never be anything but—"

"You're wrong, Becky. The sword is power. How a person uses that power is up to him. I'm going to use it for something good."

"What are you going to do?"

Don't tell her.

"I'm going to save the Nephites."

"What?"

"I'm going to Cumorah, Becky. With this sword I know I can help change the outcome. I can save Mormon and Moroni. I can save all the Nephites from destruction."

"Joshua, you're crazy!"

"Yeah, that's what I figured you'd say." I huffed, and then I turned around and started walking away.

Becky grabbed my arm. "It's not right!"

I spun back and faced her. "Don't tell me that! You of all people should know what I'm talking about. If you don't understand, I know that no one will. You were born in Zarahemla! You might as well be one of them!"

"You're right. Sometimes I do feel like I'm a Nephite. But I'm other things too. I'm also an American."

"Well, then, if you knew that America was going to be destroyed, wouldn't you try to do something to stop it? Wouldn't you do everything you possibly could?"

"Not everything. I wouldn't try to save it by doing something evil."

"Becky, there's no use talking about this. I've made up my mind. If I don't at least try, I'll never be able to live with myself."

"Josh, you're not thinking straight. The sword has twisted your whole way of looking at things."

"So now I'm twisted, eh? REBECCA, GO BACK!"

She started crying again. "I won't! You can't make me! I won't leave you, Joshua."

My shoulders drooped. I started to plead. "What do I have to do? Run away? Lose you in the storm? I'll do it, Becky. Don't think I won't."

"It doesn't matter. I'll find you again."

"Becky, you're being ridiculous. If you come with me, you could get hurt. Maybe even killed. Just go back! I'll be okay. The sword will take care of me. If I wanted to lose you, I could do it in a heartbeat. You wouldn't have found me this time if I hadn't stuck my head out. The sword told me not to. But I did it anyway. I just didn't want you to keep following me and get lost in the storm."

"I didn't see you," she insisted. "I found you because I knew where to look."

I pulled in my chin. "Huh?"

"Don't you think I've been praying like crazy? I was praying to find you, Joshua. That's how come I walked over here."

"How could you do that? You don't have the stone."

"Haven't you been listening to me? I told you! It's not the stone! It's faith! I love you with all my heart, Josh. And because I love you so much, the Lord wouldn't let you hide from me. Especially when the sword is telling you where to hide."

I gaped at her, feeling confused. Then I turned away again. "That's not true. You saw me."

She was practically bawling now. *"Joshua, please! Don't do this! I won't let you! I really won't!"*

I told you not to tell her.

"SHUT UP!"
"Joshua, stop!" Becky cried.
I stopped, but it wasn't because of anything Becky'd said. I peered into the storm. A particularly bright bolt of lightning had just struck, and near the top of the bald ridge to the east, I saw several silhouettes against the dark sky. It was about a dozen men on horseback. They were riding toward us. But they weren't silhouettes really. I made out the color of their clothes well enough, and my heart stopped. The riders' cloaks were purple.
The hill went dark again, but Becky had seen them too. "Joshua, did you see that?"
"I saw it," I admitted. "Nimrod's trackers. They must have been following us the whole time. They followed us to Salem."
"We have to go back!"
"No, Becky! I can't!"
"Yes, you can! You can give the sword to Shem. You can end all this."
"Stay close to me."
"No, Josh—"
"If you love me, then trust me just this once. I can protect you."
"I've trusted you a million times. You're my big brother. This is the one time I can't trust you."
"Then don't stay close to me," I snapped. "Go back by yourself!"
But as I began walking quickly toward the north, my little sister continued clinging to my cloak. The wind was picking up, but there was a pause in the lightning. I'd only seen the horsemen that one time. I didn't think that they'd seen us start going toward the north. I was trying to reach some trees that I'd seen during the last lightning flash, but we didn't make it all the way before the lightning struck again. It was a long one. Lightning flashed across the sky for a good two or three seconds, and the thunderclap was really loud, but when I looked back toward the bald ridge, I didn't see anyone. I almost wondered if the horsemen had been an illusion. Either that or they'd already reached the ravine below us. We continued speedily toward the treeline.

Becky hadn't said anything else for several minutes, but I could still hear her crying now and then.

"Don't cry anymore," I pleaded with her. "The echo carries every-where."

"Don't you see, Joshua? The sword led you out here so that they would find you."

"That's nonsense. The sword is loyal to whoever owns it. It doesn't matter who."

"It's not loyal to anyone. It hates everybody equally."

"Becky, be quiet! Just keep up to me."

She can't stay with us. You know that, don't you?

She can stay if I say she can stay. It's not your decision. Just stay out of it.

I'm only concerned with what's in your best interest—and the best interest of your mission.

If that's true, why didn't you warn me about the trackers? Were you just gonna leave us there to be surrounded?

I didn't warn you because there was no need. You don't need to fear your enemies, Joshua. Didn't I promise that I would watch over you?

Are they still following us?

Of course.

So what are we supposed to do?

Do you believe in my power?

"What do you mean?" I said out loud. "What kind of a stupid question is that? I'm carrying you, aren't I?"

"Josh, listen to yourself!" pleaded Rebecca. "Do you know how insane you sound? You're talking to a sword!"

"*Shut up for a second!*" *I barked at her. Then I said to the sword,* "*Yes, I believe in your power. Now what should I do?*"

Beyond these trees there is a clearing—a meadow with a large, flat stone in the center. Go there and wait.

"*Just wait?*"

Just wait.

I gripped Becky's hand and pulled her along. "Let's keep moving."

CHAPTER TWENTY

Harry

The storm had kept us airborne for hours, knocking us about, but so far we'd managed to keep the craft together and stay ahead of the worst part of the weather. Rafa finally grew too weary to fight the wind. I managed to catch him when he tried to land in the basket. Then I set him in the rear corner where he promptly put his beak in his feathers, taking advantage of the much-deserved rest.

Steffanie and I felt we'd learned a great deal about how the steering lines operated. The cloud cover remained thick, and I could hardly see a thing on the ground. Now and then the moon and stars broke through, but they never illuminated anything that looked like a viable landing site. I remained convinced that the Lord was leading us somewhere, and I wasn't about to interfere.

Jesse and Micah remained alert. They managed several steering lines of their own. These lines seemed to control the aircraft's altitude. Jesse and Micah made several adjustments as we crossed over some mountains. Gidgiddonihah seemed to have recovered somewhat from his airsickness, but I don't think flying would ever be one of his favorite pastimes. I might have wished that he wouldn't judge all air flights by this one. The turbulence was enough to nauseate *any* seasoned warrior. Yet it was Gid who first noticed the lights on the horizon.

He stood up straight and inquired, "What *is* that?"

All of us peered ahead. The lights drew nearer. It was a city— nearly as bright as any modern small town on a vast landscape. One light in particular shone as brightly as the beacons inside the city of

Enoch. As we got a little closer, Steffanie remarked, "I think . . . that's a temple!"

"It's Salem," I said, half in a whisper. "The city of the patriarchs."

I'd come to know it as the only city on earth that Nimrod and Mardon had grown to fear. Compared to Babel or Shinar it was a remarkably modest community. Yet the power of God dwelled in this place. Perhaps it was my imagination, but there seemed to be a glow about this place that went beyond the city lights.

Micah called over from his basket under the left wing, "I think it's time to land."

My poor adrenal glands were already so overworked that I didn't think there was anything left, but the prospect of landing this glider managed to squeeze out a few extra drops. We decided to land on a grassy stretch of ground east of the city that looked reasonably level. Steffanie called out to Micah and Jesse to pull down on their steering lines.

"Remember," she added, "as soon as the plane gets low enough, you guys will have to serve as the wheels. It's your job to run us to a stop."

Jesse looked dubious. Normally this glider might have landed at a slower velocity. One of Micah's steering lines actually seemed to loosen the canvas on the biplane, giving it some of the qualities of a parachute. But the stiff wind made any prospects of descent more dangerous. We'd have to come in for a straight and fast landing. I honestly feared Micah and Jesse might break their legs if they tried to use them like landing gear. The situation was tense enough that I decided to awaken Rafa. He protested with his usual squawk.

"I think your methods of landing might be a bit safer than ours," I said to him.

I held him out of the basket and released him. His chirping and squawking intensified, but as expected, he spread his wings and began to follow beside us. I gave Steffanie a nod to indicate that I was ready to attempt a touchdown. We began to pull the steering lines, attempting to guide the plane as it descended. The ground seemed to be coming up too fast.

"Not so much!" I called out to our altitude controllers. Micah and Jesse made the adjustments.

I took a few deep breaths. The more I thought about it, the more ludicrous this whole thing seemed. I'd never flown anything in my life—not even a remote-control model airplane. I couldn't even seem to make a decent *paper* airplane! Now I was attempting a real landing in a real glider. I'd often heard that *flying* a plane was the easy part. The difficult part was the *landing*. I feared I was about to learn this the hard way. The ground was now only ten or fifteen feet below us.

"Brace yourself!" said Steffanie.

We did exactly that. Micah and Jesse reluctantly hung down their legs. I might have closed my eyes, but this was something I had to see—first-time pilots landing an ancient aircraft. Besides, wasn't there some morbid part of the human psyche that naturally kept one's eyes glued to an impending accident? If so, this was true even if the accident was my own.

* * *

Mary

I saw the enormous bird with massive red wings just as Pagag and I were departing Salem to continue our frantic search for Joshua and Becky. We'd sighted it just minutes after we'd finished questioning the watchman posted near our wagon. The watchman had reported to us that he'd not seen Joshua, but that he'd seen young Rebecca headed into the eastern hills. The red-winged bird appeared to have originated from the same direction, gliding just ahead of the fast-approaching storm.

It was now crossing the sky, floating like . . . almost like one of the many air machines that I had seen in the twenty-first century. But it couldn't be an air machine. This was ancient Judea!

To my surprise, Pagag concluded that it was a man-made vehicle even before I did. "Astonishing," he remarked. "I'd heard that Nimrod's magicians had created such a machine, but I never thought that I would see it with my own eyes."

Pagag's remark caused me concern. "Do you think it might carry the soldiers of Nimrod?"

He shook his head with uncertainty. He began to run a little, eager to find out the identity of the pilots, despite the possible danger. It definitely appeared that the airplane was preparing to land.

I kept up to Pagag, an unusual feeling stirring in my heart. After another moment Pagag and I drew ourselves to a halt. The flying machine was only seconds from landing. Or rather, it was only seconds from impact. I surmised that it was moving far too swiftly for a safe touchdown. After all, the vehicle had no wheels.

From a distance of about a hundred cubits we watched it light upon the grassy field. At first all seemed to be going well enough. Runners under each of the wings were attempting to run the plane to a stop. But their poor legs simply could not spin with enough momentum. An instant later the double-winged glider overturned and flipped over on the landing strip. One of the wings seemed to break apart, but then the glider slid behind a small hill, hindering my vision of the moment when it came to rest.

Once again Pagag and I started to run toward it. As we came up over the hill, I paused again. The glider was visible in the shallow gully beyond us, one wing broken, but not looking nearly as tangled or demolished as I might have feared. We also heard the reassuring sound of laughter. The glider's passengers were laughing with relief, presumably because no one had been seriously injured.

However, there was something else about that laugh. Something so familiar and . . .

Pagag saw the sudden change in my expression. "Mary, what is it?"

My heart started fluttering like the wings of a hummingbird.

I heard a voice. It rang so clear and mellifluous, even over the whistle of the wind.

"Jesse, are you all right?" the voice inquired

"Just banged up my knee," another voice replied. "I'll live."

Tears sprang to my eyes. Such a rush of emotion swelled in my chest that I feared I'd be carried away like a petal in the waves of the sea.

I started to run down the other side of the hill, utterly ignoring the warning voice of Pagag behind me. "Mary, wait! Look at their uniforms!"

I couldn't stop myself, and I couldn't slow down—at least not until I had come within fifteen or twenty cubits of my destination. By then my legs seemed to slow down involuntarily, practically halted, as if overcome *by fear. As if stricken by the possibility that this was all in my mind. That my fantasies had somehow altered my imagination, and therefore had altered the sound of voices into something that could not possibly be.*

By now I was close enough that the passengers of the glider had all turned to note my approach and the approach of Pagag, who was only a short distance behind me. In the light of the moon and the reflection of Salem's temple beacon I could clearly perceive their faces. As Pagag had perceived, several wore the trappings of soldiers of Shinar. But as the features of those who had survived the ill-fated landing became recognizable, my heart spiraled upward in a cyclone of exhaltation.

I recognized Jesse first. Sweet Jesse! The orphan who had been with me in Ephesus and Athens. The orphan who now looked like a considerable young man. I also saw Micah, Harry's closest friend during his most difficult years in the Greek islands. He, too, looked older and more mature. They were gawking at me in disbelief. I knew now that my mind had not been misled. The voice I had heard was real. He was here. He was among them. I thought that I recognized which one he was, though his face was presently hidden behind the glider's broken wing.

Still, for some reason my feet had stopped moving, perhaps because I could no longer breathe. Or because I couldn't see very well through the wash of tears. Or because even seeing was not quite enough to convince me that this was truly happening. Did the heavens normally deliver a woman's loved one from the skies?

Suddenly Pagag sprang in front of me, his sword drawn. As he pushed me back, I tripped on a loose stone and fell. It certainly wasn't intentional, but to those around the plane, it might have looked as if he'd deliberately tried to hurt me. For a blink of an instant, Pagag's attention was divided as he stood forth to protect me and glanced back to see if I was all right. That's when the blur of blonde hair came rushing at him from the right.

It was Steffanie. She hit Pagag's side like a bull, lifting him into the air. The son of Mahonri came down hard, landing with a grunt. It happened so quickly. It was difficult to see clearly as I pushed myself up, but I perceived that even before Pagag fully recovered, Steffanie had rolled off and persons from the glider had taken over, surrounding Pagag's head. The tips of their swords were pointed at his chest.

"Wait!" I cried. "He's not an enemy! He's a friend! He's—"

But then my own attention was drawn away. I turned my eyes upward. A face loomed above me, staring down, wide-eyed, blinking, the brisk wind stirring his dusty blonde hair. He was more handsome, more breathtaking, than I even remembered. His powerful facial muscles, broad shoulders, and strong arms were illumined by the glow of the cloud-covered moon positioned directly behind him.

We gazed at each other, the surprise and disbelief almost unbearable. I watched him draw breath. He tried to speak. But nothing came forth. He reached down and took my hand. For so long I'd envisioned this moment. Dreamed it, yearned for it. Now it was here—so suddenly and unexpectedly. And also so different from how I'd first imagined. But it was better. *Sweeter! More wonderful than my imagination could have possibly conceived. Lightning struck and for an instant that beautiful face shone like the sun.*

Harry pulled me up and enfolded me into his arms. He pressed his lips to mine and kissed me. It was a kiss full of passion and tears. I no longer felt the ground beneath me. I cannot say where I was carried, but it was nowhere near the stationary earth. It was somewhere in the wind and clouds.

CHAPTER TWENTY-ONE

Steffanie

A *friend!* Was Mary kidding? The bozo with the iron sword had just pushed her onto the rocks! Was every male from this time period a colossal jerk? The man continued groveling beneath the sword points of Micah, Jesse, and Gidgiddonihah. I felt furious that such a perfect reunion between Harry and Mary had been ruined. But then I turned and saw them sharing a passionate kiss. Okay, so maybe it wasn't as ruined as much as I'd feared.

"My name is Pagag," said the stranger hoarsely. "I was only trying to protect her."

"You got a funny way of showing it, bucko," I gruffed.

Mary ended the kiss and declared, "It was an accident. Pagag is the son of Mahonri, the brother of Jared. It's all right."

Micah, Jesse, and Gid lowered their blades. From Gid's face it was plain that he recognized the name. And of course, so did I.

Mary threw her arms around my neck. "Oh, Steffanie! Jesse! Micah! I don't believe it! All my hopes! All my—! Oh, it's so good to see you!"

She embraced us all, her eyes streaming tears. But then she stopped abruptly as she noticed for the first time the face of Gidgiddonihah. Her expression blossomed with astonishment, just as I'm sure mine had when I first saw him in that line alongside Nimrod's soldiers.

"*Gidgiddonihah!*" she exclaimed.

"Hello, Mary," Gid replied, revealing his famous crooked grin.

For Mary the miracle now seemed to take on a whole new meaning. She might have wondered if she was in the presence of heavenly beings. She embraced Gid and smothered his face in kisses. After all, Mary Symeon was no different than the rest of us. Gidgiddonihah had saved her life as often as he had saved everyone else in my family. Like me, she didn't ask right away how it was possible. Just that he was here was enough. Mary started weeping uncontrollably. It looked as if she might collapse with emotion, but Harry was there to catch her.

I looked again at the man called Pagag. He'd gotten to his feet, watching closely as my brother took Mary again into his arms. He wore a smile, but it looked a little like it was painted on.

"Your name is Pagag?" I asked him.

"That's right."

"And you're the son of the brother of Jared?"

He nodded. "Jared is my uncle."

Under any other circumstances I'm sure that I'd have been more than a little breathless to meet this person. Not only was he the son of one of the most incredible people in the Book of Mormon, but he was remarkably good looking. However, I'd had more than my fill of good-looking sleazoids. Also, it irritated me to see the way he was watching Mary. Call it feminine instinct, but I could tell that he saw her as slightly more than just a friend.

Harry finally shook his hand. "I'm thrilled to meet you. If protecting Mary's life has become a regular habit of yours, then I probably owe you a great deal of thanks."

Pagag nodded. My poor, naïve brother didn't even realize that he'd just shaken the hand of his competition.

Harry turned again to Mary. "Becky and Joshua—where are they?"

Mary's face paled. "Harry, we're looking for them," she declared, as if her mind had suddenly been wrenched back to reality. "They went this way—into these hills. We were . . . We were trying . . . Oh, Harry, there's so much to explain!"

Harry's brow furrowed with concern. "Are they in trouble?"

"Yes," Mary replied. "No. I don't know. Joshua has the sword of Akish."

"*Akish!*" Harry exclaimed.

The name also went through me like a jolt of electricity.

I heard Jesse ask Micah in a low voice, "What's the sword of Akish?"

Micah shook his head.

Harry's eyes began desperately searching the area until they found Rafa. The falcon was perched on the rim of the airplane's broken wing.

"Rafa!" he called. The bird flew to him, landing on his arm.

Harry faltered, as if he was struggling for what to say, how he would phrase the appropriate instructions. Finally, he said to Gid, "I'm not sure how to word it. This is exactly what this bird was trained for, but I don't know the commands."

"You don't *have* to know them," I blurted out. "Don't you realize it yet, Harry? With our gift of tongues that bird will understand what you tell it no matter *what* words you use. It probably understands you better than it ever understood its master."

Harry smiled knowingly, as if I'd confirmed something that had already occurred to him. He just needed to hear it from someone else. The idea apparently explained many of his other experiences with the bird. Perhaps it also explained why the creature had stayed with him. It must have been quite a thrill, even for a bird, to suddenly understand so many more of the words that were being spoken to it.

Harry said to Rafa, "Find Josh and Becky. Find my young cousins. You can do it, Rafa. We'll follow."

The falcon hesitated a moment, as if it wasn't terribly thrilled to follow such orders in the face of the impending storm. But at last it took flight from Harry's arm, flapping its wings toward the east, right into the teeth of the wind.

Harry took Mary's hand. "We'll find them," he reassured. "Let's go!"

* * *

Joshua

"We have to hurry," I told Becky.

I continued gripping my little sister's hand, pulling her toward the tree line. Just before we got to the woods, I turned back to look across the hillside and down into the ravine. Another lightning flash crisscrossed the sky. In that instant I saw a dozen horses with purple-robed riders. They emerged from behind a ridge down below, making their way toward us up the slope, swords drawn.

"Come on! Come on!" I said.

We entered the trees. The ground was level now. We could finally run. Becky was the only thing slowing me down. I realized she was doing it on purpose.

"Wait, Joshua!" cried Becky.

"We can't *wait! We need to reach the clearing!"*

The lightning flashes were happening so often now that they lit up the forest every few seconds. I'd never seen a storm like this. At least not since I was four or five years old—not since that big storm in the land of Bountiful. But I barely remembered that one. To me, this seemed like the most incredible thing ever. We saw one of the bolts hit a tree about fifty yards to our right. The tree split in half and burst into flames. Becky shrieked and stopped in her tracks.

"It's all right," I assured her, yanking her arm. "Just stay close to me."

We soon reached the clearing. I could clearly see the large flat stone out in the center.

"Joshua, where are you going?" Becky demanded, still terrified.

"It's not far now. Hurry!"

The wind was in our faces. It seemed to change directions without warning. One gust would strike the right side of my face, and a stronger gust would strike the left side, but it was all basically blowing from the east. As I reached the center of the meadow, I stepped onto the stone. It was sorta oval-shaped, only a foot or two higher than the ground, and about five feet wide. As I started to climb on top, Becky finally let go of my hand.

"What are you doing?" she demanded again.

"We're waiting here."

"We're what?*"*

"We're gonna wait for them to come to us. I'm gonna fight them."

Becky sank down to her knees, the tears coming more furiously than ever. "Please, please, no, Josh."

"I can do it, Becky. Don't you remember the lions and tigers?"

Becky folded her arms and leaned over, rocking back and forth. "Please, please, please . . ."

Behind her I saw the first purple-robed horseman come out of the trees. At almost the same moment another rider came out of the woods to the north, followed by two more horses, and another rider from the south. Just as I would have expected, they were trying to surround us.

I felt the first drops of rain hit my face. I wiped my eyes and reached back to pull the silver sword off my shoulder. Becky didn't even look up. She just kept praying. At just that moment I heard the cry of a bird overhead. A bird flying in a windstorm? But there it was. It circled several times, squawking weirdly, then went away.

The riders drew nearer. I recognized several of them in the next flash of lightning. It was that creep, Githim—the guy who'd tried to kill us in the woods just before Jared showed up. I knew the others as well. These jerks had obviously been tracking us all along. Soon there was a total of twelve horses surrounding us. Several of the archers loaded their bows. I stood there in the wind and rain, holding the sword out front, ready to defend myself.

"Where is the son of Terah?" called Githim over the wind.

"He's safe from murderers like you forever!" I said. "He's in Salem!"

The horsemen looked at each other gravely, then back at me with eyes of hatred.

Githim was the most hateful of all. "You have defied the king of Shinar! The penalty for such a crime is death. Your ages will make no difference. We will return to Babel with your heads on the end of our spears!"

I moved my feet around for better balance and held the sword out a little farther, biting my lip with determination.

Githim looked at my sword with a lot of interest. He unexpectedly changed the subject. "Some men approached us yesterday. We told them of a woman who fought like a master swordsman—a woman who traveled with two children. They became most curious and asked many questions about her weapon. Is this the same sword that the woman used to attack us?"

Becky looked up. Githim's words had startled us. What men would be asking questions about the sword?

"So what if it is?" I replied.

Githim grinned and snarled, "Apparently the chancellor's infant son isn't the only thing that you have stolen." He nodded to his archers. "Now!"

The archers looked confused.

Githim looked around at his men. "Raise your weapons!"

His men still refused to obey. It was almost as if they hadn't understood him.

Finally, the rider beside Githim said, "What is your command, Captain? We do not understand these noises."

"What is this gibberish?" raged Githim. "Do as I have said!"

Becky and I looked at each other. This was bizarre. Obviously they could understand me okay. They just couldn't seem to understand each other.

Githim lashed out at them angrily. "What's wrong with everyone? KILL THEM! KILL THEM!"

His men glanced around at each other, as if checking to see if anybody else had understood Githim's words.

Finally, in frustration, Githim grabbed up his own bow and loaded an arrow. At last his men understood. Several more of them raised their weapons. Bowstrings were pulled back. Becky threw herself down at my feet, covering her head with her arms. The bowstrings snapped. In the confusion of lightning flashes, I didn't even see the arrows flying at me. But I felt my hands make the small adjustments up and down, and I saw sparks and heard the "tings" as the iron arrowheads hit the silver blade. The arrows shattered, ricocheting to the left and right. After I'd fended off six separate arrows meant to kill us, I gathered up my feet and stood tall again. I sensed the weirdest feeling inside my body. It was wonderful! I felt just like Aragorn facing an army of Orcs.

The men of Githim looked stunned. I could tell they'd never seen anything like what I'd just done. Well, except for the moment they'd come face to face with Mary. But it wasn't just shock I saw in their eyes. It was fear. They were afraid of me. I lapped it up. It was the coolest thing ever. I could actually strike terror into the hearts of grown men!

Then something awesome happened—awesome and awful at the same time. A strange power entered the sword—magnetic and hot. Its surface started to give off a weird electric light. Becky saw it too. She got up and started backing away.

"Drop it, Josh! Drop it!"

Suddenly, a bolt of blue lightning struck the tip of the sword. I wanted to drop it. I wanted to do exactly as Becky had said—but I couldn't let it go! *And then the most amazing thing occurred. The sword shot out lightning bolts of its own—a dozen separate fiery streaks zipped and zinged off the silver blade, each bolt echoing like a laser blast. The jagged blue streaks went straight into the chests of each of the riders, blowing them out of their saddles. The men screamed. The horses reared up and started stampeding in all directions, heading back toward the trees. I just stood there, confused and frightened. Most of the men landed flat on their backs; others lay there with bent and twisted limbs. All of them were silent and still. I looked at the sword, my eyes bugging out. I was frozen with disbelief. Had I just seen what I thought I'd seen?*

But as another lightning flash lit the sky I saw another silent body on the ground. It lay just ten feet in front of me. I gasped, and my lungs froze.

"No!" I shrieked.

I leaped off the stone, dropped the sword in the dirt, and gathered my sister into my arms. Just as a fiery blue lightning bolt had stuck each of the riders, it had also struck my precious sister.

"Becky!" I screamed. "Please, no! Oh, please, Becky, wake up! Pleeeease!"

I rocked her body, my mind burning up with grief. The rain started coming down hard. It felt like my guts were being twisted in a blender. It was all so unreal—none of it felt like it was really happening. I let out another cry that tore up my lungs from the inside. Then I looked down at the sword blade in the dirt, the rain splattering against its silver surface. I laid down my sister's head and grabbed the hilt with both hands.

"Why?" I demanded. "WHY?"

You knew that she couldn't come with us. It's better this way. In time, you'll agree that I was right.

I screamed again and raised the sword high over my head. I brought down the blade as hard as I could on the edge of the stone. I brought it down again and again, each crack causing a shower of sparks. Several chinks appeared along the sword's edge, revealing the copper underneath. I slammed the very tip straight down into the rock and then I threw the sword with all my might against another boulder behind me. The blade bounced off the stone and spun several times on the ground. I dropped to my knees and watched it come to a rest. As I raised my eyes, I saw a dark silhouette against the swirling sky.

The shape was standing about fifteen feet away. The lightning stuck behind the person's head, giving me a clearer outline of the person's body and the shape of his head. From just that—from his baldness and the protruding ears sticking out—I knew who it was. I might've been surprised. I might've been gasping in terror, but there was nothing left inside me to feel such things. I just gaped at him, and remained on my knees, the limp body of my little sister lying beside me.

At last the lightning struck above us, and I could see every detail of his gruesome face, right down to the buckteeth and acne scars.

"Hello, Joshua," said Akish. "How good to see you again."

CHAPTER TWENTY-TWO

Harry

"Joshua!" I cried again into the storm.

We'd seen it all. Each of us had witnessed the incredible flash of lightning. We were just inside the trees at the edge of the clearing when it hit. I'd watched the riders fall from their horses. Several of those horses had rushed past us in the darkness. I'd also watched in horror as tiny Rebecca fell. Finally, I'd observed the approach of the shadowy figure, skulking across the meadow like a demon ghost, while Joshua slammed the sword against the rocks in anguish. It was the third time that I'd shouted my cousin's name. Steffanie and Mary had screamed it too, but because the wind was carrying our voices in the opposite direction, he couldn't hear us.

We ran as swiftly as possible across the clearing. Gid and I led the way, with Pagag, Steffanie, Mary, and the others close behind. I think I sensed from the very beginning that the man poised just beyond the boulder was Akish. There was no mistaking the stench of evil all around us—and only Akish could create such an odor. That is to say, Akish and his miserable sword.

I couldn't seem to cross the meadow fast enough. The wind and rain lashed at my face. Still, I saw enough to realize that Akish had lunged forward to grab the sword. Joshua made an effort to try and stop him, but the Jaredite king tossed him aside.

Gid and I, along with Pagag, Micah, and Jesse, began to surround him. We drew our blades. I could see my fragile young cousin, Becky, lying in the grass, her body being pelted by rain. Mary made a move as if she would run to her, or run to Joshua. But Akish stood between them. He held aloft his terrible sword, grinning widely, confidently.

"Well?" he challenged. "What are you waiting for? Come and save them!"

The five of us men began tightening our circle around Akish.

"No!" Joshua screamed. "Harry stop! You don't know what you're fighting!"

But Joshua was wrong. I *did* know what I was fighting. I knew exactly what it was that Akish held in his hands. Yet in spite of it—maybe *because* of it—I felt a power surging and roiling inside me. This feeling of strength was as great as anything I'd ever felt. Yet it was no different than feelings I'd often experienced on my mission. Or experienced any other time that I was worthy and sought the communion of God. It was the power of the Spirit. The strength of the priesthood. Did Akish's sword really grant its bearer some kind of feeling of invincibility? Oh, Satan and his illusions! Akish's mistake was that I already knew what invincibility was. I'd experienced it first-hand on countless occasions. So had these other men who were closing in beside me. Akish was about to experience the most valuable lesson of his life.

The Jaredite king came running at me, his sword high overhead, prepared to smash me down like a paper cup. Instead I raised my blade and met his strike in a shower of sparks. The lightning flashed again, but this time it sent Akish reeling backwards. He landed on the ground, shaking his jowls in a bout of dizziness, his eyes wide with surprise. He couldn't seem to believe what had just happened. He looked at his precious sword, crafted in blood, smelted in the caul-drons of evil.

Then Akish leaped to his feet and came at us again. This time his sword clashed with that of Gidgiddonihah, who sent him spinning off balance to the right. Akish swung again, but this time Pagag struck back, and the silver sword with the golden hilt was knocked to the ground, looking now no more daunting than a child's plastic toy. Once again, Akish was crouched on his hands and knees in the mud.

Joshua was watching the whole thing in stark astonishment, as if this was an outcome that he would have never expected. I didn't understand why he should feel so surprised. Did Josh really think that this was somehow a battle of human strength? It might have been, except for the weapon that Akish had chosen. His choice had made this undeniably a battle between good and evil, light and darkness. I wondered if I'd ever seen the line so clearly defined.

In a flash, I think Akish realized it too. Or at least he realized *something*. In that realization he knew that this was a fight he could not win. His sword was helpless against us. The Jaredite king had been squarely defeated. But Akish had another plan. As he snatched up the silver blade, I braced myself for another assault. Instead, Akish turned and ran back toward Joshua.

I stiffened with dread. Akish seized him around the neck. And then something happened that I couldn't have possibly anticipated.

Akish raised the tip of the silver sword and slashed the air behind him. A slice of orange fire appeared. I saw it with my own eyes, and yet my mind couldn't comprehend it. It was as if a wound had been inflicted directly against the fabric of space. But then our hearts exploded in shock as Akish fell backwards and pulled Joshua with him into that wound. *They disappeared right in front of our faces!* One instant they were there, and the next they were gone.

The phenomenon was followed by a blinding flash. The nature of it was entirely different from the flash created by lightning. It was bright orange, just like the wound. For an instant the air turned ice cold, like a gust of arctic wind. And then it was gone—the wound, the orange light. The slice in the fabric of space healed over, and all that remained were the seven of us, with Becky still lying inert at the foot of the large, flat stone. We stood in awful consternation for a long moment. Mary was the first to awaken from the stupor. She rushed to Rebecca's side. Steffanie was right behind her. Becky's unmoving body was drenched and pale—no visible life. Mary gathered her up in her arms while Steffanie leaned in close and pressed her hand against Rebecca's cheek, as if feeling in vain for some pulse of warmth or movement.

"She's not breathing," Steffanie cried. "She's not breathing!"

"Do CPR!" shouted Mary. For an instant, I was surprised to hear her say it. But only for an instant. I knew of Mary's passion to under-stand all that she could about life in the twenty-first century. She'd mentioned it in every letter. I even remembered her mention in one of her early dictated letters that she was taking a course on first aid.

As Mary laid Becky down, Steffanie knelt on the opposite side. Mary listened directly for a heartbeat. Apparently there was none. Immediately Mary set her palms against Becky's chest and began the compressions. After she'd done a series of eight or ten, she listened again. Steffanie tried to move aside the broken chains that were still dangling from her wrists and pinched Becky's nose. She blew air into her lungs. Nothing was happening. The young girl's body remained pale and limp. Mary started more compressions. We all watched in excruciating suspense, our hearts ready to break.

"*A blessing!*" said Mary, her voice almost choking.

But I was ahead of her. I already had my tiny oil vial in hand. I turned to Pagag. "Do you have the priesthood of Melchizedek?"

"I do," said Pagag humbly.

"Will you help me?"

He nodded. Mary and Steffanie continued their desperate repetition of stimulating the heart and lungs while Pagag and I knelt down above her head. I handed Pagag the vial.

"It's olive oil," I said. "Will you . . .?"

"Yes, I'll anoint," said Pagag.

He did so in the name of Messiah. I sealed the anointing, and while Mary and Steff kept up the process of CPR, I recited these words:

"Heavenly Father, heal our Rebecca. Breathe air into her lungs. Restore life to her fragile heart. We can't lose her, Father. Don't let her leave us yet. It's not her time. I *know* it's not. Bring her back to her family and loved ones. The power of the evil one has attempted to take her from us. Yet Thy power is so much mightier. Tonight we've seen it topple kingdoms. We've felt it shake the earth and spin whirlwinds. We've seen it suspend whole cities in the clouds. Surely this is a small thing, Father. A little thing in comparison. Yet . . . at this moment . . . it's our whole world. Don't let this happen. Bring her back to us. Bring her back . . ."

* * *

Steffanie

Harry closed the prayer in the name of the Savior. It seemed to me that he'd expressed the sentiment perfectly. Tonight we'd witnessed fire and lightning from heaven. We'd watched as God's power had overwhelmed the greatest edifice ever created by human hands. Still, I felt we'd only witnessed the smallest fragment of God's majesty. We'd survived the most spectacular cataclysms. But were they really greater than the miracle of a child? The miracle of life? *This* miracle—the miracle of Rebecca's life—was for me the ultimate representation of God's love and power. It brought all His miracles full circle. Suddenly the destruction of Babel seemed like a trifle, while here in this seemingly simple moment pulsed all of heaven's fire and thunder and whirlwinds.

The little body gasped for breath. Air filled her lungs and a strong and steady beat resounded in her chest. I swallowed at the lump in my throat. Relief and gratitude swept over me, warming the rain and wind, burning brightly from within.

Her eyelids fluttered open. Rain was now falling gently upon her face. I realized that the wind had died down considerably. No more electricity lit up the sky. Only the warm rain continued unabated, purging and cleansing the meadow.

Becky looked up at our faces in bemusement. Her tiny voice squeaked, "Where am I?"

Mary embraced her, laughing through her tears, while Harry replied, "You're with us, Rebecca. You're going to be all right."

All at once the little girl tensed. "Josh! Where's my brother! Where's Joshua!"

With that the mood of elation faltered. None of us had the faintest idea how to answer her.

Mary replied, "We don't know, Becky. Akish grabbed him and . . ."

"Where did he go?" Becky pleaded. "I don't understand. Where did he go?"

Harry took hold of her shoulders. "Rebecca, the sword made . . . it cut a hole . . . a hole in time. Joshua disappeared. We don't know where he went. We have no way . . ." Suddenly Harry's expression brightened. He realized how to solve this riddle on his own. He reached quickly for his pocket and pulled out the small, translucent seerstone.

Becky gasped as she saw it. "Where did you find that? How did you . . .?" Her eyes widened with understanding. "At the pillar. You found it at the pillar!"

Harry nodded. "It was lying on the floor of the cave. I used it to come here. I've been using it all along."

"Then you have the gift, too!" said Becky with wonder. "You can find out where he is! We can follow him." In perfect faith, the young girl said to my brother, "Ask the Lord, Harry. Use the stone."

Harry nodded again, looking somewhat dazzled. I wasn't sure if it was because Becky's faith had overwhelmed him or just because everything was happening so quickly. He bowed his head in prayer, closing his hand tightly around the white stone. Becky suddenly clasped her own small hands around Harry's hands, shutting her eyes, both of them exerting all the power of their faith in trying to learn the word and will of heaven by exercising a very special spiritual gift. The rest of us watched, the rain drizzling down our faces. The only light that illuminated the area was the glow of a blazing moon—so bright that it pierced right through the storm clouds. Even Rafa, who was perched under Jesse, sheltering himself from the storm, seemed to be waiting in acute anticipation. I bowed my own head and prayed along with them, as did Mary and Micah.

When I looked up next, Becky and Harry were staring at each other, as if trying to comprehend exactly what they had learned.

Mary asked them hesitantly, "Is Joshua all right? Is he alive?"

"Yes," Becky answered. "But . . ."

Harry took over. "Joshua is all right, but he's . . . not well . . . not the same."

"Where *is* he?" asked Gidgiddonihah.

Harry answered thoughtfully. "We'll find him . . . in the same place that we'll find the others. In fact we'll find *everyone* there. Everyone except for my father and Aunt Jenny."

My muscles stiffened. "Where's Dad and Aunt Jenny?"

"They're fine," said Harry. "So are Sabrina and Melody. Sabrina and Melody remained home with their little ones in our own century. But Dad and Jenny went looking for us. Not long ago they survived a very close call."

"What happened?" said Mary with alarm.

I knew the answer to that without having it explained. "Akish attacked our home. He stole a photograph." I looked back at Harry. "You're sure they survived? You're sure they're all right?"

"Yes," said Harry. "Melody and Sabrina are just fine."

Gid asked, "What about Jim and Jenny?"

Harry looked perplexed. "I'm not sure. They went to the cave, but . . ."

"They leaped into the pillar," blurted Rebecca. "They leaped in without knowing where it would take them."

My heart dropped. "Oh no! They could be anywhere!"

Becky shook her head. "I know where they are. Or at least . . . I know how to find them."

"What about Joshua?" asked Mary. "What do you mean he's not well? What do you mean he's not the same?"

Harry shook his head. Rebecca didn't seem quite sure how to answer either. This caused my soul to quake. I feared that I already knew what was wrong, and it had nothing to do with anything physical. It had to do with Joshua's heart. His soul. It struck me that this was a thousand times more frightening than worrying about someone's life or limb.

"But he's together with the others?" Jesse repeated, trying to keep it straight. "You mean your cousin, Joshua, is in the same century with Meagan and Apollus? As well as Garth and your brother-in-law, Marcos?"

"I'm not sure if they're together," said Harry, "but . . ."

"They're *not* together," said Becky. "They're in the same century. But they're not together."

"And where is Akish?" I asked.

Harry and Rebecca couldn't answer this either.

"So what do we do now?" asked Mary.

Harry replied, "We find them. We make sure that we're all in one place. It's the only way to end all of this. We bring everyone together, and then we go home *together*. However, for some of us, I think it would be best if they went home now. There's a cave not far from here. It's the same cave that we've used before to travel to ancient Judea." He looked at Gid. "Do you remember?"

Gid, Micah, and Jesse all nodded.

Mary became defensive. "Just who are you proposing should go home? Certainly you don't mean *me*. I'm not leaving your side, Harry. I never intend to leave your side again."

"Someone has to take Rebecca home," Harry pleaded. "Sabrina and Melody need to know that she's all right."

"Forget it," said Becky defiantly. "My brother is out there somewhere. I'm not going home without him. I'm *not*. And you can't make me, Harry."

Harry sighed dismally. He dropped his head, but then his chin sprang up and he raised his arms in submission. "All right!" he said in frustration. "We'll go together. We'll find them. And we'll bring this adventure to an end."

At that moment the Jaredite named Pagag, who had remained silent for a long while, stepped forward. "I would also like to help, if you will have me. I don't understand all that you're saying, but I feel strongly that this is a righteous cause. If my services can be of any use to you, I wish to come."

Harry looked up at him and smiled. "We'd be grateful to have you, Pagag. *More* than grateful. We'd be deeply honored."

Oh brother, I thought. I considered voicing a protest, but I held my tongue.

Mary asked with concern, "But what about your family, Pagag? What about your father and your uncle back in Salem?"

Harry replied thoughtfully, "If I can manage it . . . I'll make it so that they'll never know he was gone. At least not by the passage of time."

Pagag still looked mystified, but his curiosity was dramatically peaked, and he looked determined to keep his word. However my womanly wiles told me there were other motives for his participation, and these motives irked me to the core. I suspected our friend Pagag had it bad for Mary, and if there was any possibility that he could win her heart away from Harry . . . Well, what's that they say? All's fair in love and adventure?

At least *some* people might say this. I was seriously afraid it might hinder our cause. And I must say, after my other experiences with men in this century, I was more than dubious about his ultimate usefulness. That's all we needed was another arrogant, cocky, testosterone-overdosed male. Yet I wasn't gonna make a federal case out of it. If nothing else, it might be fun to watch him cut down to size for thinking he could ever compete with my brother. In fact, I might even help with the whittling.

"Our fortunes may be running thin," said Micah. "How many more adventures like this can we endure before one of us—or *all* of us—experience terrible tragedy and death?"

It was Gidgiddonihah who answered—Gidgiddonihah whose fortune had been changed, and whose life had somehow been snatched away from the jaws of death. Right now Gid's answer probably meant more than it could have meant from any other soul, reminding us again of the thing we humans are so quick to forget.

"That's in God's hands," he said simply.

So with the rain bearing down on us, our party of eight, including a feathered companion named Rafa (who seemed quite content to travel beneath Harry's cloak), commenced the journey to the cave that would serve as our transport.

We arrived several hours later, cold, wet, and tired, but with an energizing flame of hope flickering deep inside us. The cave looked quite different from how I remembered it. Some of the tunnels seemed familiar, but the way that the unique powers of the cavern demonstrated themselves was wondrous to behold. I almost felt that we were seeing the window of time in its purest form—before any of the earthquakes or energy shifts of later centuries would throw it off balance and force the window to appear in different shapes and casts.

Harry and Becky led us to an overlook within the cavern. There were no sparkling stones on the walls, no raging, swirling pillars. Just a lake of sorts. A calm, soothing lake of energy. I couldn't even see the far wall. It was a mask of blackness. The energy within the lake wasn't like water. It was more like mist. This mist wafted along the surface like fog clinging to a forest floor after a rainy night. We could see into it, but not very far. Its density seemed to increase the deeper one peered. The energy revealed a variety of subdued colors—mostly purples and blues, with an occasional flicker of red. These colors seemed to be slowly rotating toward a center point that wasn't visible to us because of the mist. It was into this lake that Harry expected us to descend. We didn't even have to leap. We just walked down into it, like descending a stairway. A stairway into a world of rapturous miracles.

So we bade farewell to ancient Babylon and began our journey to the new destination. In my heart I sincerely hoped it would be our *final* destination—the last stopover before returning to our own place and time. Afterward, I was determined to stay put in the twenty-first century—at least for a long while. And while I will confess that I did enjoy seeing extraordinary sights and meeting extraordinary souls, I'd also gained a far greater appreciation for home. In our case, however, I had to wonder if there was any home left to return *to*.

But what was I saying? Home was wherever my family was, so in that respect I was headed to precisely the place I wanted to be most. And if there was another adventure between here and there, I only hoped that I would endure it well. For what else was there in this world besides love, family, and friends, and the prospects of continually increasing in all three categories? Perhaps it was a strange dichotomy that the only way to increase all of them at once was by facing adversity.

And what better way to do that than in the midst of adventure?

EPILOGUE

Garth

My back continued to ache. My thirst burned painfully in my throat. And the thought kept repeating over and over: *You're too old for this, Garth Plimpton. Much too old.*

For thirty-six hours I'd been in the same tormenting position. Marcos was near me, his arms also bound behind his back. Our feet were tied behind the trunks of the sapling trees, forcing us to support our weight on the balls of our knees. The trees had been cut short, the branches removed. A tent had been thrown up around them. The canvas was thick, turning the air muggy and permeating the area with the stench of our own sweat. This had attracted many flies, and there was nothing we could do to swat them off. Here the Nephite warriors had left us for thirty-six hours. No food, no water—only the prospects of farther suffering.

Two days ago Marcos and I had arrived at our destination. We'd leaped into the swirling silver void on Harry's cue, and emerged from a cold-water spring in a land of many waters, rivers, and fountains. I'd quickly deduced our location. I'd done fieldwork for the university in this very region. I'd also visited here as a college student. It was the Tuxtla Mountains of Southern Veracruz, Mexico.

What I could not immediately ascertain was the century. There were, of course, no roads or modern structures. But this question, too, was resolved a couple of hours later when we were confronted by a Nephite patrol. Determining their ethnicity was easy enough. I simply asked. But afterward their behavior became unduly hostile.

Marcos was about to defend himself by using a stick as a club. Fortunately, I convinced him to forbear. He and I were then bound and marched to their military outpost in the jungle.

After a few more statements from their lips, I drew my final conclusion about our proximity. They accused us of being Lamanites. The squad leader then reclassified us as Gadianton scouts. I braved another question by asking how far we were from Zarahemla. The angry response was that I ought to know, since my kings had stolen the city from their fathers. Now I could make my deduction. It was the fourth century A.D.—the time of Cumorah.

After I told Marcos where we were, he boldly requested an audience with Mormon himself. This only drew laughter. They did inform us, however, that before our execution we would be granted an audience with their immediate superior—a Nephite captain whose headquarters were some distance away.

A runner was dispatched. Marcos and I were bound. Before they left us alone in the dark, Marcos asked them how long before this captain might arrive.

"For your sake, you should hope it takes him a long time," said the squad leader. "He will show no mercy. His skin is pale, like yours."

The flap was closed.

I heard Marcos ask in the darkness. "Pale skin? Were some Nephites lighter than others?"

"Undoubtedly," I said. "There are many different tribes. Many different varieties of people. It's no different than Europe or anywhere else."

That was the last time we saw daylight for thirty-six hours. I felt sure that there were sentries just outside the tent, but they would not respond to our entreaties for water. I was beginning to wonder if they'd decided to impress their superiors by showing them our dehydrated bodies, rather than burden the Nephite captain with the trouble of an unnecessary interrogation.

My mind felt on the verge of slipping into delirium when I became aware of some commotion outside the tent. Some people were arriving.

Marcos also raised his head in response to the noise. "Do you think this is it?" he asked, sounding painfully thirsty.

"If it is," I replied, "let me do the talking."

Marcos huffed, as if he found this request humorous, maybe because I sounded even thirstier. "Be my guest."

I had a bold speech prepared to earn this captain's confidence and convince him to set us free. I'd also done a lot of praying. Marcos had assuredly done the same, but I still felt compelled to act as our representative. After all, we were here to find my children. If I could gain this man's favor, I intended to waste no time asking him about them, or else about Apollus, Mary, Meagan, and Meagan's boyfriend, Ryan Champion. Harry had informed us that our loved ones had divided into two groups. Marcos and I had no inkling of who exactly we were searching for. But if these Nephites had found *us* so unusual, they might have also found the others to be equally noteworthy. If Providence were with us, we might resolve this mystery by the end of the day.

Finally, the tent flap was tossed aside. I squinted in the bright light. The buzzing flies dispersed. Two Nephite warriors entered the domain, followed by the squad leader. These men were followed by another man adorned from head to foot in leather armor. My immediate impression was that he was quite young—late teens or early twenties. Like Mormon, this warrior had apparently come up fast through the ranks. His face was white, just as the squad leader had intimated. In fact . . . I might have sworn he was Caucasian. I decided the bright sunlight was playing tricks. I blinked and looked down to give my eyes more time to adjust.

The captain came closer. Then he stopped. Only as I glanced at Marcos did I realize that something was desperately wrong. Marcos was gawking at the Nephite commander in absolute disbelief.

"What's wrong, Captain?" the squad leader inquired.

I turned back to the captain, my gaze moving up from his feet to make it easier on my vision. For the second time my sights fell on the features of his face, his bright, red hair and green eyes. A feeling of dread and shock spread outward from my heart until it encompassed my entire soul.

"Release these men," the captain commanded again. The voice was deep. More resonant. But it was still a voice that I knew, mostly by its inflection. I felt as if my stomach was being ripped from my torso. I began dry heaving, though there was nothing in my stomach to throw up.

The cords on my hands were cut. I fell forward. The captain caught me in his arms.

"Do you realize who this man is?" he shouted angrily at the others. "He's my *father!* Bring water! *Now!*"

"Right away, Captain Josh," said the flustered squad leader.

Men scrambled in all directions. Yet I wasn't aware of anything besides the face above me. A face of strength and power. A face that filled me with wonder and terror.

The face of my son, Joshua.

ABOUT THE AUTHOR

Chris Heimerdinger currently resides in Riverton, Utah, with his wife, Catherine Elizabeth, and their three children, Steven Teancum, Christopher Ammon, and Alyssa Sariah. However, there will soon be another Heimerdinger in the family. She will be born in April, and her name will be Cecelia Liahona.

Tower of Thunder was conceived from Chris's intense curiosity about the world prior to the days of Abraham. His challenge was to take the scant information that we have from the scriptures and from statements by General Authorities and attempt to "put flesh on the bones." As with all of the "Tennis Shoes" books, it is hoped that the scenarios he creates with his imagination will broaden the mind and direct the heart to look forward to the day when such things are no longer the product of imagination. As Chris reminds us, "One day the details of the early history of the earth will be common knowledge, but only according to the will of the Lord and our preparation as a people to receive it."

Readers can soon expect another volume in the "Tennis Shoes" series. However, Chris will also pursue several other projects, including a possible feature film.

For further information about *Tower of Thunder* and other books by Chris Heimerdinger, please become a registered guest at www.cheimerdinger.com.

TENNIS SHOES
ADVENTURE SERIES

by CHRIS HEIMERDINGER

1. TENNIS SHOES AMONG THE NEPHITES

Chris Heimerdinger holds you spellbound as he introduces you to teenagers Jim Hawkins and Garth Plimpton, as well as Jim's pesky little sister, Jennifer. They accidentally stumble upon a mysterious passageway that hurls them into a Book of Mormon world where danger and suspense are a way of life.

Suddenly the names Helaman, Teancum, and Captain Moroni are more than just words on a page as Book of Mormon characters come to life. Carefully researched, entertaining, and exciting, this story will motivate young people to read the Book of Mormon and will add a whole new dimension to the understanding of those who already know and love Book of Mormon stories. *Tennis Shoes Among the Nephites* is a great educational tool that will provide fun and delight for the whole family to share!

2. GADIANTONS AND THE SILVER SWORD

Jim and Garth are now in college at BYU, and their earlier adventures in Book of Mormon lands are revisited in a most unusual way when evil men from the past (Gadianton robbers from Nephite times) pursue them and disrupt their lives with danger and violence.

This is a spine-tingling, explosive saga that transports the reader from the familiar settings of Utah and the American West to the exotic and unfamiliar settings of southern Mexico and its deep, shadowy jungles, where Jim must find a mystical sword once wielded by the Jaredite king, Coriantumr.

3. THE FEATHERED SERPENT, PART ONE

Jim Hawkins is now the widowed father of two teenage daughters, Melody and Steffanie, and a ten-year-old son, Harry. Jim finds himself embarking on his most difficult and perilous adventure—a quest for survival against unseen enemies and an evil adversary from the distant past. He must also solve the deepening mystery of the disappearance of his sister, Jennifer, and his old friend Garth Plimpton. Once again he returns—this time with his family—to ancient Book of Mormon times; but now the civilization is teetering on the brink of destruction. It's the time just prior to the Savior's appearance in the New World . . . a time of danger and uncertainty.

4. THE FEATHERED SERPENT, PART TWO

Jim and his family continue their perilous adventures in Book of Mormon times, using all of their instincts and resources to find Garth and his family and deliver themselves from the clutches of one of the most treacherous men of ancient America—King Jacob of the Moon. They encounter murderous and conspiring men, plagues, a herd of "cureloms," hostile armies, and finally earthquakes and suffocating blackness as the Savior of the world is crucified. Along the way, members of Jim's family discover their loyalty and love for one another, and the importance of the gospel in their lives, culminating in the glorious visitation of our Lord Jesus Christ to the city of Bountiful.

5. THE SACRED QUEST

Jim has just learned that his daughter, Melody, now age 20, has a very serious illness. During their last adventure in Book of Mormon times, Melody fell in love with Marcos, son of King Jacob of the Moon, who had been converted to Christianity. Now Jim's son Harry, age 15, is determined to go back in time, find Marcos, and bring him back to be with Melody. He and his stepsister-to-be, Meagan, embark on this journey, but are sidetracked and end up in New Testament times, about 70 A.D. They encounter both believers and antichrists who are consumed with finding a mysterious manuscript called the Scroll of Knowledge. The epic climaxes with a breathtaking confrontation between Harry, Nephites, and gladiators; but Harry's adventure of a lifetime has only begun.

6. THE LOST SCROLLS

Harry and Meagan continue their heart-stopping adventure as they face the awesome challenges of courage and survival in the hostile world of Jerusalem in 70 A.D. While Meagan and Jesse, a young Jewish orphan, are held hostage by the evil Simon Magus and the Sons of the Elect, Harry and his friend Gidgiddonihah must make an impossible journey to Jerusalem to find the Scroll of Knowledge, which may contain the ultimate power and mysteries of the universe. They have only a few days to find the scroll and deliver it to Simon Magus, or Meagan and Jesse will be killed. Our young heroes face breathtaking danger and high adventure as they encounter flames, swords, desperate villains, and perhaps the greatest loves of their lives in this sixth volume of the award-winning Tennis Shoes Adventure Series.

7. THE GOLDEN CROWN

Hang on to your seats as the heart-pounding adventure of Harry Hawkins and Meagan Sorenson in the land of Jerusalem and the world of the Romans races toward its thrilling conclusion.

In a nightmarish twist of events, Harry finds himself in the midst of unforeseen enemies who seek to separate him from all that he holds dear. To make matters worse, Garth Plimpton and Meagan are forced to make choices that threaten to leave Harry permanently lost in time.

Harry's father, Jim, and Meagan's mother, Sabrina, enter the fray to save their families, while Harry knows that to survive he must somehow reach a faraway land where resides a true apostle of the Lord Jesus Christ. "We're all on a golden journey," Harry is told by a very special person from biblical history. "A journey inspired by golden dreams, and at the end awaits a golden crown of righteousness."

Reenter the reeling world of the first century A.D. in this, the seventh book in the celebrated Tennis Shoes Adventure Series. This is also the final volume in Harry and Meagan's breathtaking New Testament trilogy that began with *The Sacred Quest*.

8. WARRIORS OF CUMORAH

Leave all your expectations behind as your favorite characters from the Tennis Shoes Adventure Series are reunited in a miraculous journey into worlds never before imagined, where villains old and new must be stopped to keep the landscape of history from becoming permanently altered.

Just when the children of Jim Hawkins and Garth Plimpton thought they understood the powers of the Rainbow and Galaxy Rooms, a transformation of staggering dimensions takes place. It's a mystery whose secrets can only be unraveled by a pair of small white stones—stones in a gleaming silver frame whose powers can only be harnessed by the mightiest of prophets or by one pure-hearted little girl.

Embark on the millennium's greatest adventure, an epic that one day soon will culminate in one of the most tremendous battles ever fought—a battle of tragedy, heroism, and the rebirth of dreams on the slopes of a hill called Cumorah.

DANIEL AND NEPHI

A Tale of Eternal Friendship in a Land Ripening for Destruction

Welcome to 609 B.C.! In a world of infinite mystery, when caravans rule the sun-swept deserts and mighty empires grapple for ultimate power, the lives of a young prince named Daniel and a trader's son named Nephi become entwined in an adventure that takes them along the razor's edge of danger and suspense as they struggle to save the life of a king—and the fate of a nation.

Join Daniel and Nephi as they learn the lessons of friendship, fortitude, and faith that shape two young boys into great prophets of God.

Carefully researched and scrutinized by scholars, *Daniel and Nephi* offers a breathtaking opportunity to explore the world of Jeremiah and Lehi.

"In Daniel and Nephi, *Chris Heimerdinger has once again breathed life into significant characters in biblical and Book of Mormon history."*

—BRENT HALL, FOUNDATION FOR ANCIENT RESEARCH
AND MORMON STUDIES